ICONOCLAST
A Novel by Jerome MacEvoy/Michael Jerome Connelly
©2021

Before the Story

- ~2100: Aliens calling themselves "Fomorians" invade Earth and begin slaughtering people indiscriminately. Major cities and isolated nations wall themselves off as best they can.
- ~2110: Most of humanity is dead, manipulated into killing one another by the Fomorian's psychic influence. The alien menace is almost impossible to kill.
- ~2111: Only a handful of cities and nations survive as survivors hide underground. The Fomorians seemingly die off on their own.
- 2112: Survivors emerge, witnessing a ruined world. Natural areas have begun to rapidly evolve and mutate, apparently because of Fomorian influence.
- 2113-2290: Social and technological regression, where the last of humanity tries to rebuild amidst the brutal wilderness. Many find a strange religion among the untamable outside world, forming The Martyrs that worship the fallen Fomorians. Some can tap into the supernatural power of the land itself.
- 2291: Great Britain gains footing as one of the most cosmopolitan countries in Europe. They attempt to claim more territory from mainland Europe, known as "The Outlands," while facing pushback from The Martyrs. The Martyrs destabilize many cities and recovering nations. These nations look to places like Great Britain for safety, leading to an influx of immigration.

- 2295: Aaron Sennec, a strange man with a profound gift for the supernatural, emerges as a messiah for the Martyrs, leading efforts to let people "live with nature" and leave the old world behind. The newfound unity of The Martyrs lets them push back even harder against Great Britain and other countries.
- 2310-2312: Sennec and The Martyrs lay siege to the recovering Cairo, prompting a deluge of refugees. British PM Chester Grell moves to wage war with The Martyrs, and Sennec, who was trying to surrender, is shot in the crossfires. The Martyrs are furious and redouble their war efforts, directing all their ire towards Great Britain.
- 2330: Years of war has brought exhaustion and dread. New PM Nathan Rowe approves a drastic experiment to make progress.

1   Hastings, England   18:28 November 12, 2334

Dr. Yousef looked wearily back at his patient as she waited for death to come. She passed all the tests, signed all the forms, and was ready to become a superweapon. How she slept so calmly with that knowledge was beyond him. With the results of her health evaluation on his tablet, he braced himself to share them with his boss.

The corridors of the hospital were almost black. The brightest light came from his tablet and the smoky yellow glow from the city reflected on the overcast sky. Yousef found himself staring out the window, trying to ignore the pit in his stomach.

Yousef Makkareb was tall and slender, with distinct bones showing through his fingers and face. He had kept his hair long and slick ever since he was a teenager, but the look suited him. His eyes were bright and wide, often half-lidded when dealing with the uncertainties of this experiment. Though he was never the type to sit still in the first place, he was particularly restless tonight as his fingers drummed on the window pane.

Maybe it was his own guilt eating at him, but he often had the sense that someone was giving him a dirty look. He feared that word about the FH project would spread from the Hastings military base; if the military thought they were crazy, the public would, too.

He tried to push the thought out, but it lingered. The weight of it all sunk in even more as he took another look at the tablet. Sighing, he strode down the dark hallway towards Judicia's office.

The bleak corridor seemed to stretch on forever. Jaundiced city light covered the sleek plastic floors and walls, striped by shadows from the windowpanes. He had been going over the patient's readings since last afternoon. He cracked his neck and marched on, rubbing the exhaustion from his eyes.

An artificial light spilled into the black corridor. Even from the other side of the hallway, he could hear Judicia pounding at her keyboard. He tapped on the door.

"Who is it?" Judicia demanded, not even pausing to stop the pounding.

"It's me," Yousef said.

She stopped typing. "Come in."

Yousef walked into the glow, squinting his eyes at the bright light. The office was full of computer monitors lined up around the desk, each one displaying something different. Between the e-mail inboxes and the algorithm compilers was the shape of a small woman.

Dr. Bianca Judicia, the mastermind behind the FH project. A head and a half shorter than Yousef, she had dark brown, bowl-cut hair to her shoulders and square glasses that reflected all light. Age lined her face and sunk her defined dimples.

"What's the damage? Give me the worst of it." She demanded, taking a swig from a mug of coffee on her desk.

"You're not gonna like this," He told her, half-groaning. He held the tablet out, and she took it with her free hand. "We've got bronchial infections, severe malnutrition, the first few signs of osteoporosis, and scores of muscle and tissue damage. Among many other things."

Judicia remained fixed on the device, her perpetual scowl becoming even more sour as she pored over the text. "Son of a bitch," she muttered, thrusting the tablet back into his arms. "What are her treatment options here?"

He glanced over several of the readings a second time. "I can probably knock out a few of the major infections with a medbot treatment or two, but the muscle damage and nutritional issues are gonna take a little longer."

Her head slowly turned up to him. "How much longer?" This was a rare moment where Judicia's irritation carried a genuine note of apprehension.

He looked up at her with a raised eyebrow. "Muscle damage and malnutrition, Bianca. How long do you think?" He was too tired to be afraid of what she would say. He spoke his mind, to his unprecedented relief.

She placed her coffee back on the desk, glaring at him. "Yousef, are you here to do your job or pretend that you're witty?"

He sighed, trying to maintain a professional air. "Our best bet will probably be nutritional regiments and physical therapy, which, if we're lucky, will take a month or two."

Judicia spun to face him. "A month or two?" She said, her anger genuine.

"Yes, a month or two." He met her incredulous gaze with his own. "And that's not factoring in psychological therapy or recovery time from the other procedures."

She said nothing, only stared.

"I'm sorry, but we have to postpone. This isn't the kind of treatment you can rush."

Yousef relaxed for the first time that night, feeling that he had made his point. Judicia remained silent, biting her lip. She looked down at the floor, searching for the words. After a moment, she turned back to him.

"We can't." Her tone was solemn.

Yousef was stunned. "Excuse me?"

"We can't. Postponing isn't an option."

Yousef felt his frustration revitalize him. "Did you hear anything I just said? This patient is a wreck! She'll die if we go ahead with this!"

"I can see that the girl is a mess, but we'll just have to make do." Her tone was more reserved than his, more out of defeat than apathy.

"'Make do?'" Yousef echoed in disbelief. "What are you talking about? All I'm asking for is a little time!"

"Time isn't a luxury we can afford, Yousef." She took an envelope from her desk and held it out to him.

"What's this?" He said, taking it.

"A demand from Mr. Rowe."

Yousef let the envelope fall to the floor. His hands were tense, and his fingertips bent the paper with their force.

> *To Doctor Bianca Judicia,*
>
> *I have pledged my wholehearted support to the Fomorian Hybridization- or "FH"- project for the past four years. You understand that I admire your*

ambitions and wish to foster as much progress as I can within our State. However, continuing to supply the money and resources your experiments need is no longer practical. The Martyr's Army is on the offensive: everywhere I look, I see outposts raided, soldiers killed, and graffiti of "Remember Sennec" on more and more buildings. The military is going to need every pound it can get, and I can't afford to keep funding your project without any results. However, I understand that you finally have another volunteer, so I am prepared to allow you some additional time. By May 25 of this coming year, if you have nothing of use to offer the State, I shall be forced to cut all funding for the FH project. Use your resources wisely; I want this experiment to work as much as you do.
    Nathan Rowe

  The tension in Yousef' fingers lightened, and his hunched shoulders went slack. The vein in his neck had stood sharply on end during his talk with Judicia, but now it had receded. His expression slowly faded as he processed all the words on the page.
  "Until May?" He said after a moment of crushing silence. "When did this come in?"
  "This afternoon, when you were doing the scan." She took the letter back from him. His hand hung in the air

as if he were still holding it. "We won't have the time to give her that kind of therapy. We'll have to start right away."

Yousef felt faint. A spray of aggravated sparks shot through his spine. He bent over her desk, planting his hands on the top.

"Bianca," he said, his voice as solemn as a grave, "you cannot ask me to do this."

"Yousef, we've dealt with worse than this."

"When?" He cried, beating his fist on the wood. "Are you mad? This girl is going to die!"

"Stop yelling!" She said, emphasizing her words without raising her voice as he did. She met his exasperated gaze with her own, rubbing her temple in anticipation of a migraine. "I don't like it either, Yousef! But we don't have a choice here!"

"Actually, yes we do:" he began with a mocking overtone, "Either we murder this girl or we don't." He leaned in closer to her face. "This isn't difficult!"

"'Murder?'" Judicia repeated, incredulous. "Yousef, I want you to really look at this situation."

Yousef straightened himself, folding his arms.

"We've got until May. About five months. That's enough time to run the procedure, isn't it?"

"Yeah, if everything goes perfectly!"

"It won't take long to get rid of the really big infections right?" She downed another gulp of coffee.

"No, but that's not what I'm worried about. How do you expect me to deal with everything else? Like the muscle damage and-"

"Give her a nice IV and some electric stimulation. Do whatever you can, report back to me in a week." She went back to her keyboard, turning from him.

The tablet felt heavy in his hands. He had thrown everything he had at her. All he had was a wordless gape as he tried to grapple with what she said.

"Bianca, I can't do this." He placed the tablet on the table.

Groaning, she turned back to him. "Yousef-"

"No!" He barked, almost yelling. "Three people have died in the past year alone! And then we wonder why no one has been signing up! If you're really going to kill more people trying to make this work, I don't want anything to do with it!"

Bianca strode out from behind the desk, looking straight into his eyes. "The deaths were not your fault, Yousef! We've talked about this!"

"I am the Chief of Medicine, Bianca!" He emphasized each word. "I have been doing everything in my power to help these people, and none of it has been good enough!" He clenched his teeth and shut his eyes. "Do you honestly expect me to watch another patient die?"

"No, because she isn't going to die." She planted both her hands on her hips. "I know we've made mistakes, but we've learned from each one! I know what to do this time!"

He cocked his head at her. "I am so sick of that story, Judicia. Our soldier doesn't have a chance!"

She looked to the side, narrowing her eyes in thought. "'Doesn't have a chance?' Funny- some critics had the same words about your procedure."

He opened his mouth and leaned in to reply, but no words came to him. He backed up, eyes wide. The anger left him, and he and Judicia stared at one another in silence.

"That was a cognitive enhancement, Bianca. This isn't the same thing." He said, drained.

"I took a man who huffed solvents for a living and turned him into a doctor. If that worked, why won't this?" She had the closest thing to a grin on her face, confident that she had won the argument. "This experiment needs you, Yousef. We're not getting another shot. If you leave now, everything that's happened will have been for nothing."

He pinched the bridge of his nose, clenching his jaw. "I realize that. I just don't know how we're gonna make this work."

"I'm supposed to worry about that. Like I said before: you do your job, and I'll do mine." She handed the tablet back to him. "You used to be so optimistic about this project, Yousef." She patted him on the arm. "Honestly, cheer the fuck up."

He watched her march back to her monitors, taking her mug and beating the keys. "In my defence," he began, as his feet started moving towards the door of their own accord, "I haven't had a lot of reason to be optimistic." He ducked out of the room before she could think of anything else to say.

With that last comment, he had depleted himself. He wasn't trying to be funny, he only wanted to leave that ordeal without feeling that he had more to say. And while he didn't want to admit it, she was right. The smell of paint thinner was still sharp in his memory, but not in a way that made him want more. He took a deep breath, and let it all out in a hard exhale.

A part of him knew that arguing with her was a losing battle. She would always pull the "I turned you into what you are" trick. The more he thought on it, though, the more vital to the operation the story seemed.

Genetic enhancement was all the rage nowadays thanks to Judicia's research. Usually, it was reserved for military applications, but a handful of other procedures were becoming more public. It was being used to counter neurodegenerative disorders and other facets of physical health, and it was on the verge of becoming trendy. In his experience with orthopedics, Yousef had met plenty of people who wanted to get "touched up," getting smarter or stronger. It always irked him. There were too many unknowns, and people were being too casual about it.

He stayed brisk, wanting the night to be over. The sooner he broke the news to his team, the sooner he'd be back home in his bed. He kept that in mind as he went on.

He staggered into the bright room. He crossed over to her, taking one more look at the soldier. Her head was tilted to the side on the pillows, deep in an anesthetic sleep. She looked at peace for the first time since she arrived.

She was young. He wasn't sure how young, but certainly not out of her twenties. Despite the wounds, the restless look in her eyes, there was still a youthful vigor to her. A sort of ingenuous light that kept her moving forward through all of this.

The codename Rowe came up with only perplexed him: "Andraste." He wondered what it was about her that earned her the moniker.

Judicia hadn't moved from the DNA injector in hours. She calculated amounts of cellular deconstruction formula and DNA injections to the hundredth decimal point, disrupted only when one arm broke routine to reach for her coffee thermos.

For the past four months, this was nearly every day. The soldier was buried beneath a thick tangle of tubes, wires, and protective glass, floating in a slurry of suspension fluid and IV tubes. From the view of Judicia's infrared camera, she looked like she was dissolving into it.

While Dr. Yousef and the rest of the genetics team glanced in bewilderment over Judicia's shoulder, Yousef and his team kept the subject alive, regulating IV administrations and piloting several medbots that swam through the fluid. Yousef's face was wracked with strain, and there were several red cracks in the white of his eye.

"I am not going to lose you," he thought.

The soldier's skin didn't even look like skin anymore. It was marbled and hard, like worn slate. This was mostly consistent with the Fomorian biology they were familiar with. Legends said the Fomorians were nearly indestructible and intelligent beyond human comprehension. If half of them were true, then they were delving into something much more dangerous than any Martyr's Army militia. Her skin was the first sign of that.

"All right, everyone," she said over the PA system, "it's time for Andraste to wake up."

Yousef and his team set about removing the various cables from Andraste's body, one at a time. Yousef gritted his teeth as he coordinated his medbot, maneuvering its claws and cameras as best he could.

His arms were wracked with strain. He wanted nothing more than to push away from the desk and let them fall limp at his sides. The metronome of the heart rate monitor sent shockwaves through his head with each sound, but he kept going.

Judicia refused to acknowledge such things while bringing her experiment to life. The anticipation kept her going like an immense fire lit up in her stomach, moving her tired, near-dead limbs where they needed to go.

No one got a good look at Andraste while they were working. With the tangled cables, the foggy suspension fluid, and their own fear of the unknown, each person had a different idea of what she looked like. The uncertainty sat with each person like a jagged rock in their stomachs, but they worked through it. Sighing, everyone set to removing the anesthesia and draining the suspension fluid.

She had manifested into nothingness, an incorporeal void with no memories or context. She couldn't remember anything, and there was an unsettling lightness in her mind. There was nothing to think about, and nothing to recall. She was an empty shell, drifting through space and barely conscious. The camp and all remnants of the nightmare had been swallowed up by the same nothingness.

"The Martyr's Army knows about you," said a voice. It reverberated throughout the space and echoed in a way that its words were almost unintelligible. "George Bashford isn't happy."

"Who's there?" She cried, not recognizing her own voice.

"I'm sorry," it replied, the words becoming clearer. "I can't tell you that right now. Before time runs out, know this:" It paused.

"Wait! What's going on? Where am I?" She had little sense of her body, but she could tell that she was flailing around in the space. The awareness of the emptiness was crushing, and the fear surged through her body like freezing water.

"Listen to me. You have to get out of there. They're coming."

"What? Who's 'they?' Who are you?"

"Fear The Martyr's Army." The voice trailed off. As the last few echoes began to dissipate, her sense of awareness began to diminish.

"Wait," she called after it. She wanted to scream and let her fear come bursting out, but her energy was failing her. She was fading, and the part of her that experienced the most intense fear was being buried beneath the nothingness.

She was unsure of what she was losing to this interminable void. She couldn't see her hands or her body, nor recall what they looked like. She tried to picture her hand in front of her; she felt it there in front of her face, but she couldn't muster a clear image. Everything was lost to her, and she felt herself about to vanish.

"Get out of there, Andraste." the voice said once again.

2 Unknown

From the inexorable blackness, she was pulled into existence by some invisible force. She was an unknown consciousness drifting in and out of dreams and nonbeing, not knowing what she was, where she had been, or where she was going.

Between smothering intervals of darkness, she would open her eyes to some amorphous, filtered light source. The dull flicker would grow brighter and stay longer with each crack of her eyelids, pushing away the oppressive black curtain.

It was hard for her to tell, but she was being watched. Her heart rate was rising to a more reasonable number, and the people observing her could only hope that it stayed that way.

She couldn't move. She wasn't even sure what she had to move.

More sensations became apparent as the blackness dwindled. She could tell her body was floating in an opaque liquid, as air was being forced in and out of her lungs. Several oddly-shaped white figures swam through the fluid- medical robots. It was too murky to see them clearly, even as her vision cleared.

"Y… An…" A garbled voice said. The sound echoed in the space, reverberating throughout her lifeless body. It grew louder, but no less incoherent, as she awoke more.

With the sound, came images. Shapeless blends of colors and textures would penetrate her vision with no clear pattern or timing. This was what made the fear set in. There was nothing to make out from them, but each vision carried a sharp sensation of anxiety and horror with it. Every sensation had a distinct tenor and flavor to them, and she felt like she was feeling fear in countless, indescribable ways.

She tried to block out the noise and focus on the light, but the images only grew sharper, and other voices joined in a disjointed chorus with the first one. It all came together in a frenzied whirlwind. She wanted to rip the seams of her skull apart to get some relief from the pain, but she still couldn't move. She had feeling, but no movement. Muscling herself past it as best as she could, she tried to keep her focus on the light.

Her heart rate spiked. Someone was told to fix it.

As gradually as they set in, the images began to abate. As though ice water was being pumped through her, everything went numb. The light became stronger, but she felt as though she was falling asleep again. Of other voices in the background, none were so clear that they were anything other than inoffensive static.

A blurry gray tube hissed air into her body, and the borders of this odd container full of fluid vanished into the fog. With no memory of where she was or why she was there, all she could do was drift and wait to see if something would happen.

After a long time trying to pick through the voices for some thread of coherency, she could hear the sound of water running. She could see the rippling wall of the liquid's surface sinking on top of her. Before long, the surface brushed past her face, but the sensation felt somehow wrong. Having grown used to the water, the air was sharp and cold, but the sensation of it on the sides of her head was misshapen, as if something obstructed the contours of the water.

As the water kept draining, she started to fall with it. Her limp arms, hanging down at her sides, rested on the bottom of the container along with the rest of her body.

The top of her container was, not unlike the suspension fluid, a dull white. There was a distinct crease that split the top into two sections. Some mechanism whirred for a second, and the crease began to widen.

An acute light stabbed into her eyes as the two halves came apart. She squinted, but didn't want to close her eyes for fear of fading back into the darkness. The whiteness gave way to more detail after a few seconds- she could see a sterile white ceiling with several lights hanging from it in columns, and there was an audience of chairs, computers, and people wearing scrubs in her peripheral vision.

With what little strength she had, she rocked her head to the right and let it slump. One man grabbed the rails in front of him and slowly leaned towards her.

"My God," he said, "She's alive!"

A shorter woman with dark hair rushed in front of him, pushing him out of the way. Everyone else looked on in awed silence.

She was still skin and bones, but with a different type of skin. What wasn't dark and rough, as if ravaged by frostbite, was covered in thick gray exoskeleton plates, especially along her arms, legs, and torso. There were three plates on each side of her face, frayed out like bizarre fins. Each plate was about the same shade of slate gray as her hair.

"We've done it!" The woman said, pounding her fist on the rail. "Activate the second round of stimulants!" The crowd dispersed, with several people going to the desks around the room.

A fulminant surge of mist shot down her breathing tube. A hot, tingling sensation rose in her throat and burned through the rest of her body, winding through the muscles and setting her lungs ablaze. She sat upright in a jolt, her heart pounding against her ribs. Everyone in the room recoiled at this, save the woman at the rails. All feeling had returned to her body, and every centimeter of her skin crawled with the energy.

She was twitching and taking huge, deep breaths, her breath fighting for space with the respirator. She was choking on her own air. Without thinking, she grabbed the metal-reinforced hose with both hands and wrenched it from her face. It gave with little effort, and snapped like a rubber band. It slid out of her hands and fell to the ground, hissing and twitching.

The crowd stared at her in fear and anticipation as she gasped for air. Her arms trembled as she propped herself up. She turned her head to the crowd, which gawked at her in horror of the unknown. Her eyes were even more striking, as wide open as they were. They were at least twice the size of human eyes, a bright blue gradient with no sclera. They looked like giant irises, with a proportionally large, oblong pupils, each about twice the size of a normal human eye. The distinction was sharp and unnerving. She looked at the crowd in an odd way; with the metal mask covering her nose and mouth, she could only convey emotion through her oversized, alien eyes.

She wanted to say something, anything, to try and make sense of what was happening, but simple exhales burned through her mouth like clouds of fire. Every sensation was so strong, and every experience was so intense, she could hardly stay upright. She was becoming dizzy from all the things demanding her attention. She was overwhelmed, and the crowd took notice.

Many people got up from their desks and approached, though their approaching figures and heavy footfalls only contributed to the cacophony that beat against her skull. The overload was building up in her head, threatening to get too full and burst. She clasped her hands around her temples, trying to keep it contained.

She looked at the crowd again, hoping for some solution. They were all frozen, as far as she could tell. A thin haze had settled over her spectators, blurring all of their features together. None of them seemed to be speaking, but a soft chorus of voices was becoming audible. As their complexions grew more homogenized, the voices grew louder. She covered her ears, which seemed to be folded against the sides of her head as bizarre, alien holes. The cries didn't abate, and grew into piercing, resounding shouts. Her head was splitting, and everything around her seemed to be melting.

The ground beneath her legs was dissolving into a gray paste, and so were her legs. The gray exoskeleton and dark skin were liquefying and spilling onto the floor. She looked at her hands, and the same thing was happening. When she saw the red of blood and muscle tissue drip from her fingers, she screamed. The headache was unbearable, and all her flesh was falling from her bones.

"What's happening?" A doctor said, who was nearly seeing the same thing. His vision was hazy and unclear, and he felt as though his head was going numb. Several of the other doctors were seeing what their subject was seeing, and those who didn't were having their own headaches. The subject could see the woman at the rails hunched over in pain, wringing her hand on the metal rail with every ounce of her strength.

"Get a sedative in her!" The woman said, wrestling with the pain. Her voice was mangled by the other voices and sensations the subject felt.

The building tension in her head was too much, and it was trying to get out. It clawed at the top of her skull, trying to breach the hard bone. She felt its claws loosen a piece and expose her brain. With one last push, it broke through and tore her head open, blood and screams filling the air. Several people lost their balance and fell or vomited. An older doctor began to twitch and foam at the mouth, and he fell over, writhing on the ground.

Something was slapped onto the subject's face, and she was pulled onto an operating table. The back of her head struck the firm surface and shattered the apparitions. The pain in her head was fading, and the fear and agony that gripped her vanished like a dense fog in the sunlight.

The crowd had fragmented, and everyone was either bent over in pain and fear or huddled around the man who had fallen over.

"Take Williams to the ER!" The woman cried, as two people in uniforms came in and tightened the tube on the subject's face. "Get her stabilized! Go! Go! Go!" The doctor clapped her hands in rhythm to her words, and the crowd scrambled out of the theater. "Hang on, Andraste!"

She was exhausted. A stream of ceiling tiles rushed by in an unfocused haze, which grew darker and blurrier as her entourage rushed down the hall. She wanted to know what was happening, but that curiosity was soon lost beneath the overwhelming tiredness. The name that the woman cried- "Andraste"- that word stuck in her mind, but all other things faded into a tunnel around the memory of it. The chaos around her faded into a prosaic white noise as she was sucked into another bout of sleep.

3   Hastings, England   14:18 May 5th, 2335

Yousef was laying down on the bench outside the emergency room, his head still spinning. The throbbing had gone away with some basic painkillers, but he still remembered the feeling. And then there was Williams, whose seizure would have him laid up for a while. Everyone had seen something similar when the patient woke up- blood, screaming, some bastardization of flesh- but not everyone was dealing with it the same way. While some discussed their experiences in the break rooms, others went home in horrified tears.

Judicia walked in after a while, a football-sized bag of ice on her head. She saw Yousef in his wounded state across the way, his black hair spilling over the sides of the bench. She sighed, more out of tiredness than irritation, and walked over.

"So, how are we doing?" She asked, taking the chair across from him.

Only his eyes turned to meet her. Yousef let his head fall back onto the bench. "I'm still alive, miraculously." He chuckled, trying to dull the hard sting of the awful memory. "What about you?"

"Nothing I haven't dealt with before," Judicia said, shrugging, "I've had chronic migraines all my life. That little debacle just gave me a flare-up." She pressed it harder against her head.

"What the hell happened to Andraste?"

"She's been stabilized. You saw it, then?" She raised an eyebrow.

He strained to lift his head. "Saw what?" There was silence for a moment while it sunk in for him. "You mean, the whole," he paused, making gestures that imitated an exploding head.

"Yeah. That."

Despite her nonchalant tone, her sentiment got Yousef to sat up from the bench. "So, what exactly was all that?"

"I'm still figuring it out, myself. Those stimulants are only supposed to give you a little jolt, but according to the readings, her brain activity was off the charts. Some of our neurologists compared it to a visual hallucination."

Yousef cocked his head. "Are you saying that was a hallucination?"

"It must've been. Her head is still intact, so, obviously, it didn't actually happen."

"But it was a hallucination that everyone saw?"

Judicia shrugged. "Like I said, I'm still figuring it out."

Yousef looked lost. "How do we know it won't happen again when she wakes up?"

"We don't." She sighed.

Yousef slumped back onto the bench. "Jesus. So, what options do we have left?" He said, feeling he already knew the answer.

"Simple. We get her stabilized and hope for the best." Judicia said, her response almost verbatim to Yousef's expectations. "As long as she's under, we can do some x-rays and basic scans."

"Fantastic." He said, as if holding back laughter. "Nothing else we can do, I guess." He hoisted himself up.

Judicia smirked. "My, you've come around."

He couldn't hold it back anymore. Yousef wheezed out a tired, defeated laugh. "What, you thought I wouldn't?"

"After all that whinging about 'killing' her?" Her tone was somewhere between casual teasing and hard criticism. "I wasn't holding my breath."

He shrugged. "That's fair." He paused, letting his back fall against the wall. "I guess I'm too relieved to let anything else bug me. I was so worried about all this- I mean, you certainly realize that, but still- and after all the shit we went through, she still made it." He sleeked a loose strand of his hair back over his head. "I'm so used to being worried about it, I've forgotten what it's like to not worry, you know?"

Her face crinkled. "No, I don't." She shifted the bag of ice to the top of her head. "Having something to worry about makes me feel alive. It reminds me that I'm doing something with my life."

Yousef pursed his lips. "Thought you'd say something like that." He collected his hair into a ponytail. "But personally, I'm not that upset. That was one hell of a trip, but if we managed to get the experiment off the ground without killing her, then I think we'll get through this just fine."

She glared. "Where was that enthusiasm during the experiment?"

He wrapped a band around his hair, forming the ponytail. "With all due respect, there wasn't a lot to be enthusiastic about until now." He looked at her with a mild grin. "I understand that we have a lot more work ahead of us. And trust me, it's not that I'm not freaked out by that whole hallucination business. All I'm saying is, we did it without killing the patient. At least to me, that's a reason to be hopeful."

Judicia groaned. "Whatever keeps you working." She got up from the bench. "So, how long do you think you're going to sit there? Step two is running diagnostics."

He sighed. He let his arms fall back and swung them forward, letting the momentum carry him off the bench. "I'm ready if you are." He glanced at the bag of ice. "Are you ready?" He asked, concerned.

She put the bag down. "Head over to the elevators. I'll be there soon."

Yousef did as he was told. After a few minutes, Judicia came with a bottle of painkillers dangling from her hand. Up on the second floor of the hospital, there was the makeshift containment unit.

There was a colorful crowd standing around one of the rooms. Some wore scrubs and had themselves glued to their tablets, while others wore full protective equipment and covered the room in biohazard symbols. One turned to them as they approached. They flashed their badges at him, and he cleared the path for them.

Big machines lined the room, many of which were unfamiliar to Yousef. Doctors and biohazard handlers were coordinating an intricate dance of flipping switches and recording changes in numbers. The test subject herself was behind several panes of thick glass, which was pierced by several cables and hoses that led into her body and back to the machines in some unimaginable sequence and oscillation. An airlock-like opening near the back of the room was the only way into the chamber. He wasn't sure what he would see when he went in there, and he wondered if Judicia felt the same way. She received clearance from some other employees in hazard suits, and gestured for Yousef to come with her. Having come this far, Yousef took a breath to center himself, and followed Judicia through the doors.

"Is her skin supposed to be like that?" He quietly asked. He hadn't heard of any skin problems during the procedure, so he assumed Andraste's slate-gray complexion was some esoteric side effect from the Fomorian genes.

"More or less. Didn't expect the discoloration, but no problems other than that." There was a nonchalant tone in her voice. She walked to the side of the bed opposite him, and grabbed the tablet resting on a nearby stand.

Yousef, still unsure of what he was feeling, looked back at their experiment. Her disheveled, unnaturally white hair was the same, and that gave him some reassurance as he scanned the rest of her. Draped over her cheeks were the six exoskeleton-like plates, three on each side, hanging over skin that looked leathery and coarse to the touch. Her eyes were closed, and above them sat eyebrows that seemed to be made of the same exoskeleton, segmented in a way that made them look like rows of white beetles standing opposite each other. A few murmuring doctors remarked that the exoskeleton was mostly keratin, and received its white color from her melanin-deprived hair.

"She's something, isn't she?" Judicia said; her abrasive way of speaking had an odd way of mingling with other emotional overtones. As far as Yousef could tell, it was a sort of cautious pride. She was happy with the results, but wasn't letting herself get carried away.

"Yeah," He said with a slow nod. "Something."

For two days, Andraste laid in comatose silence. Every employee approached her with a near-paralyzing sense of trepidation, making even the smallest adjustment with the most delicate touch they could manage. The researchers were having a heyday with the x-rays and MRI scans, but to everyone else, she was a ticking bomb that would make everyone hallucinate again. The entire staff would panic and hit the deck when she so much as stirred, but, to their relief, no one had to be hospitalized over the course of the post-procedural assessment.

By far the most fascinating changes, however, were in her brain. They already knew of some great and terrible possibilities with that grisly hallucination Andraste gave everyone, and the MRIs cemented that sentiment. Her synapses were noticeably more active and densely packed together than those in an average human, and she had a particularly dense concentration of folds and wrinkles in her cerebral cortex. The staff could only wonder what thoughts this once-human brain could conjure up.

Basic reasoning told them the Fomorian genes were responsible, but they didn't want to broach that topic any more than they had to. No one was excited for the day that they would wake her up, but Judicia brought it down on them soon after. She didn't acknowledge any grievances, and made it very clear that she wouldn't tolerate any further obstruction. What scared the staff the most, however, was when they showed her the scans of Andraste's alien mind. For the first time since anyone could remember, she smiled.

4   Hastings, England   9:15 A.M.   May 8th, 2335

The darkness faded, and for once, the sense of awakening wasn't as violent as it had been before. She experienced no pain; she instead felt warm and comfortable, while the voices and cacophony from that nightmare earlier had been reduced to a gentle hum.

It took some coercion for her eyes to crack open. Every part of her was heavy and dense like hardening concrete, but she fought to bring it into motion.

As she stirred in the bed, the energy in the air spiked. The voices and noise around her intensified, but not in a painful way. One of her eyes opened slightly, twitching and resistant, but it was enough for her to see a group of people in coats not too far away. Some were frozen solid, staring at her, while others ran around in a subdued panic.

"She's awake! She's awake!" A man cried as he ran out into the hall. His screams were audible for several minutes after he vanished through the door.

Both eyes were almost half open now, and there was more sense of feeling in the rest of her body. The white expanse of a hospital bed stretched before her. Beyond that, she was surrounded by thick panes of glass and a grove of tangled wires and machinery. Two hoses led from her face, while there were three of different sizes and colors embedded in her right arm. In the corner of her eye, one fell from the side of her head. The sheer number of different connections and machines made no sense to her, and she struggled to imagine what each one was for. She would have objected to the straps keeping her tied to the bed, but she wasn't feeling much below the neck, anyway.

The people beyond the glass came into focus, and she became aware of all the different eyes staring at her. Looks of horror, confusion, and panic were spread across the entire crowd. She wondered what the machines told them, and what sort of monster they saw her as.

As soon as there was enough feeling in her arm, she rubbed her hand along her head. A disheveled field of short hair ran between her fingers, with no scars or blood to be found. Her head didn't actually rupture, it seemed. And yet, she remembered the event so clearly.

The screaming man ran back in, trailed by two others: the tall, thin man with long black hair, and the short woman who was giving orders when her head burst open. They both stopped dead as they saw her. She met eyes with them, and they stared with the same shock and awe as the rest of the staff.

For a few moments, everything was still. No one said or did anything, waiting for someone else to break the silence. All the awareness directed towards her was striking, and she felt as if she was taking in a portion of the nervous energy they shared.

Eventually the thin man approached the glass, to the nervous anticipation of the others. His hands were shaking, and there was visible tension on his lower jaw, like his teeth were clenched together.

"Hello?" He said, with no small amount of trepidation. "Can you hear me?"

Her breathing hastened as she tried to speak, but her mouth hung agape and soundless. She could hear him fine, but the social onus made the simple task of responding much more of an ordeal. Words weren't an option, and she was still getting feeling back in her body. Sighing, she gave a weak nod.

"All right, excellent." There was something familiar about his voice, with its light but noticeable Egyptian accent. He turned to the others and said something- it was hard to tell beyond the glass. "Sit tight. A couple of us are coming in, okay?"

She nodded again. It was all she could manage.

The man and the short woman vanished around the corner of the glass enclosure. They passed through two reinforced doors, which swung open and closed with noticeable weight. The tall man came in slowly, while the shorter woman rushed to get in.

"Take it easy, Judicia." The tall man said. He came up to the side of the bed, walking in a slow, restrained manner. The short woman, meanwhile, stood at the foot of the bed, staring with intense, dark eyes.

"Uh," the tall man said, his voice trailing off. He shrugged and shook his head. "Hi." He finally said. "I'm guessing you have a lot of questions."

He was right, but she couldn't put them into words. Her jaw felt numb and foreign, and she struggled to create any speech. A few nonsensical sounds came out in her attempts.

"Don't force it," said the woman. "You're still coming off the anesthesia."

"I know this whole thing looks pretty mental- and it is-" he said, chuckling through the discomfort, "but you're in good hands. Now-" He pulled up a chair close by, and gently lowered himself into it. "My guess is, you don't remember much. Is that right?"

There was a disarming gentleness in his voice that she liked. She nodded.

"I figured." He leaned forward in the chair, folding his legs. "You've just completed a massive neurological enhancement." He gesticulated a lot, speaking in a matter-of-fact yet calm way. "I've gone through something similar. Try not to worry, we can try and help that."

Despite the woman's advice, a few fragments of a word were forced out. "Okay." The word was mangled and strained, but intelligible.

The man smirked. "All right, already making progress." He straightened up and gave her full eye contact. "Now, to begin: you are currently in Sussex municipal hospital, in Hastings, England. My name is Doctor Yousef Makkareb, and she is Doctor Bianca Judicia."

Their names crystallized some of the haze floating around in her head. Fragmented memories of Yousef's face and voice came into clearer focus. "I-I," she began with a heavy stammer. "I rem-m-member you." She knew what she wanted to say, but it seemed the rest of her body didn't want her to say it.

"Oh," He said, at a loss. "From when you woke up?"

She nodded.

"Alright, this is good. Don't put pressure on yourself, but is there anything else that comes to you? Anything at all?"

She felt a spike of anxiety. Some impetus told her that she had to remember something, that it was vital that she provide an answer. Without hesitation, she scoured her foggy mind for some information.

"Something called 'Fomorians,'" she began, the stutter still laying thick on her words. "The name 'Andraste.'"

"Do you remember your name?" He asked.

She stopped, nervous. "Is it Andraste?"

"Well, technically, no." He bit his lip as he pondered the answer. "But your real name is classified information."

"E-even to me?" She tilted her head.

"I'm afraid so. If it helps, I wasn't told it, either."

Andraste looked conflicted.

"Don't worry, you're doing really well." He spoke in an assuring tone. "Please, go on."

"I remember there was a crowd all around me earlier." A surge of worry, hot on her back and leading up into her head, struck her. "I started bleeding," she said, taking deep, short breaths. "Something came out of my head. People were hurt." she clenched the bed sheets.

"Don't worry, it's all right! It's alright." Yousef shot up from his chair. He put a hand on her back and one on her shoulder to steady her.

When his skin met hers, Andraste tensed up and bolted away from him, almost falling out of the bed. At his touch, heat, cold, and electricity tore through her body. It was a sharp, fulminant revulsion that cut into her in a way she couldn't explain or tolerate.

Yousef reeled in shock. He stepped back almost to the opposing wall.

Andraste straightened up, waiting for the sensation to subside. She noticed Yousef on the wall, looking at her in frenzied worry. The sight of his terror was crushing.

"I-I'm sorry," she said in a small, submissive voice. "I don't know what came over me."

"It's fine," Judicia chimed in at last. "You hallucinated the blood and pain when you first woke up. It wasn't your fault."

She looked at Judicia in confusion. "I hallucinated?"

"We're still figuring it out, but yes." She stood up and walked to where Yousef used to sit. "You were given stimulants to get you off the anesthesia more quickly, but they put you into shock instead. I understand it was scary, but don't worry. None of that really happened."

Whatever relief this brought was eclipsed by a discomfort in the pit of her stomach. There was still the lingering memory of pain, but her own pain. It was a distinct, empathic feeling that existed outside of her experience.

"But," she began, hesitant. "But someone was hurt." As she said this, Yousef slowly came back. "I'm not sure how, but I know that someone was in pain because of that hallucination." She didn't sound confident in what she was saying.

Yousef and Judicia looked at each other, confused.

"I'm sorry, I can't explain it," she whimpered. "I just have this sense that someone was in pain." It was a struggle for her to get the words out.

Judicia looked to the side as she tried to think of what to say. Yousef furrowed his brow and snapped his fingers, as if he knew what it was but it wasn't coming to him.

"Does she mean the thing with Williams?" He looked to Judicia.

"What?" Andraste cried in horror. "So someone was hurt?" Her big pupils seemed to narrow in her state of arousal.

"Yes." Judicia grunted, her voice hoarse with aggravation. She turned from the bed and kneaded her temple. "One of our psychiatrists had a seizure and was put in the emergency room."

The horror crept down Andraste's spine like an encroaching frost. "Oh my god," she gasped. She held her head in her hands as her eyes grew watery.

Judicia pressed her hand hard against her temple. She staggered a bit as she walked, then put her other hand on her head. "That wasn't your fault," she said, pained. Both of her hands squeezed to contain the sudden pain surging through her skull.

"Judicia?" Yousef called in a panic. He reached out to her and noticed that his arm was blurry. His voice was clouded and full of static, and his balance was off. He grasped the side of the bed to keep himself upright.

Andraste didn't know what was happening. Her heart was palpitating, and a whirlwind of thoughts went through her head. The memory of the blood and pain still occupied a space in her mind, which combined with the fear of the current situation to make a miasma of worry and panic.

A thin layer of smoke seemed to fill up the room, but she didn't smell it. Everything was as blurry and incoherent for her as it was for the people in the room. She could tell she was hallucinating again, and their anguish registered in her mind as well. 'Help me,' 'make it stop,'.

"I-I'm sorry!" She cried. "I don't know what I'm doing!" She tried to pry her body from the bed.

She jerked back, surprised to find several straps holding her in place. Andraste looked back at Judicia, who was writhing on the floor. Determined, she gave the strap on her arm a tug. After some considerable resistance on its part, it snapped. With her arm free, she went to work on the other ones.

"Andraste," Yousef said weakly, "what are you doing?" He was on his knees, grabbing the rails on the bed to stay up.

"Dr. Yousef, please hold on!" She broke the strap around her waist. "I can help you!" She reached out to him as best she could.

Her body grew heavy as she stretched towards him. Every sensation dulled and her limbs grew weak. Within a moment, she became too weak to support her own weight and collapsed back on the bed. There was another tube in her arm, shooting a sedative into her veins. The fear leaked away like blood from a deep wound.

Yousef stood back up and he dashed over to Judicia. With some help, she was back on her feet. They glanced back at Andraste and exchanged a brief look. Without getting closer, he said, "Try to relax, Andraste. We'll check on you later." With that, they both made their way to the door.

As the room faded, Andraste felt a dam burst, and big, hot tears fell from her eyes. "I'm sorry," she said. Her weak voice was quiet as a whisper but dense with remorse. She couldn't think once the sedative took hold.

Judicia returned to the room half-an-hour later with a huge bag of ice and a bottle of painkillers. Andraste was passed out on the bed, her face scrunched in an agitated grimace. No one was hurt, and Andraste seemed stable, but there was tangible unease in the room. Yousef approached her as she came in.

"You all right?"

"I'm fine," she said, clearly in pain, "just more of what I had earlier."

Yousef sighed, looking back at Andraste. "What the Hell are we gonna do?"

Judicia looked away. Just looking at Andraste hurt. "I don't know," she said. She turned to the monitors. "What did it look like on the scans?"

Yousef turned to the neurological records. "There was a big spike in activity around the amygdala," he said, "and her adrenaline shot through the roof. Pretty basic panic response."

"Get her some medication for it."

Yousef looked confused. "Like what?"

"Anything!" Judicia winced as she spoke, pressing the bag of ice against her head even harder.
"Benzodiazepines, SSRIs, I don't care. If we're going to

make any progress with her, we need to keep her stable. Keep those nerves in line, no matter what."

"Alright, alright." Yousef replied. "We'll see what we can do."

"Good. Talk to the psychiatric unit, and report back to me." She staggered out of the room, propping herself up against the wall.

Yousef still looked at Andraste. His face was equal parts scared, anxious, and confused, but unmistakably sad.

"I'm going to do everything I can," he said under his breath.

5   Hastings, England   11:25 a.m.   May 10th, 2335

Dr. Yousef spoke to the resident psychiatrist, who prescribed an intravenous medication in anticipation of Andraste's next panic attack. It was hooked up to a catheter in her arm, designed to release when the next bout of anxiety struck. A nurse described it as "strong stuff."

She tried to put her mind on something else as she was wheeled to her physical therapy session, put in a wheelchair and attended by two nurses. Her memories were treacherous since they could stir up another hallucination and put someone else in the emergency room. She looked ahead and stared intently at the corridor in front of her. The fear was still there, but she refused it- she resolved to keep it at bay.

She closed her eyes, to clear away the distractions. Noises faded from the background, and her thoughts came into focus.

From beneath the darkness of her eyes, she saw a pattern emerge. It was at once bizarre and strikingly familiar. She could see the silhouette of a giant gear pop out against the darkness, turning on its axis. There was a distinct nostalgic feeling at the sight of it. The tines of the gear spun with three others to drive a metal shaft sharply and precisely down a metal rod, hollowing it out and smoothing it. It was a small piece of a larger assembly line, and as the hollow barrel moved along, another section of the assembly came into the light.

She saw more gears spinning around and more intricate machinery, highlighted piece by piece. Everything from the screws to the wires came together as if she were assembling it herself.

The sequence of images felt like memories, yet there was also a pang of exciting novelty to them. She felt like the artificial intelligence running a facility, overseeing every process of the machines and every step of production- she was in control of all of it. She had no idea where these images or feelings were coming from, but she didn't care. For the first time since she had woken up, she felt happy.

"We're almost there, just hang on." The nurse said, turning to the right and pushing two doors open.

She was wheeled into a small exercise room. Yousef and Judicia were in a corner, waiting. Andraste cast aside her mechanical fantasy as she saw them, worried about any lasting effects from their previous encounter.

"Andraste?" Yousef said, kneeling to her level. "How are we doing?"

"Are you two all right?" She lurched forward in the wheelchair and almost fell out. There was no strength in her body to stop the fall. One of the attendants caught her and pushed her back into the chair.

"We're fine." Judicia said, her voice stern. "Andraste, this is all part of the experimental process. You're not giving people seizures and hallucinations on purpose, are you?"

Andraste shot up, her posture erect. "No, ma'am! I-I would never-"

"Then you have nothing to worry about. Stop worrying and get testing. Chop chop." She snapped her fingers twice, and the attendants spun Andraste around.

She was pushed in front of a long tank of water with iron bars along the sides. Yousef walked over, giving Judicia a reprimanding look. "All right, Andraste, this is just to test your coordination. And then…" He took several small gauze pads and stuck them to several spots on her legs. "These will measure the muscle activity in your legs. Prop yourself up on the bars here and try to walk to the other side, okay?" He walked to the other side. "No big deal. Take it nice and slow."

Taking a deep breath and then sighing it out, she lifted herself onto the bars and into the waist-high water.

She let out a loud whoop. "Cold!" She cried.

The attendants at her sides went tense, but calmed as she started moving. It took some considerable effort to get her numb and unwieldy legs to cooperate, even with the shock of the cold water. She knew what she wanted to do with her leg, but the impulse to move only made it twitch around.

"Remember, nice and slow. Just put a little bit of weight on your leg at a time." Yousef spoke with an abundance of caution in his tone.

She did as he instructed. She leaned forward, eager to get moving, but the pressure on her leg seemed to be too much. She stumbled and grasped the rail as hard as she could. There was a loud grinding of metal. As she regained her balance, she noticed the attendants had backed away from her.

Where her hand had grabbed the rail, it had been yanked far to the side.

Wide-eyed, she looked at Yousef, who shared her expression. Judicia had gotten close, and took a close look at the damage. She slowly nodded as she looked over it. She looked up with a perplexing smirk on her face.

"Very promising." She walked over to Yousef.

Andraste glanced between the two of them, unsure of what to do or say. Yousef noticed this in her, and shrugged. She looked to the floor.

"I don't understand," Andraste said, supporting all her weight on her arms. "How am I doing all this?"

"This is what we want, Andraste." Judicia stepped up before Yousef could come in. "The Prime Minister of England wants to get a leg up in our war against The Martyr's Army, and this is how we're doing it."

Yousef nodded. "The Fomorians were incredibly powerful, Andraste. This kind of strength is probably just the beginning."

Andraste turned away, looking back at the bent metal bars. "So, no one really knows what I'm capable of."

"No, but that's what we're going to find out," Judicia said. "Your hallucinations have actually given us a lot of insight about you mentally, and now we just need to test you physically." She stepped back. "The sooner we get those numbers, the sooner we can move on to something else. Get busy."

Nodding, Andraste tried to get her legs back under her control. Her arms did much of the work as her heavy legs struggled to coordinate themselves. After a good half-an-hour of wading back and forth, she was able to walk again. Heaving her breath, Andraste pulled herself out of the pool and took two steps before collapsing into her wheelchair.

Yousef was looking at the results on his tablet, lit up with elaborate scans of her leg muscles. "Great job, Andy."

She and Judicia turned to him with raised brows.

"'Andy'?" Judicia asked in an incredulous drawl.

Yousef shrugged. "What? 'Andraste' is kind of a mouthful, isn't it?" He gestured to Andraste with the tablet. "I mean, unless you prefer that."

Looking aside for a moment, Andraste pondered it. A nickname felt- she wasn't certain- familiar. Comfortable, even. Finally, she shook her head. "No, Andy is fine."

Yousef smiled, then glanced back at Judicia. "All right. How are you feeling, Andy? You must be tired."

"No," Andraste blurted out, very tired. "I can keep going. Don't worry about me." She took a breath and stepped onto her aching legs. Seeing the doctors calm and calling her cute nicknames was worth pushing through the exhaustion.

"If you say so," Judicia said, leading her into another room.

Inside a massive gymnasium was a roughly building-sized obstacle course, with floors that moved in waves and spinning metal hoops for her to jump through.

Andraste went limp at the sight, almost tumbling into Yousef, who was similarly struck dumb.

"The current record is five minutes, Andraste. Think you can beat that?" Judicia teased with a stopwatch.

Walking up to the starting line, Andraste got into a starting position. She imagined the gears and machinery from before to calm herself, hoping to stay calm for another round of trials. It settled her mind, and beneath the fearful misgivings, she found her strength again.

"Let's do it," Andraste told Judicia with a nod.

The latter nodded, and she started the timer. Andraste hurled herself at the obstacle course, setting a precedent for one of her many attempts at the record.

6   London, England   15:41
May 14th, 2335

The graffiti was painted on a building near St. James Park. It was distant, but not so distant that he could ignore it. As he waited for the public sanitation workers to come and do their job, Nathan Rowe sat at his desk and stared at the picture.

It was a black silhouette of what was maybe a person. Both of his hands were in the air, he was on his knees, and there were three spots of exposed tree trunk on the body representing bullet holes. There were two in the chest and one in the stomach. Cracks radiated out from these holes like he was made of glass and the graffiti had captured him mid-shatter. Beneath the silhouette were the three words that stained every act of rebellion against civilized society: "I Remember the Martyrs."

The news crew arrived before the cleaners did. The media would be ablaze with this picture. Already, he could see the headlines: *"The Martyrs' Army, in London? 'Remember The Martyrs' Graffiti in Front of Prime Minister's Office."*

Rowe scratched his beard, made of the same tight brown curls as his hair.

There were two soft knocks on the door. Rowe looked at his computer screen, pulling up the video feed. With two security guards, Adam Laurie, the Secretary of

Defence, stood outside. Rowe anticipated that Laurie would want to talk about this, and it wasn't a conversation he was looking forward to. Bracing himself for the worst, Rowe pressed the button on his desk to unlock the door.

Laurie rushed into the room in his characteristically eager way. His white hair was thick and shiny with styling products, and the Botox treatments had left him with a permanent smirk. The caricatures of him in political cartoons were never too far from what he looked like.

"Good day, Rowe." He said in an officious, bold tone.

"Hello, Mr. Laurie." Rowe said, not getting up from his chair. "I'm guessing you're here because of the new artwork?" He gestured to the graffiti outside.

"Afraid so. A whole team of reporters is swarming around Parliament." He folded his arms. "Don't know what I could say that I haven't already told them a million times."

"We'll take them in." Rowe said, opening communications with his press team on the computer. The voice prompt came up, and he said, "Prepare a podium. ETA, twenty minutes." He got up from his chair.

Laurie narrowed his eyes. "Come on, really? That picture's all over the place!"

"That's why we need to address it." Rowe moved past him, heading out of the office and towards the entrance. Noticing the knot in his tie was off-center by about a thousandth of a centimeter, he stopped to fix it.

"Let's not make this incident a bigger deal than it needs to be, okay?" Laurie said with sweat on his brow.

Rowe didn't respond for a moment, having taken the time to get his tie perfect. When the issue was resolved, he whipped around to Laurie.

"If you want to go to the press and keep insisting that their messiah had a gun or nuclear launch codes or something, fine. But I'm sick of dancing around the issue." Rowe turned and grabbed the knob on the door.

Laurie went wide-eyed. "Rowe, we're not going to keep talking about that idiot, are we? This is nothing new!"

"All the more reason to talk about it, Laurie!" Rowe opened the door. "They're pissed, Laurie, and our people are scared. They don't need more silence from us."

Laurie groaned. "Your mouth will be the death of you one day, Rowe."

Gratefully walking out the door, Rowe turned to his guard.

"To Downing Street, sir?" His guard asked.

"Yes, thank you."

The instant Rowe had agreed to meet with the press, reporters and photographers swarmed in front of the building, clinging to the edges of the podium like carrion crows.

He pushed the doors apart, and the shadow of the podium obscured the waves of light coming from the cameras. The phalanx of media reporters stretched to the sidewalk, at least twenty meters away from the stage itself. Arms, microphones, and notepads were all writhing around like the arms of a sea anemone while dozens of voices meshed into unintelligible, chaotic noise.

Rowe took a deep breath, and stood before the podium. They were all silenced as he came onto stage.

"Good afternoon." His voice carried across the open space. "In light of the recent portrayal of the Martyr's Army sigil, I have called this press conference. I am open for questions."

At the front of the pack was a familiar face: news anchor Kennedy Schmidt. It was the same dark complexion and flowing hair that announced only the biggest news, complete with her microphone and camera crew.

"If I could, Mr. Rowe?" Her crew was already focusing in on him, with their elaborate cameras and equipment poised and ready.

"Yes, Ms. Schmidt."

"We all know the story by now. The infamous 'Remember The Martyrs' graffiti has been painted nearby your office. Do you think this signifies a conspiracy to instill fear in the people of England, or is it nothing more than thoughtless delinquency?"

"Straight to the heart of the matter, as always," he thought. He was hoping for a question like this.

"I do believe there is deliberation behind these images. We have seen this picture all over the city. Whether there is a conspiracy in London or not, the fact remains that there is sympathy for the Martyr's Army among our people."

"What do you have to say about that, sir? That there is, in fact, sympathy for the people who wage war against us?"

For a moment, Rowe pondered how Laurie would respond to this question. *"There are mindless people everywhere, Kennedy. Even in our country."* Something to that effect. A self-important, dismissive wave of the hand, made to distance himself from the matter and cast an inoffensive net to catch thoughts about difficult issues.

"I don't think we have any right to be surprised about that."

Schmidt widened her eyes, and the tangle of arms stopped moving.

"What do you mean, sir?" Schmidt asked the question with a note of genuine loss.

"What I mean, Mrs. Schmidt, is that our country has much to answer for. The Martyr's Army is incredulous of our actions, and it is not unreasonable for our people to be incredulous, as well." For the sake of the Cabinet's peace of mind, Rowe would tone down his honesty about these matters and focus more on the present, but he had grown tired of it.

The crowd livened up at this sentiment. Looks of fear were exchanged, and murmurs rippled through the crowd.

"Sir, are you saying that the Martyr's Army has some justification for their actions?"

The crowd went silent at this. He knew this was the question that they would really cling to.

"There is no justification for the deaths of innocent people, much less a full-on war." He looked out at the crowd as he said this, narrowing his gaze. "Let me make it abundantly clear that I do not condone the actions committed against our country. In the past five months alone, The Martyr's Army has sacked twelve outposts, attempted three bombings within our borders, and taken no less than thirty of our brave soldiers as hostages. Their body count rises every day, and they have no intention of stopping. And it would be remiss of us not to mention the other countries and cities we have lost to their mad cult." He looked back to Schmidt.

"That messiah of theirs, Sennec, believed he understood something special about the lost Fomorians they worship. Messiah or not, they hung their hopes on him, and his death dashed those hopes."

Rowe knew he had to mention Sennec and the Fomorians at some point. The outside world defied all natural sensibilities. Rowe was sympathetic for people who had to live with that, but he wasn't sympathetic for the Martyr's Army.

"The Outlands are certainly difficult to survive in," he continued, "but the Martyr's Army chooses violence over our assistance. So, no, I am not saying that they are justified. I am saying that we are being antagonized for a reason- which is *not* the same thing. There is rampant contention over the true nature of the late Aaron Sennec- was he truly the hero of the Outlands? Do his efforts truly make him one of the titular 'Martyrs' that this rebellion trembles with fanaticism over? No one has the answers to these questions. What we know for certain is that he was a man who tried to make a difference in The Outlands."

Rowe knew this would cause a stir in the Cabinet- whenever Laurie saw this interview, it would be his fourth ulcer that month for sure. What he wanted people to understand- both the English populace and the Martyr's Army members who kept tabs on his policies- was that it was possible to admit his mistakes while still adhering to his beliefs.

"We had no intention of killing Aaron Sennec. The intent was to arrest him and question him about his involvement with the sacking of Cairo. Regardless, fire was exchanged, and Sennec was shot. I understand why The Martyr's Army is angry at us." He looked back at the crowd overall, straightening his posture. He took a deep breath and allowed his conviction to strengthen his tone of voice. "What I want The Martyr's Army to understand is that we will not stand for their ludicrous idea of justice.

"England has had an unprecedented year of economic success, as well as cultural and scientific advancements. The genetic enhancement industry has been booming, health care has improved prodigiously, and I am delighted and honored to see so many refugees calling this country 'home.' To satisfy the corpses of the Fomorians they worship, The Martyr's Army would see all of this destroyed.

"'There is no justice in government-run societies,' they say. I say, not only do we have justice, we have peace. We have a vision for the future in England- what vision does the Martyr's Army have? Tear down civilization and leave people to fend for themselves in a world shaped by unearthly forces? They are nothing more than petty, anarchic terrorists. If they want to destroy us, they can bloody well try!"

Rowe took a deep breath as the media members digested this.

Schmidt was whispering something to her tech crew. Some looked at one another for answers or insight, and others looked to the ground.

"So how do you plan to approach the graffiti, sir?" Schmidt said, breaking the silence.

"When we find whoever is responsible," he said, keeping his stride going. "We shall enforce it as we always do- the perpetrator will be charged with the destruction of property and insubordination, and shall be appropriately punished within the purview of the law." He looked straight at Schmidt again.

"What do the other members of the cabinet have to say about all this, sir?" Schmidt asked. A question like that signaled that she was at the end of her interview.

Rowe softened his expression. "I'm sorry, Mrs. Schmidt. I'm not at liberty to speak for my colleagues. I have no doubt that Mr. Laurie will have some more answers for you in person." He looked up. "Are there any other questions you'd like me to address?"

No one else said anything. Rowe expected this, and was satisfied with how it had gone.

"Thank you for your time, sir!" A voice in the back called out.

"My pleasure," Rowe said. "You shall be notified as soon as the graffiti has been cleaned off." There was a scattered, courteous applause from some members of the crowd while others dispersed to relay the story to their respective news outlets. Soon, Rowe returned to Parliament.

One person in the crowd had broken off from the throng before anyone else: a young man with a small video camera, who wormed his way past security with a false ID and the excuse that he was a "freelance journalist." Taking frequent glances over his shoulder to see if he was being followed, he took the Tube for about seven stops before going into a small flat.

"Smug old fucker," he muttered as he pulled out his phone. In his list of contacts, there was a contact for 'Pizza.' He dialed it.

The call connected, and a nasally, bored voice received it. "This is Vincenzo's Italiano, how can I help you?"

"What are your specials for the day?" They were the first few steps in a dance of codes and secret messages.

"Our meat lover's is half-off, we have a chicken parmesan, and Granny Vincenzo's Lasagna."

"Is it Granny's original recipe?"

The voice on the other side became subtly more alive as the conversation continued. "Yes sir, secret ingredient and everything."

"Give me five orders of those. For pick-up." The quantity served was an alarm level. One meant you were only checking in, five meant you had plans to discuss.

"Sure thing," said the voice, after a pause. "I'll give you another call once it's ready- about twenty minutes." He hung up.

Twenty minutes was how long he had to make himself scarce. In his drawer, there was a scanner designed to pick up wiretaps and other undesirables. A brief but thorough scan revealed no hidden microphones or cameras.

He locked himself in the bathroom, the most distant and sound-absorbent room in the flat. In the phone's charging socket, he jammed a crude device that would prevent the call from being traced.

Minutes later, his phone rang again. There was no caller I.D., but he didn't need one. He answered the call.

"David, this is Steven. What's the word?" It was the same voice from before.

"I watched Rowe's address. He's not even fazed by the paint job."

"So? How is this a code five?"

"It's a code five because he's being all smug and cavalier about it. It didn't work at all." David was wringing the fabric of his pants with his free hand. "If we really want to get our message across, we need to act now."

"You don't mean-"

"I do. I propose we conduct the operation sooner. Within the month, if we can."

"David, you can't be serious!"

David was yelling. "Fuck you, I'm dead serious! Rowe basically denounced the Martyr's Army in front of all these cameras! If we don't respond to that soon, everyone's gonna think we're soft!"

Steven was quiet for a moment. When he replied, his tone was forced and reluctant. "I'll get in touch with the others. We'll see what they think."

"There's nothing to think about, Steven! He's getting confident, and we need to knock him down a peg. Even if the plan doesn't work, an attack in the city so soon after Rowe's address will make him look like an idiot! We can't pass up an opportunity like this!"

"All right, all right. We still need to run this by General Bashford, you know. I'll get back to you in about two hours."

"Fine. Tell the others to get ready. We're bringing the war to London."

"I got it. I Remember the Martyrs."

"I Remember the Martyrs."

The phrase 'I Remember the Martyrs' was a sign of respect and acknowledgment within the ranks of the Martyr's Army. Saying it filled David with a hot, electric sense of conviction. As the feeling coursed through his body, he hung up.

In the same room, there was a loose edge of wallpaper. Pulling it away, David pulled out a cache of Martyr's Army contraband from a hole in the wall. He had dog tags, a preserved fruit that glowed in the dark, and a photo of Aaron Sennec. He took a deep breath as he saw the man's smile, reminded of his cause. The fruit reminded him of the insane nature that ravaged Europe. They say Sennec used the juice from this citrusy clump to deter a bear the size of a truck. The dead messiah seemed immaculate in the picture, with his alabaster skin and wavy brown hair. David even relished the shape of the assault rifle he held.

"Damn, I wish I could have met you."

7   Hastings, England   6:41 p.m.   May 14th, 2335

Everyone in the hospital watched Rowe's address. Judicia, Yousef and Andraste were all watching together.

After some time, Laurie had not come to comment yet, but Andraste noted Yousef's enthusiasm when another speaker arrived: Labibah Quadriyyah, another minister who was, by all accounts, Rowe's second-in-command. The crowd hushed and listened intently to this Egyptian woman in a hijab.

"We are continuing to speak with other surviving countries throughout the world in response to the crisis," she said. She was a small woman, but her voice was loud and clear. "We are uniting against the Martyr's Army on as many fronts as possible. Let me assure you, my friends, you will all be safe."

Andraste saw Yousef nodding along with her words as they watched the address. He was assigned to be Andraste's counselor, and thought that this bit of news could establish some context for her memory issues. And the staff was curious to see Andraste's reaction to it.

She was sequestered in her room, behind the glass- the television had been rolled in for her. No one was happy locking her up, but Andraste agreed it was for the best. As unstable as she was, she was willing to do whatever was necessary to ensure the safety of the employees.

"Are you a, uh, fan of hers?" Andraste asked when Quadriyyah had said her piece.

"Oh yeah, big one." Yousef nodded as he turned to her. "She was a huge help in the Egyptian refugee crisis." He shrugged. "But we can talk about that later. In the meantime, what do you make of what Rowe said? The Army and Sennec and all that?"

"I definitely remember what the Martyr's Army is. They're the ones I was sent to fight." She said slowly, voice grave. "And I recognize the name 'Aaron Sennec,' as well. I don't recall where I heard it, though."

"That's something we can work on." Yousef said, pulling up a chair.

He and Judicia were on the opposite side of the glass. Many of the machines needed to stabilize the DNA were taken out, so Yousef had converted some of the ample space into a temporary office.

"So," Yousef said, pulling out his tablet and opening the 'notes' application. "Shall we get started?"

Andraste sat upright on her bed, facing him. She was nervous as him, of too many things to count. There was a similar flavor to the fear he felt, and she felt at ease around him.

"Yes, please." She braced herself and pushed the fear down.

"Very well." He folded his legs and took a deep breath. "Now, the purpose of these sessions will be twofold: first is, of course, to help you keep your stress under control. Second is to monitor your brain activity.

We're hoping to get a sense of the different chemical responses in your brain. I'm going to share the scans with the other members of the staff, so we'll all be in the loop here."

Andraste nodded.

"First, I'd like to get some insight on your experiences." He didn't look at Andraste as he spoke, and mostly kept his eyes on the tablet. Andraste was surprised at the change in his demeanor for this situation. "We got some brain scans during a few of your, uh, 'episodes,' but what can you tell us? What were you thinking and feeling when that happened? Say, for instance, when you woke up?"

Andraste was hesitant to reminisce on that.

"That happened so suddenly, I don't feel like there's much to recall." She was being honest, but a feeling remained unexpressed as she said this.

"Anything would help." Judicia said, after a long stretch of silence. Coming from her, it sounded less like encouragement and more like an order.

"I-It's not that I don't remember it well," Andraste said, hastily, "I just don't remember what was going through my head at the time." She drew up her legs onto the bed, curling into a little ball. "I'm sorry, I don't know how to describe it. Every sensation was so sharp and distinct, like I was experiencing much of it for the first time."

Yousef was jotting down notes on his tablet. "All right, good. Please, go on."

"As for the," she paused, cogitating over the word. "As for the 'episode,' I remember feeling very overwhelmed. And it only got worse until it was unbearable. Next thing I knew, my head was splitting open." She shook her head from side to side as she said this, like she was trying to shake off the fear that the memory aroused.

"Well, you *were* in shock. We were all pretty worked up, so the overwhelm isn't surprising, either." Yousef assured her. "As for the 'new experiences,' that's more or less what we expect. When you go through a massive neurological overhaul like that, it's normal to feel like you have weird déjà vu about some things. What about the second time, when the two of us spoke with you?"

The memory of the fear and the discomfort were easy to relate, but she didn't know how she would bring up the experience of detecting other people's emotions. Fear crept up her throat at the notion of sounding crazy or unstable. So much had gone wrong, she wondered what else was risked by admitting to such an inane experience.

"I've come so far in this experiment," she thought. *"What will happen to me if I fail?"*

As that thought crossed her mind, she remembered something Yousef said: 'I'm sure you must have a lot of questions.' It had been over a week since she had woken up, and that was still the case. As it crossed her mind, a sense of helplessness washed over her.

"Should I have done more? Why haven't I asked more questions? How much necessary information am I ignorant of?" These thoughts and others fell on her like a wave.

Yousef spoke up before her mind went further. "Okay, Andy?" He tried to get her attention. "We're getting a big spike in activity in a lot of different places. A lot of epinephrine going around. What's going on?"

She took a breath. She had no idea what to say. "I-I don't know!" Andraste shuddered, letting her head fall forward. "I don't know what to tell you, Dr. Makkareb. I feel so lost."

He and Judicia looked at one another. Yousef was nervous, and that showed on his face, but Judicia gestured back to his patient, as if to say, 'get on with it.'

"It's alright- and please, you can just call me 'Yousef'. Could you define 'lost'?"

"I'm just," she said, wrapping her arms around herself. Her hands held onto her shoulders. "I feel so helpless. I hardly remember anything, my mind is playing tricks on me, and I'm hurting everyone who's trying to help. What's happening to me? How did my life come to this?"

The words came out of their own accord. They were sudden and forceful, and they left like rocky clumps shot from her chest. Whatever relief this feeling brought was offset by the negative emotion coming off the doctors. It was strongest from Yousef, and there was a definite change in Judicia as well.

Yousef was speechless. He was glancing around the room and biting his lower lip, desperate for something to say. Judicia, meanwhile, looked on in intrigued silence.

"Stupid, stupid, stupid!" She was doubled over, berating herself for losing control. *"It's because of that lack of control that people are getting hurt! I'm going to ruin this for everyone!"*

Andraste straightened her posture and put her arms in her lap. Her shoulders tingled, crying out for her own embrace, but she couldn't bring herself to do it again.

"I'm sorry." She looked at Yousef as she said this.

"Why?" Judicia spoke up. She walked in front of Yousef, and stood close to the glass. "Why are you sorry?"

Andraste was caught off-guard by this. "B-Because I lost control of my emotions?"

"What's wrong with that?" Judicia cocked her head. "I'm not trying to mess with you, Andraste. I'm genuinely asking."

It took a moment for Andraste to come up with an answer. "Because all I'm doing is complaining. Everyone involved in this project is putting so much on the line just keeping me alive. There are much bigger things to worry about than my personal comfort."

Yousef got up from his chair. "Andy, we *want* to hear about the things that are upsetting you. That's the whole point of counseling." He chuckled in spite of the situation.

The heat from him diminished. His consolation did little to console her, although he did seem to calm down.

"Andraste, understand something." Judicia said, in an aggressive reprimand. "This is one of the most important scientific experiments ever conducted. Period. We will create a new age for humanity with these results. If making scientific history means stepping on some toes, so be it."

Yousef and Andraste both looked at her, nonplussed.

She met their stares with folded arms and her own narrow gaze. "Oh, spare me. If we don't take risks, then we won't get anywhere." She looked back at Andraste. "So, you said you have a lot of questions. Get on with the treatment, and maybe we'll answer some." She went back to the wall on the other side of the room.

"So, Andy," Yousef said, clearing his throat, "From what we talked about earlier, it sounds like you don't remember much at all. And, again, that's not surprising- your brain just got pumped full of Fomorian bits. But let's see what we *can* remember, all right?"

"Sure," Andraste said, hands in her lap.

Yousef opened up a drawer in his desk and pulled out a folder. "When your brain is suddenly given so many new neural connections, your thoughts tend to get confused. As such, before someone has a neurological enhancement, we ask them to bring in some things that have distinct memories associated with them. Photos, keepsakes, that sort of thing." He reached into the folder and pulled out some photos. "Honestly, I don't know how well it's going to work for you, but it's worth a try.

" I'm going to show you some pictures. Tell me if you recognize them, or if they make you feel a certain way."

He took one and held it up. It was a picture of a scrawny woman who looked agonized just to look at the camera. There was an unmistakable look of defeat on her face with her bloodshot eyes and damaged complexion.

It had an immediate effect on Andraste. "That's," she said in disbelief, "That's me, isn't it?"

Yousef nodded.

"What happened to me?" Andraste looked at herself. The dark gray skin and slate-colored exoskeleton were far removed from the picture.

"Something to do with the Fomorian genes, Andy. Try not to worry about it- your skin isn't unhealthy or anything. Here, let's change gears."

He put the photo down and pulled a document out. "I also have your FH Project application right here; let me know when something jumps out at you." He cleared his throat. "According to your military information, you were in the army."

The word "army" had a distinct echo to it. It summoned an expanding series of disjointed sounds and images in her mind, of orders being called out and a gun in her hands. There was nothing specific about any of it, but it felt accurate. She tried to focus on the more concrete recollections, which summoned others alongside it.

"Yes," she said. "I remember, I applied for the military as soon as I finished school." More memories rose up as the instances from boot camp were cemented.

"So, this is all making sense, then? Good." There was more relief emanating from him. "After this, Andy, we have some details that are going to be harder to talk about."

Andraste raised a brow. "Harder how?"

"You were involved in a nasty incident out there, Andy," Judicia said flatly. "That's going to be a major talking point, so you should be prepared."

"Before that," Yousef said, catching the thread of the conversation, "Andraste, I'd like you to try something when you feel the anxiety." He gestured to the brain scans. "When you get upset, there's an enormous amount of activity in your mind, especially around your prefrontal cortex. I'm going to guess that, when you're anxious, your mind just races?"

There was something very freeing and assuring about those words. "Yes," she said, "That's exactly what happens."

"Well, when you notice that your mind is going too fast, here's what I want you to do: take a slow, deep breath, and count until your lungs are full- let's say to five. When they are, slowly breathe out, and count until your lungs are empty."

She tried it- she counted until she hit five, and then sighed, counting until she hit five again. She kept going, and felt herself relax. Tension in her body started to loosen, and her mind slowed down by a small but noticeable margin. Not wanting to waste time on this, she nodded.

"I'm ready for whatever you want to tell me, doctors."

"Okay, here we go," He pulled out several photos. "You were part of a reclamation squad; your job was to go into the Outlands and try to secure land for outposts. With me so far?"

She nodded, continuing her breathing.

"Your squad was attacked approaching Germany. And," he looked to the side, hesitating with the photos. "And it went very poorly."

"Yousef, come on." Judicia walked up to him. "We can't keep holding her hand with all this."

He began to protest until Andraste cut in.

"Dr. Yousef, please." She did the breathing cycle another time before continuing. "I can handle it."

"Okay then," Yousef took a picture and held it up for her. On it was the shape of the woman from before, face and equipment soaked in blood. She stood up on two rickety legs, looking ready to collapse from the weight of her supplies. The whites of her eyes pierced the coating of gore as they looked skyward.

"My god," Andy said in a whisper. That sense of stability evacuated her chest.

"Your unit was ambushed and slaughtered," Yousef said, wincing. "You were the only survivor."

When he said that, the image he was holding leapt out at her. As if it were being shown on a documentary, she saw the same fractured shadow of her former self being thrown into a firefight. Bullets tore at the trees and greenery, while the bloodshot eyes stared at her amidst the haze of forest mists and bullet smoke. Her expression did not change, even as the structure of the eyes collapsed and they melted into white pools on her face.

It was no nightmare. This long, integral memory exploded into her mind, accompanied by the fear. Tidbits of the environment came back, too. The only memory that existed beyond the picture was of a dense, inescapable tangle of vines, thorns, and tree branches. Unnatural noises surrounded her, and bizarre animal limbs reached into the mix to stab and claw at her. Andraste didn't know how she escaped, only that she had and was running through the forest as it tore her to shreds.

The experience was so visceral and so multifaceted, that she didn't know how to put it into words. There was too much information for her to communicate. Trying to focus on one particular sensation or thought would only open the floodgates to other ones. Andraste fought to bring her thoughts under control. She clenched the sheets of her bed while she took short, hard breaths.

"Andraste?" Yousef said, getting up from his chair. "What is it?"

"I-I'm sorry," she choked, breathless.

Her body sucked air in and out, but she didn't feel like she was getting any. As the first few pangs of panic crept up her back, she started breathing more quickly and violently.

"I can't breathe," she forced the words out, and she fell from the bed, onto her hands and knees.

The panic shot up into her body. She lost track of her breathing, as if her lungs imploded. The room around her faded from view as clouds of dark static filled the borders of her vision. She shuddered and twitched on the ground, subsumed by a nameless, all-consuming dread. It was a cold, bitter notion of aimless existential despair with the paralyzing terror of imminent death. There wasn't a car running into her or a gun at her face, but the presence of her death felt as real and tangible as the floor beneath her.

"Andraste, do the exercise!" Judicia cried out, her head throbbing.

Andraste sucked in air, and let it leak out. She counted to five once while inhaling, and again while exhaling. The long breaths were worrying, making her feel like she wasn't getting enough breath, but with a few repetitions, she did feel the thoughts slow down. But the panic still had her in its claws.

It's not enough, she thought. *I can't calm down.*

She wanted all the thoughts in her head to stop, but no alternative came to her.

Anything, she thought, as if pleading with her own mind. *I'll take anything!*

As these thoughts crossed her mind, revelation struck. She closed her eyes, continued to take the deep, five-count breaths, and went back to the machine.

Beginning with a spinning gear, she diverted all the focus she could muster onto the image of this machine. The gear turned in time with her breathing, making a full rotation by the second time she counted to five. After the gear, she added drive shafts, pistons, and other components. The panic began to melt away, and the deep breaths felt more fulfilling and gratifying.

A small beeping sound on her right brought her out of her trance. It was the mechanism on her arm, which dispensed a tranquilizer when she panicked. The effect was immediate.

Judicia had a hand on her head, but was still standing up.

"The pain is stopping," she said, amazed.

"Andraste, that was great!" Yousef said, standing up from the chair. There was a warm glow coming off him. Andraste guessed this was what his excitement felt like.

"You were definitely panicking, but you brought it under control!" He was smiling from ear to ear. "Did the breathing help?"

From the icy lake of the panic, Andraste felt a warm bloom of joy rise up. "Yeah," she said, hardly believing it. "I guess it did." She got up off the floor, staggered. "Tell me, Dr. Yousef," she asked, "is there anything in that folder about a factory?"

Confused, he started skimming the photos and documents, until he found something that made him stop. He pulled out the document and read it aloud with wide eyes.

"Work history: mechanic at several factories, ranging from munitions to vehicle development." He looked back at Andraste. "How did you-"

"Machines are a recurring image in my mind, Doctor." She sat back down. "Now I know why." The medicine helped the stream of memories feel less overwhelming. "I was a mechanic during those factory days. There was always something so engaging about the way all the pieces came together." Even on the bed, she struggled to stay upright. "Of all the things that pop into my head, that's the one thing that I actually like to see." She was swaying back and forth, and some of her words ran together.

Yousef leaned forward. "Is the medicine too strong, Andy?"

"Maybe," she said before slumping over on the bed.

"Andy!" Yousef shot up. "Judicia, we need to fix this."

"No, it's fine!" Andraste's inhibitions were slipping away as she picked herself up. "I can handle whatever you two need to do."

"Well, we don't *need* you to get overmedicated like this, Andy. Judicia, help me out here."

Judicia looked at him with folded arms. "Yousef, it's either this or another head-exploding panic attack. Just be glad that it works, yeah?"

"No, I will not!" Yousef was red in the face.

"Yousef, it's fine. You're putting yourself through a lot just to do this session with me." Andraste opened despite his protests. "I can feel it in your fear."

The heat from Yousef's fear stopped. It didn't grow cold, it stopped. Coolness was relaxing, heat was worrying, but the absence of any sensation was an enigma. Andraste guessed it was terror- the kind of vacuous, shocking realization that consumes your mind and leaves you mentally paralyzed.

"I know you're worried, Dr. Yousef." She rested her arms on her legs. "You don't have to make excuses. I understand."

His eyes were wide, and his sweat grew cold. He glanced back at Judicia, who had nothing but a raised eyebrow. Andraste's assessment had a startling, cutting insight to it, and the mere sight of her was terrifying. Her big blue eyes were beacons of a macabre energy, with an otherworldly magnitude that he agonized to interpret. As her inscrutable face pored over him, he could feel the cut of her gaze, penetrating and dissecting him.

"I feel it when you worry, doctor. It's cold, and it's bitter. I don't want to make you feel that way without good reason."

The light on her tranquilizer catheter went out, and she could feel the lightheadedness abate. As she got a good look at Yousef's face, she realized just how far she had gone.

"You 'feel' it?" Yousef's gaze flitted between Andraste and Judicia, looking for an answer. Several moments without one passed, so he just stood up and cleared his throat as he looked at the tablet.. "Hang on, I need to show some of these scans to our psych team." He made his excuse and rushed from the room.

Judicia perked up at this. "He'll come around." She lamented, in a calmer tone of voice. "So, you said his fear 'felt' familiar?" She folded her arms and stood near the glass. "Think you could describe that for me?"

As best she could, Andraste spilled her guts about these extrasensory experiences, and the tangibility of other people's emotions. She figured there was no point in trying to stay quiet about it.

Judicia narrowed her brow and scratched her chin. "Fascinating. You've noticed this from the very beginning?"

She nodded.

"So, we're not the only ones affected by your mental abilities. In some ways, we affect you." She paced as she thought on this. "Have you only been able to pick up on emotions? You haven't, say, read minds or anything?"

Andraste was stunned at the thought. Sensing the emotions of another person was already a daunting notion. She hadn't even considered going further.

Judicia pursed her lips and nodded. "Well, that's another thing we'll have to work on." She moved to the door. "I think that's enough therapy for today. Try to relax; that medicine will definitely put you out of sorts."

"I'm sorry!" Andraste cried, praying Yousef would come back. "If you see Dr. Yousef again, could you-"

"I'll tell him," Judicia said with a nod. "Just relax. We'll keep you updated." Judicia moved past the door before she could say anything else. Sighing, Andraste did as she was told.

The remote to the television was left in her chamber. As she settled onto the bed, letting her head fall onto the pillow, she took it and started going through the channels. She wasn't paying attention to anything that she was seeing; she clicked the remote on impulse, to ease her nerves. Football games, cooking shows, and cartoons passed by as she tried to center her thoughts.

"What does Judicia expect me to be capable of?" She thought, holding herself by the shoulders again. She could feel the tension ebb away from the muscles. *"I only have myself to blame for getting into all of this, so it's no use feeling sorry for myself. Still, I can't stop wondering: what have I gotten myself into? What have these people done to me?"*

She stopped herself at that thought. She violently shook her head, as if she would break the thought against the sides of her skull. Returning to the breathing exercise, she calmed herself before it was able to take root.

"'These people' are here to help me. If I develop a 'me versus them' attitude, it will all be over." Sighing, she kept skimming through the channels.

Several minutes and several dozen channels passed, and the nerves were creeping back. Her toes curled up, and with her free hand, she grabbed her shoulder a little harder. Breathing in, exhaling, and counting to five, the channels went by more quickly.

She stopped, however, when she saw the machine. A complex manufacturing system composed of gears and pistons and all the things she imagined to calm herself were being shown on the television, and it snatched up her attention. It was a documentary show about the process of manufacturing wind-up toys. The narrator talked about the specifications of each gear and part required for the toy, and the unique process that went into the creation of each moving piece. Metal gears were cut from templates, long strips were wound into springs, and it ended with the assembly of the toy itself. For the entire duration of the episode, she was lost in it.

The moment the episode ended, Andraste pressed "rewind" and watched it again. She did this several times, never once losing her focus. She memorized every pattern of movement, and every minute step that went into the creation of the toy. Her mind was already drawing the schematics, and by the sixth time she had watched it, she had a full mental blueprint for making the toy.

In her idleness, she became aware of how relaxed she was. She felt stable and in control of herself, with no immediate fear of causing any harm.

In the hallway, Judicia was almost ran over by an excited Yousef.

"Whoa! Sorry," He quickly said. "But while I've got you here-"

"She said she was sorry," Judicia said flatly. "I know it can be a lot, but try not to sprint out of the room in terror next time."

"What?" He was holding a folder in his hand, which went limp at the reprimand. "Judicia, I wanted to see what the scans were showing us."

On his tablet, he had a time-lapse of the activity in Andraste's brain. He slowly went through the timestamps as Judicia looked at the bursts of yellow, orange, and red blossoming over the blue brain images. Flowers of activity swirled around the radius of Andraste's alien mind, as Yousef emphasized their shapes around the middle and frontal sections.

"Look here, this was when we showed her the pictures- lots of epinephrine, like I said. And then she does the breathing, look." The flowers were shining a harsh red at first, but then they softened into a gentle orange. "It calms her down even more. Then, the medication:" The orange blooms became sunny yellow petals scattered around the gray matter. "I was worried she would pass out- thankfully not, and it looks like she's still awake. How is she?"

Speechless, Judicia's gaze flitted from him to the scans. All she could do was nod, impressed. There was silence.

"I, uh," he said after a moment, "I know it didn't look good to rush out like that. She did freak me out a little, but that's not what I wanted to see. Like I said, wanted to check in with the medication team."

"She was worried about scaring you," Judicia confirmed. "But she'll be happy to see these. What do the readings say now?"

Flipping through the other scans, he brought up the current activity monitor. The bouquet of her mind's flowers was more balanced than it had been before, with each color showing similar prominence.

"This is good," he said. "Looks like she's pretty relaxed."

"Maybe we should leave it that way, then." Judicia kept walking. "Let her recuperate from the medication."

"Oh, right." He looked back at the tablet. "Monitor the side effects."

"You did a good job calming her down in there," Judicia told him with a rare smirk on her face. "Keep it up. If we're going to get anywhere with this project, we need to keep her steady."

"Right," he said with a lingering uncertainty.

As Judicia walked on, Yousef kept his eyes on the tablet. According to the scans, this was the calmest that Andraste had been in a long time.

"I should do more for her," he thought. *"Let her know I'm really there for her."*

8   Hastings, England   3:41 p.m.   May 17th, 2335

According to her nutritionist, Andraste had to keep the mask on to prevent the disruption of her dietary regiment. Her body required a very specific intake of nutrients to function properly, and unnecessary additions could have drastic consequences.

She reflected on this fact as she brushed her fingers along it. The metal was very smooth and light, and it had four vertical holes. It was evocative of a medieval knight's mask. The center grill could retract and open a space for one of the special rations to be placed. They weren't bad- they were filling and even had some decent flavor- but it didn't feel like eating. There were distant memories of having food and going through the rigamarole of having a meal, and this had none of the ceremony or atmosphere. It nourished her, but the experience was hollow.

She only needed one ration per day, and that was all the water and nutrition her body needed. Andraste found that to be a very interesting notion; it was one of the few things that actually made her feel like the super-soldier that everyone expected her to be.

She thought the control over her strength and her mental powers were too tenuous to be worthwhile. In the grand scheme of things, she felt stuck. She was being moved to another facility in London in a few days, and they had made it very clear that they wanted Mr. Rowe to see her. The impending meeting only made her wonder what would go wrong.

    Yousef and Judicia were discussing their plan of action in another room. They said they would be right back, but after an hour with so much on her mind, it felt much longer.

    "Is your mask bothering you?" A nearby attendant asked.

    Andraste snapped to attention at this. "Oh, no, sorry." She put her hands down in her lap. "Everything's fine, thank you."

    "All right." The attendant said, and she went back to her phone. She seemed disinterested in her work. Her emotions were flat; Andraste barely felt anything coming off her.

    She noticed the emotions of every passing doctor, nurse, and janitor. Some were soft, some were intense, and no two were the same. Heat meant the mind was active or inviting, coldness meant it was relaxed or closed-off,

    As this happened more and more, she reflected on the potential of looking into another person's mind. The stories of Fomorian mind manipulation were only legends; she had no idea what to make of any of them. It seemed likely that Yousef and Judicia were talking about this exact thing just outside.

    As the names crossed her mind, the door opened, and Yousef walked in.

    "Afternoon, Andy." He said with a light tone.

She jumped at his voice. "Hello, Dr. Yousef!" She steadied herself with her breath. "Are you well?"

"I am, thanks." He grabbed a nearby chair. "I know how busy the last few days have been. How are you feeling about it all?"

She glanced to the side before answering. "It's a lot to take in, I admit." She looked back at him to answer. "But I'm looking forward to making more progress."

"That's good," Yousef nodded. He pulled the back of the chair towards her and sat in it backwards, fingers drumming along the top of the headrest. "Still, there's really not much to worry about. I know how hard things can look, but in my experience, they generally work out for the best."

His mental aura was palpable as he said this. A warm feeling came off him- confidence, she guessed- that she didn't see often before. Her curiosity took hold.

"What do you mean?" She cocked her head at him as she went from her bed to a chair closer to the glass.

"Well," he said, drawing out the end of the word, "I've been through some tough times, Andy. Nothing like becoming a human experiment, but a lot of times where I was really unsure of the future, myself. I never thought I'd be working on a top-secret government project like this, you know?"

She sensed more conviction coming from him, and it fascinated her. "I see what you mean, I think," she said. "I-if you don't mind me asking," Andraste stammered, "what sort of tough times?"

His fingers stopped drumming. With wide eyes, Yousef looked to the side as he pondered the question.

Andraste felt the confidence fade. "I-I'm sorry, I didn't mean to-"

"It's okay, Andy. I'm not upset, I just," he shrugged, "I just haven't talked about it much. Most people already kinda know my story. Wondering where to start."

Andraste leaned in. "Whatever works for you."

"All right," he chuckled. "Let's start at how I came to London. I'm from Cairo, originally."

Her eyes widened. "Cairo, Egypt? I thought the Martyr's Army-"

"Sacked it to reclaim the land? Yeah. They did." He nodded ruefully. "I was only, I think, eight or nine years old when it happened. My parents did a lot of work abroad, so we were lucky to escape. They thought London would be safest for us- away from the mainlands." Yousef shrugged. "Yet here we are, dealing with the Army again."

"Doctor Yousef," she said with a heavy-hearted breath. "I had no idea. I'm so sorry."

He sighed, running a hand through his hair. "It wasn't your fault. Thanks, though." Noticing a loose strand of his ponytail, he pulled off the band and started to re-do his hair. "Even when I was a kid, I struggled over here. I fell in with some bad crowds, got into drugs and alcohol. Nearly died from an overdose."

"My god!" Andraste was shocked.

"It's one reason I keep my hair long- I had my head shaved for a long time." He tried to chuckle bitterly as he pulled back his hair. "Kinda separates me from that time in my life."

A deep chord in Andraste resonated. The image of her past self flashed before her eyes, and she was reminded of how badly she wanted to leave that behind.

"I think I know what you mean," she said with wet eyes.

"A reminder that I've moved on, yeah." He finished his ponytail. "Once I was out of the hospital, my brain was fried. I signed up for this experimental treatment for the damage, and guess who was in charge: Judicia."

"Are you serious?"

"Yeah! Her genetic enhancement stuff started out as medical treatments." He poked at the side of his head. "Fixing the brain damage was the easy part- next up, she suggested regrowing parts of my brain in such a way that could make me more intelligent. Sounded crazy, but I was so scared of being back in the gutter, I was up to try anything new."

"A-and it worked?"

He nodded with a chuckle. "It changed everything about me. And like you, I was even missing some major memories. Got them back after a while, but God damn, it was scary."

Andraste leaned as far forward as the chair would allow. "You lost your memories?"

"Oh yeah. That must have been one of the most uncertain times in my life, kind of like what you're going through."

She sensed another warm glow off of him, but there was a different nuance to it. She presumed it was sympathy.

"Once I had all that sorted, though, I got into studying medicine and ended up liking it. One thing led to another, and now I'm working here." He gestured to the room. "I was scared, yeah, and there were a lot of times where I had no idea what was coming next."

"But you never gave up," Andraste said, feeling inspired.

"No. No I didn't," He responded, still feeling warm. "I had people all around me who had my back and had faith that I would succeed. It's not always easy to see, but the same thing can be said for you, Andy."

A little tear went down the side of her face. "Thank you so much, Doctor."

"Aww, Andy!" He looked away, still smiling. "I didn't mean to make you upset."

"Well, I'm the one who asked." Andraste wiped the tear away and did the breathing- in, count to five, out, count to five.

At the end of her breath, Judicia came in with a third man. It took a moment, but she recognized him. It was the doctor who had a seizure when she woke up.

"Hello there," he said, with a wide grin on his face. "How are things?"

The man radiated discomfort. Something about him sent shivers down Andraste's spine. He had the same receding brown hairline and slight hunch, as the last time. The memory of this man convulsing and dying on the ground filled her with dread. His warm and inviting body language was once a set of violent jerks and contorted limbs.

"Andy, this is Professor Williams." Yousef gestured to him. "He's going to be help us prep for the trip to London."

More and more people had been calling her 'Andy,' but Yousef did it most often. The informality of it was comforting, and took the edge off for a moment.

"It's nice to meet you, Professor." She said, imagining a spinning gear to calm herself. "Are you-"

"I'm fine, Miss Andraste." He said, chuckling. "Please don't feel bad about that little mishap during the experiment. It was just an accident." He wrung his hands together. "In fact, that's why I'm here; my team and I have been working on some medication that should help your panic and hallucinations. Should be much more effective."

She sat straight up as he said that. "Really?" She said. She closed in on the glass, and propped her hands against it as she looked at him. "I was just talking with Doctor Yousef about that! You think it will help that much?"

He put one of his hands parallel to hers on the glass. "Possibly- it's still experimental, but we figured we would go ahead and try it before we meet with Mr. Rowe."

"Thank you so much, Professor." She said, her voice trembling. "That is a massive relief."

"Finally," she thought, *"I can stay in control!"*

"Think nothing of it," Williams said, "I'm happy to do whatever I can to help you." There was a massive smile on his face.

As he said this, Andraste became aware of the discomfort again. His emotions did not add up- there was no warmth in his words, only a bitter cold. For someone who was so inviting to her, the coldness was strange.

"What is this?" She thought, moving away from the glass. Saying you felt a certain way while feeling another

way altogether- she didn't want to believe it, but nothing else made sense.

"Is he lying? But why?"

The attendant opened the door for him, and the discomfort deepened as he drew closer. When he held out his hand, the coldness jutted out into her space.

"If you'd come with me, please? We can go ahead and get started."

She glanced at Judicia and Yousef. She didn't know what to tell them, but she knew she couldn't stay quiet about this.

Yousef came around to the entrance of the glass enclosure, and gestured for her to approach. Judicia only raised an eyebrow.

From Yousef, it was encouraging. His disposition was warm and inviting, and implied a level of trust with Williams. That was enough to get Andraste to follow the man out of the room.

Yousef walked by her side as Williams led them down the hallway. Judicia walked ahead, and showed Williams something on her tablet.

"What's wrong?" Yousef whispered. "You looked tense a moment ago."

"Something about him is very wrong," she whispered back, "his words and his emotions don't add up. I don't know if he's telling the truth."

Yousef didn't respond for a moment. He glanced at Williams, then back at Andraste. "Let me try something," he said.

"Hey, Professor?" Yousef said, gesturing to the man.

Williams turned from the tablet. "Yes, Yousef?"

"Andy had a question about this new medicine. From what I heard, her usual stuff makes her a bit loopy. What can she expect from what you've been working on?"

Williams froze. In that moment, there was a rush of heat from him. Andraste knew this was her time to test him.

"Well, it's complicated- it's similar to what you were given earlier." Mumbling the words, Williams wrung his hands.

It was easy enough for Andraste to feel the nervousness. His words were rushed, and she could see the sweat beading on his forehead. As he began to explain, Andraste focused.

There was the same coldness that he met her with earlier. The more she dwelled on it, the more pervasive it was. It was an all-encompassing, numbing sensation that you got from stepping in ice water. All other impulses and feelings were lost beneath this coldness. She pushed aside all of her own thoughts as best she could, and narrowed her focus onto Williams.

"Asshole!" His mouth did not move, but Williams' voice was clear. *"Stop wasting my time!"*

The cold became sharper, bordering on painful. There was unmistakable vitriol in his tone, directed at Yousef. Following that outburst, Andraste didn't hear crisp, distinct words- she experienced the hatred with Williams on a physical level. His mind repeated small phrases over and over again, and his stomach tied itself into countless knots with anger and anticipation.

At this point, Andraste could swear she was feeling all of this herself. She could detect every trickle of sweat and twitch of the hand, and, with more clarity than any other sensation, the convulsions in his mind. Williams was struggling to maintain a straight face and an agreeable disposition amidst the anger that bubbled in his head.

Williams glanced at her. "Andraste, are you all right?"

She heard the words, but they were muffled behind the violence in his mind. He had visions of a syringe going into her arm, followed by grisly pictures of her writhing in pain and coughing up blood. As he watched her movements slow, he stood over her and felt a cruel pleasure in witnessing her death.

"No!" She thought as the images resolved themselves. *"Stop it!"*

Williams staggered as she thought this. His anger turned to worry. "Who said that?" He asked aloud, looking back and forth at Yousef and Judicia.

"Said what?" Judicia snapped, still holding the tablet.

The voices broke Andraste's concentration, and she found herself back in her body, as if she had woken up from a dream.

"I know I heard someone say something! Was it you, Andraste?" Williams gasped, the strain on his face incongruous with the pleasant smile he had on.

Andraste's head snapped forward, looking straight at him. "What did you put in that medicine?" She spoke with unusual clarity and conviction.

He backed away as she snapped at him. "Why, Miss, what do you mean? I just explained to Yousef-"

"You're trying to kill me!" Andraste's voice was a blend of terror and anger, albeit an anger buoyed by that same terror.

The panic in Williams spiked. He backed away from her, before centering himself and saying, "Miss Andraste, there must be some mistake!" He shrugged emphatically. "I would never want to hurt you!"

Again, there was the cold. She honed in on it, and felt him struggle to contain the rage.

"God dammit! She'll ruin everything!" His thoughts were frenetic and hard.

Andraste knew this was the time to strike. She returned to her body, and called him out.

"And what exactly will I ruin, Professor?" Andraste demanded, closing the distance between the two of them.

Williams grew weak in the knees as he backed away, tottering slightly.

Yousef approached as well. "Is something wrong, Williams?" He spoke in a harsh tone as he narrowed his gaze at the man.

Williams couldn't maintain his façade. He was trembling as the two approached, while Judicia watched with a raised eyebrow.

"Yousef, why so hostile?" He was breathing fast and hard. "Don't tell me you believe this nonsense!"

"I dunno, Professor." Yousef shrugged. "Andy has a way of reading people."

"Why, I never- Bianca!" He turned to Judicia.

"If Andraste is mistaken, then you have nothing to worry about." She held the tablet under her arm. "So why are you so nervous?"

Once again, Andraste entered his mind. Everywhere, there was pandemonium.

"No! I can't go out like this!"

"And how is that, Professor?" She said, raising her voice to a hitherto unheard-of register. "How were you hoping you would go out?"

As she said this, the fear he felt bubbled over, and all his emotions exploded out of him.

"Get out!" He clutched his temples and screamed. "Get out of my head!"

Judicia was closest to him. His arm shot out and grabbed her shoulder, and he pulled her close. With his free hand, Williams reached into his coat pocket and pointed a small handgun at Judicia.

"This ends, right now!" The tip of the gun was pressed against Judicia's temple, but that didn't stop his hand from shaking. "Both of you, hands over your heads. Make your way to room 308. The freak gets on the bed," he gestured to Andraste, "and takes the medicine without any problems. If either of you tries to make a move, I'm blowing her brains out!"

Yousef and Andraste put their hands up as he instructed.

"You sabotaged the medicine, then?" Judicia said, her voice calm. "You went to such great lengths to smuggle a gun in here- why didn't you just use that?"

"I didn't think your pet monster would be so easy to dispose of. Besides," he said, gesturing Yousef and Andraste down the hall, "I only need one bullet for you. If the medicine doesn't work, I'll put the rest into her."

"What is your problem?" Yousef growled.

"That monster is my problem! Give her some basic stimulants, and she nearly kills a man!" He prodded Yousef in the back with his gun. "You can put all the drugs in her you want- this experiment was doomed from the start! The sooner I put this freak down, the better it will be for everyone!"

Andraste had felt secure in this hospital until now. Usually there was someone there to help when things went downhill, but here, she was alone. The only thing standing between her and murder was this man's gun. The determination to stay alive overpowered her fear, and she was spurred into action by it.

Doing her best to keep pace with Yousef, Andraste focused on Williams' state of mind again.

He was brimming with eagerness, which manifested as a heat that tickled his insides. The hatred in his voice resonated through his body, a sadistic expression of power.

"This is what cruelty feels like," Andraste thought. She felt Williams reminisce on each word with a satisfied sense of self-importance and indulgence, making the experience even more crushing for her. She had been paranoid of making someone regret their role in the project, but encountering this kind of intense loathing for it was uncanny.

As much as she hated it, Andraste concentrated harder than she had ever concentrated before, forcing all distractions away.

As easily and inexplicably as she had done earlier, she entered his mind, staring through his eyes. Yousef was in front of him, and a bushel of Judicia's dark hair was in his peripheral vision. She felt the cold metal grip of the gun rattling with his hand. She didn't know what she could do, but she was willing to try anything. He had responded to the impetus of her thoughts earlier, and she wondered if he would respond to anything else when she was in this deep. She made a focused attempt to move her arm.

Williams stopped. Judicia could feel his heart beat faster against her back. The gun against her head jumped, barrel scraping her temple.

She had done something, but it wasn't enough. Andraste tried again, focusing even more. She visualized the gun moving away from Judicia, and William's arm jerked again. An equivalent force pulled her arm in the other direction when she tried to move it. It was Williams, fighting back.

"What are you doing to me?" He said, straining. "Stay out of my mind, damn it!"

As he said this, an impulse shot up his arm and led into his finger. Andraste funneled all of her focus onto the trigger finger to fight against it. Unrestrained, electric panic surged through Williams as he became aware of Andraste's invasion.

Williams winced, and almost released his hold on Judicia. His hand was convulsing and shaking, and his forefinger had gone rigid. The tremors crept up his arm and into his shoulder, as if a dozen threads tied to his bones were pulled in different directions.

Yousef was watching all of this, frozen. He glanced at Andraste, who was shuddering all over. Her eyes were wide, and the pupils had gone narrow, almost into vertical lines. Even they shuddered. He wanted to call to her, but the fear of the unknown had paralyzed him into stillness.

Andraste was using every ounce of her strength to pull the finger away from the trigger. Every effort to resist was like a blow to her entire being, and she struggled to hang on. Her mind was one with Williams, and the physical conflict mirrored the mental one as turbulent thoughts and sensations from both of their minds collided.

"Whatever you're doing, stop!" Williams cried. "I swear, I'll shoot!" This was a lie. He had been trying to shoot Judicia for several minutes. There was no longer any feeling in his hand, though it still jerked around. His thoughts became fragmented and chaotic, and he struggled to focus on anything.

Feeling had returned to his hand, but the arm beneath it had gone numb as Andraste moved her focus onto it. Slamming his finger back onto the trigger, the forearm was yanked out of the way before the gun would fire. A single bullet shot out into the ceiling.

The experience was such a shock, he let himself to go slack, and Judicia ducked out of his grasp. She dashed to the wall and pulled the alarm handle.

"No!" He went to go after her, but the arm holding the gun stayed in place. The alarm blared and red lights pulsed along the hallway, worsening the discord in his head.

Andraste also felt it as she kept his arm from moving. Every image and sensation grew sharp and painful, stabbing into the mass that she and Williams occupied. Hate, anger, indignation, and other hot, searing emotions strangled her, and her focus was gone. She maintained her hold on Williams as if her hands had been welded onto him, while her mind succumbed to the chaos. The room was a crude combination of two different perspectives, which warped and twisted and overlapped like a pod of disturbed animals. She could hear the distant cry of an alarm as she tumbled through the madness, which buoyed what was left of her cognition- all else had descended into the viscera.

"*Hold on,*" she thought, "*don't let go.*" She cycled through the same few words to help her through the mindlessness. As it went on, she thought she saw faces in the distorted room, screaming at her. Either way, even this anchoring thought was lost, and evolved into something she understood even less:

"*Don't run away.*"

She failed to notice it, but her grip on Williams was coming loose. He struggled to pull his arm from the air, jerking on it with his free hand.

"*Don't run away.*" The thought came again and again, as if someone else was saying it. The faces in the walls developed more features and repeated it: "*Don't run away.*"

Several security guards were already closing in. Two from behind Williams and three from behind Judicia and the others. There wasn't enough energy in his arm to be able to fight back. Wresting it back under his control as best he could, he held the barrel against his own head.

"*Don't run away again.*"

In the gap between the alarm sounds, one bullet was fired. A bright red ribbon of blood flew as Williams fell, the recoil from his gun knocking it out of his hand.

When he hit the floor, Andraste had stopped shaking. Her pupils bulged back into their full size, and she took a sharp breath of air.

"Andy!" Yousef said, rushing to her side. "What happened to you?"

She said nothing, only stared straight ahead as she held her breath. She sighed, and the feeling left her legs. Her eyes closed, and she collapsed into Yousef's arms. He could still feel her moving as he held her.

"What happened here, doctor?" A guard asked.

Judicia walked over to the two of them, not looking at the guard. "Andraste just saved our lives."

"She's having a seizure!" Yousef cried as Andraste convulsed in his arms. "Get her to the ER!"

9 Unknown

"That was excellent," said a voice. "You're coming along wonderfully."

The sound evoked a primal, instinctive memory in Andraste, unearthing a long-lost experience. She remembered hearing this voice before she woke up, warning her about the Martyr's Army.

"You again?" She said, or possibly thought- she couldn't tell which.

"We were unable to talk last time," it said, in a much more relaxed tone than their first meeting. "Let me take the time now."

Slivers of blue light cracked out from beneath her feet, radiating outwards and colliding at several junctions before spreading out again. The light expanded outwards in waves, as if a luminescent fluid were flowing through the ground. They stretched on and on into the seeming horizon, coating the flat plane in a soft pulse. It looked like a field of neurons, with transmissions flowing into eternity.

She looked down, and saw the blue lines and junctions climb onto her body. It was only along the gray of her exoskeleton that the lines were visible, as her skin faded into the surrounding darkness.

"Hello?" Andraste asked the open air, her voice trembling.

In the distance, she could see several of the glowing lines straighten with tension. A large, swirling ball of light came over the horizon, pulling the pattern into it. As it grew closer, Andraste could see that it was made entirely of the neurons, and that all the pulses of light fed into it.

"Hello, Andraste." It said, the voice no clearer for its tangible point of origin. "I must get straight to the point: why are you still in England?" The voice delivered every word in a soft, unflinching tone. There was no emotion in its inflection, and there was none to detect in the air.

"What are you talking about?" Andraste asked, her voice was hoarse and exasperated. "I don't even know what you are! Who are you and how do you know so much about me?"

The being maintained its monotone. "I don't know."

Andraste only stood there. "What?"

"Funny, isn't it? I'm just like you- I don't remember a thing. Maybe answering my questions will answer things for both of us." It floated closer to Andraste. "Until then, here's my question: why are you still in England? Didn't I say that you were in danger?"

"England is safe!" Andraste cried. "The only people who can keep me alive are here!"

"One of them just tried to kill you."

She expected a response like this, but she felt no less indignant for hearing it.

"It's hard to believe that the Martyr's Army has already wormed its way into military research. In all fairness, you dispatched him very well."

"Martyr's Army?" Andraste demanded, resentful of the patronizing words. "Williams wanted vengeance because of the seizure! Are you saying he was-"

"He reached out to the Martyr's Army the instant he was out of the hospital. Were you not aware?"

Andraste wasn't sure how to respond to this. She began to shudder. "Wh-what do you-"

"You were inside his head, Andraste- you really didn't notice? Perhaps you're not as far along as I thought."

The words hurt. With each verbal blow, she shook a little more. She practiced the breathing exercise before thinking of a response.

"I don't understand," Andraste muttered as her head slumped into her chest.

"What don't you understand?"

She grabbed her shoulders and continued the cycle. Breathe in, count to five, breathe out, count to five.

"Anything," Andraste began after a pause. "What does the Martyr's Army want? Why is any of this happening?" Her knees weakened and her breaths became ragged. "What am I doing in the middle of all this?"

The question seemed to echo in the space. It was one of the few times Andraste had said something without stammering, and its loud, violent exodus from the depths of her mind sent shockwaves through her body.

"Don't be stupid, Andraste," she thought.

"Why was that stupid?" The voice said.

She jumped at its question. "Excuse me?"

"You just told yourself 'Don't be stupid.' I fail to see why that question is stupid."

Andraste lost all feeling in her legs, and she fell to her knees. She wrapped her hands around her chest, like it would physically keep her from falling apart.

"I understand, Andraste. In your position, this is a valid question. I've felt the same way." The voice sunk towards the ground, closer to her. "If you truly do not have an answer for my original question, then perhaps you can answer this one: What *are* you doing in the middle of all this?"

Andraste looked up at it, hands still gripping her shoulders.

"Why did you participate in the FH project? What outcome did you anticipate?"

As Andraste pondered these questions, her hands loosened.

"I," she began, almost choking on her words, "I don't remember."

"You cannot lie to me."

"But I don't!" She barked before regaining her cowed tone. "At least, I don't think I do."

"You doubt yourself?"

"I'm sorry, I don't know what to tell you." She fell forward, supporting herself on her hands. "All these hallucinations, all these disfigured memories and images- I barely know what's real anymore." Andraste looked up at the ball of light. "I don't even know if you're real. Am I dreaming? Hallucinating? What's happening?"

There was a long pause before it replied. "So, you do doubt yourself."

Her shoulders slumped.

"To doubt oneself is a terrible thing. You must stop."

Andraste felt the energy rise in her chest, and she rose from her prostration. "What do you want from me? You say that as if I can change it like a light switch!"

"If you cannot stay in control of yourself, who can?"

For several moments, Andraste stared. She held up her trembling hands, begging for some shred of insight to fall into them. Letting out a cry of frustration, she clasped them to her face.

"Where there is doubt, there is truth. What do you remember that you doubt?"

Her arms fell, and she took a long, deep breath.

"'Don't run away again.' When I was controlling Williams, that thought ran through my head over and over. I don't know what it means." She said, resigned.

"What else do you remember? Perhaps more information about your past will contribute some insight."

She told the voice about the session with Yousef and that horrid photo of her old self.

"What do you remember about your old self?"

A current of withering energy ran down her spine. She didn't have specifics, but the suggestion of looking back on that time filled her with dread. Fighting the feelings, she attempted to reassemble the loose pieces of her mind. All she remembered was a flat apathy, a lack of feeling.

With more focus came more memories, and the apathy remained even when she recalled x-rays and a sterile medical space. They held her in a special room to prepare her for the procedure, where she laid still as a corpse without a single anticipation in her head.

"What is this?" She thought, knowing the voice would hear her. As though in response, a wave of feeling from these past images came over her.

Whether the FH Project was a success or not, it would end the same way for her. It was a military-funded experiment designed to create a new generation of super-soldiers, and the onus of that was on everyone but her. Either she became one of those soldiers or died, and she accepted both outcomes. She could feel herself lying there in peaceful resignation.

"I knew the project was dangerous," she told the light, not believing her own words. "I just didn't care."

"What were you running from?"

The photo came to mind as the voice said this. The photo of her twisted, injured, broken old self. The memory filled her with disgust, and the fact that she used to be that pathetic creature was intolerable. Upon reflection of the few concrete moments before the procedure, she noticed the same loathing.

"I was running from myself," she gasped. "I think of who I used to be, and all I feel is hate. Even before the experiment, I felt that way. I volunteered," she paused, the weight of the realization bearing down on her shoulders, "to erase myself. To wipe away my failures."

The words came out of their own accord. Andraste focused on the deep breathing as the orb of light hovered before her in silence. A burden had been lifted from her mind, while greater depths of confusion filled the empty space left behind.

"I see." The voice commented after a long, agonizing quietude. It began to move away.

"Wait!" Andraste started after it, though she lacked the strength to rise to her feet. The blue patterns in the distance faded. "Don't leave! I have so many questions!"

"I know," it said, "but our time was not managed well. You are about to wake up."

"Please," she begged, voice weak. "I'm so confused. Please, come back." Uncontrolled tears trickled down her face. They were bright blue like the pattern on her body, bursting into small fireworks when they hit the ground.

"Soon, Andraste." No matter how far away the light was, the voice never seemed to move. "You're too fascinating to abandon. I will be back."

She had no power to voice her protests. The sphere vanished over the horizon, and the glow that covered the ground began to recede. The lines of the neurons raced back to her, vanishing into the darkness. They ran up her body, and she was struck by a feeling of imbalance, as if she had tripped.

10   Hastings, England   6:41 a.m.   May 18th, 2335

She stumbled back into consciousness and saw the familiar ceiling of the hospital. Her whole body was numb, and a tangle of different cables were attached to her head and neck.

"Andy!" Yousef rushed over and leaned into her line of sight. It took some effort for her to turn to him, even sitting on a chair at her level. Judicia was leaning against a wall. "Oh, thank God. How are you feeling?"

She struggled to sit up on the bed. "I'm fine, I suppose." Her speech was slurred and her head lolled from side to side.

One of his hands shot up. "You just went through hell, Andy. Don't push yourself, all right?"

"I know you're going to ask," Judicia chimed in, "so let me go ahead and say: Yousef and I are fine."

She sighed with relief. "What happened to Williams?"

Yousef pursed his lips and looked away. "Well," he said, putting his hands together, "once we called security, he got desperate." He looked back at her. "Please don't blame yourself for this: he shot himself."

Her posture straightened as he said this. He was right, and she knew that, but she couldn't help but feel the guilt.

"What's done is done." Judicia walked over. "Now, let me ask you: from your perspective, what exactly happened? Williams started having spasms in his arm, and you started having a fit."

She didn't know what to say. Her mind was still on that dream with the talking neurons. Andraste realized that she would have to tell someone about it, especially if the voice kept its word and returned, but there were still too many questions that she couldn't figure out.

"It will have to wait," she thought, wondering if anyone was listening.

"I told Yousef that I didn't trust Williams," she said, breathing deep. "I tried to focus more on the discrepancy in his thoughts. He visualized himself giving some poisoned medicine to me and watching me die."

Yousef's eyes bugged out of his head. "Are you saying," he started, holding the last consonant sound for a few seconds before going on, "that you read his mind?"

Judicia's gaze narrowed.

The current of his confusion and awe rushed over her. "Um," she said, wringing the bedsheets, "I-I'm sorry, I don't really know what to make of it myself." She looked away from him, fidgeting with her words. "I didn't feel like I was 'reading' his thoughts. It seemed more like I was experiencing them."

Judicia leaned in. "How do you mean?"

"It wasn't like reading off a tablet. It was like being in his body, feeling everything he felt. With enough effort, I was able to move him, too."

"My god," Yousef wheezed, shaking his head in disbelief, He looked away for a moment to collect his thoughts. "So, you not only stepped into his body, but you also controlled it?"

She didn't have to focus on the aura of his emotions to realize how scared he was. Williams had made his feelings very plain, calling her a 'freak' and a 'monster.' She couldn't help but wonder if anyone else felt this way, even in passing frustration.

"Yes, I did." She admitted. "But I barely knew what I was doing! I didn't kill him!"

"Andy, I'm not saying you did." He spoke in the most comforting tone he could manage.

Judicia stepped in. "We can't worry about that. If anything, this is good progress." She pulled out her tablet and started to make notes. "Andraste, this new ability of yours is going to be the highlight of our report to Rowe."

Andraste looked at Judicia with a start. "Wh-what? Judicia, I think it's terrifying that I can do that."

"For our enemies, yes." Judicia pulled up the findings on her tablet. Scans of the brain and swirls of color to signify the flow of neural activity glowed at Andraste. "We're still making sense of it all, but you may have heard about the mind powers the Fomorians had. It's said that just one of them could control an entire squad of soldiers!"

A chill descended on the room when Judicia said that. Worse yet was the rare smirk on Judicia's face as she contemplated it all. Yousef and Andraste could only anticipate what frightful dreams this resurrected power inspired in the good doctor.

"Judicia," Andraste began with trepidation, "A-are you hoping that I'll be able to control an entire group of enemy soldiers?"

Judicia almost chuckled, making some harsh, dry sound instead. "Well, why not? Think of how helpful it would be. A group of soldiers has their guns trained on you, so you make all of them turn to one another and then shoot each other in the face. Easy."

"Judicia!" Yousef cried. "The Fomorians did that to us when they invaded! We don't really want that back, do we?"

"Oh, don't give me that." Judicia only shook her head. "You're making incredible progress, Andraste. The sooner we get moving, the sooner we can get you fighting in the field. What do you say to that, private?"

"Private" echoed in her head. All went still for Andraste, a bristle going down her back as she felt herself clutch the sheets on instinct. Fear, dark and oily, welled up from an unknown place.

"P-private?" she said aloud. "I-is that what they called me?"

She found herself staring off into space without heeding either doctor. With this gruesome new power to move a human body against its will, she would return to the place where death and violence waited.

She could see it, overlaying the hospital room. Green leaves and tall grass were layered in with dense humidity that built weight in her lungs. Distant gunshots grew closer, bullets whizzing past her head and digging into flesh. She heard the screams and smelled the blood as she stood straight and still. A forest surrounded her, where soldiers hid behind trees and took potshots at an unseen enemy while clutching their wounds.

"I'm seeing things again," Andraste tried to say aloud, but the thought only vanished into an echo. Yousef and Judicia had vanished.

"Private!" A voice called from ahead. A vague figure of a man was looking back at her with no eyes and distorting features. "What are you doing, private? Fight back!"

She tried to move, but was stuck in place. She felt the strain in her arms and legs as she tried to move them, fearing they would crack like ice if she overexerted herself.

"Private, god damn it!" The man shouted again. "Private Andy!"

"What?" She willed herself to ask. The vision was fracturing, each gunshot sending cracks through the scenery as the sprays of blood melted into the landscape.

"Andy!" The soldiers around her cried. Each voice cracked under their pain, and she felt every ounce of it. Looking down, she saw herself cracking as the sounds rolled through her.

"Andy!" They chanted. The world melted into indistinct colors.

"Private!" Voices swelled around her as she fell into aching pieces. "Private Andy!"

"Help me," Andy shuddered to think. *"Someone!"*

Guilt and shame filled the gaps in her crumbling shape. The sensations built and buried her, about to collapse until she heard a clear gunshot close to her chest. Shattering glass was heard for a split second.

"Andy!" Yousef called, his hands on her shoulders.

Gasping, his face was the first thing she saw. Chest heaving with tears in her eyes, Andraste looked around and saw the hospital room again. Judicia was pressing her head against the wall as the catheter in her arm beeped.

"What just," Andy sputtered. "I didn't- I-"

"Andy, it's all right!" Yousef said, giving each shoulder a light squeeze. "You're fine now."

"O-oh. Okay." She put a hand to her face to brush a tear away. To her surprise, they soaked her face plates. "I'm sorry. I don't know what happened."

"We'll work on it." Judicia said in a prolonged groan. "Christ, my head!"

"Just let the medicine work for a bit," Yousef assured Andy. "Judicia, you okay?"

"I'll be fine," Judicia grunted. "I'll walk it off. Yousef, come see me when you have the chance. Rowe has a message for us." With this, Judicia slogged away.

Andraste looked at her hands, grateful she could move them but worried what was happening.

"Andy?" Yousef pulled up a chair. "Want to talk about it?" He shrugged, a subtle urge for her to open up.

Her heavy head shook to the side. "I don't know what to say." The tranquilizer was taking hold. "Judicia said something, and I started seeing things again. I don't-" The words were a struggle. "I don't know what's happening with me."

"Was that a flashback? You were literally scared stiff."

Sighing, Andraste relayed her experience in as much detail as she could manage. Every painful moment of this new episode exhausted her to recollect, but she was confident in sharing it with Yousef.

"Sounds like a flashback," he said as he jotted down notes. "Your commanding officer called you pri- er, that title. Must've been a tough thing to see."

"I'm not an expert on these flashbacks or hallucinations," she began, "but they're still so strange. And the way they affect Judicia, I think something about my Fomorian power is affecting them."

"That makes sense." Yousef nodded. "It won't be easy getting your other memories back, but try not to fret about it."

"How can I not?" Andraste protested, but the medicine made her voice weaken. "Can you predict anything about me? You're all in danger just being around me!"

"Come on, Andy, it's not as bad as that."

She looked at him squarely, noticing the coolness coming from his emotions. "You're lying," she said quietly.

Yousef pursed his lips and let out a sigh. "Andy," he said, looking away from her, "I don't know what I can tell you." He let his head slump forward. "And I don't think anyone else will have an answer, either. We didn't know what we were doing when we put you together, and even now, we just start grasping at straws whenever we need to make a move." He sighed. "I'm sorry."

She shut her eyes at this sentiment. He was being honest, though.

"But don't worry," Yousef followed up. "We're going to get you through this. One way or another."

Andraste gave a weak nod. "Thank you," she said, trying to mean it. "The medicine is really kicking in. You shouldn't keep Judicia waiting." Andraste let out an earnest yawn.

"Sure." Yousef got up. "I'll send in a nurse to check on you in a bit. Hang in there, Andy." He smiled thinly.

"It all goes back to my memories," she reflected as he walked out. She sat up and leaned back. She did the breathing and mulled over the machine in her head, but some negative sensation still stirred inside her. *"Whenever I try to recall who I am, I end up hurting someone. What can I do?"* That final thought was carried with her into a light doze as the medicine took hold. *"I have to change this, somehow."*

Yousef fretted the whole way to Judicia's office. Once there, he shared the story as Judicia nursed her migraine.

"So it was something I said?" She asked in an exhausted drawl. "My fault, then?"

"I didn't say that," Yousef said, his tone silently confirming that yes, it was her fault. "We'll have to watch what we say next time."

"Noted. Next time I get a migraine, we'll know she's upset."

"So, did you get in touch with Rowe?" Yousef asked, trying to clear the air.

"Yes," she said, turning back to the computer. "I told him about Williams and his connection to the Martyr's Army. He's already responded."

There was a brief response to an encrypted e-mail: *Get her over here, now.*

"If you need to pack for the trip to London, go and do it now." She closed the computer and went for the door, rubbing her eyes. "The train leaves at 1500 hours. Be back here by then."

"Today?"

"Yes, today." She stopped at the door and looked at him. "Williams could have compromised our entire operation. We're putting everything in jeopardy if we stay here."

He was struck dumb by the immediacy of these events. "Well, where are we going?"

"Central Base, beneath the Shard." She tried to exit out the door again.

"Is that safe? Williams could have leaked that!"

"I don't know, Yousef!" She stopped, exasperated. "Anywhere is better than here!" She went out into the hallway, holding the door by her fingertip. "1500 hours." She released and let the door slam.

Under the guise of a shipping train, only the most necessary personnel of the FH Project chauffeured Andraste to London. After everything that had happened, the fake shipping containers rattled along in tense solemnity.

Andraste didn't make a sound. A huge, thick book full of engineering schematics was laid over her legs, and she wasn't so much reading it as staring at it with a hung head. Her concentration as elsewhere, even as they pulled into Central Base.

Central Base was established beneath one of modern London's most iconic buildings, the Shard, when military applications for genetic enhancement were proposed. Some feared that putting it beneath a building as conspicuous as the Shard would make it harder to hide, but as military, medicine, and politics further overlapped, critics soon agreed that a centralized location for all of it- hence the name- would work best.

Andraste was assured that only the best of the best were allowed to work at, much less know about, Central Base, but the quality of her care was one of the last things on her mind.

What she found the most thought-provoking was her identity with the old soldier. These memories, these flashbacks- she wasn't sure how much was her and how much was empty spectacle. These were the remnants of the tragic precursor of the super-soldier that now walked among the rest of humanity. If she left her past behind, then it would affect the present less.

There were a lot of things that Andraste didn't know about the soldier, but she didn't care. That wouldn't be her problem anymore. It would probably crush Yousef, but something crossed her mind: she didn't want to continue the memory treatments. She spent the whole trip wondering how to bring it up, but silently thinking it would finally make some progress.

Once they had pulled into Central Base, Andraste was too tired to even think straight anymore. All she wanted was sleep. Not pass out or get hooked up to anesthetic, but to lie down in her own bed, close her eyes, and sleep. By that point, she had been tranquilized and sedated enough times to know the difference.

She didn't focus on the security clearance procedures or pay attention to the eyes ogling her. No part of the facility registered for her, despite a few members of their entourage going "ooh" and "aah" at the elegant, contemporary furnishings of the place. All else was white noise and hazy backdrops.

Among her few belongings was a table clock, gleaming "21:03" at her. It was early, but she let the bed envelop her all the same.

11   London, England   10:38
May 19th, 2335

After spending all the preceding night planning a new regiment for the memory treatments, Yousef and Judicia heard Andraste wanting to talk about that exact thing. Thinking a change of scenery would be welcome, Yousef proposed that they have the conversation on a balcony on the upper level.

That morning, Andraste woke up refreshed for the first time in a while. She went about her morning with a renewed sense of vigor and determination, buoyed by the decision to distance herself from her old life. This sense of confidence in herself was unfamiliar, but welcome. She felt like she was making the right decision.

Yousef got her from her room and led her down the hall. As they walked, she finally had an opportunity to take in the sights of Central Base. The hospital in Hastings was nice, but that was just a hospital, bound to the world of normalcy by its tile floors and drab panel ceilings. Central Base teemed with energy, its interiors kept polished a near-blinding white as giant cables as thick as a human torso lined the hallways. She let a sense of childlike wonder grow inside her.

Yousef looked back at her and noticed a distinct levity to her steps.

"Doing all right?" He asked.

Andraste snapped back to attention when he said this, "Yes sir!" She said on impulse.

For a few tense moments, neither of them said anything. The cables in the elevator shaft whirred, keeping the space from occupying a state of total silence. Eventually, a smirk grew on his face, and he started to chuckle.

Andraste let out a sigh of relief, and she couldn't restrain herself, either. A few weak laughs rose out of her.

When he heard this, Yousef stopped. He narrowed his eyes. "Wow," he said, "I don't think I've ever heard you laugh before."

She perked up. "Really?"

"I mean, not that I remember." The elevator doors slid open, and he led her inside. "I didn't mean to startle you." He leaned back against the handrails.

The elevator breached the darkness of the underground and slid through some layers of the building. Many were too fast to take in, but the light from the city was no less striking for it. London sprawled around the Shard, spreading off into the horizon to bask in as much sunlight as it could. Sleek skyscrapers came out of the underbrush of small houses and stone streets.

She moved closer to the glass, magnetized by the sight.

"Impressed?" Yousef said.

"Uh-huh." She propped her hands against the glass and stared, not even blinking. Knowing she was in the middle of all this splendor filled her with a sense of home.

He laughed again, much harder this time. "God, you seem like a different person today."

She turned around at this sentiment. "Wh-What do you mean?"

He moved away from the wall, towards her. "What I mean is, you look like you're in a good mood, and that's great. Especially after all that madness back in Hastings." Yousef settled in front of the window. "Any particular reason for this?"

The elevator came to a stop at the 58th floor. The door slid open behind them as the city descended into a dense pattern split in half by the Thames.

"I suppose there is," she said, unsure of where to begin. "Maybe it'd be best to mention it in the conference with Judicia."

"Fair enough."

In front of the glass doors and partitions that divided the floor, a huge, open space sprawled out. Judicia sat at a café table. Yousef waved hello as they approached, while Judicia only watched.

Her expression was hard to read, with elements of anger and disappointment mixed in with overall resignation. "Rowe will be here in less than a week," she grumbled, taking off her glasses and kneading the bridge of her nose. "We can't waste time with pleasantries when we have so much to prepare for."

"We've already discussed this, Judicia." Yousef leaned over her shoulder. To Judicia's unmistakable discomfort, Yousef got close to her and pointed to Andraste.

"I'm sorry for what happened yesterday."

"You don't have to apologize, Dr. Judicia." The others looked at her, incredulous. "If anything, it gave me an idea that I want to talk to you two about today. Hopefully, it will expedite the process a bit."

Judicia grinned. "It's good that you feel that way, Andraste. I'm glad you appreciate how much has been invested in this project." She looked over the city, and her face reverted to its usual sourness. "Speaking of 'investments,' however, there's no avoiding the fact that Rowe and some other Cabinet members will be here soon."

Andraste cocked her head. "What exactly do they want?"

"They want to evaluate us," Yousef chimed in, taking a seat next to Andraste. "Nathan Rowe went through hell to get this project up and running, and he wants to convince his fellow politicians that it was worth all that money."

Andraste grew tense.

"Don't be nervous, Andraste," Yousef said despite the worried aura that came off him. "We have a few days, and we were just discussing how to budget our time and make some progress." He pulled out his tablet and brought up a calendar application. "Let me show you what we've come up with."

According to Yousef's notes, there were six days until "ROWE ARRIVES," and, twice a day, in stretches of several hours, he had written down "Memory Treatments."

'This is it,' Andraste thought. Her insides rolled around at the thought of being so forward, but this seemed to be the perfect time. *'"I'm sorry, Dr. Yousef, but I don't think it would be in our best interests to continue the memory treatment. Here's why I feel this way:" Okay, let's go.'* It was all rehearsed in her head, and she braced herself for his confusion and disappointment as best she could. She took a deep breath and dove in.

"I'm sorry, Dr. Yousef." With a gentle hand, she put the tablet aside. A current of fearful anticipation came from him.

With three pairs of eyes on her, her dismissal hung in the air like a beacon of awkwardness. No words came to her, and a sensation like falling came over her. She was screwing it all up, defying every line that she had worked so hard on. Yousef and Judicia stared in anticipation. She tried to force out something, anything, but in that moment of scrutiny, she had forgotten how to communicate.

"I-I-I don't want to continue th-th-the treatments!" The words were forced out like a confession.

The others were silent.

'No, no, no!' She yelled at herself in her mind. *'This isn't how you stand up for yourself, idiot!'* She grasped her shoulders, but it offered little comfort. The whole idea of abandoning the treatments fell apart as the humiliation ripped through her.

"Interesting," Judicia said, interlocking her fingers. "Why not? Has Dr. Yousef done something to upset you?"

Yousef sprang to attention, switching his gaze between the old woman and his patient.

"Wha- no!" Andraste said, breaking out of her self-deprecating trance. "Dr. Yousef has been wonderful to work with! I only have reservations because," she trailed off. As she searched for the right words, she laid her hands on the table. "Because I don't think it would be helpful."

A cooling wave came over Yousef as she said this. Andraste hoped to assure him even more. "Under any other circumstance, I think it would be very beneficial, but not in my situation." Without thinking too hard on it, she let the words come out. "There's so much that I don't remember, and trying to bring it back always causes some problem. I wonder, is it even worth it?" Her thoughts came out coherent and reasonable. A swell of confidence came from her clarity. "The person I was before the experiment- she's gone. I would feel much more comfortable if I distanced myself from my past life as much as possible."

Judicia scratched her chin. Andraste couldn't tell if she had convinced them, but she was content with how she had expressed herself.

"I don't know, Andraste," Yousef said, his leg twitching. "I know the sessions can be a bit rough, but it seems like a pretty drastic-"

"She may have a point." Judicia interrupted him. "One of the main driving points of the FH Project is the aspect re-inventing yourself. What good is it if you spend your new life trying to re-capture your old one?"

"True, but-" Yousef tried and failed to enter in the conversation.

"Besides, think of all the time that we could free up by cancelling the sessions. We still have a lot of physical tests to cover."

Yousef leaned in. "Judicia, maybe if you would listen-"

The discussion went downhill from there. For a few brief moments, Andraste was filled with pride about winning Judicia over, but that pride was buried beneath the chaos of the doctors' argument. They seemed to forget about her as animosities and frustrations boiled over. She felt the need to avert her eyes.

The sky caught her attention- a huge gray blob began to roll over the building, its wispy white edges filtering the sunlight. For its size, it eclipsed the sun at considerable speed, dragging a far-reaching cloud curtain over the point of the Shard. She glanced over at the city, and saw the great shadow spreading across the rooftops.

The sense of belonging returned. Hastings was so distant and so impersonal, but London was embracing. This was her city. At some point, she had most likely felt this way about Hastings, but that was the experience of that poor, dead soldier. For Andraste, everything was new, and everything was even more intense because of it.

The sun vanished behind the clouds. A few darkened spots appeared on the patio, followed by a few dozen more. She hadn't experienced much weather before now- something about the rain created a moth-to-a-candle effect inside her.

She held her arm out. The raindrops were sparse, but eventually one struck her. The cold splashed into her skin and sent ripples of sensation up her arm, diverging between her head and her spine. Andraste chuckled, yanking her arm back for a moment before holding it out again. Another drop hit her, further up towards her wrist, and the same wave coursed through her body. She was overcome by the wonderful ability to feel, and she was starving for more. Eager to leave the squabble, she stepped out from under the awning.

"Andy?" Yousef called. The argument had stopped.

She didn't respond. Andraste staggered into the gathering rainstorm, holding both of her arms out to catch the falling skies. Thunder sounded in the distance as the thick drops fell, cutting through the numbness she felt after so much uncertainty. She breathed faster and harder, drawing life into her body through the sweet summer air.

No one could see it, but Andraste was smiling. She was light as a feather, unbound by her troubles. As the rain fell harder, the intensity grew. Her breaths turned into half-formed laughs as the feelings overtook her. And as the rain came down in waves, she fell to her knees.

It was all so new to her. She knew what life was before the hybridization, but she had no idea what it was like until now. All the testing and preparation- even with Williams' affront- seemed to exist in a vacuum. There was nothing in her old life that was like this, she was sure of that. All the more reason to leave that horrible time behind. In that moment, she was completely, truly alive, for what may have been the first time. Andraste was fully there.

"Andraste!" Yousef called. He stepped into the rain and his shirt was soaked within seconds.

Again, she didn't respond. The look on her face caught him off-guard. It was the first time, as far as he knew, that she looked happy.

"You okay?" He didn't know what to make of it.

She turned to him, vision blurred by the sweet rain. "I'm perfect," she said, speaking with unusual clarity.

Yousef only stood there, lost.

She turned her face back to the direction of the rain. "I really wish you knew what this felt like."

Andraste looked away from the rain and back to her audience. She saw their confusion and got up from her repose.

"I'm sorry," she said, walking over. "I needed a distraction." Her clothes had been soaked through, and her hair clung to the sides of her head.

"What's come over you, Andraste?" Judicia asked. "You seem ten times as self-assured as you usually do."

She sighed, and spoke clearer. "The thought of leaving my past behind me- abandoning the experiences of the soldier and re-inventing myself- it's invigorating. I suppose, by focusing less on my past, I can focus more on the present." She took a seat at the table and glanced back at the rain. "Everything feels so new and intense. If it's not too presumptuous of me, I would really be happy to continue this way."

Judicia and Yousef glanced at one another.

"You've already heard my input about it." Judicia poured herself a glass of water. "If you don't miss your memories, then you don't miss your memories. It could free up a lot of our time and energy, and we'll need plenty of both before the Prime Minister shows up."

Yousef didn't respond, but his wide-eyed expression betrayed his unease. After a few indecisive moments, he let loose:

"Are you two mad?"

Judicia was more annoyed than upset, but Andraste felt the sting of his indignity.

"Dr. Yousef, I'm sorry!" She interjected. "I'm not trying to make a statement about you or your methods. You've helped me so much, and I'm extremely grateful."

"That's not what bothers me! What bothers me is that you're proposing we quit cold turkey!" It was a shock to hear him speak in such an exasperated tone. "I understand that you're frustrated, but you can't drop the treatment and expect everything to resolve itself! That's not how this therapy works!"

"In people," Judicia said, taking charge of the discussion. "Let's not look past the fact that Andraste is, after all, part alien." She leaned in closer to Yousef. "Dance around the issue all you want, Yousef, but her mind doesn't work like ours. And that's exactly what we want."

Yousef reddened. His speaking abilities were reduced to frustrated gibbering, ready to burst with indignation. His emotional aura was sizzling, and Andraste rushed to his relief.

"Well, this is mostly an experiment, Dr. Yousef. If things don't go as planned, then I would be more than willing to resume the treatments." She homed in on Yousef's mental state, and her concession did seem to help him.

"Nonsense, Andraste." Judicia said, re-igniting Yousef. "It's good that you're taking some initiative." She stood up and shot a sour look at Yousef. "As long as we're making progress, we should establish a schedule for the upcoming tests. Sound good?"

Before responding, Andraste looked back at Yousef. His mind was crying out for support, screaming "help me." It wounded her to see Yousef this way, but there Judicia was, offering the alternative that she wanted so intensely. It was now or never.

"I'm sorry, Dr. Yousef. I should go with Judicia on this." Andraste said and followed her back into the building.

Recalling the incident with the balance beams in Hastings, one of Andraste's more unorthodox physical tests was bending metal bars. After six days of this, on top of the bruises, blood, sweat, fractures, and pulled muscles, Andraste was able to twist a length of rebar into a pretzel with her bare hands, and even punch clean through the hood of a car. This was done in addition to rigorous sparring sessions and obstacle courses, with varying- albeit substantial- degrees of success.

Andraste had been showing fewer signs of stress and anxiety over the six-day period. She was optimistic and eager to work hard, willfully researching techniques to control her emotions and keep her powers under control. She even completed some more wind-up toy blueprints. Some doctors patted her on the back for her initiative and insight, while others went so far as to criticize Yousef for using "harmful" therapy. Andraste herself insisted that she was grateful for his help, but he couldn't dismiss even a small bit of disappointment. In the meantime, he tried to focus on being happy for Andraste.

Despite her improvements, the imminence of Nathan Rowe's judgment filled a significant space in Andraste's mind. She said that she wanted to focus on the present, but she had forgotten that the present entailed impressing the British government, which could spell life or death for the project. Excitement became indistinguishable from terror as the day approached, and in situations like this, all she could do was breathe and hope for the best.

12   London, England   10:38 a.m.   May 25th, 2335

The security screening was over quickly, and he was relieved to see Central Base kept in good shape. There was a general atmosphere of tension in the air as the security staff led him inside.

Further into the facility, the guards outside a door held it for Rowe and Laurie. He was met by Yousef and Judicia in the latter's office. Yousef was fidgeting in a chair while Judicia was at her computers. When Rowe walked in, however, Yousef sprang to his full height and met the man's eye.

"Mr. Rowe." Yousef blurted as Rowe approached. "A pleasure to meet you in person, sir."

"It's a pleasure to meet you, Doctor Makkareb." Rowe extended his hand, and Yousef responded in turn Their hands clapped together, and Rowe gave it a solid shake. "I've heard some terrific things about your role in this project.

Yousef shrugged. "I do what I can, sir. And please, you can just call me 'Yousef'."

He looked past Yousef at Judicia. "Is Dr. Judicia available for comment?" He spoke loud enough for Judicia to pick up on the message. She didn't respond, and held herself up on the desk.

The easygoing atmosphere grew tense as Judicia stood. She wasn't doing anything on the computer or pressing any buttons, only clenched her fists on the table.

Rowe turned to Judicia. "You don't need me to remind you of all the opposition we've faced. I know how important this project is. And I know how utterly brilliant you are, Judicia." He pulled out his tablet, and brought up a picture of Andraste. "If all else fails, I can promise that your work will be remembered, and that Andraste will be taken care of- one way or another." There was a lack of conviction in the latter half of his assurance.

Andraste stood as upright and still as she could manage, but it didn't stop her from shaking. Andraste took deep breaths, counted to five, and imagined the blueprints for an intricate machine, which abated the nervousness, but it spiked as the doors swung open.

A second later, the actual Nathan Rowe rounded the corner and walked through.

"Thank you." Rowe said to the guard as he passed, followed close behind by Yousef and Judicia.

Rowe, wearing a sleek navy suit, was every bit as striking in person as he was in the news headlines. Taller than Judicia but shorter than Yousef, his hair was a short, loosely packed bushel of graying brown curls. It wrapped around his chin in a robust beard.

Andraste was simultaneously comforted and unsettled by him. The sharpest pain came from the most unexpected sources, and she prepared herself for the worst.

Andraste fought hard against the desire to fidget and twitch, yet several unintentional spasms came through. She went cold as Rowe approached her.

Rowe's eyes widened when he saw her. He gave Andraste a cursory scan, then raised an eyebrow and smiled.

"My," he said, chuckling, "look at you!"

Andraste felt sharply self-conscious and nervous when he said that. He seemed kind, but she felt his eyes digging into her all the same, dissecting her and peeling apart the layers of mental safeguards. Her breaths became short and staggered, and she wrapped her arms around herself.

Rowe turned to Judicia. "Is something wrong?"

"Andy, it's okay!" Yousef said, his palms in the air. "Mr. Rowe is very impressed with you; there's nothing wrong!" He placed a hard emphasis on 'there's nothing wrong.'

Andraste tried to focus on those words as she centered herself. She slowed her breathing down, and took longer, more deliberate breaths. The fear subsided somewhat, but she still shook.

Rowe kept his distance from the glass. "I'm sorry." His voice was plain and undemanding. "Let's start over. My name is Nathan Rowe. It's nice to meet you, Andraste." He spoke slowly and without pretense, and the stability of his mental state gave off a soothing warmth.

She stood up and saluted him. "I-It's an honor and a privilege to meet you, sir!"

He laughed and saluted her back. "Thank you, but there's no need for such formality. Please, have a seat."

Andraste rushed back into her chair.

"The doctors have shown me some impressive things about you, Andraste. What has it been like, having all this power?" Rowe pulled out his tablet and opened a folder of videos.

Andraste tensed up when she saw the security camera footage of the training center and fully unfurled obstacle course. What followed were several moments of her trials and errors captured in glorious high-quality video footage.

Monkey bars rose higher as she climbed across them, and gave her farther to fall even as she clambered across them. Watching herself felt like seeing a spider navigate an old comb, clumsy and uncomfortable in this bizarre, violent landscape. The spider then tumbled through a gauntlet of spinning foam bars, each level knocking the wind out of it at least once.

"You made great time on that one!" Rowe cheered, enjoying Andraste's trials far more than Andraste.

She felt scrutinized and alone, even through her proudest moments of jumping through hoops with 30 kg weights in each hand. Andraste could only see her failings and every milestone she hadn't reached yet. Rowe kept pointing at the footage and sharing how impressed he was, but it didn't reach her. This performance evaluation was vivisecting.

"You'll be able to topple any enemy who-" Rowe stopped when he turned to her. "Andraste?"

Arms tense and shaking, Andraste battled an urge to retreat. Tears pooled at the corners of her eyes.

"No!" she thought, her shock almost eclipsing the fear. *"Idiot! There's no worse time to do this!"*

Yousef stepped up. "Andy, don't forget your breathing!"

"I am breathing!" She said, her words forced through a jagged filter of shame. Her hands clasped her shoulders. "I'm sorry," she looked at Rowe as she said this, "I've tried so hard to act brave and not be a burden. I don't know if I've actually been performing well."

Mr. Rowe seemed unfazed. While Judicia and Yousef turned away in hair-pulling distress, the Prime Minister kept his eyes on the experiment.

"What was it you said? You've been 'trying so hard to act brave' or something?" Rowe turned to the side, scratching his beard. "In light of all you've been through, you consider what you're doing an 'act?'"

"Act" came out on impulse, and she genuinely didn't remember saying it until he brought it up. As she cogitated on it, though, the implications of the word set in.

"I-I suppose so," she said, demoralized. "Everyone talks about how I'm 'the future' or 'the perfect soldier' or whatever they want me to be, but whenever I make progress, I feel like it's by mistake." She couldn't bear to look at him. She buried her face in her hands.

Rowe pursed his lips and nodded. "I can't speak for your experiences. But I can say, with uncompromising certainty, that there's nothing 'fake' about you."

Andraste looked up. "Wh-What do you mean?"

"I can tell just by talking to you," he said, leaning forward. "You've experienced and suffered more than most people can claim. From the beginning, you've fought to survive." He spoke with great emphasis. "You fought to make it into the military, you fought to survive in the Outlands, and you've fought to make it where you are now, helping us make a better world. It takes a rare kind of strength to become what you've become, Andraste."

Her posture straightened. "Strength?" She asked in disbelief.

Smiling, Rowe nodded. "Absolutely, strength! Someone who has seen the worst that the world has to offer, and then shows up to fight and make a difference anyway. That is strength."

Elation poured into her heart. She went to wipe her tears, but stopped when Rowe put up a hand.

"Let them flow, Andraste. There's nothing shameful about tears."

The tears came out uninhibited. Andraste felt like all the shame and fear was pouring out from her body. It didn't feel like a sign of weakness, it felt like healing.

"Does that help?"

She nodded.

"I'm glad," he said, with a warm smile. "People don't cry because they're weak. People cry because they know what it's like to be strong."

The tears subsided on their own. "Thank you, Mr. Rowe." She made clear eye contact with him. "That really means a lot to me."

"My pleasure, Andraste. Everyone involved with the FH Project has a lot to be proud of." He stood up from the chair and approached the glass. "Especially you, after stopping that rogue professor. Anyone who single-handedly stops a terrorist attack is nothing less than a hero."

She stood up, as well. "I am glad I was able to take care of that," she said, and the two chuckled. "I can't help but have my reservations, however."

"Oh?" He asked, arms folded.

She put up her hands. "I'm not arguing with anything you've said. It's a relief to hear your feedback and praise, but when you really look at it, this experiment has just started. I've struggled a lot just to be able to function, and I still have a long way to go."

Rowe shrugged. "I suppose I can't argue with that." He stepped back from the glass. "Of course, that's reasonable at this point. We're not expecting you to turn water into wine right away. But rest assured, you *are* the future, Andraste."

That comment stuck with her. *"The future,"* she thought.

He pulled his tablet out of his backpack, and started putting down some notes. "Now, since it's not entirely my decision, don't get used to it just yet,"

Yousef and Judicia, who had been watching wide-eyed from a corner, perked up and approached him. Rowe glanced at them and smiled.

"But, I see no reason to cut the FH Project's budget." He held the tablet under his arm.

Andraste got up and pressed against the window.

"Really?" Andraste trilled, her voice high-pitched with delight. "You're not going to cut our funding?"

He put up a hand, stopping her. "Like I said, it's not entirely my decision. I need to run this through Parliament, after all. I'll do my best to make a case for you, but I'm feeling optimistic." Showing his tablet, he looked over to Yousef and Judicia. "I've already reached out to several other members of the Cabinet, and I have shared the details you've given me; I'll reach out to you as soon as I get some feedback from them."

Between Yousef, Judicia, and Andraste, the atmosphere became rich with excitement and relief. Yousef looked at Judicia with uncontainable joy and had to physically stop himself from hugging her. It was tough to tell what Judicia was feeling, but the relief she felt was palpable.

"As for you, Miss Andraste-" Rowe turned back to the young woman, standing upright and at full attention.

Andraste perked up, standing in the same way as him.

"As impressed as I am, there's no arguing with the fact that you do, indeed, have a lot of work ahead of you. Can I count on you to get that work done?"

For no better reason than feeling like she had to, Andraste saluted him again. "Yes, sir! You can count on me."

He saluted her back. "Excellent. At ease, soldier."

He opened his satchel and slid the tablet in. "Furthermore, I'll need all the relevant data I can get if I'm going to convince the rest of the cabinet to keep this project going. Andraste, I want to be as transparent with you as possible."

"S-sir?" Andraste asked, cocking her head.

He smiled. "I may not have too much time before all the data is compiled, but if there's anything you'd like to ask me, Andraste, I'm sure I can answer it for you."

The moment the words left his lips, Andraste strained to think of something, even as she glanced at the doctors, who either shrugged or looked away. In the next instant, a rush of inspiration struck her.

"W-Well, it's not something that's really been on my mind that much, but now that you're here," she said, tension building up inside her. "I've heard before that you wanted to keep my identity secret, and I'm not going to question your decision on that."

The man seemed surprised to hear this. "Indeed, for security reasons. But we're discussing this in confidence. You're saying you don't want to know who you were?"

She took a deep breath. "Yes, sir. I'm content to leave that behind me."

"Very well, then." He gave an uncertain nod, glancing at the doctors. "In that case, what would you like to know?"

"Instead of who I used to be, I'd like to know more about who I am now. Where does the codename 'Andraste' come from?"

Rowe paused for a second, reflecting on the question. "Hmm, that's a great story. Tell me, are you familiar with the story of Boudica?"

Andraste sat down as well. "Boudica? I don't think so."

He looked back at Andraste and took a deep breath. "Boudica was the queen of the Iceni tribespeople in ancient England. Thousands of years ago, during the time of king Nero in ancient Rome. The Roman empire was reveling in an era of unprecedented power and expansion, and Boudica was far from pleased.

"Boudica was a proud woman, and a fierce rebel. She refused to tolerate the oppression of the Romans, and roused her entire tribe into rebellion against them. And the goddess that Boudica prayed to- a symbol of victory and invincibility- was named Andraste."

Andraste's eyes opened wider, and she was shocked into silence.

"Again, I'm surprised you weren't familiar. There's even a statue of Boudica not far from Parliament."

"B-But," she began, "I'm still not sure I understand. If Boudica is the symbolic one, then why not call me 'Boudica?'"

Rowe pursed his lips. "I had a feeling you would ask that." He leaned forward. "You see, for all of Boudica's strengths and grandeur, she was only human. You are more than that, Andraste. By tapping into power that is greater than what we have here on Earth, the FH Project is not unlike Boudica's invocation. We are taking advantage of a force that is as close to godlike as anything ever encountered. You aren't just a rebel, Andraste, you're an augur of victory and invincibility. A goddess, if you will. One that will bring about a perfect world, at long last."

There was a look of manic intensity in Rowe's eyes. He was radiating with excitement, yet Andraste was quite put off by it.

The guard tapped on his watch intently. Rowe turned. "Ah, it seems I must go. I hope I explained that well enough."

Andraste nodded. "Thank you for taking the time to see me, Mr. Rowe. I-I'm so grateful."

"Of course," he said, radiating warmth. "It was an honor and a pleasure, Andraste." He said goodbye to

Yousef and Judicia as well, and led his entourage out the door.

"Fuck yes!" Yousef yelled. "Holy Christmas, we did it!"

"That's no reason to shriek like a banshee!" Judicia said, clasping her hands against her head.

Yousef wasn't fazed by her. "We secured our funding! Aren't you happy at all?"

"Of course I'm happy, but that doesn't change the fact that you nearly shattered my eardrums!"

Andraste wasn't paying attention to them. After the shock of Yousef's outburst, she let her gaze fall to the floor.

It was reassuring to meet Rowe in person, and it was terrific to see his support for the experiment, but the way he said "goddess" worried Andraste. "An augur of victory and invincibility." She took some deep breaths and envisioned some machine parts coming together to ease her mind.

Yousef looked up from the argument for a moment, and saw Andraste.

"Andy?" He asked, rousing both her and Judicia from their concentrations. "Are you all right? You looked awfully upset there."

"Well," she began, unsure of where to begin. "It was lovely to meet Mr. Rowe, but something he said seemed off." She looked away, hesitating to continue. "He called me a 'goddess'. Also, why is everyone going on about a 'perfect world'?"

Yousef nodded. "Yeah, I heard. He's, uh," he glanced to the side and scratched his temple. "He's a grandiose thinker, that man."

"The 'goddess' comment?" Judicia pulled off her glasses and kneaded the bridge of her nose. "Don't think too hard on that. Right now, we have other priorities."

Yousef and Andraste both stood up.

Judicia put her glasses back on and continued. "Rowe managed to buy us some time with his approval, but that makes it all the more important that we get him some results as soon as we can." She looked straight at Andraste. "Your training will have to become a lot more intense if you're going to convince the Cabinet that you're worthwhile. Think you can handle that?"

On impulse, she went rigid and saluted. "Yes, ma'am! I-I'll do everything I can!" She began to shiver as she held her position.

Judicia sighed. "Make no mistake, Andraste, you've worked hard to get where you are. I'd be lying if I said I wasn't proud." She spoke in a stilted, exaggerated way, as if she couldn't believe what she was saying. "But the fact is, we still have a lot of work ahead of us, and we can't afford to celebrate just yet."

Yousef, usually striving to offset Judicia's pessimism, shrugged. "Can't argue with that."

As she took in and released another deep breath, Andraste could feel the tension ebb away from her body. Albeit a small one, the meeting felt like a victory, a success. Her hard work had paid off at least a little bit.

"I'm prepared to do whatever you need me to do." She said, knowing that she meant it.

Yousef had a reassuring smile, and even Judicia managed to smirk.

"Let's get busy, then," she said.

13   Somewhere in The Outlands
4:38   June 2nd, 2335

A man wearing goggles and a black balaclava walked into the tent and answered the video call. On the front of the balaclava was the familiar sigil of the Martyr's Army, a white silhouette shattering into glass shards. It was their contact who had been to Rowe's conference.

"David, internal contact number 41, reporting in." He said, sweating.

"What's your status?" The man asked.

"The smuggled supplies have successfully been delivered to us, and all the necessary tools have been properly distributed. My allies have been informed of the plan, and we will be making our move in seven hours."

"Hang on while I fetch the General." The man moved away from the video screen.

"What? Wait!" David called after the man. "Please, it's not necessary! I'm only reporting in!"

"He will want to know. Stay on the line." Ignoring David's protests, he moved out of the tent.

General Bashford's regiment had been established in the forest for some time now. One of several monolithic trees was at the center of it all, and the soldiers had set up camp around it in a wide, saturnine ring.

If he focused on the ground with each step he took, he could feel the pulse of the Outland's Heart. The influence of the Fomorians he and his comrades worshipped was all around them, subtly projecting its lambent energy into the land. Those sensitive to it, like him, could see its gentle flow.

Even after a lifetime in and around the otherworldly wilderness of The Outlands, the soldier never found these sights any less breathtaking. He found himself looking up at the tree in reverent awe as he traced its prodigious circumference- no one had taken the time to measure it, but he guessed that the trunk at its widest point had a diameter of about 20 meters. Most of the other soldiers were asleep in their tents, and the black "I Remember the Martyrs" flags hung in the dampened breeze. A chorus of ungodly animal sounds came from the surrounding blackness.

A high-pitched chittering came from his left. On impulse, he raised his rifle to the sound. Through his sights, he saw an oblong figure of a similar color to the tree. It chittered again, and he saw a pair of shivering wings, catching the light at such an angle as to appear iridescent. The cicada turned towards the top of the tree and began to climb.

He sighed, and kept going towards the General's tent. Two other guards were stationed outside the structure. They regarded him, and he told them about the message.

"Don't waste his time!" One of the guards said in an emphatic whisper. "He must rest!"

"No need for concern," a voice said at a clear volume.

The folds of the tent parted, and the General walked out: George Bashford, a tall Englishman with striking white hair and matching mustache. For all the lines on his face and starkness in his gaze, he had an unmistakable energy about him.

"General Bashford," the guards all stood at attention and gave the Martyr's Army salute: three fingers over the heart, one for each bullet fired into Aaron Sennec. Bashford returned the gesture, and the soldiers were at ease.

"I overheard something about a message," Bashford said, scratching his chin. "Is it from that young man in London?"

"Yes, sir."

"Very well, I'll see to it." He left the tent and made his way towards the communication center. "You're dismissed."

Bashford traced the circumference of the tree without the need for night vision tools. When he approached the tent, he saw the faint glow of the computer from inside. He smiled at the thought of seeing the young agent again.

David was still on the screen, and his face blanched at the sight of the General. Bashford came closer and met the face on the monitor with a warm smile.

"Hello, David," Bashford said, saluting the young man.

"An honor and a privilege, sir!" David replied, three-finger salute firmly planted on his chest.

"I was informed that you have a message for me?" He cocked his head. "I do hope it's important."

"W-well," David looked to the side. "I wanted to inform my superiors that all the weapons and tools have been successfully delivered," he said before mustering the strength to look at Bashford again, "and that we're ready to make our move at 1200 hours later today."

"Fantastic," Bashford said. "And everyone has been informed of their roles?"

"Yes, sir. All the participating agents have been briefed and properly outfitted."

Bashford folded his arms. "Excellent. I must say, I'm looking forward to the outcome of this little venture."

"I am too, sir," David said, wearing a forced smile. "I'm afraid that's all I had to report, sir. I wouldn't want to waste your time with-"

Bashford put up a hand, silencing David.

"You're not wasting my time at all, friend. If anything, I was hoping for a good opportunity to talk to you."

David stared at his commander, mouth agape. He was cordial and easygoing enough, but David couldn't tell what was beyond that inviting demeanor.

"Unless you're otherwise indisposed, of course," Bashford commented, breathing life back into the conversation.

David snapped to attention. "Of course not, sir!"

"Good." Bashford pulled a notebook and pencil out of his breast pocket, full of questions and points that he wanted to delve into. "With that in mind, let's get to it: I would like to know more about the information you got from the informant. Williams, was it?"

"Yes, sir. He was a pharmacology professor involved in the FH Project- he approached another one of our units with some information."

"And what was this information?" Bashford knew the answers to all these questions. He was measuring David's responses.

"T-two things, mostly," David was fidgeting and shaking, but otherwise resolute in what he was saying. "First, that it was a human experiment. They created some Fomorian monster that can give people seizures."

Bashford could sense the intense fear in David's eyes and voice as he described this supposed monster. This was what Bashford wanted to see.

"Second, that there's a secret military base built beneath the Shard. Williams attempted to assassinate the creature shortly after we got in touch with him, but he was compromised."

Bashford scratched his chin. "Such a shame- we could have used more help like his." He smirked, looking David straight in the eyes as the latter stood ramrod straight. "I must say, David, I was dubious of launching an attack on Great Britain so early. However, considering all this new information, I think now is the perfect time to strike."

"Y-Yes, sir, I agree!"

"Now, before you go in, I want you to keep something in mind: We need that monster."

David was quiet. "We do?"

"The Fomorians still rule this land, David. Without someone like Aaron, we cannot hope to appease the forces out here." Bashford's expression darkened at the mention of that name.

"A-Aaron Sennec?" David risked saying the man's full name.

"The same," Bashford said, composed again. "This Fomorian hybrid the English have created could perform miracles for our cause. Bring it here at any cost."

David nodded with hesitation. "Yes, general."

Bashford was quiet. There was no expression nor tic to betray it, but he looked over David's face with great scrutiny.

"I must say, David, something has been on my mind," he began, twirling the pencil between his fingers. "I wonder if you understand the implications of 'any cost.' You know your way around a can of spray paint, but do you know your way around a gun?"

David gave the three-finger salute. "Oh, don't worry about that, sir! I've gotten plenty of practice at shooting ranges!"

"That's not what I mean." Bashford motioned for David to lower his salute. "Any fool can pick up a gun and pull a trigger. It takes a soldier to hold a gun and take full advantage of it." His look became more intense and his tone was grim. "Many, many people swear their lives to us. More than a handful of new recruits feel invincible with a gun in their hands, but the instant they see a gun pointed at them, their resolve breaks and that invincibility fades."

David struggled for a response. "W-Well, sir, my crew and I will-"

"We have lost thousands of soldiers this way, David." Bashford's commanding voice shocked the young man into silence. "Thousands of young, promising people with entire lives ahead of them, either dead or traitors to the cause. So far, David, all you have offered me is promises. And you can't measure the worth of a promise until the time comes to keep it." He leaned over, almost touching the screen with his face.

From David's perspective, the screen had stared him down. He still stood at attention, doing his best not to look away from the man.

"What I'm trying to say, David, is this: I truly, desperately hope that you won't be among the thousands who lose their nerve. I don't want to see your life squandered, either with a bullet in your head or our knowledge in enemy hands. Do you understand?"

"I offer myself up to the cause, sir!" David cried at the height of his voice.

Bashford narrowed his gaze at the young man. "More promises," he lamented, moving away from the screen. "The whole world will be watching when you hit the Shard, David. And by that point, I'll have my answer about you."

David began to protest, but Bashford killed communications before he could say anything. He walked out of the tent, satisfied.

14   London, England   11:38 a.m.   June 2nd, 2335

The moment Rowe left Central Base, Andraste was thrown into a regiment of physical and mental tests more intense and rigorous than anything they had tried before. The obstacle courses were bigger, the weights were heavier, and the time limits were shorter. She charged headfirst into every challenge they put against her, whether it was sparring or endurance testing, and Andraste was often the one to propose running these gauntlets multiple times, to Yousef's dismay. She was not going to stop until she could do these challenges properly. Her muscles were strained and her bones ached, but she refused to stop.

There was no denying the toll it was taking on her. Her sparring partner was begging for her to stop during their sessions, and not because he couldn't beat her.

"Andraste, I really think you should take a break."

Andraste was on the ground, gasping for breath. Sweat dropped out from the seams in her sparring gear and padded gloves.

"I can do it," she said, gasping between each word. "Please, sir, don't worry about me."

Sighing, he got into a stance.

Andraste swung at him with all her regular gusto, but the exhaustion made her slow and predictable. She went in for a roundhouse kick, which went wide and missed him completely. The momentum made her pirouette in place before she dropped to the floor.

The man stood over her, wagging an enormous finger at her. "Andraste, as your teacher, I instruct you to stop fighting and rest."

Andraste's head fell to the side in resignation. "Yes, sir."

The man turned to the side and peeled off his sparring equipment, tossing them in his gym bag. Andraste couldn't pull herself off the floor yet. She opened the Velcro strap on her helmet and slid it off, which was all she could manage before letting her arms fall flat on the floor again.

'Will I ever be ready?' She wondered, staring at the reinforced lights hanging above her. Fighting against the soreness, she hoisted herself up and went for the ladies' locker room.

She had become very fond of water ever since she stood in the rain on top of the Shard. For health reasons, Yousef and the others had insisted that she didn't immediately sprint outside whenever it started to pour, so she started to find the same kind of solace in the shower.

"*Maybe one day,*" she thought as she rubbed shampoo through her hair, "*When all of this is over, I can move on.*"

Andraste stopped herself before the thought could take root. "*I have a lot to do before any of this is over. I can't get comfortable yet.*" She sighed and hung her head, letting the water flush out the soap. "*Will I ever get comfortable?*"

It was another thought that she knew wouldn't end well. She swiped at the faucet and turned it from hot to cold. A rush of frigid water came over Andraste, shocking her system.

She anticipated that the cold water would purge the negative thoughts from her mind, but they remained. While so much was going on, she couldn't afford to dwell on any possibilities for the future. Shaking the thought out of her head, she went for her towel and dry clothes.

As she left the locker room, gym bag slung over her shoulder, a red light blared. Several alarms went off, followed by an automated message:

ATTENTION,
ALL PERSONNEL, PLEASE REPORT TO THE NEAREST PANIC ROOM. THIS IS NOT A DRILL.

Every square inch of the structure tingled with the intensity of the situation, as if the base itself came alive to share its panic with Andraste. Other footsteps and voices alongside the alarm made the area vivid with intensity.

It was so overbearing, Andraste almost ceased to think. In this absence of thought, she began to run, bag sliding out of her hand. Whatever soreness was left in her body was abandoned in the wake of this panic.

Several crowds of people were rushing up and down the hallway, following bright red arrows that were lit up along the sides of the halls.

"Andy!" Yousef broke out of the throng and grabbed her by the wrist, pulling her down one of the paths.

"What's going on?" It was all that Andraste could say as the people and lights rushed by.

"There's some lunatic in the Shard with a gun!" He jerked her down another hallway. "I don't know much else, but it sounds bad!"

Down the hallway was an open steel door. Yousef pulled her inside, where Judicia was waiting in a darkened room. The door slid shut, and Yousef led Andraste to a chair. Armed guards lined up outside.

"Dr. Judicia!" Andraste called once they were inside. "What on earth is happening?"

Judicia gestured to the TV as she looked to Andraste.

On the screen was a live news broadcast, with the familiar anchor Kennedy Schmidt. The base of the Shard was visible in the corner of the screen, behind all the blaring lights and sounds of the ambulances and police cars.

"All that we know for certain at this point, ladies and gentlemen, is that a man with a gun on the 5th level of the Shard, focusing on Argosy Hospital, has taken numerous doctors and patients hostage."

"Oh my God," Andraste said, propping herself up on the table.

Schmidt continued to talk as the camera moved. Several people from outside of the frame came into view. "Several eyewitnesses were able to escape the building. First was nurse Blake Myron." The camera came over to a heavyset man with glasses and blood-stained scrubs. He was pale and shaking. "Nurse Myron, I'd like to get straight to the heart of things: from your perspective, what happened?"

The man took a deep, shuddering sigh before speaking. "Well, it was a normal day, same as always, until we heard a patient from an emergency clinic was being transferred to us." He was talking fast and struggling to breathe. "I was assigned to assist the surgeon on what we assumed was a shattered rib cage, but then the man jumped us!" Myron looked at the blood on his scrubs. "He grabbed a knife and started stabbing the other doctors. When he pulled out the gun, I panicked and ran for the stairwell. I didn't stop until I reached the ground floor."

"Could you describe this man? Had you heard anything about his injuries before being transferred to your hospital?"

"I, uh," Myron gasped, struggling, "I had not heard anything about him before then. I didn't get a good look at his face, but he was a tall white man. Came in fully clothed, with a gigantic trench coat on." He pulled his glasses off his face and rubbed his hand over his sweaty features. "Sorry, that was all I saw before leaving."

"Thank you, Mr. Myron." The camera panned away just as the man turned. Kennedy followed the camera as it moved over even more. A man dressed in riot gear entered the scene.

"Next, we have Commander James Abbadi," As she approached, the man removed his helmet. He was a dark-skinned, tall man with bright eyes and a well-trimmed beard. "Commander, can you summarize the situation for us?"

"Absolutely, Miss Schmidt." He said curtly. "The man is surprisingly well-armed, possessing more ordnance than any civilian could easily acquire. He has established a solid perimeter around entire sections of the hospital, trapping doctors in with critically ill patients. We have dispatched a specialized police force to the floor, but security forces already present in the Shard have informed us that he has at least fifty hostages."

Acute chills ran up and down Andraste's spine. "Fifty?" She blurted out, too shocked to hush her tone. "W-What do we do?"

"Hope that nothing about Central Base is compromised," Judicia declared, fixed on the screen. "A lot of our genetic surgeons come here through Argosy."

"N-No, the man with the gun!" She stood up, and her chair tumbled backwards. "What are we doing about the man taking the hostages?"

Judicia finally turned to her. "I said, we're hoping that nothing about Central Base is-"

"And that's it?" She demanded, cutting Judicia off. "Don't tell me we're just going to sit here and watch!"

"Andy, take it easy." Yousef stood up as well, putting himself between her and Judicia. "I get it, this is an awful situation. But we'd expose this entire place if we sent anyone up there." He silently turned her from Judicia. "Besides, the situation should be fine. Abaddi's one of the finest officers we have. He'll have that madman taken care of, no worries."

Andraste took a breath and sat down again. She trusted the report, but still felt agitated. If there was ever a situation where someone with superhuman abilities was needed, it was here. In a time where the lives of her countrymen were in active danger, she couldn't do anything but watch. Her optimism was only buoyed by the sentiment that the situation was in good hands.

With a wave of static, the crisp, high-definition camera shot was supplanted by a grainy, darkened view of a hospital room. Andraste's optimism plummeted.

Six beds protruded from the sides of the walls. Between the beds were the huddled figures of other doctors and patients, clearing the rest of the floor space for the figure in the center of the room. A patient out of the camera's view was softly whimpering, trying not to let their sobs escape.

The camera was focused on a gigantic, bald man in the center of the shot, hefting a tremendous rifle in his grip. True to Nurse Myron's description, he was wearing a large coat that covered enormous bulk, but the shape and contour of his size looked unnatural. It was in sharp contrast to his well-built face and hard features.

He approached the camera, walking with a heavy gait and resounding footsteps. His gaze was narrowed and intense, but it broke into a wide grin when he stopped.

"Hello, London." His voice was quiet but distinct, and he savored every word he spoke. "Some of you may recognize me. To those who don't, let me fill you in: my name is Corporal Alex Gattis, 502nd division of the Royal Air Force." He leaned in close. "That's right, I'm a fucking soldier. I'm not from the Outlands, I'm not being blackmailed, and I'm not being hypnotized or any bullshit like that. I joined the Martyr's Army because I wanted to. I wanna see the Fomorians return!"

The look on the man's face cut into Andraste with surgical precision, and the mention of the Martyr's Army only deepened the wound. Gattis reminded Andraste of Professor Williams, the way he relished the pain and anger.

"I want you all to remember that going forward. I'm not a sleeper agent, I'm just a guy taking a side. And there are a lot more of us than you might want to believe. We're in your offices, your neighborhoods," he paused and smiled, "your homes."

The weeping patient let out a cry, drawing a staggered breath into their body. Gattis jerked away from the camera to face them with wide, intense eyes. He walked over to the bed, grabbing the camera and facing it towards the patient.

The patient was a young man, boyish in stature and face, wearing a neck brace and a bandage around his head. He shrank back from Gattis as much as he could, but most of his reddened face and eyes were still visible to the audience. More tears went down his face as the gunman got closer.

"What's the matter?" Gattis said, leaning in close to the man. "Are you scared?"

Andraste was boiling. Her fists were clenched and her mind gave substance to a maelstrom of violent and hateful thoughts. In her waking dreams, she wedged herself between Gattis and that helpless patient. She would wrench the gun from his hand and knock him to the floor, sending him flying with one punch.

"What are you so scared of, little man?" Gattis said, a facetious tone in his voice.

It took several deep, strained breaths for the patient to respond. "S-sir, please," he finally said, pained to do so, "I don't want to die." His voice was then lost between sobs.

Gattis leaned away. "No one does. We have lives so we can live them- not that any of you fucks would appreciate that!" His voice was loud and intense, and he spun the barrel of his gun in an arc.

The hostages flinched at his insult, curling into tighter balls and pressing themselves closer against the wall.

Gattis went on. "It must be nice. Everyone in Great Britain sleeps so soundly, pretending their lives are the only ones that matter. I haven't lived in the Outlands- like I said, I'm a Brit just like you fuckers. But the fact that you all ignore what's going on in Europe is what makes this necessary." He moved the camera back into its position. "Aaron Sennec was going to teach *everyone* how to live and survive and get along, and then, not only do you murder him, you pretend that the Outlanders are fucking barbarians."

His voice and movements were becoming more emphatic. "The Outlanders are tired of always fighting for their lives. The Fomorians, our Martyrs, are still with us, and they're preparing the world for their return!"

"What is he on about?" Andraste whispered, begging.

"They worship the fucking Fomorians, that's what he's on about." Judicia muttered.

" And to top it all off, you act like it's not even your problem. Let me teach you a little something about responsibility."

Still keeping his hand on the trigger of his gun, he went for the zipper on his jacket and pulled it down. He pulled the flap aside, revealing a thick tangle of wires and lights. As the jacket was held open, the camera got a full view of clusters upon clusters of plastic explosives, comprising his unnatural size. On his right side alone, there must have been at least twenty bricks of explosive material.

A frigid sense of panic surged up Andraste's spine. The room was filled with a painful silence, apart from the horrified shrieks and sobbing of the hostages on the TV.

"I'm not just another bad dream, England. I'm the real fucking deal!" He held his arms apart, voice buoyed by enthusiasm. "You can't ignore us anymore; the war of the Outlands has come to London!" He began to roar. "I'm Alex Gattis, and I Remember the Martyrs!" He hung his head back as red lights began to flicker in the cluster of bombs. A split second of his explosion was captured before the TV screen went blank.

In the panic room, there was a reverberation of shock waves like a close strike of thunder. Andraste placed both of her hands on the table, taking deep gasps of air. The shaking was soon over, but Andraste propped herself up on the table all the same.

The news network displayed a "please stand by" screen, while they and their audience waited to find out what the hell was happening. Andraste was stiff and trying her damnedest to center herself. A terrible energy raced through her body with no clear outlet. It ran into her hands and twisted her hands into trembling, pained fists.

Yousef got up from his chair and turned away. Andraste could hear him taking deep breaths too, and felt him experience shock and bewilderment not unlike her own. Judicia sat in her chair, still ogling the TV.

Intense sensations and situations had the tendency to precipitate panic in Andraste, but she found the familiar sensation absent. Panic was always so cold and hostile, like a parasite eating away at you. She felt something hot and oddly addicting, a feeling she almost reveled in- anger. Fire surged up her spine. The vengefulness came back- she imagined herself tackling Gattis to the ground and beating his head against the floor. She would have faced the Martyr's Army head-on, and torn them apart with the shards of their own broken pride.

After its long, painful silence, the news on the TV came back to life. Instead of Kennedy Schmidt, the screen showed a blacked-out silhouette on a higher level of the Shard. Sunlight filtered through the nearby windows as the occasional plume of smoke from the explosion cast a shadow.

"Hello," The voice was of another man, notably younger than Gattis. "This is far from over. Mr. Gattis was just the beginning."

"Oh God, now what?" Yousef sat down again.

"My fellow soldiers have made excellent use of Mr. Gattis's sacrifice- we have moved up to the higher levels of the Shard, and we have hostages on over thirty floors. Make sure this message gets to Nathan Rowe: unless you want ten times as many casualties as the Argosy bombing, you will comply with our demands.

"We know all of your secrets, Rowe. We know about Central Base, we know about the FH Project, and we know about the monster."

All three of them took a sharp breath, and the room became frigid with fear.

"Only a few people know what I'm talking about. Rowe, you're going to go on the air and fill in the blanks: tell the people everything about the FH Project. And you'll send the monster to us, on the 43rd floor. Send her to us restrained and unharmed. If we have any reason to believe that you're trying to sabotage us, everyone will die. You have an hour to comply." As quick as he came, he was gone, and the network returned to the 'please stand by' screen.

Silence filled the room. All three of them stared at the TV, too stunned to move, respond, or even think. It wasn't until Judicia's phone rang that anyone reacted.

"Hello?" She answered with her usual deadpan, which somehow seemed even more monotone. "Yes, I saw it."

After the voice went on for a few more moments, Judicia got up and turned to Andraste. Her arm jutted out with the phone clenched in her hand.

"Mr. Rowe wants to talk to you."

Andraste, almost completely numb, stood up and took the phone. Judicia's pale complexion was completely pale.

"H-H-Hello?" Andraste couldn't keep her voice still.

"Hello, Andraste." Rowe's voice on the other side was solemn. "I'm sure you're aware of the situation we're in here."

"Y-Yeah."

"We have less than an hour, Andraste. I don't have a problem with telling people about Central Base and the

FH Project, but I'm not sure how to approach their demand to see you."

"What do you mean, sir?"

Rowe sighed. "Andraste, you're too much of an asset. I can't just hand you over to them!"

"So, what are we going to do?" Andraste asked with vehemence.

"I don't know, Andraste!" Rowe responded in turn. "Give me a moment to think. Sit tight until I call you back." And he hung up.

A cascade of conflicting thoughts and emotions rose inside her. After so much time spent battling, wondering, and preparing for an encounter with the Martyr's Army, they were overhead, and she was helpless to stop them. Indignity, anger, fear, and so many others filled her head in a chaotic mass.

"Andy?" Yousef asked, gently taking the phone from her. "Are you okay?"

"How do they know about me?" Andraste limply sank into a chair.

"Williams, I bet," Judicia said. "If Rowe asked us to stand by, then that's what we're doing. Whatever those idiots want with you, we're not letting them have it."

"Judicia, come on! People are going to die if we don't do something!" Andraste protested.

"We will do something, Andraste!" Judicia kept going. "But whatever you're planning, you are NOT ready to fight them yet. Don't get any ideas." Yousef tried to help, but she interrupted. "End of discussion," she said with a jab of her hand.

Slumping in her chair, Andraste couldn't help but ruminate. The scene in Argosy Hospital returned. She remembered the weeping patient in the bed, and all the terrified people forced against the wall. Only the patient spoke about how scared he was to die, but in their heads, she knew every other hostage was screaming the same thing. After ten minutes passed without word from Rowe, she covered her face with her hands when her imagination conjured the sensation of the hospital bombing.

"Andy," Yousef pulled out a chair next to her and sat. "I know this looks bad, but we've dealt with worse than this."

She looked at him, trying to feel relieved.

"We're safe here. Running up there without a plan isn't going to help anyone."

Andraste nodded, but her heart wasn't in her agreement. "You're right, of course. But," she looked away, gripping the cloth on her pants. "But how can I just sit here? I can't put all those hostages' lives over mine!" She shook her head as her hands clasped her shoulders. "I'm supposed to be our ace in the hole! Is there really NOTHING I can use against them?"

"Andy, remember to breathe."

She did her breathing, but the impotence lingered. A cloud of prickling uncertainty came out from Yousef even as he tried to stay composed. The sense of frustrated powerlessness was mutual, and even he seemed to notice it from her.

Another twenty minutes passed in twenty ticks of agonized silence. Judicia nursed a headache with a bottomless thermos of coffee as her phone laid flat on the table, and Yousef was thumbing through random pages on his tablet. Thirty minutes were left until the deadline. Andraste was surprised that her tranquilizer hadn't gone off during the whole span of the tragedy.

As she turned to look at it, the despair left her. Something akin to hope began to fill the space as an idea took form in her mind.

Andraste stood up as she looked at the catheter, her finger spinning as she imagined gears and mechanical systems to give structure to her thoughts.

"Andy?" Yousef asked after a moment. "What are you doing?"

Andraste's eyes were narrowed as her mind's eye drew the schematics of her newest, most insane idea yet. The most detailed plans centered around her medicine.

The psychiatric department had given her the tranquilizer because moments of intense emotion could affect other people. Entire rooms of people could suffer violent hallucinations without it, but maybe that was what they needed right now. It wouldn't be a fun experience, and she acknowledged that her idea might not work at all, but she was willing to try anything.

"Hello? Andy?" Yousef got up and started to follow her.

"What now?" Judicia asked as she turned to them.

Finally, Andraste let the tension fade from her face. "I have a plan," she said with quiet determination.

Judicia and Yousef shared a glance.

"Andraste, what did I say about getting ideas?" Judicia said exhaustedly. "You're going to go down there and have another episode, I know it."

"Exactly!" Andraste snapped her finger and pointed, breaking the room's tense silence. "I can't imagine how they would be prepared for that. I'd go up to them, have a little breakdown, and then Rowe's forces would be able to come in and take them out!"

"Are you completely mad?" Judicia demanded.

"Andy, we-" Yousef started, then caught himself before going on. "We may be low on options here, but that's far too drastic."

"What other options are there? We haven't heard anything else from Rowe!" She gestured to Judicia's phone. "Just call Rowe, and we can discuss it with him! If he says no, we'll come up with something else!"

"Andraste, calm down." Judicia sighed. "Let's give him five more minutes."

"Do we *have* five minutes?" Andraste protested.

Yousef looked at Judicia with uncertainty. "He can help us," he finally said with a shrug.

"Fine, but don't expect much." Judicia picked up the phone and started to dial, her sentiment like that of a tired parent to an unruly child.

When they were through to Rowe, they explained Andraste's idea. Much like the doctors, his initial response was dumbfounded shock.

"Andraste, do you hear yourself?" Rowe said when he finally found his voice.

"I do hear myself, sir. Loud and clear." She took a breath to steady her voice. "Unless you have a plan already, we *cannot* afford to wait."

"True as that may be, Andraste, you are too valuable! You're our goddess!"

Still unsure of how to process the 'goddess' sentiment, Andraste kept going. "Do you think it won't work?"

"W-well," Rowe replied, his hesitation saying it all.

"I joined this project because I want to help people. And there are people directly above me who need help. Please, just let me try!"

The air in the room was heavy with anticipation. With her fists clenched, Andraste's short, hard breaths were the only dominant sound. All eyes were on the phone as they waited for some response.

"You're not going alone," Rowe finally said.

Yousef jumped at Rowe's voice. "What?"

"Directly behind you, we'll be sending in the special forces." Rowe spoke quickly and seriously. "The moment something goes wrong, they'll come and clean things up."

"You mean," Andraste said with an airy gasp, "we're using my idea?"

"In a way, Andraste," Rowe answered heavily. "We'll let them think we're complying, and that'll give us some more time to respond. If you can handle them, that's splendid, but your priority will be surviving. Is that clear?"

"It is, sir!" Andraste nodded. "Thank- thank you for having faith in me!" She sputtered, caught betwixt validation and terror.

"Of course," Rowe said. "A goddess needs faith, after all."

This comment took them all out of the moment, but Rowe continued:

"I'll communicate this to our specialists and then respond to the hostage taker. If you can be ready after a few minutes, go on upstairs to them."

He hung up after that, leaving the three of them in silence.

"Again with the 'goddess' stuff?" Andraste mused aloud.

"Andy," Yousef reached for her, voice trembling. "Do you realize what you've just signed up for? You're still doing physical therapy, and now you're trying to fight the Martyr's Army!"

"Dr. Yousef, please." She turned to look at him. "I know this is dangerous. But they're not going to wait around until I'm ready to fight them. I appreciate it, but please, don't try to stop me."

He steadied himself. "I'm not trying to stop you, Andraste. I'm just," he shrugged, "I'm just reeling from this whole thing." He sat down. "I lost over a dozen patients to this experiment. Most didn't even wake up from the genetic surgery." Andraste felt a chill. "When you pulled through, I thought I had finally done my job and saved someone. Now you're walking up to people who want you dead."

His sentiments weakened her knees. All at once, the implications of her failure surged through her mind, and she dropped into a chair next to him.

"Dr. Yousef," she began, struggling to find the words, "You've done so much for me, and I-I'm incredibly grateful for all of that. B-but this is what I've been preparing for!" Andraste chuckled weakly, trying to coax a smile out of him. "This is how I'll finally be valuable to the

FH Project. After so many mistakes, I can help with Rowe's 'perfect world' idea, or whatever he said."

He scoffed gently, meeting her eyes. "You have value *now*, Andraste," he wheezed. "You think everything is your fault, but it isn't." Yousef shook his head with a sad smile. "As for the 'perfect world' idea, I wouldn't cling to that. Nobody is perfect, ever, and it's ridiculous to expect it."

This tore into her soul. Words of encouragement from someone she had consistently pushed away for her own ends. As she felt a sob rising.

"O-oh," Andraste muttered.

"Honestly, I don't really know what Rowe's on about when he brings it up." He shrugged.

"Don't worry about it, you two." Judicia finally said. "We have other things to worry about. You said it yourself, Andraste: we can't afford to wait." She tapped her watch, not looking at either of them. "If you're going to go, you should go now."

Her resolve shriveled, Andraste slowly got to her feet. She looked between Judicia and Yousef, the two people most eagerly waiting for her to come back from this in one piece. Or at least, Yousef was.

"I," she started, but the words were tangled in her throat. "I'm s-s-sorry, Dr." Andraste looked at Yousef, while the rising bundle of words in her throat pushed out a few tears. The pressure was too much, and she turned from the room and towards the elevators.

"I'm sorry!" Andraste finally said, clinging to fragments of this grief to fuel her attack on the insurgents.

Taking a deep breath and drying her eyes, she grabbed the catheter and wrenched the needle out, taking care not to break the cable. The rest of the way up, she pressed down on the exit wound to stem the blood flow.

15 London, England
13:34 June 2nd, 2335

No matter how she tried to put it out, Andraste couldn't keep the image of the patient out of her mind. He was agonized and terrified, and just from the cadence of his voice, she knew his state of mind. Horror beyond belief was all too common in her environment, and she was noticing patterns between each instance of it. There were similar looks in people's eyes, common nuances in their fearful twitching, and the abject terror that strained their voices all sounded alike. She didn't want to entertain the notion that she felt the same way as that patient.

The service elevator wasn't fast. It was designed to be subtle and not draw attention. It made very little sound, which forced Andraste to endure her thoughts. She leaned against the wall opposite the door, arms folded. She stood still, without any visible movements to betray the cacophony in her mind.

Her breaths were as deep as her body could allow. She put all her effort into imagining another machine, but she was too distressed to keep it together. The gears would get caught on one another and pistons would fly off and embed themselves in the dark recesses of her imagination.

"I'm not scared," she repeated, over and over again. At one point, she started to see that sentence spelled

out in the teeth of her imaginary gears. The sentence no longer held any meaning, but it became a habit she was scared to break.

"You idiot, you just finished talking about this with Rowe." She unfolded her arms and let them hang limp. *"You're ready for this. You're not scared."*

No amount of self-abuse would make the fact congeal. She hung her head back and started to say it aloud.

She still didn't believe herself, and the machine she tried to imagine morphed into several dark forms. They had no features, but she knew one of them was the silhouette on the TV. In her mind, she knelt before these figures, powerless and unable to move. A glint of silver broke the darkness. The hostage taker's silhouette had raised a gun to her, the barrel at eye level. As she shut them, a bullet was fired.

Curled in a shuddering ball, Andraste struggled to catch her breath. She grabbed her shoulders and wept painfully. Every part of her body shook as the adrenaline started its course, her arms resisting as if trying to straighten themselves. She had never been sure why she had this habit, but the important thing was that it calmed her down. But there was too much on her mind for it to fully calm her down.

The past month was full of enough calamity and uncertainty to fill several lifetimes. Only recently did Andraste feel like she was assuming control over her bizarre abilities and learning how to help the people around her. Before that, she had been a burden.

The shame dug into her with a thousand needle points in her chest. She curled into a tighter ball as the pain grew more intense. Deep breaths had only been marginally helpful, and her mind was too overclocked to divert its focus onto anything that would calm her.

Her rebirth as a Fomorian Hybrid was a stream of trouble, even before it happened. It was trouble to get the project approved, trouble to go through the hybridization procedure, and trouble to keep her alive and functioning. The worst part, she thought as her fingertips dug into her skin, was that her life was going to be validated by her death if she failed now.

"All I've done is hurt the people who care about me." The tears fell in heavy streams as she thought this.

"You have value, Andraste," Yousef's words came back. She clenched her fists, lamenting that his attempt at kindness was fueling this dissonance inside her. But deep down, she felt gratitude for him welling up.

"The people who care about me," she mulled, with a sense of renewed determination, *"are counting on me."*

The elevator finally stopped and slid open. Andraste was met at the door by a young man with an assault rifle. His eyes bulged and he almost dropped the gun when he saw her.

It wasn't the one giving the orders on the TV, but they appeared to be of a similar age. He was a wiry person with glasses and bright blonde hair, which stood in sharp contrast to the black bandana covering the lower part of his face. Like the defining feature of most other Martyr's Army soldiers, it had a white render of the "I Remember the Martyrs" graffiti.

"David! The monster's here!" He called back, looking away from Andraste. The instant he noticed his vulnerability, he whipped back around and pressed his gun onto her. "Don't fucking move."

His gun trembled like the leg on a newborn fawn. His grip was wrong, as well, with two digits on the trigger.

She had no more time to think before another set of doors flew open. It was David, the same silhouette that had ordered her to arrive, illuminated by the light in the room. He had short dark hair and hard eyes, which matched his Martyr's Army sigil perfectly. He had the correct demeanor for an insurgent, with deliberate, understated movements and no forced impression of being "tough." Also, he was holding the rifle correctly. He brushed past his fellow insurgent and stared Andraste in the face.

"Are you serious? This is the monster?" He rushed Andraste and grabbed her by the shirt. "Are you the one who killed Williams, bitch?"

Andraste did her best to stay calm. She couldn't make her move until the perfect moment.

"No," she said, looking back into his eyes, "He killed himself."

David thrust the butt of his rifle into her stomach, which knocked the wind out of her and brought her to her knees.

"Don't try to act tough, freak!" He and his friend grabbed her by the arms and dragged her away from the elevator.

Instinctively, Andraste wanted to catch her breath, but she knew it would be best if she didn't. She didn't want to calm down, for the first time in ages. She felt her heart rate go up as she allowed herself only short, staggered breaths.

The rest of the floor was dark, with no lights on and most of the blinds drawn over the windows. The floor was undergoing renovations and had been largely cleared out. Almost the entire space was visible, so the lack of personnel was conspicuous. She wanted to look into one of their minds to try and find some insight, but she risked discovery.

The rebels pulled her towards one of the more well-lit areas of the building, where three other people were. They let her fall, and her head smacked the ground.

"Terrifying, isn't she?" David addressed the others, facetious. "Get the camera ready."

Andraste turned to look at the others. Like David and his friend, they were all young adults, twentysomethings with assault rifles and black bandanas. Another man and two women, all with their guns trained on her.

The fear in the air was tangible. Every single one of them, near-frozen with fear and anchored by the heavy ordnance in their arms. They braced themselves against the unknown with the knowledge that they could shoot their way out of a problem. Beneath the cold, however, was a vein of heat, a passion that they fought for.

David prodded Andraste with the barrel of his gun. "Get on your knees. Hands behind your head."

Andraste did as she was told. In front of them was a cheap-looking video camera connected to a large antenna, which one of the women operated.

"Are we good to go?" David asked. The girl gave a thumbs-up.

Andraste took her chance. Starting with the woman at the camera, she did as much as she could to focus on her feelings. She would have started with the other man who dragged her in, but he seemed too unstable to be sensitive to her scrutiny.

She saw the woman's point of view, fiddling with some buttons and making sure the camera was properly centered. Through the camera, Andraste saw herself, a skinny, slumped-over enigma with a weird gray exoskeleton covering some of her char-black skin.

"What the hell did they do to her?" The woman's first coherent thought came through. This, followed by a miasma of concerns with the camera and the way her gun kept jamming, told Andraste that there was nothing to find within this woman. As the camera turned on, Andraste disengaged with her.

"Hello, people of London." David spoke, his face visible except for the bandana. "If all goes according to plan, Nathan Rowe will soon be telling you all about our guest. Behold, ladies and gentlemen," He grabbed Andraste by the arm and held her in front of the lens. "The results of the FH project! The world's first Fomorian Hybrid, here with us today!"

It occurred to her that everyone in Great Britain and beyond was watching this. The attention of millions was focused on her, filtered through a single glass eye. Pangs of self-consciousness and fear struck her. It was a welcome addition to the other feelings she harbored.

What Andraste wanted to do was panic. When she first woke up, she put people in the hospital and nearly killed a man. If she could produce the same effect here, she might be able to wriggle her way out of this and save some lives. She severed her connection to the medicine so it wouldn't sabotage her, and she tried to focus on every stressor and fear that she had. Recognizing how backwards the entire plan was, it was her only option.

"You heard me correctly, good people: the British government, your beloved Nathan Rowe and his flying circus, have been trying to revive and weaponize the Fomorian menace!"

Her only hesitation was the idea of any backup from the Martyr's Army. She wanted to search their minds, to see where the hostages were and if there were any countermeasures in place if something went wrong for them.

David continued to go on about Rowe's deceitful nature and the madness of the British government. Not holding back any longer, Andraste embraced the mind of the wiry man from earlier.

Thoughts raced through his mind at incomprehensible speed, the sweat running cold down his back. Classic performance anxiety, but it wasn't the kind of thing Andraste could work with. She concentrated even harder.

Beneath the fear and anxiety, she found an ill-fitting emotion. It was a delicate but distinct sense of excitement and enthusiasm, which was especially strong as he looked at David. Her curiosity piqued, she moved away from his fear and onto that sensation.

"It's really amazing how he's doing all this," he thought. She wondered, in this focused vein of thought that he had, if there was more to find on David's plans.

"I didn't think we'd get as far as we did with Gattis, and now we're here. The five of us, pulling off something this big!"

Andraste pulled herself out of his mind before her own thoughts made an appearance in his.

"These five people," she began, doing her best to keep her wide eyes away from the camera, *"are the only insurgents here."* It would be absurd if they didn't have some other measure in place. Calming herself, she closed her eyes and went back into his mind.

The number of layers that existed in the insurgent's emotions surprised her. Beneath the veil of courage, there was fear. Beneath the fear, there was admiration. And beneath that admiration, there was a nuance of disbelief. She wondered what the disbelief and admiration coalesced into.

"David is the bravest lunatic I've ever met," he thought, as his grip on the gun started to relax. *"I need to remember that, no matter what, we've won here. Even if we get captured or killed, we'll take the Shard with us."*

That confirmed Andraste's suspicions about a contingency plan. After that bit of knowledge, the insurgent's thoughts focused more on his movements and breathing. She ducked out before he could take note of her.

"It's pretty sad, the way you could put so much faith into something so insane! Just look at this!" David shouted at the camera.

Before Andraste could think of her next move, David grabbed a clump of her hair with his free hand and forced her to look at the camera. His grip wasn't strong enough to hurt her, but his touch sent waves of electric discomfort across her scalp, and she could feel the vitriol in every mangled strand of hair.

"They say that the FH Project was going to produce the ultimate soldier. Is THIS what you call the ultimate soldier?" He shook Andraste. She could feel some clusters of hair being ripped out, and the blood that trickled from those points. "This weak, unstable abomination?" He leaned in closer, getting right next to her. David's face pressed against hers felt like fire. "Look at what Rowe is prepared to do. He's taken an innocent human life and warped it into this sick monster! He wants to bring the apocalypse back just so he can say that he's won! Well, what now, Rowe? What will you do about the Martyr's Army after we take your secret weapon?"

Andraste couldn't stop shaking. The cold and numbness in her limbs, the heat and anger from David's hateful soliloquy, and the electric thorns that surged up and down her spine were overwhelming. The longer she was forced to look into the camera, the more she felt its gaze cut into her. She tried to breathe, but even the smallest mouthful of air was forced out before she could bring in more.

David stopped talking when he noticed her agitation. He moved away and loosened his grip on her hair. Without his support, she almost fell forward.

"Look at this." He gestured at her. "Look at how she suffers. Is this what you want, ladies and gentlemen? Do you want to put your future in the hands of this pained, tragic creature?" From what Andraste could detect about him, he believed he was showing sympathy.

"Don't worry, Andraste." David reached for the grip on his rifle. "You'll be among people who understand soon enough." He grabbed one of her shoulders and pushed her back.

As David continued to talk to the camera, he mentioned martyrdom, sacrifices, and held up his photo of Aaron Sennec. Andraste focused everything onto her fear, trying to force the panic. Her mind raced, her pulse quickened, and her breaths became shorter. All the pieces were in place, but nothing.

"What's wrong?" She thought, as the fear continued to pile up. *"Why isn't this working?"* There needed to be inexorable, all-consuming fear, or this plan wouldn't work.

Remembering her awakening, which had served as the inspiration for the entire scheme. All these different elements came together to produce the panic- the chorus of voices from the onlookers, the sensory overload from the world around her, and her own confusion had all laid the foundation. All those elements were present here, but they didn't bear the same results. *"What's missing?"*

As David started to tell something to the other insurgents, she remembered something. She was given stimulants to get her off the anesthesia more quickly, and those sent her into shock. What she needed was a jolt.

"All right, now listen to us, Andraste." David said, the first coherent thing she had processed from him in some time. "Do as we say, and we'll keep you alive."

Her legs were locked in a painful kneel before them all. She looked up at the gun barrels pointed at her to demand obedience. Already sorry she didn't have a better idea, she leapt upon the first thing that crossed her mind.

The insurgent she had been examining earlier still held his gun with unease. She dove back into his mind. In his focus, he was easily thrown off-guard. She forced the gun's sights away from her torso and onto her left shoulder, and then made him pull the trigger. One slug of hot metal tore into Andraste's shoulder, stopping at the bone.

It was the jolt she needed. A lurid hallucination erupted as the pain struck her.

Plumes of fire and sparks burst from the entry wound, while the agony and panic from the impact sent energy into the world around her, cracking the floor and walls like glass. Andraste howled as the metal seared into her flesh with molten intensity, and cascades of bloody lava gushed out of her mouth and eyes, melting away her mask and face plates.

David and the other insurgents all backed away from the flames, putting up their hands and arms in meager protection. Cracks and sparks came from David's friend, and he began to shatter as he held his hand in shock. His and Andraste's screams formed an eldritch harmony that reverberated and echoed, shaking the room like an earthquake.

He collapsed onto the floor, and the other rebels fell to the same influence. One of the women had a chunk of her forehead explode off her face, and she cried as the same sparks and fire shot out.

The heat and liquid continued to rise until only David was left standing- all the others had fallen into the neon fluid, kicking and screaming. Their last few twitches would send ripples and bubbles through the lava, but Andraste could still hear their cries. David had somehow managed to resist it, grasping onto his temples in immense pain.

"What the fuck is happening?" David's voice sent shockwaves through the space, deepening the cracks, and agitating the lava. His words made Andraste's head throb at an intensity almost equal to the throbbing in her shoulder. Her ears rang as he stopped talking.

As he stopped, she heard a familiar beeping sound, foreign to the hellish world that she had found herself in. Working her way through the agony as best she could, Andraste felt around the burning mass of her arm until she found a loose cable. As best as she could, she found the needle point on the cable and jammed it into her vein.

A gap was formed in the lava, which deepened as a welcome cooling sensation traveled her shoulder and into her head. A rush of relief came over her scalp and down her face, washing away the fire and torment. The floor of the room and its natural lighting reappeared around her, pushing away the world of her hallucination. She took a deep breath, and felt the horror flush out with her sigh.

Some of that horror returned when she looked at her shoulder. A hole had been ripped in her shirt and a stream of blood leaked onto the floor. This was the first time the legendary resilience of the Fomorians seemed to come into play. The pain finally did start to fade, and she feared the blood loss would be much more profuse than it was.

The hallucination faded, and four of the five insurgents were on the ground. Three of them were dead, while another still twitched and foamed at the mouth.

David, to her astonishment, was still standing, staggering back and forth as he clutched his head.

She didn't have time to tend to her wound or think about the camera. Gathering her strength and muscling past the pain, she got on her feet and charged. She went for one of the discarded guns, settling for the twice-discharged gun that had hit her.

Her arm shot out and grabbed the handle. As she turned to point it at David, she was met with the barrel of his gun.

The two of them were locked on one another for several moments, eyeing one another maliciously. There was a horrified frenzy in David's face, accentuated by the ruptured vessel somewhere in his left eye. Andraste was too drained from her breakdown to pick up on anything he was feeling. All she focused on was the gun in her hand and the man she was going to shoot.

"You," he finally said after several moments of strained breathing. "What the fuck are you?" He kept the sights on her and took a slow step backwards.

"Don't move!" Andraste got up on one of her knees, squeezing the rifle grip to cope with the pain. Her left arm hung limp at her side as blood trickled down her fingers, warm as it bled out but cold on her hand.

"What's your game, monster?" David's crumbling resolve was apparent by the tremble in his voice. "Do you even know what you've done?"

There was too much pain for Andraste's voice to convey her anger. "My name is Andraste," she said. "S-stop talking to me like I'm some kind of animal!"

"Okay, 'Andraste,' do you have any idea what you've done?" His eyes shot lines of daggers at her. "Do you actually have a goal in mind, or are you just following orders? Is Nathan Rowe going through with that address of his, or is he waiting for his little attack dog to bring some bodies home?"

"Sh-Shut up!" She took care not to squeeze to hard, lest the gun break in her hand. "Don't pretend that you know me!"

"And you think you know us, bitch? What do you even know about the Martyr's Army, or any of the things we've lost to your shithead politicians?" He leaned in, tightening his grip on his gun. "Do you even know who Aaron Sennec is?"

She went along with it for now, hoping to buy some time for backup. "Of course, I know about him. You all want revenge for his death."

"You mean his murder." He barely blinked during his interrogation. "He was giving the world the political revolution it needed, and then you all come in and slaughter the man. He was going to save all of us, but now no one can be saved!"

"What?" Andraste was baffled.

"The Outlands can't be controlled without him, you dumb broad! England has screwed everyone over! And if the Outlanders are going out, we're taking you all with us!"

She was inclined to ask what he was talking about, but her curiosity would have to wait. Worse things were afoot. "I don't have time for your lunacy! Either give yourself up peacefully, or face consequences!"

"You can't touch me!" He yanked his hand away from the gun and drew a small device from the pocket of his vest. It had a small antenna and a button with a familiar red light.

Andraste staggered. It was the same kind of light she saw on Gattis.

"Caught on?" David backed away from Andraste, towards a nearby staircase. "I've got bombs. And it's not just the button- if my heart rate stops, this will still go off. One wrong move, and I'll bury you." He was at the staircase. "Now drop the gun."

Indignation made her hand go rigid, and the gun almost straightened. She gave him a hard look, while he shook the detonator for emphasis. She shut her eyes and started to lower the gun.

With the little empathic sense that she had, the relaxation in him was enough to spur her into action. She pulled the trigger and released a volley of bullets into the ceiling. She popped her eyes open, and saw David flailing in panic, but unharmed. With the split second that she had to respond, Andraste took to her feet and ran at him. As he looked back at her, she was already barreling into his chest. Her speed was enough to knock him off his feet, and with her hands clenching his, she pinned him onto the stairs.

The burning in her shoulder started anew as she held him down, with one hand restraining the gun and the other restraining the trigger. Blood gushed from her wound with renewed intensity, dripping onto David's face. He scowled and tilted his head away from it.

His loosened grip on the detonator had pulled the button away from his hand. Tightening her grip, she pulled back and slammed his wrist against the edge of the wooden step, snapping the bones and contorting his fingers.

She grabbed the detonator and looked over it- the device was crude, with exposed wiring and a rudimentary design. From her engineering research, she could piece together which component did what, and how they worked together to send a signal. It was something she could dismantle.

They fought over the detonator, Andraste's combat training holding strong. Twisting away from him to keep the detonator out of reach, Andraste maneuvered her fingers through and between the proper wires, ripping out the ones that carried signals to the antenna.

She looked back at him and yanked his gun away. "What now, David?"

"What now, yourself?" With his destroyed hand, he reached for another pocket on his vest. He looped a limp finger around a metal pin.

Andraste jumped back, landing on the floor and covering her head. There was a loud bang followed by a sharp ringing sound. She was expecting worse than a flashbang. When she looked back up, David was sprinting up the stairs. Andraste hefted her assault rifle and sprang to her feet, going after him at a full gallop.

The pain in her shoulder was becoming unbearable. It hurt when her arm swung under its own momentum, and it hurt when she exerted some force to keep it still. Each time she rounded a corner on the staircase, it felt like a circuit was completed and rivulets of electricity tore through her flesh. She kept her gun up, and she prepared herself for anything.

For at least three floors under construction, Andraste chased David. The stairs seemed to go on forever, reminding her for an eternity of how painful the bullet wound was. To stay focused and alert, she reminded herself: she had a gun, and he didn't. The situation was in her favor, for better or for worse.

After the billionth flight of stairs, Andraste saw the blood trail go off onto one of the floors. It was distinct with its high, vaulted ceilings and intricate network of glass. She looked over and saw a hunched-over figure at the same balcony where she stood in the rain. The blood led straight to him. It was a painful sight, like his presence had fouled this beloved place.

She pushed through the doors and took aim.

"Get up! Hands over your head!"

David turned to her with a frenzied look on his face, eyes wide and brows arched. He was clutching his damaged hand, and every part of him twitched. Even his pupils seemed to shake.

"Bloody proud of yourself, aren't you?" He stayed still.

"I said get up!"

Finally, he stood up. His hands were at his sides. He gave the impression of being calm and collected, but Andraste could see through the façade. A familiar coldness came off David- fear. Shuddering, uncompromising fear.

"Put your hands over your head, now!" Andraste almost didn't notice, but she was exhausted. She staggered just staying upright, and she couldn't summon any decent volume when she tried to raise her voice. Her gun shook and traced wide circles in the air.

"Or what? You'll shoot?" David was still. "Did you forget about the bombs hooked up to my heart rate?"

A chilling pulse of fear came from him when he said that. Confidence betrayed by fear- Andraste had seen this before. It was a lie.

"Enough, David." Her tone of voice calmed, which matched the tired cadence. "There's no such thing. That remote was all you had."

The cold fear turned into frigid horror. The only sign of it was his widened eyes. He didn't move or respond.

"Hands over your head. I won't say it again."

David was paralyzed. She didn't know what else she could do to get him to comply. He was defenseless, but she knew she would miss with the gun.

"Please," she thought, stopping herself from speaking aloud. *"Let it end. I'm exhausted, and so are you."* She allowed herself a deep sigh. *"Let the pain stop."*

As that thought concluded, her mind was silenced by the sound of chopping air. The news helicopter flew over from the side of the building, righting itself as the lens caught David and Andraste in its sight.

Movement in the corner of Andraste's eye broke her concentration. David was running towards the edge of the balcony. About four meters away, the tile patio ended and poured onto the streets below. David reached the guard rails and kicked off into the air.

As if a switch had been flipped in her mind, Andraste automatically threw the rifle aside and sprinted after him. She dove to the edge and grabbed David by his fragmented wrist.

"David, stop! Please!" Andraste begged, feeling a tear accumulate in her eye. "No one else needs to die today!"

David looked up at her. "Why do you even care?" David called back, the chilling fear replaced with flat resignation.

"You can help us, David! You have options!"

"No." He closed his eyes. "No, I really don't. I promised the General I would deliver you, and now I can't keep that promise." He reached back into his vest, and pulled out some folding tool. It opened into a hook-like implement with a wiry edge- an angled plasma welder, overclocked and built for combat. He flicked a switch, and the edge grew white-hot.

Andraste flushed when she realized what he was going to do. "David, no! Please!" The tears began to fall alongside the blood from her shoulder. "This isn't the answer!" She tried to pull him up.

"It's the only answer!" He said, his own tears mixing with Andraste's. "There's no hope for a perfect world anymore. We're all done." He drew the blade over his shoulder and dragged the hook through, slicing the arm off the torso.

Andraste could only watch him fall. From the massive crowd around the base of the Shard, screams filled the air.

16   London, England
15:42   June 2nd, 2335

"No one, and I mean no one expected this, viewers!" Kennedy Schmidt was exploding with emotion. "One shocking revelation after another followed by an equally shocking rescue by the terrorist! The result of the mysterious FH Project, a young woman subjected to strange genetic experiments, has single-handedly saved the Shard and all its hostages from a horrible fate! The woman was shot in the ordeal and is currently receiving intensive care, while coroners are investigating the deaths of the other terrorists, who have all been identified as local Londoners."

The paramedics came and scooped her up off the balcony twenty agonizing minutes after David killed himself. The entire Shard was evacuated, the hostages were secured, and they shut down access to Central Base until they were unquestionably certain it was safe.

They poured veritable buckets of neurochemical regulators and painkillers into her, as potent as the FH doctors could prescribe. Her arm was numb and lifeless, rigidly held in place with a cast crowned by the gauze and IV cables that mummified her shoulder. Two bags hung over her, shaking and tugging the cords as the medics moved and turned.

The painkillers made everything hazy and the neurochemical treatments intensified every sensation; fluorescent lights were blinding and the din of the crowd outside battered her eardrums. Even picking up on emotions from others became troublesome. Most of the time, it was like white noise that she could tune out, but now every tidbit of emotional arousal had the impact of a defibrillator.

Andraste felt lifeless and numb, fitting for all the blood loss, as well as the shock from seeing David die. Outside was the press, which had a gruesome front-row-seat to his death. The pressure of the situation sat in her chest like a stake of depleted uranium.

Everyone on the FH Project had been struggling to develop their own satisfactory answers about her, and now all of London was looking for answers. Andraste didn't know how much she could answer, having many questions herself, but keeping secrets was exhausting. Judicia and Yousef were waiting for her in the foyer.

"Andy!" Yousef dashed to Andraste. "Are you all right?"

"I-I'm fine." She groaned, her voice cracking. "Wh-what do we do now?"

He pursed his lips, casting worried glances out the door. Judicia stepped up and filled the silence in the room.

"All those idiots outside are braying to see you. If it weren't for the guards, they'd likely have flooded in already." She said, casting a contemptuous look outside. "I'll handle them." Judicia walked to the entrance, talked to the guards, and they let her breach the doors to address the crowd.

Looking at the crowd, Andraste felt physically buffeted by them all, like a gale from a snowstorm. "What's happening?"

"We need to wait for the elevators to Central Base to be cleared, but you should be in intensive care *now*." Yousef put himself between the crowd and Andraste, but she still tried to peek around him. He was monitoring her vitals and making hasty notes of all the ways she had been hurt.

First, Andraste heard the din of clamoring voices and saw the blinding fireworks of the flashing lights. Shortly after that, she was pressed further back into the wheelchair by the torrent of emotion that came flooding in through the doorway. Cold, paralyzing fear, more than anything else, with a few negligible veins of anger and exhilaration.

She heard people gasp and murmur as they looked at her. The cold seemed to intensify. Despite all the guards in place, the crowd was eager to stick in their microphones and cameras.

Several of the reporters looked at one another, trying to decide who should go up first. After some exchanged glances, most eyes fell to Kennedy Schmidt. She and Andraste locked eyes, and a circuit connected, sending sparks and shivers down both their backs. Her grip around the microphone tightened, and she turned to her camera.

Judicia stepped in, gesturing to Kennedy for the camera to be on her.

"Turn it back on," She told the cameraman, who obliged. A light along the top of the box came on.

"Welcome back, people of England. I'm here at the Shard, where the creature codenamed 'Andraste' is being hurried to safety."

"Turn that off!" Yousef pleaded. "Please, she's very hurt!"

"I'm right here, all of you." Judicia folded her arms and looked at the press. "If you have questions, aim them at me."

Kennedy backed off, but the others managed to rise above the din. "We have a lot of questions here for you, Doctor. If you don't mind, I think I'll get to the most pressing question: what happened in the Shard? When the insurgents broadcasted, one of them shot early, and then they all began seizing up. What was that about?"

Andraste hadn't considered that most everyone had seen her do that. Not only that, but that no one knew she had done it.

"Andraste was the one who caused the insurgent's seizures."

The entire crowd gasped, and terrified murmurs were carried along the cold currents of fear that they were giving off.

The weight of all the eyes came bearing down on Andraste.

"Guards, any updates?" Yousef called out. "I know they had to check the elevator for bombs, but come on!" He was making harsh scrawls on his tablet.

"You mean she manipulated him?" One voice crept in.

"Well, yes," Judicia continued the conversation, despite Yousef's urgency.

"So the rumors of Fomorian mind manipulation are true?" Said another, before she could process the first question.

"Was she able to see his thoughts as well?"

"Can she do that at will?"

More and more questions were cropping up, and none of them registered as anything more than a flicker on Andraste's perceptive range. Judicia looked like a wave breaker during a hurricane.

"For god's sake," Judicia muttered as the barrage intensified.

It was one volley of questions after another, carrying intense fear and curiosity with every shot, exploding and rushing over Andraste time and time again. Great waves of emotion crashed over her, and it took every ounce of her fortitude to resist them. She could barely move in the wheelchair, yet the torrents of the crowd seemed to be throwing her back and forth. The most injuring feelings came from the general onlookers, normal people who had gathered outside to see what all the fuss was about. Hearing a baby cry gave her an urge to cry herself.

Panic and terror rose up in her body, and poured into the open from a thousand agonizing bullet wounds. The cold winds of the crowd's fear had become so intense it started to burn, and any resistance she put up against it was just as painful. She shuddered and bowed her head. Unbeknownst to her, the questions had stopped, and she sat in the chair shaking and straining to breathe.

Finally, the elevator came. Yousef and the other emergency doctors pushed Andraste in, while Judicia kept handling the questions from the crowd.

Andraste passed out, and the emergency operators got busy handling her wound. The crowd livened up as the elevator doors closed.

Judicia sipped on her coffee as the news network cut away from grilling Rowe, who had opened up about the project.

The anchor did everything he could to pad out the description of Andraste's two minutes in public, referencing previous studies and rumors about genetic experimentation, as well as similarities between Andraste's appearance and the few surviving photos of the Fomorians. They also keenly replayed the footage they had of herself talking to Schmidt.

"We are actively keeping in touch with the researchers and scientists who are maintaining Andraste," the anchor seemed to say directly to Judicia.

She had to restrain herself from yelling at the investigators on the other end of the line, telling them to leave her and her workers alone so they could do their goddamn jobs, but she knew that wouldn't go over well. Her reputation was shaky enough as it was, especially now that she had been outed as "some kind of modern Dr. Frankenstein," in the exact words of the headline that ran across the electronic newspaper. As the black coffee slid down her throat, she mulled on her bitterness, already fending off an annoyed migraine from Andraste's inevitable confusion.

For a while, the anchor kept talking about the lies that Rowe had been telling and all the tiny hints that he had been doing something unethical or wrong. She wondered if they were even aware of the suicide bomb in the Shard.

When Andraste looked up and down and realized she was back in the same hospital bed, there was no hiding her frustration.

She turned to Judicia.

"What happened this time?"

Judicia shrugged. "You almost went into shock again. The nurses bailed you out before anything bad happened."

"That was it?" Andraste leaned over to Judicia as far as her injury would allow her. "No mass hallucinations or anything?"

Judicia shook her head. "Imagine, nothing going wrong for once."

There was a small signal of relief from Andraste, but it was eclipsed by the rest of her feelings. "What about Rowe?"

Judicia pointed to the TV. "See for yourself."

The news network had shifted its focus away from the anchor and was back with Kennedy Schmidt. Nathan Rowe was hunched over a podium with an expression like a waterboarding victim.

Schmidt had to shout to be heard over the other questions and interviewers. "When we have the opportunity, we will approach Mr. Rowe with our own questions, but hearing the inquiries and responses thus far should sum up the mood here, ladies and gentlemen."

The camera went back to Rowe, who faced each question with a palpably failing energy.

"Yes, Andraste was a volunteer. She signed up for the project with complete informed consent."

She tensed up at this. They were discussing *her* on the news.

"How did they teach her to control people's minds?"

"We haven't been teaching her how to do that!" Rowe was sweating.

"If she can give people seizures, can she give people heart attacks as well? Strokes, even?"

"That was unintended!" Rowe raised his voice at this question. "She has never given anyone a seizure on purpose!"

"How much control do you have over her?"

"Are there any more like her?"

"Has the creature put up any resistance against the scientists who created her?"

Too many questions came up for Nathan Rowe to answer at once. He was able to take control again, but Andraste was too fixed on the nature of the questions.

"Creature?"

"Have they been asking about me the whole time?" She turned to Judicia.

"Yes." Judicia said, her voice flat and lifeless. "We tried to keep the hounds away when we got you out of the Shard, but they're tenacious bastards." She sipped her coffee again

"But, they," she stumbled over her words as she looked for the right one. "Do they even know that I'm here to help them?"

"I don't know. The interview hasn't gotten very far."

"They think I'm some kind of monster!"

Judicia sighed. "It seems so."

Andraste was dumbstruck. Emptiness filled her head.

"Are you really surprised by that?" Judicia chimed in again.

"But I'm here to help them! Don't they know that?"

Judicia took a long drag from her thermos. "Andraste, you're a mind-manipulating crossbreed of some ghost from the past. How do you expect people to react?"

Judicia's bluntness pressed hard into Andraste's chest. "But, once they know I'm here to fight in the war-"

"Don't fool yourself, Andraste." Judicia cut her off. "If you ask me, this is something you should just accept. There's no doubt in my mind that even Rowe was afraid of what you would become."

Andraste was stunned. She looked at Judicia, and Judicia looked at her.

"Are *you* afraid of me, Dr. Judicia?" There was no stammer in Andraste's voice.

Judicia glanced away, lips pursed.

"Oh, Andraste." She closed her eyes and shook her head. "Anyone in their right mind would be afraid of you."

A heavy silence filled the room. Andraste looked away from her, back at the interview on TV. Judicia did the same.

190

17 Somewhere in the Outlands
10:30   June 4th, 2335

"It would seem that the rumors were true," General Bashford said, poring over the images taken of Andraste. "I'm not sure what I was expecting, but I'm surprised nonetheless."

The lights in the bunker room were low, just enough to make the details on the photos visible. Heavy iron doors kept the information from leaving the room. General Bashford and General Scarlet were the only ones there.

Provisions were made as soon as "General Scarlet" was mentioned. Most soldiers knew to put on their best behavior when she was around, but even at their best, her presence terrified. Long lengths of wavy auburn hair trailed behind her as she looked ahead, her dark green eyes as placid and glassy as a shark's. Her freckled complexion was smooth and clean, which was uncanny for all the battles she had been in. Countless battles staring the enemy in the face, gouging throats and slashing arteries, and she didn't have a single visible scar. Unwise rumors went around that she wasn't human- the most ignorant among them said she was some kind of witch. The ones who started such rumors were never around for long.

Scarlet looked at the pictures with her usual expression, flat and unreadable. With her free hand, she rubbed her thumb along the hilt of her knife.

"It was a waste of good life," she said. "Finally, a handful of promising young people prove themselves worthy of joining our cause, and they are thrown to this creature." Her accent was of indeterminate origin somewhere in Southeastern Europe, spoken like a robot.

"No life spent in service to the Martyr's Army goes to waste, General Scarlet." Bashford took a handful of the pictures and put them into a folder. "They knew what they were getting into. Most importantly, we've drawn Andraste out of hiding. While the couriers died, their message went through all the same. Rowe is keeping secrets, and London is in a perfectly justified uproar about it." He sat in one of the chairs, straightening out the contents of the folder. "The cacophony will spread, and Rowe's death grip on the country will finally loosen."

Scarlet continued to stare at one of Andraste's pictures, holding a gun up to David before he threw himself from the ledge. "And what of her?" She stroked the flat image of Andraste. "When do we get our hands on her?"

Bashford shrugged, his head cocked. "All in good time, General."

Scarlet slammed the picture down on the table. "Don't try me, George." She eyed him like a predator about to slaughter its prey, yet her tone didn't change. "We can make that time. Don't get content just because of this one victory."

He raised an eyebrow at her. "It's even more dangerous for our agents in London right now- we need to be careful, Scarlet." He stood up. "Besides, we don't know what their next move will be yet. Once we have that intel, we'll make our move."

"No intel yet, but I've heard rumors."

Bashford came around to her side of the table. "Rumors of what?"

"One of our agents overheard plans to move Andraste out of England. This may be our opportunity to get a hold of her."

He glanced at the picture- she was still pinning it to the table, her hand on Andraste. "You seem eager."

"The rumors are true, Bashford." She said. "I am actively keeping in touch with our reconnaissance team."

He nodded. "Good."

Scarlet went for the door. "I'll get in touch with them right away, then." She touched the immensely heavy door and lightly brushed it to the side.

The underground bunker sprawled out in front of her, with soldiers, agents, and refugees scattered throughout the makeshift hallways. It was a large, open space divided by columns and sheets of tarp dividing different areas into residences or clinics. A soldier was cleaning blood off their uniform next to a group of children playing with a tablet. Families were cooking boiling pots of food next to operating tables, the smells of blood and spices mingling in the air.

Deeper in the base, they built a chapel, and Scarlet approached in silence. In an umbrella of roots, people had built statues and woven tapestries of the Fomorians. Each person inside was clinging to a root and muttering to themselves, eyes rolled back in their head.

"Reclaim these lands," said a man with glasses. He shook with energy coursing through him. "I remember the Martyrs. The Fomorians who will reshape the world."

"Heretics are trying to reclaim Paris," a woman whispered as she held her baby. "I remember the Martyrs. I pray they do, as well."

Scarlet nodded as she walked by, confident in the faith of her people. Before she reached out for a root herself, another voice caught her attention.

"Please help my papa," said a little girl behind her. "He fights for you. Please keep him safe. He's going north of here. I can see him there." She pointed to nothing. In her mind's eye, she saw her father trekking through the woods. "I remember the Martyrs," she added hastily. "Thank you."

Scarlet watched her closely, relieved that her eyes returned to normal when the child released her grip. This deep below the earth, touching the roots was especially potent, and it wasn't clear if they were safe for children. She made a note to report this to Bashford.

Scarlet took hold of a root and felt her awareness take flight. Her vision was filled with kilometers and kilometers of wildlands, speeding through the roots and natural channels of the Outland landscape that their Martyrs had created. It was through these roots that they were connected to the world around them, and the Martyr's Army was given vision. It was here that Scarlet hoped to catch sight of Andraste.

18 London, England
16:43   June 4th, 2335

One of Andraste's greatest frustrations was her lack of tools. Whenever they did renovations around Central Base, Yousef usually got her some bits of scrap metal, springs, or anything else she might need to bring one of her wind-up toy blueprints to life. Obviously, it looked easier on the TV, but actively putting the instructions into practice without proper resources was still aggravating.

With this confounding situation before her, Andraste got creative. With enough strength and concentration, Andraste was able to turn random pieces of scrap metal into whatever resource she needed- a 10 by 20-centimeter piece of aluminum could be made into coils, legs, gears, and winches with enough ingenuity. Most of all, it was one of the best ways to exercise her fine motor skills without aggravating the bullet wound.

This work brought her immense relief, even though the design was just a four-legged contraption that skittered around with an unbalanced weight. It was agony to watch all the coverage of the terrorist attack- "The Battle of the Shard," as they were calling it- and to endure all the prying government officials and journalists who were trying to see her. In the twisting gears and bent metal devoted to the little silver bug, she found great solace.

Solace offset by confused obligations, however. Whenever she felt the most comfortable and happy with what she was doing, her state of mind was invaded by the sense that she was running away.

And that was only one thought. She nearly froze whenever she was reminded of Judicia's comment: *"Anyone in their right mind would be afraid of you."*

"Hey, Andy!" A security guard called to her. She looked up and saw him gesturing to the door. "You have a visitor coming in."

"Visitor?" She set the toy down. "I thought we were keeping people out."

"Not this one," he said wryly as he disengaged the lock.

The heavy security doors opened wide. The size of the doorway was accentuated by the lithe figure that stood there: a tall woman in a silk business suit and lilac hijab. When she met eyes with Andraste, she smiled.

"Hello, Andraste. I'm sorry to come in unannounced like this." She walked towards the glass wall, taking a seat at the provided chair. "But I've been wanting to meet you for a while now. I am Labibah Quadriyyah."

Andraste perked up. "Chancellor Quadriyyah?" She pulled her own chair away from the desk. "It's an honor to meet you, ma'am." Quadriyyah's presence was soothing and warm; much more appealing than anyone else who had forced their way in.

"Are you doing all right, Andraste? That wound looks serious." She put the case on her lap.

"It's doing better, thank you." Andraste's tone was flat.

Quadriyyah tilted her head and smirked. "Don't worry, I'm not going to interrogate you about the incident. I know a lot of government employees have been doing that. And believe me, we're doing everything we can to get them to stop."

Andraste was stunned for a moment. "Oh, um, thank you." She stuttered out, feeling awkward and inept.

She chuckled. "On that topic, I've been wondering: how many of them have shown any kind of gratitude?"

Andraste was stunned again. "I-I'm sorry, I'm not sure what you mean."

"I'll take that as a 'no.'" She leaned over, closing in on Andraste. "The terrorist attack is the only thing that anyone talks about. And I'm sure you've seen more than enough of the media coverage." She looked to the side. "No one seems the least bit grateful for what you've done. Not even a 'thank you.' Argosy was a travesty, but it would have been a hundred times worse without your intervention."

These words resonated with Andraste, sending shivers of warmth down her spine. Quadriyyah was meeting her for the first time, and she was showing a remarkable level of understanding.

"Well, it's a difficult situation to make sense of. The FH Project was forced to go public immediately afterward, after all." Andraste shrugged.

Quadriyyah scoffed. "Good of you to show some empathy, but if you ask me, that's a pitiful excuse. Not everyone has all the answers immediately."

"Respectfully, Chancellor, I think there's more to it than that." Andraste glanced to the side, recalling the crowd at the bottom of the Shard. "People are," she paused as Judicia's words came back to her, "afraid."

"Well, they shouldn't be. After all, you're here to help us." She smiled at Andraste as she spoke. "From me, from the Cabinet, and from everyone who struggles against the violence of the Martyr's Army, you have more than earned our gratitude. In short, thank you."

A swell of relief, joy, and satisfaction bloomed inside of Andraste. As if a sheet of ice was melting and sloughing off her shoulders, a sense of pervasive warmth went through her body at the sight of Quadriyyah's smile. She had no words for what she was feeling, only that it was good. Sweet tears began to coalesce at the corners of her eyes.

"Th-Thank you, chancellor." She wiped one of the tears away. "It was an honor to serve."

"Well, that's good to hear." Quadriyyah pursed her lips after she said this. "Unfortunately, I'm here for a less heartwarming reason."

Hearing this, Andraste sat up straighter. She took another quick swipe over her eyes to banish the tears.

"There has been talk of your deployment, Andraste. And of moving you to one of our bases in the Outlands."

Andraste almost leapt out of her chair. "Already?"

Quadriyyah gestured to the bandages over Andraste's shoulder. "Once that heals, of course." She raised a brow at Andraste. "Is this really the first time you're hearing about this?"

"W-well," Andraste shook her head, trying to recall other conversations that people were having. "I know that we were talking about our next steps, but I don't remember-"

"Interesting," Quadriyyah said, standing up from the chair. She put a hand on her chin and started to pace. "It's true, we only recently finished up our plans for it- the Cabinet and the staff here at the project, that is- but this is still a surprise to me."

Andraste stood up and started to pace with Quadriyyah when her voice became hard to hear through the glass. "You've been talking with Dr. Judicia and Yousef?"

"Mostly Judicia. Tough nut to crack, isn't she?" She looked at Andraste while tapping the side of her head.

"Yeah," Andraste said with a sigh. "She's a tough one."

"I've been planning the flight with them and covering information about the base. Nothing too intense, but it's still a foreign land by all accounts. I'll make sure they properly brief you on it all." Quadriyyah started to pace the other way, and Andraste followed. "But it all does make me wonder- if Judicia isn't telling you about deployment plans, what else is she not telling?"

Andraste stopped, even as Quadriyyah kept walking. "Wh-what do you mean?"

"She's not the most communicative, Andraste. Even with us in the Cabinet." Quadriyyah finally stood still. "Rowe eats up everything she says, but I feel like it's not the whole story." She looked at Andraste. "She's been so focused on your progress that a lot of questions have gone unanswered."

The point of Quadriyyah's words dug into Andraste, and she was eager to answer. She leaned closer to the glass. "What kinds of questions, Chancellor?"

"So, we all know why we funded this project: to win the war with the Martyr's Army. But what happens after we win?" She raised a brow at Andraste. "What do we do with you then?"

Andraste's eyes widened. A little noise creaked out of her throat when she tried to speak, but it was all she could manage. The question settled heavily on her mind.

"So you haven't had that conversation, then?"

Scanning her mind for anything that might follow up on the question, Andraste stood in silence as she slowly shook her head.

"Interesting," Quadriyyah sat back down.

"I guess it never really occurred to me," Andraste said as she propped herself up on her chair.

The chancellor shrugged. "I can understand that, with the war effort. But I've been trying to ask Judicia what her plans are, and- not surprisingly- she hasn't given me an answer, either." Biting her lip and lowering her voice, Quadriyyah asked, "do you think she wants to make more hybrids like you?"

This stopped Andraste's train of thought, and she could only focus on that thought: "More?" She looked down at her hands, examining the strange gray exoskeleton. "Why would she want to make more people like me?"

"Well, why wouldn't she? After all the effort to make the experiment work?"

"I was made to be a soldier." Andraste was walking herself through her own logic, speaking slowly. "Why make more soldiers when the war is over?"

"A fair point, but what about you?" Quadriyyah leaned forward in her chair. "Were you only made to be a soldier and nothing else? When the war is over, Andraste, what do you want to do?"

Andraste hadn't even thought of the war being over, or conceived of a time where there wouldn't be a Martyr's Army to fight. The scope of her life centered on preparing her for that exact task. Now, asked to imagine a world without them, she felt like she had to describe a color no one had seen before.

"What do I want to do?" Andraste said aloud, muttering to the floor. "I-I don't know. I feel like I'm just a soldier." She glanced at her desk and saw the toy sitting there, having completely forgotten it.

"Hm?" Quadriyyah followed her gaze. She stood up and walked towards the desk, putting a hand on the glass as she ogled the wind-up toy. "Andraste," she said with a breathless smile, "did you make that?"

"Y-yes." She chuckled gently. "It's just a little side project." She walked over and picked it up, feeling a strange tenderness for the contraption in her hands.

"Does it work?"

"Um, I think it does." Hesitating, she wound the key on its side a few times. The spring tightened and tension built in the tiny motor. Fearing the worst, Andraste put it on her desktop.

The toy began to buzz as the weight spun around, making the long legs dance and skitter as the toy rollicked on the desk. Trembling on its spindly frame and racing around in an unspecific dash, it moved with an ungainly but charming gait like a foal still learning to use its legs. Quadriyyah's eyes went wide, and Andraste held her breath as she waited for something to go wrong.

Then the toy took a fall over the edge, and Andraste dove to catch it. She examined it closely for damage, breathing hard as she checked all the little gears and springs.

"Andraste, what a brilliant little thing!" Quadriyyah said with a wide smile.

Andraste was still for a moment as she caught her breath from the near fall, but softened as she comprehended Quadriyyah's words.

"Y-you think so?" Andraste asked, bashful. She shrank away from the chancellor just a bit, putting her body between the toy and the rest of the room.

"Of course!" Quadriyyah pointed to it, emphatic. "You can clearly do so much, Andraste! 'Just a soldier,' she says!" She scoffed playfully. "You could open a store when we're all done here."

Andraste chuckled, gingerly putting the toy back on the desk. "Maybe we can show Mr. Rowe and see what he says."

"Hmm," Quadriyyah responded. Hearing the name, her expression faded somewhat. "Has he been going on about that 'perfect world' idea with you?"

Andraste became vigilant at Quadriyyah's change of tone. "He's mentioned it. Why?"

"Because I'm still wondering what he means when he says that. Defeating the Army is one thing, but his notion of 'perfection' doesn't sit right with me." The chancellor folded her arms and shrugged. "I hope he hasn't been preoccupying you with the idea of being perfect all the time."

"W-well," Andraste hadn't thought about that- it was one of several new thoughts for the day. Her ruminations on being a soldier came back to her.

"There's more to life than war, Andraste. And there's definitely more to life than chasing perfection- you'll be running forever."

They both looked over at the toy again.

"More to life?" Andraste quietly said, ruminating on the words.

The doors opened again, with no warning from the guard this time, and Judicia walked into the room. When she looked up at the room, she stopped.

"Who's there? Step away from the hybrid!" She demanded, picking up her pace. "What's your authorization?"

"Judicia, it's okay!" Andraste spoke up.

"It's not, Andraste! Security, we have an-"

Quadriyyah turned around, eyes wide.

"-intruder." Judicia's harsh tone faded.

"Oh dear," Quadriyyah stood up, glancing back at Andraste. "Maybe I've been here too long."

"Why *are* you here, chancellor?" Judicia tilted her head.

"I had to speak with Andraste on the government's behalf." Quadriyyah started to walk towards the door. "I've said everything I need to say, doctor. I won't get in your way."

Andraste looked quizzically at Quadriyyah; it seemed she had more to talk about.

"Take care, Andraste. You too, Judicia." With an affable nod of the head, Quadriyyah walked out of the room.

Judicia and Andraste watched her leave with equal measures of uncertainty.

"What was that about?" Judicia asked, sounding sincerely puzzled about it.

Fondly, Andraste told Judicia about the conversation. She held up the wind-up toy for emphasis.

"She said it was 'brilliant.'" Andraste said, beaming with pride. "Thank you again for lending me those engineering textbooks, Dr. Judicia."

"Sure," Judicia said, nodding in disinterest. "But don't forget, we have to get you ready for deployment."

Shoulders going slack, Andraste put the toy aside. "Right," she admitted. "What's our first Martyr's Army target?"

"One thing at a time, Andraste." Judicia shook her head. "We're not moving out until you heal, and even then, we're going to get some field reports before committing to anything major."

"Oh. Okay," Andraste said, uncomprehending.

"The base is in Berlin. We finally took it back from the Army a few years ago."

"Berlin?" She said with renewed spirits. "I've heard it's beautiful!"

"It's not a vacation, Andraste. Just focus on what's to come." Andraste pulled up her tablet. "Here, let's cover a few things."

"Actually, Judicia," Andraste took hold of the conversation. "Quadriyyah has me wondering: what are the plans for the FH Project after the war?"

Judicia set her tablet down and heaved the heaviest groan that Andraste had ever heard. "Andraste, please. One thing at a time."

Shrinking in her chair, Andraste was quiet. "Yes, Doctor. Sorry."

All throughout the briefing, Judicia could tell that Andraste's mind was elsewhere. Quadriyyah had filled her mind with too many questions for her to deal with.

Judicia let the doors slam behind her, hoping the noise would hide her aggravated sigh. Her glasses kept bothering her, and she lost track of how often she had to take them off to massage her eyes or the bridge of her nose.

She put them back on to see Chancellor Quadriyyah leaning against a wall, giving her an indignant look. Her arms were folded and her eyes were narrowed, giving Judicia another urge to take her glasses off.

Judicia groaned. "You were listening?"

"How could I not?" Quadriyyah shrugged. "I think we should all be clear with each other on what's happening in the experiment."

Judicia pressed her lips and sighed. "You're not just here to check up on her, are you?"

"No." The chancellor said bluntly. "I was hoping to talk to someone about the other plans for Andraste."

Judicia's brow folded, and she looked at Quadriyyah with a start. "What are you talking about?"

"I was hoping you could tell me," she said with such quickness as if anticipating Judicia's response.

Quadriyyah was silent for a moment as she and Judicia bored holes into each other's piercing stares. She unfolded her arms and drifted away from the wall, standing in the path of Judicia. The chancellor dwarfed the woman.

"Tell me, Dr. Judicia," Quadriyyah began, "what *are* the plans for Andraste when the war is over?"

"Chancellor, what are you getting at?" She shrugged. "If and when Andraste survives the war, she'll be a gift for genetic surgery research and understanding Fomorian biology. She could probably lead seminars about the war."

"And that's all?" Quadriyyah cocked her head. "Have you talked to Andraste herself about it?"

"Not yet," Judicia said, impatiently glancing behind Quadriyyah. "With all due respect, Chancellor, I have work to do."

"I'm sure you do. But I know there are more plans than that." Quadriyyah tilted to the side, keeping her face in Judicia's field of view. Judicia went to the other side, and Quadriyyah did the same thing. "The way Rowe talks about the FH Project, it sounds like he has more planned than making this one soldier."

"Well, maybe he has the answers, then." Judicia's tone betrayed her diminishing patience. "I'm sorry if our methods aren't to your taste, Chancellor. But right now, what matters is that she is bound and determined to do her job. We need to be prepared for anything, and we need to collect as much data as we can. Our soldier is part of a large plan, yes, but we're handling it one thing at a time."

"Before she was a soldier," Quadriyyah lamented, "and before she was your guinea pig, she was a person. She's been through so much, and you can't even have the decency to be honest with her?"

Judicia closed the distance between them. "Let me emphasize that Andraste knew what she was getting into. There would be tests, there would be harsh realities, and there would be discomfort. I'm here to make progress, not to give her hugs and kisses when she starts crying."

"That's not what I mean." Quadriyyah started to lean over, into Judicia's face. "I know it goes beyond her. Rowe keeps calling her 'the next step in evolution,' and I can't say I like the sound of that. He's not just being grandiose, he's planning something. Do you plan on making more hybrids like her?"

A single bead of sweat appeared on Judicia's forehead. She turned to the side before Quadriyyah noticed it.

"Well?" Quadriyyah kept the momentum of her inquiry going. "Why is it so hard to ask what happens next?"

"Because we need to know what will happen now!" Judicia finally snapped. "The super-soldier Rowe commissioned is a stuttering wreck who breaks down in tears each time she actually fights someone! And I have people working around the fucking clock just to keep her heart beating! Forgive me, chancellor, for being a bit preoccupied!" She was panting from her words. "And if you don't mind, I have a deployment to prepare for." Judicia moved past the Chancellor.

"You always were a sympathetic sort," Quadriyyah's voice echoed down the hallway.

With a massive groan, Judicia turned back around. "What do you want from me? I'm not her mother, for God's sake!"

"I'm not saying you should be! I just," she stopped, and within a blink she her aggression decayed into frustrated sadness. "I know you have more planned after this. And she won't be happy to hear it."

"In that case, we'll deal with it as it comes. Only thing we can do with all these unknowns."

"Fair enough, I suppose," Quadriyyah said, more out of lament than continuing the conversation. "Answer me this, then: what do *you* want out of this experiment?"

Judicia softened at her sentiments. She unfolded her arms and released some of the tension in her body.

"You've been working on improving the human condition for decades, now. Would you say the FH Project is the culmination of your studies?"

"An excellent question," Judicia said as she glanced to the sides and pocketed her hands. "I want to see what the results of this project are before I move on."

Quadriyyah nodded. "How have you put it in the past? You're 'always working to make us better', was it?" She glanced to the floor. "How much better can humans be?"

"I've wondered the same thing," Judicia began, "all my life."

Quadriyyah looked up at her.

"As far as I'm convinced, all the world's imperfections are just part of human nature." She glanced back at the doors to Andraste's containment center. "That's one reason I'm doing all this."

Quadriyyah looked back as well. She looked back at Judicia with wide eyes.

"What are you-"

"*Human* nature seems to ruin everything, doesn't it?" Judicia said, with some twisted semblance of a smirk. "With any luck, Andraste is our first step towards curing it."

Quadriyyah was silent. She looked at Judicia, then back at the door, then back at Judicia. The latter had also gone quiet, as if waiting for a response.

"'Curing' it?" She finally said. "Is that what Rowe is getting at with that 'Iconoclast' thing he's mentioned?"

Judicia's body went rigid and her face went pale. The most she could do was turn away from Quadriyyah.

"Judicia?" the chancellor asked. "Does that mean something to you?"

Shaking off the rigor, Judicia took a breath and kneaded her forehead. "I don't know what he's on about most of the time. I've heard it, but," she rubbed her temple harder. "God, I can never tell what he's getting at."

There was an actual migraine forming in her head. She blessed her good fortune for this chance at getting out of the conversation. Quadriyyah could see the anguish.

"I'm so sorry, chancellor, but I really must get going."

The chancellor cleared her throat and straightened her clothes and hijab. "Understood. I hope I didn't waste your time," Quadriyyah lamented. "I really should be getting back to Parliament.

"Very well. Have a safe trip back."

Quadriyyah went down the rest of the corridor until she finally disappeared.

Judicia stood there, statuesque in her pensive stillness. "She's onto me," She mulled over it, out loud. The more she thought on it, the more she envisioned Andraste's face. The glow in her eyes, and the potential she showed. Maybe she did deserve an answer about the 'Iconoclast' plan, but Judicia knew this would be a bad time.

As she turned to go back to her office, the thought still lingered. Quadriyyah could certainly make an impression if nothing else. *"I know what I'm doing. And I'm not stopping."*

19 Unknown

"Wake up, Andraste."

Genderless, lacking a tone, and altogether inhuman; it was the voice from her dreams.

Andraste's eyes popped open. She didn't remember falling asleep or being tranquilized, only that she was in this place again. The pattern of light blue neurons lit up her exoskeleton and surrounded her on all sides like a still ocean.

She turned to the side, and the orb hovered nearby.

"You!" Andraste cried, sitting upright in a hurry. "What are you doing here?"

"It's been too long since we last spoke," it said.

It did feel like the incident with Williams was ages ago, but something about the voice's familiarity made it feel like there was only a momentary lapse in their last conversation.

"The situation with Williams was certainly impressive, but the way you handled the Shard- I couldn't look away. Truly a sight to behold." Its monotone fractured and gave the slightest impression of excitement. "You've come along even farther than I thought."

From anyone else, this would have been flattering, but there were too many questions surrounding this being.

"Why am I so important to you?" Andraste backed away, but the sphere didn't seem to get any further from her.

"Because I think I see answers in you, Andraste." It hovered around her in a small arc.

"Answers to what?" She tilted her head at it.

"To everything." It spoke without emphasis, as if she was expected to know what that meant right away. "In the meantime, you're doing quite the job of making the Army fear and hate you."

"Wh-what?" She felt shrunken by these words.

"Andraste, that's okay! I think it's amazing how you gave that group of soldiers seizures." There was a hint of delight in the way it spoke, which withered her further. "You should try and do that again when we get to Berlin."

"What are you talking about?" Andraste shuddered. "Don't you remember how dangerous that was?" She shook her head, feeling an echo of the piercing headache from the aftermath.

"Of course, I remember. That was what made it worth it. You won't get anything done by constantly playing it safe." It closed the distance between them, looking through her with unseen but distinct eyes. Its presence and tone cut through her, and she felt the need to shuffle away from it.

"I don't understand you!" Andraste turned from it. "If I'm not careful, I could hurt all these people here at Central Base!"

"They knew what they signed up for." The spirit kept getting closer. "You can't let them constantly hold you back."

She got to her feet, tired of its derision. "Stop talking like that!"

"Oh, please. They're only humans."

Something broke. Words and human communication became impossible for Andraste, and her body moved as if possessed. She sprang from her seat on the floor and leapt at the orb.

The orb didn't move, and Andraste fell through it like a floating ball of loose threads. It maintained its composition despite her assault.

Andraste was undeterred. She got into her stance and threw every ounce of her strength into her punches and kicks. Every earth-cracking fist and puncturing knee didn't affect the stoic blue light. Still, Andraste's incoherent fury carried her, and she cried in exertion with every blow.

"Please stop."

The longer Andraste went on, the less organized her movements became. Her repertoire had become less like proper combat training and more like a wild animal.

"Andraste, control yourself."

The sphere's words only angered her more. She screamed until her vocal chords were raw, defiantly trying to rip the thing apart. Soreness began to set in after several minutes of continuous thrashing, and some tears began to collect at the corner of her eye.

It was at that point that her senses were coming back to her, but she didn't stop. Tears began to fall as she inanely flailed at the thing. She showed no signs of stopping until the tiredness began to encroach further along her arms. The attacks slowed down, and her destroyed voice couldn't even force out a proper cry. Finally, she gave a slow swipe before her arms hung limp and she fell to her knees.

"Do you feel better?" Asked the voice, monotone but judging.

She took some time to catch her breath before responding. "No."

"Can we keep talking, then?"

"Just help me understand." Andraste pleaded with it, too tired to sound angry. "We are talking about people's *lives*. What is so important for you to learn that you would talk about other people like that?"

"Interesting use of 'other people,' Andraste." It loomed closer to her. "I understand that you consider yourself to be part of these 'people.' Do you think I do the same thing?"

"What?" She squinted at it. "W-well, why wouldn't you?"

"I thought I already told you," the sphere said as it drifted away, neuronal branches going slack. "Much like you, I don't remember anything. You have documentation about being human and living with these people. I don't." The way it moved and spoke, the sphere gave an affect of shrugging and incredulity. "I'm not assuming anything that I haven't seen for myself. But your power?" The branches went tight again, and it shot back towards her. Andraste recoiled. "That feels familiar. I see you manipulating minds, and it feels *right*. Something clicks."

Looking at it up and down, Andraste tried to comprehend its emphatic energy, but only found herself perplexed.

"Think about it like that toy you made- it works best when all the little pieces *click* together. You want answers, don't you, Andraste? Well, so do I. And I think that once we're out there, we'll find plenty of them." The sphere backed off as Andraste rose off the ground. "In the meantime, if you're so concerned about these Brits, then fine. Ride it out until we get deployed."

She didn't like the way it kept saying 'we.' Her eyes narrowed as that thought crossed her mind, and Andraste scanned the orb to see if it noticed.

"What's that look, Andraste?" It finally said in a way that goaded her for a response.

"They don't know about you," Andraste told it, feeling like she was revealing a secret. "I was never sure how to talk about you, this," she paused as she felt out the words, surprised at herself when she eventually said: "this voice in my head."

The neurons sparked, and a pulse ran through the entire field. "Me, a voice in your head?" It shouted. "Actually, that makes sense." The pressure it exerted immediately vanished. "Your hallucinations are well-documented, and it stands to reason that your 'dreams' would be just as inane and insubstantial. They really would think you were insane if you told them about me."

Andraste shook her head, shaking off the force of its shout. "W-well, not necessarily."

"Don't worry about it," The orb said. "They would only get in the way. It's best you don't tell them."

Andraste felt a surge of anger when it said this. "Get in the way? Are you serious?"

"Yes, I am serious. That's what humans love to do more than anything: get in the way. I wish you would have a little more trust in yourself than in them."

"And why should I trust you? Better yet, why am I even talking to you?" Andraste closed the distance between her and the orb.

The orb backed off a bit at her confrontation.

"You said it yourself, 'your hallucinations are well-documented, and your dreams would be just as inane.' So why have I listened to you at all?" She turned away, arms outstretched in her own disbelief. "It all makes sense. You're just another hallucination, aren't you? All this time, I've been talking to myself!"

The orb was silent.

"You know, a lot of the doctors have drawn comparisons between my mental activity and schizophrenia. I was wondering when I would start hearing a little voice, but it looks like I've been hearing to one this whole time!" She whipped around, pointing a rigid finger at it. "I'm not taking lectures from you! You act like some all-powerful Fomorian," she paused, "deity, or whatever you want to call it, but really, I'm hallucinating all this!"

Still, the orb was silent.

"When I wake up, I'll be sure to talk to the doctors. One little change in medication, and you're gone!"

It remained silent, but not still. It rose and began to drift away.

"You want me gone? Fine. See how well you do." In a blink, the orb vanished.
She was left alone in the neuronal sea, hunched over, and fuming at nothing.

"I can't keep this to myself anymore." She stood up. *"I'm going to tell the doctors everything. Keeping me alive is enough guesswork as it is- I can't be withholding information, too."* Her fists clenched. *"I'm such an idiot- this isn't about me. It's never been about just me."*

The light around her feet began to fade. She looked back down, and sighed with relief. Her eyes were clouding over, and the intricate pattern was becoming a blur. She was waking up.

"This is about everyone."

20   London, England
8:21   June 5th, 2335

Andraste kept her promise to the sphere of neurons and told the doctors. It brought puzzlement and vexation, especially to Judicia, who couldn't imagine why Andraste hadn't told them sooner.

"We can't have you having delusions on the battlefield, Andraste! For fuck's sake!"

She looked to Yousef for support, but he offered her none. "We can handle this, Judicia."

He penciled in a small addition to her medication, nearly losing track of it as the base prepared to move out. Judicia moved with silent indignity and fervor, double-checking everything after she triple-checked it, as Yousef helped Andraste with her own things.

"How do you feel about all this, Andy?" He asked as he helped organize her books. She had finally settled on using the Dewey Decimal system.

"I'm not sure yet," she said as she taped a box shut. The words lingered strangely on her tongue. "If I can be honest, that weird orb was getting to me."

Yousef nodded as he took the box from her. "Are you having second thoughts?"

"No!" She cried. "I-I mean, no." Andraste took a breath to catch herself. "What I mean is, I think I'll have some clearer thoughts once the medication kicks in and I stop seeing that thing."

"Ah, okay." Yousef had dealt with patients with vivid hallucinations before, but Andraste's story didn't sit right with him. "You know, Andy, your story about the ball of neurons really piqued my curiosity. Believe it or not, it sounded familiar."

Andraste raised a brow. "Familiar? What do you mean?"

"Well, you've heard all about the Army saying that 'The Outlands are alive' or 'The Fomorian will lives on,' right? Stuff like that?" He spun a book around between his palms. "Well, there have been a few stories of people seeing spirits or ghosts out there. I looked those stories up, and a few of them actually mention something similar to what you've been seeing."

Her eyes went wide and her arms went slack, making her drop her favorite engineering textbook. "You're serious?"

"I am, Andy." He picked up the book, fingers drumming the cover. "I don't know if it means anything, though. Maybe it's just a coincidence." He offered the book back to her.

She limply took it in one of her hands. "How can you be sure? They're saying the Fomorians still affect the world, and, you know," She looked at the cover and traced her fingers over the illustrated gear system, feeling soothed by it. "I'm half Fomorian. Maybe I'm seeing something that others can't."

He pressed his lips together. "It's possible, Andy. It's certainly possible."

She felt the conflicting emotions radiate from him as he said this. The heat of his false confidence cooled as the chilling uncertainty came in.

"Whatever happens," she said shakily, holding the book close to her chest, "I feel good having you and Judicia around for it."

His expression softened into a smile, and he nodded. "Thank you, Andy."

Noticing his emotional aura settle, it was a relief to her as well to see that he meant it.

The rest of the books were sorted and packed, and Andraste kept a small box of them to have at the new base. She hoped to spend more time with them all, but she understood that her deployment came first.

The rest of the days were filled with moving equipment onto the plane and making Andraste's room portable. Vital sign monitors, reinforced glass and cases of medicine were all built into an empty cargo container and then loaded into the back of a stealth craft. When they arrived at the base, the whole container could be unloaded and installed in the next location in only a few steps. As Andraste helped with the construction, she wondered if she had been on a plane before. No memories arose to answer the question, but she prepared to see some after takeoff.

"I'll let them know right away if something happens," she reminded herself.

As they worked with her medicine, Judicia was glad to hear that Andraste wasn't dreaming of blue neuron spheres, though not as glad as Andraste herself. She was quietly prepared for another experience when they landed, but decided to accept her progress as a sign of remission for now. Hoping to put it out of her mind, she buried herself in one of her textbooks until they were ready to go.

A night of reading passed quietly, and when her alarm went off, Andraste opened her eyes to two walls of text.

"Rise and shine!" Judicia's voice came in over the loudspeaker.

Andraste shot up in her chair, a page from the book caught on her mask and tearing away with a harsh shear.

"I'm coming!" Sliding everything on her desk into her bag, Andraste dashed to the door and met two escorts, who showed her to the plane. There was only a sliver of dawn on the horizon, and she realized how little she had slept as she staggered aboard.

Yousef was the first to meet her. "Long night, Andy?" He pulled the scrap of paper off her mask.

She gave a soft chuckle, too tired for the embarrassment to come all the way through. "Sorry, am I late?"

"No, you're fine." Yousef gestured towards her improvised room. "You can rest a little longer on the way."

"Thank you, doctor." Sheepishly making her way into the room, she let herself fall onto the bed. Leaning back, she pulled out her book to fall asleep to it again.

The engines revved, and soon they were off not long after. Yousef himself was eager to shut his eyes, but Judicia kept the energy alive with the astringent smell of her coffee. Glancing back at Andraste, he saw her nodding off until the book fell on her face. He smiled to himself as he pulled out his tablet and opened his favorite farm simulator.

"Hang in there, Andy."

Some time passed, and Andraste was woken by a lurch in the plane. Eyes popping open, she saw a smear of black text and smelled the pages of her textbook. Pulling the book from her face, Andraste took a deep, cleansing breath before any anxiety set in. Breathe in, count to five, breathe out, count to five.

Her shipping container didn't have windows, to her dismay. From the pressure built in her eardrums, she could tell they were far above the ground. Her first instinct was to ask Judicia or Yousef what was happening, but recalling that she was alone in her room, she turned to the door. What she saw made her gasp.

A haphazard layer of tarp had been put in front of the glass, cutting her off from the rest of the plane. She looked around the space for the button that summoned a nurse and saw it hanging from the ceiling.

It lit up and she heard the small buzz of a transmission. Whoever was closest would usually respond right away, but there was silence over the radio.

"H-hello?" She spoke into it. "Is anyone there?"

A sound came from the other side of the tarp. Not a voice, but movement. A reaction to her. It was distant, but she could detect several emotional auras: all familiar ones, those of Judicia and Yousef. They were too far away for her to read in detail. It was a comfort to know they were close, but also a source of fear for their silence. Her query was met with more static from the unused communicator.

"Please, can someone respond? Did I do something wrong?"

After some more jostling on the other side of the tarp, the communicator finally came to life.

"No, Andraste, you haven't done anything wrong." Yousef came through on the other end, his voice exhausted.

"Oh, um, a-all right." She said. "So, why is there a tarp covering my room?"

"Wha- what?" Yousef asked. "Tarp? What are you talking about?"

The dumbness in his tone settled on Andraste, and she had to blink it away before going on. "Doctor, there is a tarp stretched over my door. I can't see the rest of the plane."

"Well, that's news to me. Uh, maybe Judicia didn't want you seeing something. Let me check with her."

"All right. Thank yo-" She paused. A feeling crept into the room, unwanted and unanticipated. It was cold and malevolent, and it was making an advance towards the other doctors.

"Andy, what is it?" Yousef asked, urgent.

"Who else is on the plane?"

"What? Um, just a few guards, another doctor and the pilots. Why do you-"

"Hands over your head! Now!" A third voice entered the conversation, barking at Yousef. In the background, she could hear him falling to his knees.

"Hello? What's happening?"

Further down the plane, she heard an electrical implement being crushed, and in her room, the grating static that accompanied the death of the second radio in the conversation.

Where Yousef and Judicia were, a cacophony of feelings started to whirl through the cabin. The flame of hate, the icy crush of fear, and the general static of disorder. Voices were muted behind the glass, and the only movement was implied by slight twitches of the tarp.

Without thinking, Andraste went for the door. By design, it was supposed to resist impacts and bullets- and, ideally, the budding strength of a Fomorian hybrid. Andraste put every ounce of her strength into her push and pull of the door, to no avail. She could feel the reinforced material bend and flex with the pressure, but remained shut.

The door handle broke the stalemate by snapping off at the foundation, sending Andraste hurtling into the back wall. She ran towards it and started beating her hands against the seal, sending thunderous beats throughout the plane.

"Yousef! Judicia!" She cried as her fists pounded on the semi-elastic glass. It was exhausting to battle against the rebound of the material, and Andraste was breathing hard after only a handful of impacts.

She pressed her palms against the glass and centered herself. Breathe in, count to five, breathe out, count to five.

"If this is the Martyr's Army, they won't risk going against me again." She thought, noting the tarp. *"They must have put this up. As long as I'm stuck in here, I'm cut off from them. What are my options here?"*

The door was impervious, and these mental states were too foreign for her to close in on. There was no face, and no eyes for contact. She feared the worst, imagining they had the doctors on the floor at gunpoint.

"The doctors!" An idea came to her then, one of tremendous audacity and potential harm, but hopefully none greater than a bullet in the head.

She sat down and relaxed her body, back against the protective wall. She closed her eyes and began to concentrate. Gently peel away the outer layer, and focus on the controlled chaos of Judicia's mind. She was distant, but nonetheless identifiable.

She saw through Judicia's eyes with unanticipated clarity. The blurry world sat on the peripherals of her glasses, and a flash hider on an assault rifle was pointed at her face.

"Dr. Judicia!" She thought, hoping that Judicia would catch it the same way Williams did.

The eyes widened. *"Andraste?"* Judicia's voice came through the ether.

"You can hear me? Oh, thank God!" Andraste was speaking to Judicia in her mind as if it were as clear as any other conversation. *"What's going on?"*

"Take a wild guess. More Martyr's Army insurgents."

She glanced up at the man holding the gun. He was much more well-fortified than any of the bombers in the Shard. He had the telltale balaclava on his face, along with goggles and a bandana over his head. The "Remember the Martyrs" symbol was grafted onto his equipment wherever it would fit, even on the assault rifle. No twitch or movement gave any insight into his mental state, and Andraste couldn't pick it out for herself. It seemed he was trained for this.

"Is there anything we can do?" Andraste asked.

"This isn't the time for any of your dare-devilry, Andraste." Judicia responded. "The only reason they haven't shot us is because we're kilometers above the ground. This is no place for a shootout."

"All the more reason to get me out of here! If they won't shoot me, I can overpower them, easily!"

"They have control of the plane, Andraste. The pilot's been taken out, too. You would only make things worse." In all her pessimism, Judicia's tone of voice never wavered. Even in this mysterious realm of telepathy, she kept her monotone.

"I would save our lives! How could I make things worse?" There was no hiding her anger.

"You'd find a way."

Andraste was nonplussed. When all hope seems lost and guns are aimed and loaded, Judicia makes time to make a jab at someone.

She moved down the list. He would be scared, but Yousef would probably be more receptive. She could feel the chill of his fear seated next to Judicia.

She focused on the chill and spoke to him.

"Dr. Yousef!"

He flinched at the sound of her voice, and everyone noticed. He nearly jumped out of his chair, catching the attention of the insurgents. Just as Andraste's vision coalesced with Yousef's, one of the soldiers slugged Yousef in the face. Knuckles met flesh, and Yousef was forced back into his seat. Andraste felt the same impact as he did, and the same strain on the neck. The exoskeleton on her face offered no resistance, as if the blow had passed those and went straight through to the skin beneath.

She fought against the pain, remaining fixed on Yousef's mind.

"Yousef," she thought, keeping herself calm by repeating the breathing exercise. She kept the numbers going in the back of her mind- breathe in, count to five, breathe out, count to five. *"It's me, Andraste. Please, don't speak, just think. Is there anything you can do to open the cell doors?"*

"What do you mean? Do you have a plan?" He replied, repeating the numbers in sync with her.

"Not really," she began, going over the words slowly, *"But I didn't have the most specific plan when I faced the insurgents in the Shard, either. If I can get out of here, surely, I can do something!"*

"Andy, they've taken over the plane. They killed our pilot, and we have no idea where we're going. Even if you take these guys out, then what? A British Plane flying around in Martyr's Army airspace is doomed!"

She didn't need to hear this a second time. She went after him with more vehemence. *"Can you get me out of this cell or not?"*

He was taken aback by her tone. *"Okay, fine. It's not like things could get much worse."* He sighed, which had a deeper sound than before when audible through his own ears. *"There's a 'panic' function built into the system, which will force us to slow down and lower our altitude- there's an auditory cue to activate it, but these people won't be happy to have it go off."*

Andraste was stunned. One verbal expression was all it took to defuse an emergency, and it took two mental intrusions and a punch to the face to get to it.

"Ideally, I can deal with them by then." Andraste finally said, trying to keep her indignation and anger separate from Yousef's experience. She would channel it into dealing with the insurgents. *"Yousef, please."*

"Okay. You'll know when it happens."

Andraste stepped out of his mind, returning to the wall of her cell. She stood up and poised herself, ready to burst out of the door at a moment's notice. The tension building in her body was enormous.

Yousef's voice broke through the calm. "Alpha Upsilon Theta Omega!"

One of the insurgents tackled him back into place, but this sound was diminished over four consecutive beeping noises went off before the cabin lights went dim and the sound of a dying electric surge was heard.

A red glow filled the darkness, and the walls were lined with blinking white lights. Over the speakers, a voice repeated: *"Emergency systems activated. Please remain calm. A distress signal regarding your current situation is being broadcasted to the Royal Air Force."* The mental energy in the air became intense, like lightning woven into the oxygen. She could hear gas masks dropping from the ceiling and doors sliding open. Finally, her own door popped open and tore the tarp away.

She saw two of the insurgents and made a dash. She didn't even register their faces as she charged for them and envisioned breaking them apart.

The charge stopped when her foot failed to make contact. The doctors were strapped in, and the insurgents held onto nearby wall mounts for stability, so only Andraste went airborne when the plane started to dive. Her container was thrown onto the ceiling and slid towards the back of the plane, finally gaining purchase on the wall of her room. There was a loud whoosh as the plane depressurized and slowed.

With the plane stable, Andraste could move around more freely. She drifted back to the wall of her cell and then kicked off, shooting herself at the nearest soldier. The force of her tackle knocked him into the other insurgents, and they were all sent towards the cockpit. They flew several meters before crashing into a wall.

In the split second she had, she tried to go for one of the guns. She didn't care about damaging the plane at this point. Her arm went out and grasped the barrel of one.

Before she could pull, a spray of mist was blown over her face. She gasped, and her mouth and lungs started to burn. She saw the silhouette of a can of mace before she squeezed her eyes shut, as if she could crush the sensation beneath her eyelids.

"Restrain her!" Cried a foreign voice. "Take her alive!"

Her body went numb, and the notion of stopping insurgents on a plane became a vague fantasy at the back of her mind. The immense pain had dislodged her from the present. Hands from the far-off reality of the soldiers were on her and forcing her still, binding her arms and legs in cords.

Their shock and Andraste's dissociation were brought to an abrupt stop when the plane stopped diving and leveled out. Andraste was slammed onto the floor, head rebounding with the whiplash, and the soldiers were thrust back. They all called out to Andraste, but she couldn't process anything- everything was a haze that stung the eyes and throat. She tried to sit up, but her body refused to cooperate.

Mentally, the plane compartment was a hotbox of rage and terror. Andraste hated being in this moment, but she had no choice of being anywhere else, at least not yet. Seizing her advantage over the minds of the other passengers, she reached out to Yousef again.

"Dr. Yousef," She begged, sounding ragged even in her mind, *"I need your help again. How can I get you all out of here?"*

"Andy, I don't know!" He was glancing frantically around the plane as the soldiers buzzed around keeping the scene secure. Only Judicia was calm, trying to reach for an oxygen mask as she fought off blackouts. *"The plane is depressurizing, so maybe one of the doors can-"* Yousef stopped when he saw a solid red light among the blinking red ones. Beneath it, he saw the words "rear cargo door open." Her container-room had flown back hard enough to dislodge the door.

"Yousef, keep your eyes on that!" Andraste continued. *"I have a plan now."*

Thus began an awkward dance of violence and audacity that would risk everyone's lives. Her own eyes full of mace, she would be looking at this through Yousef's eyes.

Two soldiers were still hunched over her, holding her down, and they took her stillness for compliance. In a rush, she swung her arms up and knocked them both back. The half-done binds they had on her came undone, and she made her way towards the emergency light.

Beneath it was a control panel. The AUTO alert had disengaged the emergency override, so just as a soldier was getting his taser out, Andraste looked through her own wounded eyes and turned the key. She shook off more of her numbness when the loading bay in the back finally opened.

She staggered to the door, and saw a field of dense, uninterrupted treetops spreading out into the horizon. The deafening sound of the wind and engines and her own awe had stunned her, even as the floor moved beneath her feet.

The soldiers and doctors were all reeling from the turbulence Andraste had brought inside. As compartments opened, she saw parachutes, survival kits, and other things made for an emergency. With the soldiers disoriented, Andraste grabbed as many kits of whatever was closest, at least three parachutes, and tried to get to the doctors. She had a hand on Yousef, hoping to push the parachute into his arms. He only looked at her in bewilderment as she went for his buckles.

Another man wedged himself between them. A soldier had pushed her away and held his gun to her. His taser was up and crackling with energy.

She ducked out of his way and tried to kick him back, but lost her footing as the inclining metal floor started to grind.

Wires were being pulled from walls and some safety belts snapped as the container started sliding. The sound of the wind became a violent shriek as the metal crate filled the rear door.

"Oh no," Andraste eked out in shock, looking away from the soldier for only a second. As the last of the container's straps broke away, the plane lurched one final time from the weight, and her tenuous footing failed as she went airborne. With a parachute in one hand, Andraste was thrown flailing out of the plane.

"Andy!" Yousef shouted for her as they vanished.

The moment was perfectly lucid as Andraste fell. The container just below her, the plane speeding away into a dot on the horizon, and the green and blue panoramas of the sky and the ground filling the background overtook her sight.

The shock of the situation was immense, such that it almost came full-circle and nullified Andraste's panic. She felt numb and cold, overcome by a feeling of vulnerability that paralyzed her. She wanted to move, wanted to do something, but that feeling wouldn't spread to the rest of her body.

"Do something, you idiot!" She yelled at herself, halfheartedly at best.

"Why aren't you moving? You're going to die!" Andraste wasn't listening, only watching. She was hurtling towards death, certain and inescapable, and she was helpless.

There was a bundle of energy swirling around in her head, with some impetus to seize the parachute and save herself, but it was contained by her utter despair. There was no panic. She didn't need to breathe deep or visualize a machine. She didn't even move. Her hands didn't go to her shoulders in self-comfort, nor did her face express anything but a blank stare. What separated this feeling from other feelings of fear and failure was the acceptance.

The doctors were gone, the Army had the plane, and she was in free-fall. She was so stunned, her eyes were so wide with shock, that she saw everything at once but processed none of it. The facts settled into a flat layer around her head that wouldn't fall into her comprehension. The wind howled as leaves spun around her, and finally she became cognizant.

Almost without realizing it, tears started to fall from Andraste's eyes. No sobbing, no emotion to justify them, only tears. She assumed it was the fear, and the knowledge that she had been beaten. The feeling crushed her chest.

"So this is it?" She thought. It wasn't the same inner critic from before, it was her. *"This is how I die?"*

Some feeling in her body returned when she heard this voice. She was able to adjust for the distorted equilibrium and spread her arms to stop her tumbling. Her own voice, not one of cruel reprimands or the mutterings of some clump of neurons. It brought her comfort, and energy.

"Is death so easily accepted?" The longer she went on, the more she was able to move. *"Is that it?"* A shockwave of energy was sent through her body as she thought this. *"Did I come back from the brink of death in the Shard only to give up now?"*

The numbness emptied from her body as she flung the parachute over her shoulders. Arms in the straps, she started to fasten herself in. Not daring to see how close the ground was getting, she only hesitated when one of her books went flying out of the container. With another breath, she was in, and pulled the cord.

As the cloth billowed behind her, the rushing stopped all at once. Choked and breathless as it pulled her out of free-fall, Andraste had a moment to survey the environment. Nothing but endless expanses of green surrounded her, some trees reaching far above others in distorted fractal patterns of leaves. It seemed still, and the silence following the panic of the plane was disorienting.

Her chest heaved, and finally Andraste noticed how thin the air was. She had been low on oxygen ever since the plane depressurized, and now she was feeling it. Getting re-adjusted after she landed would be a challenge, but that didn't even approach the issue of landing. All at once, problem after problem came into Andraste's mind: where she would land, where she would find shelter, and then how she would explain all of this to Rowe and Quadriyyah, but before that, she had to find a way to get in touch with England again. Every issue with her situation mounted on her chest as she dangled from a parachute.

Wood snapped and metal crashed as the shipping container met a tree. A ripple of force was almost visible throughout the woods where the container landed, and Andraste finally had a plan: land where it had landed and see what she could salvage.

"It's a start," She thought as her vision started to fail. Deeper breaths weren't helping; there simply wasn't enough oxygen. Turning her parachute around as best she could, one of the last things she saw was the dense tangle of boughs where the container had fallen. The colors and greenery had blurred together by the time she had the metal box in view. The last thing she heard was the zip of the ripcord when she had the parachute attached, and blacked out when the resistance stopped her fall.

21 Somewhere in the Outlands
15:45   June 7th, 2335

"Oh God," he said under his breath. "God, no!" After the fifth time, he couldn't hide it. As Yousef and Judicia were being carted off the plane, bags over their heads, Yousef was showing his panic. He had nearly leapt out of his chair as Andraste fell from the plane, and had been in shocked silence until now. They were led into a tent once they met the ground, and Judicia was put on a respirator.

"Hurts, doesn't it?" The nearby soldier prodded him with his gun. "To lose someone you care about? Someone who gave you hope?" He jabbed Yousef, knocking the man out of his trance. He grabbed him by the hair and yanked him back into place, meeting him face-to-face with the Martyr's Army sigil on his bandana: the same silhouette shattering on impact from the bullets. "Trust me, we know all about it."

Yousef saw the homage to Sennec through his clouded eyes as tears fell. Still, he gave the soldier a hard look. His anger was the only thing that kept him from feeling so defeated.

The flap of the tent was swept open, and the room went silent. All the soldiers turned to the entrance, guns still trained on their hostages, and gave the three-over-the-heart salute.

"So, you failed to apprehend the target?" She asked with a cold bite.

"Yes, general." One of soldiers responded, head hung in admission. "She bailed out of the plane."

"We know," Scarlet said as she walked over to Yousef. "We had a visual of her opening a parachute over the shipping container. Another team will be sent to retrieve her."

"She's alive?" Yousef blurted out.

Scarlet turned to him, focusing her glassy eyes on his hopeful face. With her silent reprimand, he remembered his place.

"Don't worry, Dr. Yousef Makkareb." She knelt close to him. "We have no plans to kill her. Once she is in our custody, you can be of assistance in making her cooperate."

"You know me?" He felt predated by this woman.

"I do, Doctor. Especially how well you've been trying to look after Andraste." She leaned in close to his face. "You have my sincere gratitude for that. I want her to be in the best possible condition when we get her."

"You're still trying to kidnap her? Why?" Yousef couldn't back away from her, to his dismay.

"You'll understand eventually. Until then, cooperate." Scarlet stood up, nodded to the other soldiers in the tent, and left. Yousef tried to protest, but was met with another bag on the head.

One tent oversaw communication, and Scarlet burst in, making all the workers jump. On her left, a man saluted her.

"General Scarlet," he said, "a team of elite soldiers has been deployed to the crash site."

"Excellent. With whose leadership?"

The communicator took a deep breath before responding. "General Listev is with them."

She dove in front of him and looked at the monitor, which displayed the statuses of several units in the field. One, marked "FH Retrieval," consisted of a dozen highly-trained marksmen and one of the generals, Eric Listev.

"What is their mission?" Scarlet demanded.

"In the case that the V.I.P. is dead, retrieve the body and the plane's black box. If the V.I.P. is still alive, retrieve."

Scarlet nodded in acknowledgment.

22 Somewhere in the Outlands
14:55   June 7th, 2335

Like the gradual lifting of fog as the sun burned it off, Andraste became cognizant of the world. It smelled like blood and leaves, full of flashing lights and cacophonous beeping.

Undoing the buckles of her parachute, she tried to take a deep breath, but felt something jab into her from beneath. All the calm was flushed out as she cried in pain. Her hand went to the point at the bottom of her rib cage, and the sensation worsened.

"What the Hell?" She gasped, hushed. Her hand was covered in blood. Anything deeper than a gasp would beget more pain. Even with the tranquilizer, she felt a jolt of fear when she saw the growing red stain on her shirt.

Expecting the worst when she lifted her shirt up, like the exposed spike of a broken rib, she was shocked to see the pain was coming from one of her exoskeleton plates. It was cracked and oozing blood like a smashed toenail, almost purple beneath the segments of keratin. The tranquilizer had all but numbed her, and she assumed it was the only reason she wasn't doubled over in pain.

In the same tree canopy, there was the battered container that had fallen out before. Carefully as she could, she dropped out of her parachute and landed uneasily on the branch below. It was an easy enough climb among the massive tree branches towards the crate, and she glanced inside from the door that had popped open. She sat up and felt her head bump into the open door of a drawer. The safety measures present in the drop pod had all gone off, more in response to external shock than the emergency signal from before.

Stranded in nebulous no-man's land with no assistance and paltry resources, the impulse to worry filled her, but only the impulse. Panic was usually her go-to response in a situation like this, but the tranquilizers had her in a hazy chokehold. Instead, she clenched her fists and fumed. On the side of her body that wasn't ravaged by the injury, tension began to build.

She slammed her fist on the wall, bending it beneath the impact of her fist.

"Shit!" She cried, releasing some of the tension. Sighing, she stood up, keeping a hand on her injury.

Andraste checked the locker behind a chair. A backpack and some first aid kits were near the front, with welcome cold compresses and bandaging for her wound. Beneath the backpack were some handfuls of rations and refills of her tranquilizer. With a few steady breaths, she started to imagine a machine to keep her mind occupied.

The machine visualization reflected her state of mind. Just as the clear image of a gear or shaft began to coalesce, she lost sight of it as she tried to correct herself. At each aggravation of her injury, the entire structure risked flying apart. The haze of the tranquilizer was wearing off, and she found herself needing some comfort.

She was beginning to get used to her injury by the time she had scoured the entire room. There was about three days' worth of rations and three units of tranquilizer. Andraste's first instinct was to refill it, but she didn't want to be so off-center. Everything else was in the cargo hold, and she had little faith in getting down there.

The door to the container hung open, and that led out into a vista of the woods. A panorama of green sprawled out in front of her, and a wide branch was in jumping distance. Before she went, she paused.

It was a long drop from her platform to the branch down below. If she fell, she would strike that first, crushing the rest of her ribs. There was no telling what the rest of the fall would be like, if she was still alive by then. It was probably just as far and just as rough the whole way down. She would be mangled and dismembered before she even hit the ground.

She shut her eyes and gripped the metal. She was almost hyperventilating, undeterred by the pain it caused her.

"No," she told herself, without the usual vehemence. *"Don't. Are you giving up so easily?"*

Her knees became weak, and the sense of height made her dizzy. Up her back and into her head like molten metal, subdued panic set in, and the catheter on her arm started beeping, crying out for a replacement. She fell to her knees, head hanging out the side of the plane.

No deep breath or visualization could bring her out of this. They helped, but it wasn't enough. She grabbed one of the bottles of tranquilizer and slammed it into the dispenser. A numbness came over her within moments, and the thoughts slowed. She pulled herself up, her mind a blank slate.

Having exhausted her other faculties, she fell back on something from long ago.

"Don't run away again."

With a sigh of strange relief, she strapped her backpack on and opened her eyes. Before the tranquilizer held on too strong, she closed her eyes, got into position, and leapt. Both feet landed on the branch, and she stood up straight without any trouble.

The creak of bending metal brought her attention back to the container. There was a heavy indent where she had kicked off. The corner was scraping down the trunk, tearing away at the bark.

Andraste fell to her knees and grabbed onto the bough. The gnarled sections of the bark were thick enough to make handholds.

When the corner scraped down, all the weight was caught on the branch, and it cracked with a sound like thunder. The container started to tumble down the tree, with a deafening slam from each impact. Birds and other animals began crying and filling the air as the metal box crashed through. Eventually, the crashes stopped coming, leaving Andraste to wonder how much damage she had caused.

Regardless, she had made it, and she was set on making the climb down.

23 Somewhere in the Outlands
16:04   June 7th, 2335

For all the anticipation, the climb down the tree wasn't so bad. The bark was sturdy enough to reliably hold her weight, and there were enough divots and spaces for her to gain purchase.

It was slow going, with the continuous ache in her side and the sluggishness brought about by the tranquilizer, but she knew it could be worse. There were enough branches on the way down for her to stop and rest every so often.

Something was on her mind, however. There was something familiar about descending from the tree, and she found herself relying more on muscle memory than on the layout of the tree itself. For lack of a better understanding, the tree seemed to be "speaking" to her. There was an unmistakable dialogue between her touch and the textures of the branch. This level of familiarity with climbing Outland trees was unsettling. Andraste wondered when she had the time to climb trees before the experiment, her amnesia leaving some echo of familiarity that she was discovering now.

She followed the route of the container, going along the same gashes and cracked tree boughs. The green canopies beneath her seemed to be getting closer, at least.

Fog billowed almost as high as the treetops. The clouds in the air swallowed the horizon as they grew denser with distance.

Looking where she thought was down, another tree branch came into sight. She caught herself on her feet and arms, and though the impact was painful, it didn't seem to inflict lasting damage like the container crash did to her ribs. She looked out, and it seemed that she had landed on one of the roots.

Andraste took to her feet and started to sprint. Her wrists and ankles were aching, but she didn't let herself stop for anything. She could see other points she could jump or run to amidst the fog, but she knew the fog wouldn't keep herself safe forever. She continued almost mindlessly.

"God damn this fog," she heard a foreign mental state amidst the silence, and it sounded close. She concentrated on it as she attempted to keep her footfalls silent, hoping this would be her opportunity to get out alive.

Finally, Andraste's feet touched ground. Tall grass and other greenery offered a different terrain, and some of it stood taller than she did. She pushed through with no small amount of difficulty. It was denser than it let on. She had to find a place to hide and get into the mind of the sniper, and a sprinting monochrome mutant wouldn't be safe in tall grass for very long.

She fought against the tangles and density of the underbrush, until she saw the silhouette of a tree. The silhouette grew darker and clearer as she approached, thinking she was closing the distance, but it was deceptively large and distant. She could only see it better because the fog was lifting.

Andraste ducked her head and charged through her opposition.

She heard another gunshot, which struck the ground behind her. It gave her an extra burst of adrenaline, and sent her tearing through the grass. She didn't stop until she tripped on a root and bashed shoulder-first into the tree. Scrambling to her feet, Andraste snuck around to the other side of the trunk and pressed herself against it.

Opening her mind, she looked for the mental aura again. It was closer, in the tree she was up against. There were no words, only the aggravation that followed the loss of their target. She sighed, centering herself and shutting her eyes.

Another man's sight overtook her own. There was a compact sniper rifle in his hands, and a second man sat nearby with a pair of unique binoculars. He was whispering something to the spotter in a foreign language, and the latter started climbing to a higher vantage point.

"Damn it!" The man thought as he looked back through the crosshairs. *"I hope Listev knows what he's doing. If that monster dies, we're all fucked."*

Andraste pulled away, realizing that her assumption was correct- something was wrong with the way these people were shooting. They weren't shooting to kill, they were shooting to scare her towards them.

She had heard of him before. Listev had sacked countless outposts and cities. A veteran of Cairo, that grim smile of his was familiar from the newscasts about the city's burning.

Andraste prepared to step back into the marksman's mind but re-considered. The spotter was nearby, with a cooler mental state than the marksman. This gave her an idea.

She entered his vision, and saw a thermal view of the field. There was no fog, only a vivid panorama of rolling grass and rustling leaves.

If she imagined herself speaking, people would hear it, and if she imagined herself moving, she could make people move. She thought she could imagine herself seeing something. The best of it was this spotter had a view of the plane.

From the corner of the scope's vision, she envisioned a red blip moving up from the peripherals and up to the wreckage- the heat from her body, dashing through the grass towards shelter.

The spotter reacted with shock, crying something out to his sniper and to the other spotters in his earpiece. They all barraged him with questions and apparent refutations.

Andraste moved to the sniper, whose crosshairs were moving to the wreckage. She envisioned herself about to dive into the metal refuge, running and vaulting over the detritus. The sniper said something, and pulled the trigger, deliberately missing his target.

Relieved, Andraste backed out of their minds. A small ruckus rose from the trees, and she heard more gunshots piercing the fuselage of the plane. She took to her feet and started running into the wilderness as the confusion covered her escape.

It was more of the same, running through dense underbrush and bizarre plants. More of the same scenery lay ahead, gigantic trees and the slightest hint of fog. As she ran, the sounds became distant.

Her relief was interrupted when another shot went out. It was a tremendous, heavy sound that sent shockwaves through the air, and the sense of impact almost made her stop. It must have been Listev, firing a huge-caliber round at a suggestion of her presence. Even without seeing or sensing him, she had a sense of how terrible his anger would be, and she was addled by the thought. The sense of being hunted chilled her, and she almost stopped moving.

She was about to look back, but she caught herself. Taking as deep a breath as her injury allowed, she counted to five, then exhaled and counted again.

Andraste ran in what she thought was a straight line for a long time. The same scenery passed by ad infinitum, tall grass with trees all around. Her eyes started to glaze over with the repetition, and soon her legs were moving on their own. Another tree appeared in the center, and she prepared to run around it, as she always had, but she kept going. She leapt onto it, grasping the bark, but she didn't feel anything in her hands. There was no texture.

She tried to tighten her grip, but as she did, there was a pain in her chest. Andraste blinked and backed away, and her back struck a tree. Everything became clear again, and the haze was gone. No tree stood in front of her.

"Wait, what?" She thought she had woken up from a dream with no memory of falling asleep. As if she were

in someone else's mind, the experience seemed foreign and distant. *"Was I just-?"*

Before she could think more, there was a surge of intensity in the air. It rose from the ground and reverberated through the trees, unleashing an intense, primal scream of anger and terror. She only heard it in her mind, and she fell back against the tree as she grasped her temples. In the same way she felt the tree "speaking" to her, the entire earth around her was echoing out some wretched cry. A red haze settled on everything like an otherworldly reflection. Her soul was filled with dread, an acute, pervasive horror she had never felt or seen before. She shut her eyes as the world fell into an incomprehensible turmoil. It died down after a few minutes, but it wasn't gone. Rather than vanishing, the noise retreated.

The gunshots had stopped. Andraste felt safe, perhaps unwisely, and decided to sit down. Her rib was aching, agitated from overexertion, but that seemed to be the only issue. She caressed her arms and shoulders, cementing a sense of physical presence. She had wormed her way out of a life-or-death situation, and felt the need to center herself. She dismissed the visions and red haze as a hallucination, a sure sign of exhaustion.

She let her back rest against the tree, which relaxed her entire body. She envisioned a machine, slowly and methodically, with gears and drive shafts coming in at a painstaking crawl. She needed some time like this. Andraste had no idea where she was or where she was going, but she was resolute that the situation wouldn't get the better of her.

24 Somewhere in the Outlands
17:20   June 7th, 2335

Save the occasional ditch, rock formation, and plant tangle, Andraste's route was a straightforward one. Listev and his team were surely tracking her, but she thought the best thing she could do was to keep a level head and keep going. The red haze was long gone, so Andraste dismissed it as a hallucination.

A stream led to a small cliff, which poured into a deep pool of water. A misty waterfall brushed her face and emphasized the heat and exhaustion that ravaged her own body. Andraste didn't sweat. Another reason she only needed one ration a day was because her body clung to every nutrient and drop of water that was put into it. It made her metal mask necessary so nothing else would disrupt her metabolism.

She felt as if she had been sweating, though, inexplicably disgusting and unclean. Her excess body heat was wicked away by her exoskeleton, in a fashion like copper coils of a refrigerator, but, like sweat, it wasn't a perfect solution. Mindful of the wound, she set her backpack and clothes aside, and waded into the water.

A film of dread and exhaustion washed off her body when she dipped beneath the surface. The pool wasn't too cold, but it was a welcome change from the humidity. She especially felt the temperature difference on her exoskeleton, as the collected heat and aching dissipated into the water. Her wound finally stopped bleeding, but she kept her hand on it to keep the water out. She allowed herself to stretch out and relax, grateful for the rest this brought to her aching legs.

"Enjoying your deployment, are we?"

Andraste shot up when she heard the voice. The same one from before, that she had decried as a hallucination, a meaningless spasm in her brain. She looked around but didn't see the same ball of neurons. Andraste rushed out of the water and hurried to get her clothes back on.

"You never struck me as the type to be lounging in a pool in enemy territory, Andraste." It appeared in front of her, hovering at the same height and speaking in the same monotone as always. "Rest assured; I didn't see anything you wouldn't want me to see."

Andraste had no response. After applying new disinfectant and bandages to her wound, she slung her backpack over her shoulder and walked on, moving past the orb.

"I'm talking to you, Andraste."

Andraste fumed in silence. She started walking faster.

"I see what's going on." It appeared in front of her, making her jump. "You still don't think I'm real, do you?"

"You're not real." Andraste spoke in a low, aggressive tone. "I have nothing to say to you." She passed through the orb and kept walking.

"Well, that's troublesome. I won't mince words, Andraste: it's more important than ever that you start listening to me, so you'd better start believing otherwise."

The orb was talking to Andraste's back. She kept her stride.

"Oh, please. The silent game is only charming when toddlers try to do it. Besides, you don't even know where you're going."

Andraste finally stopped.

"You don't know where you are, you don't know where you're going, and you don't know how to help yourself. I'm not criticizing you, I'm just stating facts."

Andraste turned on her heels and yelled. "Get away from me!"

"At last, conversation." It didn't move, despite her approach. "Maybe we can finally start talking about important business."

"There's nothing to talk about." Andraste stood straight, clenching her fists. "You are not real. I'm only seeing you right now because of how exhausted I am." Andraste turned around and kept walking.

"Yes, yes, the 'schizophrenia-like symptoms' you mentioned." The orb followed her close behind. "I will say, I don't hold it against you for not believing me. However, it's vital that you start believing me and listening to me now."

"And why on earth should I do that?" Andraste kept walking.

"Because I'm the only way you'll survive out here. I can help you navigate to safety, and to find the doctors."

"Of course, because you know bloody everything, don't you?" Andraste glanced over her shoulder. "Collins, Judicia, and Yousef were hurled out of a plane. How could you possibly know where they landed?"

It vanished and then appeared in front of her, stopping her in her tracks. "The point is, you're here, you're stranded, and you need my help. Now, will you please stop being so obstinate and work with me?"

Andraste was silent. She straightened up, folded her arms, and stared at it.

"I have no reason to believe anything you're saying."

The orb seemed to stare back, looking for the correct words.

"Fine," it said. "You're well-aware of the fact that Listev's men are after you, right? After the delightful trick that you played on them earlier, they're more determined to reach you than ever. If I'm correct, one of their marksmen should be lining up their sights on you as we speak."

Andraste, unmoved, decided to mentally scan the area, to see if anything was out of the ordinary. On the very border of her range, she sensed a hostile coldness.

"Duck, Andraste."

She bent her knees, and a gunshot rang out. It screamed right over her head before embedding itself in a tree. Instinctively, she broke into a sprint.

"Do you believe me now?" The orb said, keeping an easy pace with her. "That seems pretty definitive, if you ask me."

"All right, all right!" She cried between breaths. "I believe you! You're real, you're omniscient, and you want to help me! Fine! What should I do now?"

"Well, I wouldn't say 'omniscient,' but that's very flattering."

"What should I do?" Andraste begged, her voice ragged with exertion.

"Turn left at the forked tree and keep going straight." The orb dissipated, leaving her alone.

With no other recourse, Andraste kept running. The gunshots sounded closer than last time, but they were every bit as inaccurate. Listev must have been with them, and they were setting her up.

Panic began to overcome her again, in all the same places where she had just washed it off. The orb was right- she was incomparably lost, and she needed whatever help she could get. But for all she knew, the orb was a major force behind the Martyr's Army. Whatever was left of the forked tree was as likely to doom her as it was to help her.

More sprinting and gunshots later, she saw a tree that seemed cleaved down the middle. Its modest trunk split into two, and the two large limbs mirrored each other almost perfectly. She was told to go left, but she didn't trust the source. She didn't know what was to the right- maybe that was the safe haven, and the left was some kind of trap. Maybe it was the other way around.

Steeling herself, Andraste sprinted even harder and went down the path to the left.

"I'm going to regret this," She thought, too tense and frightened to sound truly angry at herself. *"This will end badly. I'm dead. I'm dead, I'm dead, I'm dead."*

The path ahead of her was well-trodden and wide, with the same monstrous grass trimmed all the way down to knee height. The hailstorm of bullets had stopped, but that didn't make her feel better.

It was unsettling, how pristine this route was. Levelled out, minimal plant life, straight except for a few wide, sweeping turns. Where enormous roots usually were, there was a layer of thick sod that kept the area under reasonable control. Translucent flickers of the tall grass from before layered over her vision in sporadic bursts. She saw nettles with knife-like spikes and leaves that wound around another in a helix. Trying to ignore the visions, she turned the corner and saw an almost sheer layer of earth, fresh over the previous material. Andraste jumped off the road and into the side ditch to obscure her footprints.

Further ahead was a metal sign, wrapped around a tree with chicken wire. The sign was old, but the wire was newer, and there were numerous circular markings in the tree, as if it had outgrown each previous attempt at holding up the sign. She couldn't tell what it said.

"It's in Polish," the orb said.

Andraste jumped back. The being had manifested next to her. "Where have you been?"

"Making preparations. The owners up ahead know you're coming, and I'm sure they'll help you once you reach the farm.

"Wait, what? Farm?" Andraste turned and asked, but the orb was already gone. She groaned and kept going down the path.

Past the sign, there was more of the same stretches of re-sodden pathways and curves. Eventually, her wandering brought her to an iron gate, simple but tremendous and imposing, with another sign in Polish dangling above it. Andraste guessed it was something along the lines of, "Go Away."

Having no more faith in the orb's words despite the reduced gunfire, Andraste felt unsteady in climbing the fence. She grabbed each horizontal bar with deliberation and care, hauling herself up and over at a steady pace.

A distinct type of tree began to appear at the end of the path. Its leaves and build were different from anything she had seen so far. The bark had been stripped back, leaving a bronze-colored mast of exposed flesh underneath. The wind blew towards her, sending a sharp but sweet scent towards her- cinnamon. The aroma was unmistakable, but it was off. It was akin to a pesticide rather than the spice that Yousef liked in his coffee.

Looking closer, she saw the perimeter of the endemic nature stop at the base of these cinnamon trees. The grass petered out, and the trees wouldn't grow past them, as if the branches were all trimmed along a line. These were Outland spice trees, and another strange memory for her. Their scent killed the visions of the tall grass from before.

Further ahead, there was the end of a concrete driveway. It was cracked and perforated by some errant sprouts.

The road led through enormous fields of different vegetables and plants. She could identify a few, like the chard, the carrots, and the potatoes, but everything beyond that was a speculation. There were bumpy, pear-like fruit with stark white skin and giant pink melons that grew in trapezohedrons.

An engine growled, and she felt vibrations in the ground below her. She stopped and prepared herself to sprint.

"Don't run," the orb said, appearing behind her. "They're going to help you."

Andraste didn't turn to look at it. She was frozen in the middle of the street.

"You still doubt me. I suppose that's fair. If you want me to prove myself, then consider this the perfect opportunity: if these people walk up to you and say, 'we're going to help you escape Listev' in one way or another, then it will be because I asked them to help. Is that acceptable?"

Andraste still didn't move. "And why would they listen to you?"

The sphere went quiet. "A fair point. You'll find out soon enough."

Before she could reply, the sphere vanished. A massive truck rolled down the road towards her. It was supported on an enormous chassis with wheels that came up to her chest. Turrets were mounted on the front and the back, with a narrow viewport to supplement its tank-like appearance. Its bright lights went out before they could blind her, and it came to a halt.

The passenger side of the car swung open, and a stout, older man jumped out, landing on the ground with both feet. He wore a blue collared shirt and black jeans, contrasting his salt-and-pepper hair. A double-barrel shotgun was at his side, not used to menace or threaten her.

The most aggressive thing about him was his stare, scrutinizing Andraste with narrowed eyes and furrowed brows. He was short, but well-built and bore experience in his rugged face. He had the look of a soldier.

She was still in her defensive stance, looking at the man with wide eyes. She didn't know Polish, and she didn't want to look away, even to glance at his mind. There was no heat, so he wasn't being aggressive, but there was a cool cautiousness to him, as well. He didn't know what he was looking at, which Andraste understood.

"You," he finally said, pointing at her. "You running from Listev?"

Andraste remembered the orb's words. Relaxing, she came out of her stance, showing her hands to the man.

"Yes," she said after a few moments of painful tension.

The man hefted his shotgun over his shoulder, then turned to the truck and nodded. The engine growled to life again, and the man climbed up the steps to the passenger side.

"Ride in back," he said to Andraste, before climbing in himself.

Awestruck, Andraste didn't move. The situation was baffling and dizzying. Her already small view of the Outlands hadn't prepared her for something like this, and its existence was difficult to register.

A great sound exploded from the truck as it honked at her. She jumped, and then dashed to the back, not wondering about anything else as she clambered on. The bed of the truck was lined with gardening tools, dirt, and assault weapons in equal measures.

Already feeling like she was imposing, she curled into a ball with her hands on her shoulders as the truck lurched forward and turned around.

25   Former Polish Territory
19:01   June 7th, 2335

The truck was parked in an enormous, homemade garage, separate from the rest of the house. Three other people got out of the truck, and the older man told Andraste to stay in the garage. He didn't say why, and responded to all inquiries with a firm finger pointed at the ground and the word, "stay." Sighing, she did as she was told.

It was starting to get dark. The descending sun cast long strips of light through the cracks in the wood, and several nocturnal creatures were starting to get loud. A cicada started to spin up its deafening, metallic call in the distance, while other cicadas followed its example and joined the chorus. The walls of the garage didn't halt the sound the tin roof seemed to rattle from the vibrations. She felt crushed by the sound, being pummeled into dust by the oppressive sound waves.

Andraste looked around the empty garage, deafened by the bugs outside and diminished by the incoherent authority of these people. As she sat in prostration, legs drawn up to her chest and arms clutching her shoulders, she could only dwell on one thought:

"What the Hell am I doing here?"

"You're getting the help you need, Andraste." The blue glow of the orb bloomed next to her.

Andraste turned to it, sighing. "Knowing that you listen to my thoughts and appear out of nowhere- It's not even upsetting anymore." After speaking, she relaxed her posture. "Are you here to say that these are the people you reached out to? How did you convince them to help me?"

"You'll find out in just a second." The orb moved to the side, behind the truck.

The giant steel lock on the door unlatched, temporarily eclipsing the deafening symphony of all the bugs outside. The door swung open, with ponderous creaking that shook the entire space. Andraste stood up, looking for the figure that was coming in.

It was the older man from earlier, who still carried his shotgun with him. He saw Andraste and didn't take his eyes off her even as he pulled the door closed again. Dissatisfaction was plain on his face, and he approached Andraste one slow, cautious step at a time. His eyes were wide and alert, narrowed at Andraste along his bushy eyebrows. The gun wasn't aimed at her, but he was ready to use it.

"You run from Listev." He said, keeping his intense gaze on her. "Listev after you?"

"I believe so," Andraste began, as she got back on her feet. "I crash-landed here, and the next thing I know, I'm getting shot at."

The man pursed his lips and shut his eyes. "Don't understand."

Andraste began again. "Sir, I'm being hunted by-"

"Allow me, Andraste." The orb moved out from behind the truck, and hovered in between the two.

A small bundle of axons reached out from the orb's body and slipped into Andraste's ear. It was a gentle attachment, not an invasive gesture, though Andraste was still baffled by it.

"Now try to explain."

Andraste looked at the orb, then back at the man. "I'm sorry, sir, I don't know why Listev is after me. I was on a plane, it crashed in the woods, and the next thing I know, I'm getting shot at."

"He must think of you as a special quarry," the man said, in clear, perfect English. "This is serious." He looked to the sky. "Thank you, Spirit."

Andraste's eyes almost shot out of her head. She pointed at the man with a resolute jab. "You can speak English?"

The man stepped back at Andraste's cry. "I'm not speaking English. The Spirit of the Outlands is translating for you. You should be grateful to them."

Andraste was dizzy with all the information that had been put before her. "'Spirit of the Outlands'?" She looked at the orb, and gestured to it. "Are you telling me the orb of neurons is real?"

Hearing this, the man's brow furrowed. "'Orb'?" He echoed in confused shock.

"It's a long story," they said. "Right now, I think you have more to explain to this gentleman." The spirit disappeared to let them speak.

The man stepped in before Andraste could respond. "I know who you are; you stopped the attack in the Shard. Your name is Andraste, right?"

He had caught her attention. Before speaking, she took a deep breath. "Yes, sir. I'm sorry if I've seemed rude. I'm very grateful for your help." She extended a hand to him. "What is your name, sir?"

He took her hand and gave it a light shake, with Andraste cautiously regulating the force she exerted.

"I am Sergei Holacksi, owner of this farm." He lifted the shotgun over his shoulder, finger off the trigger. "We do not support the expansion of the Super-States, but we do not support the dominion of the Martyr's Army, either. I'm sure you realize the risk that I am taking by sheltering you. Understand?"

She looked into his serious expression and nodded her head. "I do, sir. If I can elude Listev, I'll never cause any problems for you or your family again."

"Somehow, that is doubtful." He had a pronounced frown, and his brows rested heavily over his eyes.

Sergei held the shotgun in both hands again. "Now, we cover the plan. There is little doubt that Listev and his team have already tracked you, and that will inevitably lead them here. A skirmish is the last thing we want. The Martyr's Army recognizes our independence, only so long as we offer them our crops and resources. If something happens to Listev, and then word of it gets out, the rest of the Army will crush us. We just want to live normally, understand?"

Andraste nodded. "You want to avoid confrontation. I will not intervene when he comes by."

"Yes, good. Now, when he does come by, he is sure to have a druid with him that can detect you. Hiding you won't be as simple as locking you in a basement."

"Druid?" She thought.

Andraste didn't ask out loud, assuming it was another long story. "So, what will we do?"

"We have way of silencing you," he said, reaching into his pocket. He pulled out three brown ovals, almost shiny enough to seem varnished.

She grabbed them as Sergei tossed them to her. They didn't look like anything that she had seen or read about. "What will these things do to me?"

"They will hide you from the druids." He said, turning away. He gestured for her to follow him.

Andraste was pulled out of the garage. Sergei led her down the cobbled road, his attention darting from one point of the farm to another. The sun had gone down behind the line of enormous trees, already diminishing the visibility. An amber light was covering the area, which Andraste would have found beautiful under more peaceful circumstances.

Near a modest orchard of unrecognizable fruit, the road led to a fortress. There were sheer concrete walls covered in video cameras, automated turrets, and topped with sparking razor wire. A woman with a scoped rifle was walking along the top, who stopped and stared when she saw Andraste and Sergei.

A heavy door kept the place sealed off, which Sergei walked up to with authoritative familiarity. In the middle was a handprint scanner, where he put his hand. A green light flashed, and the door slid open.

Behind the heavy doors, a large, colonial home stood. It had three levels of windows on a red brick building. Andraste recognized this kind of home, more as a relic of the past than anything that would be seen or used in a modern setting, but she supposed that Outlanders didn't have much of a choice in real estate.

"Don't touch *anything*," Sergei commanded as he led her to the door, then swung it open for her.

"Yes, sir." Andraste stepped softly onto the hard, wooden floor.

The air was heavy with the same scent of antiquated pulp as an old book. The walls and floors were covered in paintings, photos, and knitted, crocheted images with Polish phrases written on them. Varnished wood tables and wardrobes filled the space. It was pleasant to look at, but Andraste felt out of place. Like a fine painting, everything seemed to exist in its own world, and Andraste's presence therein was jarring. Two steps in, and she felt profound discomfort, a fulminant sense of not belonging as the floorboards creaked beneath her.

She jumped when Sergei prodded her with his shotgun.

"Keep going. We don't have time for this."

"Right! Sorry!" She hurried down the hallway, trying not to get distracted.

The hallway turned into a huge kitchen, covered on all sides with porcelain tiles and marble furnishings. Baskets full of vegetables hung alongside hooks of dry-aged meat and suspended pots, pans.

She stopped when a small presence manifested in front of her. A mental presence brimming with life and vivacity like she had never seen before. It was a delicate warmth, like a freshly lit candle.

She looked down and saw a small child looking up at her. A short-haired blonde boy about four or five years old, holding a toy bow in one hand and toy arrows in the other. His bright green eyes looked too big for his head, and they stared at Andraste. She stared back, frozen.

A wide smile grew on his face, and he spoke with a voice larger than his size would imply.

"Hi!"

Andraste recoiled, and the back of her head rang one of the pots like a bell. She clasped her head with both hands, unaware of the enormous dent in the pan she struck.

"What is it now?" Sergei walked ahead of her.

"Is this her, Grandpa? Is this Ander- um, Ando-"

"Yes, Ivan, this is the girl." Sergei's voice softened. His entire façade went from rough to gentle when he saw the boy. "Remember, there will be some men from the Army coming by to ask about her. Do you remember what to do?"

"Uh-huh! I'm gonna tell them that I was helping Granny pick onions! And since I *was* doing that earlier, it's not a lie!"

Andraste, recovering from the pain, found herself amazed by the boy's fortitude.

"Great job, Ivan. You're being so brave!" Sergei tousled the boy's hair.

"Thanks, Grandpa!" He rushed over to Andraste and jutted his hand out. "It's nice to meet you! I'm Ivan!"

She was stunned. "Oh, um, i-it's nice to meet you, too. I'm Andraste." She used the gentlest exertion of her hand to shake his.

He shivered with excitement at the returned gesture. "Wow, cool! You kinda look like you're from a comic book!"

She pulled back. "Uh, comic?"

"Do you have powers? What kinds of stuff can you do?" The boy's eagerness was strange. There wasn't the slightest hint of fear in him, as there was in most everyone who saw her.

"Ivan, please. Andraste has important things to do." Sergei came between them. He put a gentle hand on Ivan's shoulder. "Why don't you do some target practice?"

"Okay!" He took one of the arrows and nocked it in the bow. "I'll be ready for anything!" He ran off, and the excited, warm aura was carried away by his laughter.

Another heavy hand landed on Andraste's shoulder as he ran out of sight. Sergei came up to her side, his softness gone.

"I have a lot on the line here, Andraste. You realize that, right? I don't have to explain that to you?" He started to squeeze.

"Yes, sir. I understand." She was shaking, feeling the weight of his grip and the situation, both crashing onto her shoulders. As he moved through the house, she allowed herself to be guided by his touch.

It was the first time she had seen a child, but certainly not the first time a child has seen her. She tried not to think about the broadcast from the Shard. The looks of terror on people's faces when they saw her were too easily imagined. Andraste knew she was frightening, and she was haunted by the notion of a child crying at the sight of her.

Now there was Ivan, running up to her like she was some star football player. There was always fear, always something going wrong, always something that people were running away from. In Ivan, she saw pure bliss. Andraste tasted moments of excitement and happiness from the people around her, but this was in its own category. It was the epitome of everything Andraste wanted to cultivate and preserve. That feeling of bliss, where you weren't in danger, you weren't afraid of something, and you weren't anticipating some dreadful outcome. The rest of the house didn't even register for her as Sergei guided her along.

She came back to reality as Sergei led her down a flight of stairs. The pulpy smell of the house got even stronger as they went down, with a subtle smoky aroma. They turned to the right, and she was ushered into a wide lounge area. Taxidermy animal heads were mounted on the walls wherever they could fit, and enormous hunting rifles filled glass cases.

Sergei saw her glance at the guns. "Don't even think about it," he said.

She snapped to attention again. "Yes, sir."

Past the lounge, there was an underground detachment from the house behind two steel doors. Sergei opened the first one, and the smell of smoke grew. He opened the second one, and the scent blew over Andraste like a weighted fog. A dim light hung overhead alongside several slabs of unidentifiable meat impaled on hooks.

Andraste was stunned. "What's all this?"

"This is the smoker," Sergei said, nudging her inside. "One of the most secure and remote places in the house. Those nuts I gave you? Crack them open."

She pulled out the rock-like nuts and did as he asked. Each one burst open with a fierce crack.

He stuck his hand out, and she dropped the broken nuts into his palm. "The smoke from these will hide your mental presence from anyone who's trying to look for you. So, breathe deep, stay calm, and don't make a commotion." Sergei went over to a small metal box in the center, filled with ashes and sticks. He tossed in some small twigs and lit the tinder at the bottom. "Stay here until I come and get you. Can you do that?"

Andraste was nonplussed at the entire situation. Despite the reassurances, she couldn't move past the feeling that she was about to be cooked alive.

"Yes, sir," she said.

"Good." He dropped the nuts into the fire. "Don't make a sound." He said as he turned and slammed the door shut behind him.

26 Former Polish Territory
20:15　　　June 7th, 2335

The crucible disgorged giant plumes of smoke as the wood cracked and sputtered inside. Andraste had her eyes shut against the sting of the acrid air, as if a lattice of microscopic needle points were being loosed into the chamber. She had huddled close to the ground, where an unsteady stream of fresh air was being sucked in from beneath the door. She knew some of her bodily fluid was being stored in her exoskeleton plates, and she feared she would see them boil or rupture from the fire.

The hickory smell was most overpowering, but there was another, chemical-like scent that dazed and almost intoxicated her. She presumed it was the nuts that were thrown in. She was physically exhausted, as if her body weighed metric tons, and she couldn't bring herself to move. Her mind was blank and unfocused, but she was wide awake. Eyes closed, flat on the floor, trying to breathe as her body tingled with heat, pain, and a lack of clarity, Andraste was a conscious lead weight stuck on the floor of the smoker.

"What am I? What does my existence mean?"

"What kind of question is that?" A toneless voice asked.

The spirit came into view, blue light textured by the smoke.

"Oh. H-hello." Andraste's eyes went wide, despite the stinging. "Wasn't expecting to see you here."

"You heard what that Sergei man said. Sit and wait. So, we've got some time to kill." It hovered closer to her. "Tell me, what more have you been remembering?"

"Well," Her head fell heavily to the side. "Sorry, but I'm feeling a bit off right now. Whatever Mr. Sergei put in that fire to 'put me out,' it's working."

"'Outland Walnuts,' in the common parlance. Inedible, but known for acting as a powerful depressant on certain parts of the brain when smoked. Most people use pipes, of course, but this works, too."

She focused on the spirit, jerking her head up to get closer to it.

"Well, what about you?" Andraste demanded with some indignation. "You tell me you don't remember what you are, but then people call you the spirit of the outlands, a-and then you know everything about their walnuts. What are you remembering?"

"More bits and pieces, like what I've showed you. Making it back to these lands has definitely been a benefit, however. To both of us."

In the smoke, a vista was created. Shades of green billowed out of the featureless gray and coalesced into shapes of trees and plants. The spirit was conjuring a scene of a simple meadow.

"When the Fomorians were defeated, the land began to change. Perhaps it was their plan all along- their corpses became terraforming equipment." The blue tendrils of its neurons snaked into the landscape and began to wind through the picture. The trees grew at blinding speed while flowers burst into garlands of fantastical colors. A deer came bounding through, bewildered, before grazing on those flowers. It too began to grow, twisting into a beast with tangled horns and exoskeleton plates just like Andraste's.

Looking at her own arm, Andraste felt a shudder go down her back at the implications.

"The Fomorians are changing the landscape, then?" She glanced at her own hand. "But how? And why?"

"Why," the spirit echoed. "That one word is perhaps my primary driving force. The answer to that question is what propels me forward." The changing landscape it created in the smoke became still. "Maybe in answering that, I can answer your question, as well. What you are and what your existence means."

She nodded weakly, though it took some effort to move her head. "Any idea on how all this is working?"

"Yes. The ecosystem in the Outlands is like a brain. The trees and plants are the dendrites coming from an infinite array of neurons and synapses." The blue tendrils of the spirit's form glowed through the misty landscape it created. "When people say that the plant life in the Outlands is 'alive,' they're not too far from the truth. Every living thing is trying to survive, of course, but here, it's not on an individual basis. Everything is branching out from somewhere."

"And there's another question," Andraste said sleepily. "What is that 'somewhere'?"

"The heart," The spirit answered quickly. The image shifted, panning out to a birds-eye-view of the land. Appearing on the horizon was a massive red blip that effervesced in the smoke, giving off its own luminance. "The heart of the Fomorians, perhaps figurative and literal."

"Is that," Andraste was pulling herself up from the floor, "is that the source of it all? Of all the ways the Outlands have changed?"

"I'm sure it is," The spirit said with quiet intensity. "Once I- or, once we find it, I believe many things will be made clear."

"That red color," Andraste said breathlessly. Her chest was about to implode from the pressure the smoker put on it.

"Oh, yes. I'm sure you recall that dreadful screeching and red energy after you eluded Listev."

Andraste had almost put that out of her mind. "That wasn't a hallucination, was it?"

"No. That terrible energy is very real, and it is what fuels the fears about another apocalypse around here. When the Martyr's Army talks about the end of the world, that energy is what they are referring to. No one is certain what it is, but there is no avoiding it."

Andraste had no response.

"Moreover, I have yet to see or feel a stronger response from it until you arrived. For lack of a better description, the Outlands are responding to you."

"Great," she sighed the word out. "What am I supposed to do about that?"

"You fight, Andraste." The spirit let the smoke-scene fade and floated closer to her. "It's what you were made to do. You fight the Martyr's Army, and you fight to understand it all."

Andraste leaned away, and almost fell flat on her back while trying to push away from the spirit.

Those words stuck in her chest- "made to do." She was reminded of Quadriyyah's visit in London, and all the notions that Andraste was left questioning afterwards. The spirit was right- she was made to do this, to fight the Army and dissolve their plans, but hearing it aloud rattled her.

"Don't let that woman's words affect you, Andraste." The spirit said.

Andraste turned to it with a start. "Excuse me?"

"Don't you want to give this everything you have? To rid the world of this destructive army and understand more about yourself?"

"W-well, yes, but-"

"Don't you want to save lives and help people? To live in a perfect world?" The spirit's monotone did not change, but Andraste noticed a greater weight in the room.

"Not you, too," she balked on hearing the words 'perfect world.'

"Whatever you want, Andraste, you need to focus on the here and now. If you don't give everything you have, then the world as we know it could end."

The spirit summoned the pictures again, focusing on the glowing red heart. The blue dendrites that flowed into the surrounding nature glowed, showing an entire landscape crisscrossed with blue. It reminded her of the field of neurons in her dreams.

The blue became shrouded in red. Spreading out from the heart, the same dark red of the malevolent energy pulsed through the land and burned into the wilds. Death, as both a sensation and a phenomenon, became apparent as the picture leapt out at her. The now-red dendrites curled and warped the trees. Red tendrils flung out of the wood and grabbed Andraste, sending a hideous signal through her body that stung and numbed her. The world she was watching screamed without a voice. The Fomorian impulse was vivisecting the world, and that sensation was traveling into her.

"This will happen the world over," the spirit said intensely. "You need to focus, Andraste."

Andraste staggered, feeling as if these images sucked the blood out of her. She propped herself up on the wall, struggling to breathe and stabilize herself.

"Oh, God." Andraste slumped back onto the ground. Her head lolled to the side and her arms were limp.

"Come now, Andraste. You've come out of worse situations."

"The entire mainland could kill me," she said, beginning to shake. "I'm not safe anywhere." Andraste was overcome with tremors.

"Andraste?" The spirit approached. "What's happening? Don't tell me you're having a panic attack."

"I-I don't know! I c-can't stop!" Her words were spat out in a barely-intelligible clump, and she moved with the same look of terror and uncertainty one would see from someone getting shocked.

The tranquilizer activated, but the usual beeping was replaced by three sharp, consecutive trills and a flashing red light. She fumbled with the dispenser until she got the capsule out. All the liquid was coming in wisps of steam, and the medicine had settled into a smoldering lump of sediment on the bottom.

"Oh, no." Andraste let the plastic canister slide out of her hand and clatter on the floor.

27 Former Polish Territory
21:20   June 7th, 2335

Clawing at the door, Andraste opened the seal of the smoker and barreled out into the lounge, scrambling for her backpack. Her vision grew blurry and the arm going for her pack looked foreign to her. She ripped into her supplies, throwing aside rations and bandages until she finally found a capsule of medicine and shoved it into the dispenser. The incessant red beeping stopped. She was on the ground, hunched over, taking breaths as heavy as she could manage.

"Andraste, what happened?" The spirit was close behind her. "Did I trigger something?"

She forced words out between heavy gasps and near-sobs. "No, that wasn't you." Her fingers curled against the ground. "That was me." She looked towards the stairs. "It's all my fault. Listev must be on his way right now."

As she said this, they heard footsteps racing down the stairs. Andraste's pulse quickened, and the haze from the medicine started to take hold. Before the daze began to set in, she dashed for the gun cabinet. She tore off the door and pulled out one of the rifles. She checked the magazine; it was fully loaded.

"You think you can fight them off? Sergei said he wanted to avoid a conflict." The spirit said.

Andraste felt it was mocking her. "They know I'm here. There's going to be a conflict no matter what I do." She took a deep breath and pulled back on the charging handle. "I've caused more than enough problems for these people. The least I can do is try and fix some of them."

Knowing it wouldn't be quite enough, Andraste found cover behind some taxidermy monstrosity in the approximate shape of a bear. It was covered in bark-like armor and had claws as long and savage as combat knives.

"I'll leave you to it, then." The spirit backed away and vanished.

The door leading to the stairs was kicked open, and a soldier came in. He scanned the area, sweeping the muzzle of his gun from one side of the room to the other. Andraste could sense his uncertainty, punctuated with each heavy, deliberate step he took.

Several others were close behind, two carrying a young man, and another man in darker clothes, wielding a rifle that almost scraped the ceiling. He was smiling with warm, murderous intent.

"Listev," Andraste thought. Her arms shook as she readied herself to shoot.

"Don't waste your ammunition, monster." Listev spoke, his robust voice carrying throughout the room. "We have everyone upstairs at gunpoint. Unless you want them all dead, you'll come out with your hands up."

Andraste thought of Ivan, and her resolve shriveled.

She peeked around the corner of her cover. None of them were looking at her, and Listev seemed like he was addressing the open doors of the smoker. The two men carrying the younger person caught the most attention. The teenage boy was wearing some dense, heavy helmet that looked like it was crushing his head. He was limp in their arms except for his weak, twitching hand which pointed in her general direction.

When she was finished sizing him up, his head rolled to the side and looked at her. She felt a force overcome her. It was concentrated in her mind, but it seemed to affect her entire being. She felt the muscles and joints in her arms and legs move of their own accord, agonizing for the resistance she put up against them. Unlike the spirit, which appeared as a mental image, this felt like a physical presence in her mind, pressing on her brain with a palpable pressure.

"We have you now," said a voice. It was weak, but still harsh and grating, sending shockwaves through her body. She could tell it was coming from the teenager, whose mental presence was almost absent. As if his mind had detached itself from his body, it was joined with Andraste.

"Get away from me!" As Andraste concentrated, she closed her eyes and found herself in a familiar place- the field of neurons.

Appearing as an absence of light, a male figure that resembled the teenager stood across from her, the blue light bent around him in a withered gray hue. Like an unwanted touch, she felt a rush of sensations when he stepped on the lattice of neurons: heat, cold, electricity, everything that disturbed and clawed at her.

"Give yourself to the General," he said. He stepped forward, and the sensations worsened. Dying like plants, each neuron he stepped on turned gray. "Maybe we'll let the Holacksi family live."

"Get out of my mind!" She took a strong step forward, and blue light radiated throughout the area, which knocked him off-balance. The faded neurons returned to their original luminance.

"L-Listen, you don't know what you-"

Before he could finish, Andraste charged at him. She gave off her own light, which spilled onto him. Like black fabric, his shape was illuminated, but there were no features. She planted a hand on his face and pushed him onto the ground. She concentrated, focused, and narrowed the entirety of her cognitive prowess onto beating him back.

"Please," he cried, confidence vanishing from his voice, "don't do this! Leave me alone!"

Andraste pressed on him harder. The blue lattice of neurons spread from her arm onto his face, and it began to define a face, features, and everything necessary to convey his terror. He screamed as the light intensified, and wisps of gray steam began to rise from him.

"I said, get out of my mind!" With one final push, she crushed his head into the ground, and he burst in a thousand directions, gray smoke and particles shooting off like geysers before vanishing into the air.

Before feelings of self-confidence could set in, she was drawn back into the real world by screams of pain and strangulation. She looked up, dazed from the sudden shift, and saw the soldiers bent over and clasping their heads, while the teenager writhed and convulsed on the ground. Even Listev was hunched over.

Without pause, she dashed up the stairs. Through the door, she could see everyone- including the family- doubled over and moaning in pain, grasping their temples. Hefting the gun, she let out a volley of shots against each Martyr's Army soldier. She killed the ones near the kids first, and the front door flew open. An unfamiliar adult with a gun took down the others before rushing over to the kids. The gunshots seemed to startle them out of their stupors, and Andraste ran over to Sergei.

"Sir!" She gave him her arm and lifted him to his feet.

As the haze over his eyes cleared, he saw the dead bodies and the gun in her hand. His face, though mollified by his exhaustion, soured as he looked at her.

"What did you do?" His voice was strained, somewhere between outraged and horrified. "I told you to stay quiet!"

"Sir, I'm so sorry! Right now, you need to get out of here! I don't know how long we have until Listev comes to!"

"Listev? He's still alive?" The horror overtook the outrage.

She paused before answering, shutting her eyes and looking away. "Yes. I had to make sure you were all safe first."

Sergei broke out from her assisting grip and snatched the gun from her. "None of us are safe, now that Listev knows you're here!" Turning to his side, he helped Misha to her feet, and she rushed over to the weeping grandchildren. "Didn't I warn you, monster?"

His words struck her like a sheet of ice. She went rigid, and she struggled to speak. She only whispered meaningless sounds.

Sergei leaned in, eyebrows raised, waiting for her to reply. "Didn't I warn you?" He emphasized each word. "You fucking freak of nature?"

"Dad!" The Holacksi man spoke up, holding a bawling toddler in his arms.

At last, Andraste was able to speak, in a voice that trembled and shook. "Y-yes sir."

"Grandpa, don't be so mean!" A familiar voice cried out, and it stomped over to them.

They both turned to see Ivan, looking at Sergei with narrowed brows and an assault rifle in his arms that was taller than he was.

"Andarta just saved us!"

Seeing Ivan breathed new life into Andraste. Her rigor dissipated, and the coldness was gone.

The younger man leapt at this sight. "Ivan, you put that down right this inst-"

Two gunshots from the doorway stopped them, and they all ducked. Sergei responded in turn, and shot two Martyr's Army soldiers in the head, who went limp and tumbled down the stairs they climbed. There was more scuffling downstairs, with the unintelligible but unmistakable shouts from Listev.

"Come and get me, you jerks!" Ivan pointed the gun towards the doorway.

Sergei yanked it away. "Ivan, go with Granny and Daddy. They'll keep you safe." He looked up. "Misha!

Adam! Get the kids to the surveillance office! Check the cameras and see where the other soldiers are!"

Adam, the younger man, carried some while Misha led others by the hand, but they both struggled to get Ivan.

"Grandpa, I want to help!"

"Then live to tell the tale!" He leaned over and pushed him towards his father, who swept his son up and got his family out of sight.

"And you," he said to Andraste, pointing at her with a trembling finger. "You want to help us?"

Andraste squeezed her eyes against tears. "More than anything, sir."

He shoved the fallen soldier's gun into her hands. "Then make yourself useful. Take some cover and help me with these idiots in the basement."

She looked at the gun, and felt empowered, reminded of Ivan's conviction when he held it.

"Yes, sir." She dove behind a couch, positioning herself to shoot whatever came out of the doorway. Widening the scope of her senses, she tried to look into the mental auras of the others in the basement. There was only Listev and another soldier, not moving.

Both her and Sergei tensed when they heard soft steps seeming to come up the stairs. There was nothing in the doorway yet, even as the wide-open door beckoned something to happen.

Neither of them could react in time to a metal click and an impact on the wooden frame. Something struck the door and rebounded into the dining room, drawing Andraste's attention. In the split second between the metal payload hitting the ground and its activation, Andraste gasped at the words, "Incendiary Munitions."

There was a sound of rushing air as it ignited, followed by the deafening explosion. Balls of flame surged from the grenade, sticking to the floors and walls.

"Napalm!" Sergei choked out, moving from his position. He took a step away from the inferno, and two shots tore through him. He fell to his knees, and two more went through his neck and chest.

Andraste turned to the door, and the man who fired the shots was already putting his gun to her. She turned and took him down with three shots. Trying to reach Sergei, she recoiled, as the fire had already engulfed the dining room and was spreading to his body. The fire alarm was sounding, and the lights blared as the deafening siren shot into her ears.

The sights, sounds, smells, and heat were becoming too much. She started to shake, and her senses dulled. Smoke filled the air, which burned across her throat and into her lungs as the chemicals blazed. She moved away from the inferno until her back hit a door, leading outside. Abandoning her position was stupid- they would walk right into her- but she couldn't bear the sensory overload.

She opened the door, resigned that she couldn't fight back in this situation. Before she could decide on what cover to take, strong rush of wind brush against her. She hit the ground as best she could.

Fire and smoke burst out of the doorway and filled the room, sending a hot shockwave over her. She shut her eyes as it singed her hair and skin.

"You idiot," she thought as she scrambled to her feet, *"you made a backdraft!"*

Andraste looked up and saw the fire climbing up the sides of the house. Hoping the surveillance office was somewhere safe, Andraste looked around for cover. This was the backyard, a fenced-in patch of mowed grass covered with toys and a paddling pool. Steeling herself, Andraste vaulted over the fence and started running.

Within moments, she knew she was being watched. She dashed to a nearby orchard and ducked beneath a tree as an enormous shot went out, splintering the upper half of a tree. Dodging the falling branches, she turned to see Listev silhouetted against the inferno of the house.

The sun was long gone, but there was enough ambient light to make out his bright eyes, his rough complexion, and, most prominent, his smile. His hair and beard swayed in the wind with the tips of the flames, and a floating cinder would pass by to lend further definition. To Andraste, he looked like death.

She turned her gun to him, and he responded in turn.

"I was beginning to lose hope, monster." He spoke in a soft tone that was somehow audible over the inferno. "But it's all fine now. At last, I can put an end to your scourge."

Heat from her own anger eclipsed that of the fire. "*My* scourge? You hunt me like an animal, destroy this farm, and call *me* a scourge?"

She could see his hand tense around his gun. "If you didn't force your way into these people's lives, none of this would have been necessary. You're so eager to abandon your own humanity, that you've completely abandoned your concern for actual humans."

A current of shock went down her back, leaving a hairline fracture in her resolve. "You don't know anything about me!"

Her grip tightened on the gun, and her finger ached to feel the trigger pull.

"I know everything I need to know. Everyone who has so much as looked at you does." He relaxed his grip and let his grin fall into a placid line. "Put down the gun before you hurt someone, monster. It doesn't even have any bullets left."

She pulled the trigger and heard a dry click. One of the windows on the house broke from the temperature shock when she felt something shatter inside her.

He scoffed, in a way that almost sounded like a chuckle.

"Ahh, Frederich. So trigger-happy, yet so irresponsible about reloading." He focused the gun on her. "Do you even remember who he was?"

"He was one of your lackeys," she said, putting up a weak facsimile of courage.

Listev shook his head. "32 years old, 159 cm tall, born in former German territory. Married his long-time girlfriend seven years ago, and their first baby is due in October." He looked at her with a frown. "Fred was no lackey. He was a strong soldier, a doting husband, and a good friend. And he died trying to get us to you."

Andraste threw her gun to the ground. "What are you playing at, Listev? You spend all this time and effort chasing me, and now that you have me this close, you stand there and lecture me?"

"What I'm playing at, monster, is that you need to know how important you are. The fate of more than just the Martyr's Army is in the balance here. And you can tip that balance in our favor."

"You can't be serious!" She gestured to the spreading flames. "Why should I do anything for you people after what you've done here?"

"Because we're not giving you a choice. You love to think you're helping people, don't you?" He tilted his head, speaking incredulously. "You're not helping anyone by continuing to serve those idiots back in London. We're the only ones who truly care about the fate of the world."

Andraste's fear gave way to indignation. "Bullshit!"

He gestured towards her with his gun. "Watch your tone. Don't tell me you never thought about it? Why Nathan Rowe allows these experiments?"

She calmed herself, and took her deep breaths. Breathe in, count to five, breathe out, count to five. "We're trying to win the war."

"And that's it?" Listev cocked his head. "It doesn't bother you that modern science has created a living, breathing replacement for humanity?"

She was lost. "'Replacement?' That's not the objective at all!"

"Of course not," he jeered, "it's to open more opportunities for people, right? Opportunities to oppress and subjugate." He narrowed his eyes. "Governments and economies only thrive by oppressing the weak. The advent of enhancements was bad enough, when the powerful and the greedy were able to decide who was weak and who was strong. But you," he said, savoring the emphasis on his words. "You have finally cemented it. Now, the government has rendered humanity meaningless. They can decide who gets the power and who doesn't. You're part of a plan far greater in scope than you realize."

Ideas of what to say came to her, but nothing solid. "Y-You have no idea what you're talking about!"

"Your doctors have shed a lot of light on the subject," he said, and his toothy smile returned. "Once you did your duty and returned to England, the FH Project would go into mass-production. Rowe wants fewer humans and more freaks like you. Next time you see Judicia, just ask her."

His words ran through her like bayonets.

The indignance returned. "Lies! All lies!"

He laughed. "Have I struck a nerve? Good. Perhaps now you finally understand."

Andraste responded by trying to enter his mind, the same way she went into the mind of Williams. She was making a dangerous gamble.

Through Listev's crosshairs, she saw herself, shuddering with narrowed pupils. There was a reaction from Listev, and she tried to replace his impetus with hers to jerk the gun out of the way.

Nothing.

"You thought I didn't anticipate this?" She heard Listev's thought, echoing in his mental space like a shockwave in a metal room. *"I've worked with plenty of druids. I know all the tricks."*

His focus was off the crosshairs for less than a second, long enough for her to create the illusion that she hadn't moved. When he returned, he saw Andraste sprinting at him, then felt a sharp tug as his gun was flung to the side.

Andraste had the gun by the barrel. His fear was like a cool breeze on a hot day. She swung it like a club and drove it into the ground, demolishing the gun as Listev jumped out of the way. The barrel warped, and the scope burst into shards of metal and glass.

"I'm not one of your goddamn druids."

"You bitch!" He went for the holster at his side. "People died getting that gun!" He swiped a huge pistol out and took aim.

Andraste dashed back behind the trees as the first few shots went out. Each bullet was closer than the last, and she knew Listev would have hit her if it weren't for the cover of the trees. She had to keep running.

"Andraste!" He shouted her name over the din of the bullets and fire. "You're only delaying the inevitable!" Every so often, she would look back and see him raising his gun. "I'll just keep hunting you, and you'll just keep running away!"

As he said that, Andraste froze. A clear stream of clarity fell upon her, and the haze of her agitation sloughed off.

"He's right," she thought.

Since she landed in the Outlands, running away was all she had done. She ran to this farm and let an innocent family fight for her. She ran at the first sign of gunfire after bailing out of the plane, and she was tempted to run away from life when looking down the trunk of the tree.

A core of ice grew inside her, and it froze her insides with stoic resolve. The mantra, still ambiguous, came back as forcefully and meaningfully as ever. *"Don't run away again."*

She turned on her heels and ran towards the sound of Listev's voice. He was about ten meters away, eyes wide at the sight of her turning around. She wove her way through the trees, ducking behind one and kicking off another as Listev struggled to hit her. When his gun stopped shooting, Andraste tackled him, swatting the gun out of his hand and pinning him to the ground. Pressing on both of his elbows, she stuck him into the sallow earth.

Her arms tingled with adrenaline, and she took big, heaving breaths as she stared him down.

He smirked. "Pinned by a wild animal. How ironic."

"Shut up!" She pressed harder and felt the tug of his shoulder as it was being pulled from the socket.

"What now, monster?" Listev kept smiling, struggling against the pain. "Are you going to kill me?"

Andraste softened her grip and caught her breath.

"Go ahead. Prove my point."

"What are you talking about?"

He laughed. "From what I heard, the FH project costed a few billion pounds. A few billion pounds dedicated to outclassing humanity. To creating a new means of subjugation that can't be fought against." He put his hands on her forearms. "What's a human before a god grown in a lab?"

The weight in her arms seemed to fade, and she felt herself drifting away from him. She didn't move, but her sense of orientation and bodily awareness was fading. As if time had slowed down, she was looking at a still image of her pinning Listev to the ground.

The sensation was lost when she felt a hard jab in her chest, right on the fractured rib. She came back to reality and saw that Listev had driven his knee right into her gauzed, bandaged wound. She collapsed, curling into a ball from the pain. Andraste looked at the hand that covered the wound and saw blood seeping out onto her fingers.

Listev got to his feet again, stretching his arms where Andraste had gripped them.

In the background of the flaming orchard, she heard the terrible screech again, that insidious herald of the Martyr's Army apocalypse. The sound deafened her as she staggered, forcing her eyes shut. It wrenched her insides to know that there was some force of death and destruction in the Outlands. With a cry so wretched, it couldn't have been anything else.

"You see it, don't you?" Listev cried. "The Fomorians live, and they're going mad! They need to be controlled!" He picked his gun up from the ground, barrel aimed at her. "I'm making this as clear as can be. Either you come as you are, or I'll drag you there hobbled and bleeding."

His hate was as palpable as the heat from the fire. She tried to take a breath, but the sting of her injury flushed her lungs. The list of options was running thin, and she was in too much pain to think clearly.

"Fine," she said, clutching her wounded side. "But how do I know y-you won't massacre the survivors here?" Shifting to rest her back against a tree, her only thought was to stall until the pain faded and a better idea came along.

"That depends on them. They fight us, we fight back. It's out of my hands." Listev shook his head as he spoke.

Hideous sentiments reminded her of a hideous experience, and a grim idea crossed her mind. Focusing on his mind, she recalled how she had handled Williams back in Hastings. Seeing the world through Listev's eyes, she focused on moving his wrist.

The gun pointed straight up. Despite his shock, he muscled through her control with ease.

"Don't even try." His tone was solid, but the anger was still there. He was a different beast than Williams, and demanded a more robust approach. Moving down from his wrist, Andraste focused on the elbow. Listev's arm bent accordingly.

With grace, he tossed the gun to his other hand and fired. He missed her leg by a centimeter.

"You're only delaying the inevitable!" Listev shook the invaded feeling out of his empty hand.

His resolve ran deep into his body like a steel rod. Andraste struggled to penetrate it the same way she did with Williams. His hands would be a struggle to manipulate, so she again moved down.

Listev tried to close the distance between them, but he turned. His leg twisted to the side, and his balance was gone. Even as she sat, Andraste felt the loss of equilibrium as Listev's world spun.

When he tried to catch himself, Andraste focused on his other ankle. His foot fell hard on the wrong side, with a subtle pop in his leg that shot a column of pain up his knee. Listev grunted in pain as he fell to his knees.

"You can't keep this up forever!" The man kept fumbling with his gun while Andraste leapt from his legs to his arms and back again. He moved like a puppet with distorted strings, fumbling with the gun over his twisting fingers. The longer he fought, the more control he kept over himself.

Andraste tried to stand up, supporting herself on the tree trunk, but the torsion between her and Listev's perceptions made it a struggle. Hesitant to kill him at the risk of making another martyr for the Army, she looked round for signs of the Holacksis. She trusted they knew a good hostage when they saw one.

Heavy gunfire and screams drew her attention. Beyond the orchard, the enormous truck from before was chasing down several Martyr's Army soldiers. Most of them fell to the heavy machine gun mounted on top, while another stumbled and was crushed beneath the tire.

"Hey!" Andraste called to it. Her voice was strained from the pain and disorientation. She shut her eyes to block out her own sight and render her proprioception only to controlling Listev. "Over here!" Waving her arms almost made Listev do the same.

The focused cold of fear ran through Listev. He fought even harder to turn the gun on her before they noticed.

Andraste saw his impetus and seized it. The sights wavered too close to her, but risked it all the same: with one more jerk of his wrist, she made the gun fire. A bullet dug into the ground, spewing loose dirt. Again and again, she did this, staccatos of gunfire filling the air until it finally clicked empty.

A light on the side of the truck swiveled over to them.

"Hands up!" Cried a man. Andraste opened her eyes, nearly blinded from the light, and held up her hands. She had released Listev, to her relief, but he did not oblige.

He dug into his jacket for another gun magazine, and two shots rang out from the truck. Both burrowed into his chest, knocking him onto his back. He was dead on impact.

It was too fast for her to comprehend, and Andraste stared at the body without blinking. She didn't believe he was stupid enough to turn a pistol on an armored car, and then she realized his intent- to make himself a Martyr. Let the retrievers of his corpse think that Andraste had killed him, and encourage the Army to bring out their full force against her.

Misha leaned out from the driver's side window, and she gestured towards the car.

"Andraste! Get in!"

Mindless, she broke into a sprint towards the car. The side door was pushed open by an unseen hand, and Andraste dove in. She took a seat next to several adults that she hadn't seen before, her small frame easily crammed into the space.

The door was slammed, and the truck sped down the road. In the rear-view mirror, Andraste could see the house engulfed in flames, collapsing in on itself and billowing more clouds of fire. Listev's body was far away, soon to be incinerated beyond recognition. A silent horror crept in as the car sped away, realizing that these people would be considered accomplices to the death of a general. Whatever the Army would bring upon her, they would bring upon these people.

28   Somewhere in the Outlands
09:20   June 8th, 2335

Judicia and Yousef had been moved around with bags on their heads ever since they were pulled off the plane. A full day had passed in near-total darkness, with only vague context clues and shoves in certain directions to guide them.

A handful of soldiers had gossiped about Listev, but there were no concrete stories about what had happened to Andraste. It felt like torture, kept alive in uncertainty and discomfort without being outright beaten or maimed.

After an eternity of darkness, the sacks were finally taken off their heads, and Yousef was almost blinded by the dim light in the room. Judicia, as always, remained obstinately quiet and unresponsive to them.

They were brought into a large concrete space lit up with fluorescent lights, casting shadows from the columns.

Straight ahead of them was a larger column with a giant door in the center. The soldiers escorting them forced them towards it, pushed ever forward by the spiked flash hiders digging into their backs. Yousef stifled a pained grunt. The space was unfamiliar, surprisingly pristine and well-maintained for a place supposedly deep in the heart of the Outlands.

"Welcome to the Outlands, doctors," a deep voice announced in clear English.

Both of them looked forward and felt their hearts plummet into their stomachs. Standing over two meters tall, with white hair combed towards the back of his head, stood a man in military fatigues.

"George Bashford," Yousef muttered, trembling.

"'General' Bashford if you don't mind." He walked towards them, taking ponderous footsteps that echoed throughout the entire space. "It's an honor to meet you two. Your work has put the Martyr's Army in a very unusual situation."

Yousef was doing his deep breathing technique. It wasn't helping.

"Y-You," he sputtered, "You're the one who defected."

Bashford looked over to him.

"You killed your whole unit and joined Sennec." Yousef started breathing harder.

Bashford pursed his lips and nodded. "Why, yes I did." He put his hands together and walked towards Yousef. "I trust you know the rest of the story, Dr. Makkareb?"

Yousef was rigid. He looked at Bashford in the eyes and gritted his teeth before saying, "The Martyr's Army destroyed my home."

"Hm," Bashford grunted. "That's right, you're from Cairo, aren't you? I hope you'll understand, Dr. Makkareb, that it was necessary at the time."

"You're a monster." Yousef took a hard breath.

"That's a pretty common version of it nowadays." He walked towards the other doctors. "I followed Sennec, he was callously murdered, and now the world doesn't stand a chance at surviving."

"Fucking absurd." Judicia spoke up. "If you won't tell us what's happening, then how do you expect anyone to believe that so many people are going to die?"

Bashford's expression hardened, but not to the point of anger, only attentive deference. He shook his head.

"You're both doctors; you should understand how serious a palpitating heart is." He spoke solemnly. "I know it sounds grandiose, but the Fomorian heart of the Outlands is palpitating. And if it isn't brought under control soon, the world will have a veritable heart attack."

"Are you serious?" Judicia shrugged her shoulders alongside this outburst. "It's the same lunacy as always! You people are mental, plain and simple!"

"Does the multitude of men and women carrying guns and laying waste to your countrymen mean nothing? Millions of us are putting our lives on the line to prepare for the return of the Fomorians."

"So, it's a spiritual crusade?" She looked up at him. "Just because so many people believe in something, that doesn't mean it's real. Do the ignorant masses prove that God exists because millions of them go to church?"

Bashford chuckled. "Touché, Bianca." He sat down in front of her, cross-legged. "But you're actually not far from the truth. In your insulation, Great Britain and the other states have become ignorant of the energy suffused throughout the Outlands. It doesn't have a face or a shape, but it still speaks. And with the death of Aaron Sennec, it began to scream in pain, like a man with a knife in his heart. To those who can see it, the entire world goes red." Bashford flexed his fingers. "Let me show you."

He pressed his hand onto Judicia's face. Her initial discomfort expanded into a wide-eyed gape at the ceiling. Her eyes were unfocused and twitching, as if she were in a dream. Always a soft breather, Yousef was shocked to hear her taking deep breaths. Sweat was accumulating on her brow.

"Judicia?" He turned to Bashford. "What are you doing to her?"

"Hold on, Yousef." Bashford kept looking at Judicia, his gaze intense. "I think she's starting to see."

The longer Bashford held his hand on Judicia, the more frantic she became. Her breaths became strangled gasps, she began to shake and twitch, and tears began to run alongside the sweat. It astonished Yousef to see a look of genuine terror on her face.

Bashford pressed into her harder. Her eyes went bloodshot, and her deep breaths grew into full-on screams. The fluorescent lights overhead began to buzz and flicker, and even the other Martyr's Army soldiers began to shake and hyperventilate.

"What's happening?" Yousef cried, fighting against his restraints.

"Do you see now?" Bashford roared at Judicia, tears running from his own bloodshot eyes around his clenched teeth. "Do you feel the pain suffused throughout the life in the Outlands? The cries of agony that can only signal the onset of some tremendous disaster?" Red streaks began to fall from both his and Judicia's eyes. "This is the world that we live in! This is the collective fear, suffering, and dread of the people that you so readily dismiss!" He grunted in exertion as Judicia continued to scream, and bloody tears streaked their faces.

Judicia tried to pry the arm away, but the strength was sapped from her hands. All she could do was paw at Bashford's intense grip, and he was undeterred.

The energy inside Yousef boiled over.

"Stop!" Yousef threw himself at Bashford, the grip on his restraints lost from the guard's weakened coordination. He barreled into Bashford's chest, knocking the arm away and sending them both onto the ground.

Yousef looked up at Bashford, and reflexively hurled himself away from the stern expression and bleeding eyes. It struck him all at once that he had just attacked the leader of the Martyr's Army. His mind left him as the impulse took hold, and now it returned to imagine the dreadful repercussions of what he had just done.

Yousef looked up and saw the barrel of a gun. For a millionth of a second, time stopped for him. His mind went to Andraste, Judicia, Yousef, and everyone else he worked with on the project. All the sleepless nights, all the doubts, and all the joys that swirled around in his head blurred these different faces together. The only thing that tied any of these images together was the fear that they were all about to fade.

A bullet went out, just missing Yousef's head. It pierced his ear instead, and he screamed. He twisted and spun in pain as blood trailed behind his head. Except for the one who had shot Yousef, the other guards went to steady him.

"No!" Bashford shot up, looking down at Yousef. He looked up at the guard with the discharged rifle, who seemed just as stunned at the whole affair. "You imbecile," Bashford fumed, dragging his sleeve across the blood and tears that streaked his face. "We need him!" He lunged at the soldier.

All the lights went dark for a split second, while another gunshot went out and there was a grisly crunch of bones and a body hitting the floor. When they came back on, the gun smoked, a bullet was lodged in one of the columns, and the guard was lying on the ground in a smashed heap. The body was mangled in impossible ways, his limbs bent where there were no joints, and his head slumped to the side as if it lacked bone. Blood was profuse, and the guard left a red pool around him almost as big as Yousef in the mere seconds that he had been killed.

Turning around, Bashford took a knee near them.

"I must apologize to both of you," he lamented. "I thought our soldiers were trained better than this. I brought you all here to make a point, and this is what happens."

Judicia was slow to respond, as she fought against the blood and tears. "What do you want from us?"

"In summary, answers." Bashford stood up. "Andraste is still out there, somewhere. She's a tough one-you all trained her well." He looked down at Yousef and sighed. "I know she has a great deal of trust for you both. I hope we can take advantage of that when we seize her."

"What the fuck do you mean, 'seize her'?" Yousef was struggling against the grip of the guards who tried to keep him from shaking out of his restraints. "What do you even want with her? What does it all mean?"

Bashford regarded him with furrowed brows. "Andraste could be essential to bringing the Fomorian Heart under control." He gestured for the guards to be at ease. "The energy of the Outlands is reacting to her, almost the same way it reacted to Sennec. It knows when there's someone strong enough to handle Fomorian energy."

"What are you on about?" Yousef began, invigorated by the guards off his shoulders. "Andraste is a poor victim of circumstance, not some 'chosen one' to further your insane-"

"Yousef." Judicia interrupted him, looking like her soul had been sucked from her body. Her eyes were wide, her jaw was slack, and the tears and blood kept falling. "Bashford is right. We need to get her here, as soon as possible."

29   Former Polish Territory
09:45   June 8th, 2335

Andraste looked around and saw the familiar rotation of adults sitting next to her. The car was still moving, and the light of the day had illuminated the foliage outside. She didn't remember falling asleep, only sitting in the car in a shocked daze as a pervasive sense of vitriol hung in the air. Apart from some whispers near the front and the occasional switching of drivers, they were all silent.

She looked around, groggy, trying to get a handle on the situation. The impetus to form words reached her mouth, but no words came. The dread mounted, as she inexorably felt responsible for the death and destruction at the farm. She shuddered to imagine what they would find if they returned- smoldering ruins, charred bodies of enemies and loved ones, verdant groves reduced to desolate ashes.

She was taken out of her thoughts when she saw Ivan, poking his head out from behind the seats.

"Miss Andy is awake!" He beamed as he said this, loud enough to shatter the oppressive atmosphere of the car. His volume and enthusiasm shook Andraste out of her grogginess.

The man sitting next to Andraste turned to the boy. "Ivan, indoor voice!" He said in an emphasized whisper.

Ivan shrunk at the admonishment but kept his eyes peeking over the chairs.

The adults all turned to Andraste. Misha leaned over from the passenger seat, as well. Their gazes seemed to pierce through her.

"Um," she said, voice trembling, "good morning."

The only response was the slowing of the truck and gradual grind to a halt.

The passenger-side door opened, and Misha turned to walk out. "Andraste, come with me, please."

"Yes, ma'am!" She pulled her seatbelt off and jumped out of the car.

Outside, the environment was much of the same. Giant trees and strange plants similar to what she saw when chased by Listev, but with defined, rough terrain for roads. The sun was out and lent new definition to the colors and shapes of the world around her. She looked out in all different directions, hoping she could find a source of the sense from before.

"Andraste." Misha spoke, loud but not harsh.

She was taken out of her trance at Misha's outburst. The elderly woman before her was short, but the weight of her conviction and emotion gave her a strong presence. Her eyes were red, and her arms were shaking at her sides.

Andraste didn't know what to say to this woman. Misha's home was destroyed, her husband was dead, and the rest of the family was on the run, all because Andraste had led a madman to them. Andraste couldn't begin to imagine what Misha felt.

Andraste tried to force something out, her voice creaky and weak. "Mrs. Holacksi, I-"

"Don't." Misha shut her eyes and turned away. "You did everything you could." Tears started to leak out from her squeezed lids. "We knew what we were getting into when we helped you. It's not your fault." She put her hand over her face to suppress her sobs. "Things would have been worse if you didn't fight back the way you did."

It was a brazen lie, trying to act so certain when she was going through a whirlwind of emotion and questions. Andraste hated to dismiss the woman, but it seemed worse to dismiss the guilt Andraste felt she deserved over the situation. Looking at this woman weep, trying to cope with the disaster while comforting the one responsible for it, she was rigid and shaking.

"Mom, get out of the way!" A voice from behind demanded their attention.

They looked to see a man, the one disciplining Ivan, controlling the heavy machine gun on top of the truck. The muzzle was directed at Andraste. His arms trembled as he gripped the handles.

"Don't waste your sentiments, you know this is all her fault!" He pulled back the charging handle, prepping the belt of heavy bullets to fire. "Fucking bitch, we should have just handed her over!"

Andraste still couldn't move. Resignation came over her, even as she recognized his voice from the shooting of Listev.

"Adam, what are you doing?" Misha's cries were jagged and strangled. "For the love of God, get down from there!"

"Mom, get out of the way!" He shouted at her, tightening his grip. "If we keep her around, we'll only have more problems!"

Misha stood in front of Andraste, not meeting her full height.

"Adam, please!" She was sobbing even more. "Let the killing stop!"

Andraste noticed Adam's resemblance to Sergei. He had the same heavy brow and intensity in his eyes. Beneath that searing anger, she also detected a deep sadness. To be expected, he was devastated. Despite Misha's protests, this man's feelings seemed justified to Andraste. Between these two people, she was frozen in place.

"Look at us! We're in the middle of Martyr's Army territory, hot off the heels of a fucking massacre! The killing won't stop! The killing won't ever stop!" He aimed the gun upwards, towards Andraste's head. "But if we kill her now, maybe there won't be as much killing later. Now, get out of the way!"

The other adults had filed out of the car, watching Adam and Misha scream at each other as Andraste stood still.

Everything had gone blank for her. She wasn't thinking, she wasn't seeing, and she wasn't hearing. Deafened and shocked into stillness, her mind went somewhere else to fill the space.

She was overcome with heat. She saw a red glare in a man's eyes, and the glare of her own eyes reflected in the scope of a rifle. Andraste was seeing Listev again, staring her down with his gun. She couldn't move. It was the same vista from before, but hazier, with soft, sticky earth that crept up her arms and trapped her in place. Listev's gun didn't tremble or change focus as it did during their conversation.

Like the feeling she had with Adam and the turret on the truck, the sight didn't frighten her. There was no sound, and no voices arguing over what to do with her. The only audible input was the clicking metal from Listev's gun as he pulled tighter on the trigger. At the end of the assembly came the bullet, and she heard the ignition go off as the bullet exploded out of the chamber.

She shut her eyes and waited for the hot lead to burrow into her skull. The sound of the ignition hung in the air, echoing off whatever space she was trapped in, but the bullet never reached her. Stuck and confused in this strange memory, she was compelled to open her eyes when a familiar voice joined the fray.

"Daddy, no!"

Andraste was shocked back into reality when she heard another gunshot.

Smoke rose from the barrel of the turret's gun, tilted upward as a pair of small hands restrained it. Adam was supporting himself on the rails as he stared in horror. Ivan had forced the gun out of the way as it fired. He shrieked and sobbed as he gripped his right hand with two fingers shot off.

One of the women scrambled up the side of the car and grabbed Ivan, looking at Adam with a piercing stare. She hugged Ivan tightly while extracting some tools from a first aid kit.

Everyone else had gone silent. They looked at the man who fired the gun, the child screaming in pain, and then at the smoldering, steaming blood on the hot gun barrel. As this new situation arose and drew everyone's attention, they seemed to forget about Andraste.

She couldn't look away from Ivan, who clenched his teeth as his mother wrapped his hand in bandages. He was inconsolable, no matter how his mother comforted him. Her guilt grew as she looked at the weeping boy.

"Look at this, Adam." Misha spoke up at last. "Is this Andraste's fault, too?" Her voice was hoarse as she choked back bitter sobs.

Adam bent over the side of the rails. He was pale, and his knuckles were white.

His voice trembled as he spoke. "Sasha, I didn't-"

"Shut up!" The woman barked at him, holding Ivan close to her. "You could have killed him!"

Finally, Andraste found the ability to speak.

"I- I'm sorr-"

"Andraste, no." Misha intervened, putting a hand on her shoulder. "This isn't your fault."

Adam got down from the turret, walking around in a shocked daze before he crumpled over and vomited. The others turned to Andraste, carrying a different feel with them. What was once intense and hostile had become calm and inviting.

Sometime later, Ivan had finally stopped screaming, though his face was still warped with pain.

"Miss Andy," he began, struggling to keep his voice coherent, "I don't wanna see anything bad happen to you!"

His mother spoke up, as well. "Neither do I."

Andraste felt some guilt slip away, but it still lingered. "I owe all of you so much," she said.

"We owe you, Andraste." Misha said with a gentle smile. "It's about time we stood up to the Martyr's Army. And, for what it's worth, you did some amazing things back there."

Some time passed as they brought out the medical supplies. In rapid succession, they went through bandages, stitches, and a cornucopia of painkillers. After some time, Ivan's shrieks were stilled.

Sasha, his canny-looking mother, was adept at handling both the medical supplies and her child. "There's my little hero," she said after Ivan had toughed out the on-the-fly procedure. She eventually gestured to Andraste, who had helped dig through all the equipment.. "Miss Andy's like a superhero, isn't she?"

Ivan managed a weak smile when she said that. "Y-yeah!" The tears still fell, but his smile was sincere.

Andraste was surprised but didn't let it show. "Thank you," she said, not letting their sentiments stick. She wanted to change the subject. "But, where do we go from here?"

"Well, we can't stay in the Outlands any longer," Misha said, "so our best bet is going to try and get smuggled out."

Andraste lit up. "You're going to try and leave?"

Misha turned to the side, pensive. "We've made a handful of connections through our work, so hopefully we can arrange something to get us out of here."

"Maybe I could get you all to England!" Andraste exclaimed.

Everyone turned to Andraste when she said this.

"Mr. Rowe is a huge supporter of helping Outlander refugees! I'm sure I could talk to someone so you're all-"

"You're not talking to anyone, Andraste." Misha spoke up, pulling Andraste to the side. "You're public enemy number one. The bounty on your head is ten times anything that we could offer."

Andraste's heart sank.

"Anyone who catches a glimpse of you will turn you right over to the Army. If you want to help us so badly, then please, PLEASE, stay out of sight."

"B-but, we could get a good doctor for Ivan's hand! If we found a British outpost, we could-"

"Andraste, please!" Misha grabbed her by the shoulders. "We can't take any risks! I'm glad you want to help us, but any place a near a super-state outpost is a war zone. We couldn't possibly risk that."

All of Andraste's resolve was flushed out. She was coming up with solution after solution, but Misha shut her down at each turn.

"There's too much at stake. We need to do this as carefully as we can."

Andraste closed her eyes and sighed. "Yes, ma'am. I-I'll keep a low profile."

Misha sighed. "Thank you."

One of the other adults spoke up. "Mom, we can't stay here! The Army could have heard that gunshot!"

The others perked up and started making for the truck. Misha nodded, then gestured for Andraste to follow them. Sighing, she obliged.

Ivan was clearly still in pain. Andraste saw him contorted in his mother's arms before she sat down herself. His father was in the back seat, head still hung in his hands.

She knew the others were right. It wasn't her fault that Ivan had been shot, but she still couldn't move past the feeling that she had started it all. All these dreadful circumstances arose because of her, yet all the people affected by it were telling her not to feel bad. The smell of blood hung in the air, and his occasional whimper shook her to her core.

She looked at Sasha. "W-will he," she trailed off.

Andraste's voice was weak and quiet, but still enough to get attention.

"Will he be okay?" Andraste sounded like she was whimpering herself.

Sasha shut her eyes, holding Ivan close.

"I-I," she began, clenching her teeth the same way as Ivan, "I know he will." A tear ran down her cheek.

That was a lie.

Hot cascades of embarrassment flushed Andraste. She wasn't even sure why she asked that question.

"How on earth would she know that, you idiot?" Andraste's thoughts were quick to take advantage of the situation. *"These people are already terrified, don't open your fat mouth and make things worse for no reason!"*

The engine roared to life again, and the truck was back on the road. The monstrous vehicle was rumbling through the wilderness again, and the familiar vista of trees and greenery started speeding by.

Andraste thought back on what Ivan said when they were trying to reassure her. Comparing her to that superhero was flattering, sure, and done only with the best intentions, but the word "superhero" left a strange impression on Andraste. Maybe in her most naïve of visions for the future, she saw herself as something like a superhero, but she stopped when she remembered why she applied for the FH Project in the first place: to run away. She didn't care about other people then, only herself.

Her vision glazed over, and her focus was taken off the forest. She saw her own reflection in the window, and was confused by what she saw.

Her mind was still on "superhero." The implications of it, the sound of it, and all the ways it had been defined and re-defined in the movies were still picking away at her.

"What am I, if I'm not a superhero?"

As she thought on this, she went back into her backpack and pulled out the wind-up toy she made. It was still in its box, unscathed by the brutalities of the Outlands. This seemed indicative of something. As always, she tried to divorce herself from the "old soldier" who first applied for the project. She was the one who wanted to run away, not Andraste.

Maybe "superhero" was over-romanticizing her role, but, if nothing else, it was something to aspire to. She was reminded of all the things she had done: saved Judicia from Williams, she had stopped the bombing in the Shard, and she had stopped the Martyr's Army from murdering the Holacksi family. There wasn't anything she could do about the situation they were in right now, and instead of helpless, she felt accepting of that fact. She sighed and allowed this small light of self-kindness to shine on her, letting it abate all the other dreadful feelings she had gone through that day.

She looked out the window again. She knew this feeling would fade and she would be thrown headlong into another conflict, but she was determined to hang onto the experience as much as she could. Calm but wary, she gazed at the rolling landscape and let the sense of well-being pervade. She wondered what Yousef or Quadriyyah would think of her sentiments as she scanned the forest.

30 Former Polish Territory
12:35   June 8th, 2335

A small clearing in the woods let the Holacksi family take a much-needed break from the car. They set up some folding chairs when they were done stretching their legs, and lunch was brought out.

Andraste took her daily ration earlier, so she had to sit out of the meal. She didn't feel hungry, but she couldn't help but look at them as they ate. Someone with a finer palate had managed to swipe some prime cuts of cured meat before they evacuated, complemented with jars of pickled onions, radishes, and fennel.

Andraste's metal mask kept her from eating anything outside of her nutritional regiment, which she understood was important, but knowing that she could never sit down to another regular meal again was nonetheless troubling. Andraste was not physically capable of sitting down with someone for afternoon tea, and that bothered her.

"Miss Andy?" Ivan hobbled over to her on his numb and uncoordinated feet, his face still drooping from the residual exhaustion of the painkillers.

She was stirred from her pondering. "Hello, Ivan," she said, trying to put her grief away.

"Did you want any?" He slurred his words as he swayed from side to side.

Ivan's trembling hand was squeezing an amalgam of meat, cheese, and pickled vegetables between two crumbling pieces of bread.

Her grief came back. "Oh, um," she strained to find the right words. "N-no, no thank you; I think you need that more than me."

"Naaah, I'm okay!" He waved his bandaged hand around to dismiss the idea, putting on the biggest smile he had to offer. "It's not fair that you don't get any- it's really good! Uncle Alex makes the onions better and better each time!"

He held it closer until it almost brushed her face, and she only felt worse. She was enticed by the smell of the vinegar and spices in the onions.

"Ivan, I really do appreciate it, but I actually can't."

"Ohhhhhh," he said in a long draw. "Do you have an allergy?"

"Wha- no, my mask doesn't-"

"Granny? Do we have any hypoalla- um, hyperall- anything that Miss Andy's not allergic to?"

Before she could respond, he was teetering his way back to Misha.

She sighed, unsure if the sadness or the flattery was stronger. Although the sandwich was crushed in a child's hand, Andraste would have been delighted to take it.

"He's a wounded child, and you're a superhuman," she thought in a familiar reprimanding tone. *"They're already taking all these risks to protect you, and now you*

want their food? How much more can you demand of them?"

She could hear the discussion of Misha and Ivan in the distance, as well as the strain of her futile attempts at explaining Andraste's condition to a small, heavily medicated child. The grandmother tried to keep her voice steady as Ivan's slurring voice asked more questions and raised more objections.

"Don't worry, Andraste," a familiar voice called out. "They're happy to help, remember?"

She spun around in her chair so fast she nearly twisted herself out of it.

"Spirit!" She almost spoke, but feared of what the family would say. *"Where have you been?"*

Andraste knew how much the entity liked to interject when she was doubting herself or wondering what was going to happen next, and looking back on the past few hours, its absence was conspicuous. It didn't even show up in one of her dreams.

She stood up and looked out into the wilds, looking at the trunks and branches reaching ever upward and outward. It reminded her of the spirit comparing these offshoots to the dendrites of a neuron.

"Spirit?" She called out again in her mind, feeling the signal echo and rebound off of the world around her, sound waves hitting and curling around the extending branches and tree trunks.

"Try not to-" The Spirit began, its voice full of garble, "about th-them."

"What's happening to you?"

"S-s-something," the spirit struggled to say. "Some-something big is al- here."

Andraste got to her feet. A chill ran down her spine. "Run."

"What? What's going on?" The strain on the spirit's voice warranted a sense of urgency.

"You- get away-" the spirit's voice kept flickering in and out, growing less comprehensible with each word. "They're- coming- Army-"

Following the Spirit's mention of "Army," she saw a clear vision of a squadron of helicopters hovering over the trees, all emblazoned with the Martyr's Army sigil. A woman was sitting next to the pilot of the one in front, looking ahead in a way like she was staring at Andraste.

"I see you." The vision spoke to her before it vanished.

Andraste came into reality with a violent jerk of her head. She staggered and clasped her temples, tamping down the sense of pressure in her head.

"Hey, Andraste!" Sasha rushed over to her, catching Andraste before she fell over. "What's going on? Are you okay?"

As Andraste looked up at Sasha, with a gentle push to get the unfamiliar touch off her, she gained an awareness of a powerful presence appearing on the horizon. The hostility it gave off stung like an approaching inferno.

"We need to leave!" Andraste stood straight up and spoke loud enough to address everyone in the camp.

"What are you talking about?" Misha got up from her chair.

"Please, we need to get out of here! Th-they have helicopters!"

The others all stopped and looked at her in quiet incredulity.

"Does this mean you don't want your sandwich?" Ivan said, holding up another mangled bundle of meat and bread.

A growing sound diminished the rustling of leaves in the wind. A long way off, but unmistakable: the chopping of helicopter rotors through the air. Andraste took a sharp breath, which ran cold down her insides. She felt a palpable mist of terror fall over the area as the others heard it.

"We need to go!" Misha called out, and everyone rushed to gather things.

They picked up tools, food, children, and anything else they could get their hands on. Most of the camp was left behind with the burgeoning sound of the rotors, and the truck was almost running before everyone got aboard. Within seconds, the tires ripped through dirt and loose rocks before tearing down the road.

Desperate parents tried to quiet their crying children, and the sense of raw, inarticulate despair they radiated almost moved Andraste to tears.

"Andraste, how did you know they were coming?" Misha asked as she struggled to stay still in the car.

"I-I heard the Spirit of the Outlands, and it told me to run; then I saw the helicopters! Martyr's Army sigil and everything!"

"Son of a bitch!" Adam spoke up as he fought against the steering wheel. "How did they find us so damn fast?"

Andraste remembered the woman in the helicopter, and that lacerating stare. Andraste wasn't imaging that the woman was looking at her, she knew that she was being stared at.

"I think they're chasing after me," Andraste said, almost inaudible.

"What else is new?" Adam replied.

"No, I mean they must be tracking me! They must have a powerful druid with them or something!"

Adam didn't have a response to that. There was a chill in the car.

"Andraste," Misha began, "when you had your vision, what did you see? Was there a woman among them?"

Swallowing whatever was caught in her throat, Andraste spoke in dread of what Misha would say. "Yes. A woman with wavy red hair."

"What?" Adam roared, his voice peaking. "Are you saying that General fucking Scarlet is after us?"

"The radar is picking something up," said one of the other male adults. "It looks like," he paused, voice shaking. "It looks like five helicopters, less than ten kilometers to the southwest."

"Shit!" Adam said, pounding a fist on the dashboard. "We're so close to the border! They'll be right on top of us!"

"The border- between Poland and Germany?"

A thought came to Andraste then. Every rational part of her brain and body told her not to act on it, but she decided not to listen.

"We need someone on the gun! Keep them off us!" Adam kept yelling while wrestling with the controls of the car.

"I got it!" Andraste spoke up and went for the hatch before anyone else could respond.

Despite vocal protests from the rest of the passengers, Andraste clambered through the sunroof and met the oncoming wind head-on. She did her best to steady herself as the unsteady road bounced the car along. She turned to the back and made her way towards the tremendous gun mounted to a homemade stand, fumbling with her footing a few times before finally standing up and getting a grip on the handles.

There were safety straps on the guard rails around the turret, but she wouldn't use them. She looked back and forth between the gun's sights and the road ahead as they went along.

The line of trees was becoming thinner and less dense the further they went, and she saw the telltale specks of approaching aircraft in the distance, in the exact same model and formation she saw in her vision. She couldn't see General Scarlet yet, but Andraste knew she was there.

Approaching up ahead was a bridge, exactly what Andraste was hoping for. There was a makeshift border control center bearing the Martyr's Army sigil, and they weren't expecting a gigantic truck covered in guns and refugees to come speeding along the road. The guns in front started blasting while someone else leaned out a window and started going after stragglers with a carbine.

The person with the carbine ducked back inside, and Andraste heard her say, "the bastards are on us!"

Close enough to fit within her sights, Andraste started to shoot. The helicopters swayed to the sides as the bullets came in, dodging the volley. They dispersed and started coming in at more angles. The bridge was getting closer.

"You are harboring a dangerous and highly wanted war criminal," a voice said from nowhere. *"Surrender her immediately and you will be granted leniency."*

It wasn't directed at Andraste, it was like a loudspeaker. Everyone in the vehicle was being addressed.

"I'm not the only one who heard that, right?" She heard Adam say.

From the side of the road, they heard a roar and felt an uneasy rumble. Trees were being toppled in the same direction as the roar, and the same creature bellowed over a chorus of splintering wood.

A bush was ripped out of the earth as a bear the size of their car tore its way towards them. It was the same as the taxidermy monstrosity that was in the Holacksi's trophy room.

"Oh, fuck!" Cried the person with a carbine as they spun to shoot it.

The bear tried to get in a swipe, not at the car but at Andraste. She leaned back as the car swerved to the side, nearly throwing her out. The guard rails were almost bent from her exertion.

It kept roaring as their marksman put bullets into it. The charging didn't stop, and it didn't flinch from any of the shots. The bear didn't even look at the one shooting it. Andraste could tell it was glaring at her. It roared again, natural voice warped and distorted from the same Fomorian influence that turned its fur into long segments of brown exoskeleton.

As Andraste mounted the gun again, the bear moved away, as if anticipating it. It backed away from the truck, narrowing its gaze. She began to fire, and the bear leapt out of the way. Even when Andraste looked back down the sights, the bear leapt to the other side of the road. When she swiveled it around to hit it, the bear dodged again. It leapt back and forth to anticipate the cumbersome swivel of the gun, all while keeping Andraste in its sights.

Overhead, the helicopters closed in. The bear seemed to move in formation with the craft, which staggered Andraste to see.

"Aim for the choppers!" Adam cried. "One of them must have the druid controlling it!"

They were on the bridge now. The helicopters bored down, and the bear was still going steady. Andraste decided it was time to make her exit. She looked down and saw the Oder river had swelled into rapids. It was perfect.

"I'm sorry, everyone," Andraste said as loud as she could. "They're not after you, they're after me. Get to Germany and get out of here. Thank you for all the help you've given me."

She took her hands off the trigger. She got her footing on one of the guard rails, and kicked off, clearing the bridge's sides. She braced herself to hit the water, as well as whatever else the rapids would throw at her.

    Mentally and vocally, she heard the others in the car cry out as she fell. She shut her eyes and tried to put their horrified faces out of her mind, but the images were deeply etched. Even the bear turned to witness this. Andraste only folded her arms and straightened her legs as the rapids approached, her grasp firm around the straps of her backpack. Right before the terrible sense of free fall set in, she felt her feet strike the water, and everything went black as the current caught her.

31 Former Polish Territory
17:07   June 8th, 2335

The Oder River slowed to a picturesque, meandering waterway as it went further along the Polish border. It offered a welcoming, cool respite from the summer heat, even along the borders of the densest woodlands.

Washed up against the roots of an enormous tree, Andraste felt herself come to. The daylight was dredging her up from the deepest depths of unconsciousness, and a labored awakening came over her.

Her eyes were filled with haze and her head was full of fog. Nothing coalesced except a few spots of light from between branches. She was half-submerged in the water and limp against the roots, arms and legs splayed haphazardly atop the wood. Nothing looked broken, but she couldn't relax yet. She tried to move a limb- any limb- and found them stiff, stuck to the roots as if part of them. All she could do was sigh.

She heard movement in response to her sigh, and it gave her enough adrenaline to turn to the source. Through the blur of her eyes, she saw a figure. Dark brown and white, with a cream-colored tangle atop its head. Its bright blue eyes gleaming in the shadows roused her attention the most. She was able to make a slow lurch away from it, but she was as clumsy and inept as she expected. Even as she squinted her eyes to force some clarity from them, the figure didn't move.

The figure solidified into an approximation of a deer. The colors of the fur on its cervine countenance were fitting, and the tangle above its head, though staggering in its complexity, was indeed a pair of antlers. Like a Celtic knot, the intricacy was staggering, even beautiful. Further clarity showed it didn't have fur as much as armor. Not unlike Andraste's own exoskeleton, the deer bore layered scales of hardened material, from its legs and torso to its face. The armor seemed to be fighting for space with its fur.

The deer was fixed on her, statuesque in its focus, while she shivered and struggled to breathe. No words passed between them, but Andraste felt the sense of communication all the same. She had only seen pictures of the creatures that roamed the Outlands, and to be this close to one was a true interaction. She wondered what the deer was thinking as it stared at her, its stillness broken only by a delicate twitch of its ear. It seemed so much like her, with its armored hide and bizarre eyes. Two creatures, both alike in alien stature, neither one threatened by the oddness of the other.

A soft voice filled the air.

"I'm sorry," it began.

Andraste looked up. The deer was still.

"I can't stick around for this one," it said again. "Something about her, about this Scarlet- she's diminishing me." Andraste recognized it this time as the Spirit. "I think-

I think she might have some answers. I'll try to be back soon."

As it finished speaking, the blue glow faded from the eyes of the deer. It looked to the side, alerted, before turning around and leaping away.

"Spirit, wait!" She reached out to it as it ran off, wanting the strange sense of kinship to remain. "Don't go," she said in weak protest. Her arm lost its tension and she fell forward, remembering how exhausted she was.

Several mental auras began to appear on the horizon, and they inspired a sense of urgency that lifted her out of her stupor. Somewhere in the background, there was that red curtain of dread. She clambered to her feet and tried to get a sense of those approaching, but they were too far off for any concrete details to arise.

Stumbling over the roots, she was relieved to find flat ground, and started sprinting along the edge of the river. She looked out and saw that the river had dramatically widened from the narrow rapids that she jumped into, and assumed- or rather, had such an intense hope that it felt like an assumption- that the bridge was far behind her. She tried to find comfort in her intended goal that the Army was harrying her instead of the Holacksi family, but that didn't change the fact that they were behind her.

The mental auras on the horizon were getting closer, but still unreadable. She was standing prone and unprotected; this situation usually warranted fear, but she wasn't having it. The first pang of worry and panic turned into resolve and anger. She was tired of running, tired of being the coward. Andraste had fought and won before, and she was in the mood to do it again. She let her indignity fuel her fighting spirit.

A hand clapped on her shoulder from behind.

"Hello," said a voice.

Andraste spun around, trying to grab the wrist, but found herself gripped. The woman with curly red hair was holding her steady. Despite Andraste's strength, the woman didn't move, and stared at her with a flat expression. Her eyes didn't blink, and the pupils didn't even twitch.

"Don't resist," she said with a voice as stoic as black glass.

Twisting to throw her elbow at Scarlet's arm, the woman seamlessly dodged and grabbed Andraste's other shoulder. Ducking, Andraste tried to sweep Scarlet's legs, but she leapt over Andraste, supporting herself on the same shoulder. The entire time, just like the bear from the bridge, Scarlet never broke her gaze on Andraste.

Andraste rolled forward before Scarlet could land. She went in for a punch, which Scarlet mechanically deflected. Andraste's elbow was met with another block, and a feint leading to a knee was easily dodged. The general was a machine of iron resolve and fortitude made to perfectly counter or dodge everything Andraste learned in self-defense training. The whole time, Scarlet didn't so much as blink, moving with inhuman precision and poise.

"This is a waste of time," Scarlet said, grabbing Andraste's wrist. She flung Andraste over herself, smacking her on the ground like a ragdoll. With her breath knocked out of her, it was simple to put Andraste in a steely headlock.

Andraste had no information on this woman. There was no mental energy to detect: no heat from excitement, cold from focus, and not even the string of incoherent thoughts of the normal person. Scarlet was hollow.

"Wh-what are you?" Andraste managed, struggling to breathe properly.

"Never mind that," Scarlet said as she kept an unflinching grip on Andraste. "You're coming with us, monster."

Andraste, fueled by a surge of indignity, tried to dive into Scarlet's mind. If the minds of other people were like oceans of discordant thoughts and sensations, then Scarlet's was a still lake. The sight of Andraste caught in her grasp was uninterrupted, as if she knew and could anticipate everything in the world around her. For a moment, Andraste thought Scarlet's vision was clearer than her own.

"Don't waste your time," Scarlet said aloud.

"Fine," Andraste said aloud, imagining her hands behind her back.

"Excellent," Scarlet said as one of her hands loosened.

This gave Andraste enough of a chance, so she twisted around and tried to shove Scarlet away, only to shove herself away more. Regardless, Andraste had escaped and was back in her fighting stance. Scarlet only folded her arms.

"What do you want, applause?" She shrugged. "You're only delaying the inevitable, monster."

"Stop calling me that!" Andraste roared. "I'm not going anywhere with you!"

"Yes, you are. Sooner or later, you'll realize it's for your own good. Give yourself up quietly, and things will be so much easier for you."

"Why the hell would I do that?" Andraste fell back on her anger to hide her fear. "Why would I cooperate with you when you won't even call me by my name?"

"Fine, I'll call you by your name." Scarlet shrugged, her voice changing tone for the first time. "It's for your own good," she paused, "Private Claire."

As a reflex, Andraste took in a sharp breath. She couldn't place its origin, but a surge of numbing panic came over Andraste when she heard that name. Her hands went slack and she started to shake.

"Wh-What did you say?" Andraste finally said.

"You heard me," Scarlet said, head cocked. "Claire. Claire Dillon."

Andraste's shaking intensified, and her breaths became agonized gasps. "What are you doing to me?" Her knees buckled as her legs went numb.

"I'm not doing anything. I'm just using your real name, like you asked." She took a single step closer, and it shook the ground beneath Andraste.

Andraste's hands shot towards her shoulders and she took deep, jagged breaths. She didn't even hear the rest of what Scarlet had said.

Seeing this, Scarlet got on her knees and looked Andraste in the eyes. "This is only part of the truth you've been evading for so long."

Andraste couldn't make anything of what was coming over her. The name "Claire Dillon" meant something to her, but she couldn't tell where that meaning came from. Whether it was self-delusion or memory repression to such an incredible extent that the name had been forgotten, Andraste knew the awakening of these memories would be a torturous experience. Yousef and the abandoned memory therapy came to her mind.

"I know you've been trying to eliminate your past." She reached down and lifted Andraste's face up by the chin. "If you keep fighting us like this, then I will have no choice but to remind you of everything."

Andrate processed that much. A surge of anger rose within her, and she lashed out at Scarlet. She swung her fist with such force, she felt the torsion throughout her whole body.

Scarlet held up her palm and caught Andraste's hand. She didn't so much as twitch from the force.

As she turned, she saw the palm of Scarlet's hand strike her face.

Scarlet didn't look strong, nor was she pushing hard enough to make an impactful blow, but Andraste felt herself being thrown back, tumbling over herself as she skidded across the ground. The shock wasn't to her face as much as it was to the threads of her innermost being tying everything together.

Through blurry, dazed eyes, Andraste got her bearings in the field of neurons cultivated by the Spirit. Glowing blue lines crisscrossed the ground, creating an infinite plane of synapses and cell bodies. There was red on the horizon. Leading up from the ground, she saw another figure: Scarlet, appearing as herself. No neurons touched her.

"I know this raises more questions. But this isn't the time to answer them."

Andraste scrambled to her feet, trying to get on Scarlet's level. She dashed at her, but Scarlet held up a hand, sending a pulse of energy that resisted Andraste's movement. She was trapped in the suspended animation.

"Stay calm and watch."

As she hung in the air, the darkness behind Scarlet started peeling back. A blue sky and rolling grass hills were hidden behind the blackness.

Andraste was able to touch down, though she felt as if she were floating in a dream. Gravity had left her, and any of her attempts to move were suppressed by the density of the surrounding images.

The landscape vanished, colors melting together like clouds of ink before re-shaping and forming new vistas of color and texture. As the images came together, Andraste felt a pulling sensation in her head. It was as though someone had taken hold of her gray matter and was unraveling the threads of her mind.

With a faded echo, a bright light and the scream of an infant came into view.

"Your first breath," Scarlet's voice said in a cadence of mild awe.

"Impossible," Andraste wheezed, near-paralyzed at the sight and sensation. "How could I remember this?"

"We hide a lot of things, Andraste. Especially from ourselves."

"Vanessa, it's a girl!" A male voice cried in joy.

With the impact of a lightning bolt, Andraste felt a shock to her system when she heard the voice.

Tears waterfalled from Andraste's eyes. "Dad?"

The scene faded again, and it formed a complex painting of gears, steel, and metal. The smell of oil was dense in the air.

Andraste saw it and recognized the patterns on the gears and moving parts. It was all the same kind that she visualized when she had to calm herself down.

A pair of young, scarred hands came into view, putting machine-cut pieces together with springs, latches, and screws. She brought her heavy arms to her shoulders, feeling exposed at the sight of it all. Gripping her shoulders hard, she saw the hands work to build the receiver on a gun; the first thing that she saw when she started visualizing the machine parts.

"Even as a child, you were part of the British war machine. You volunteered as soon as you were able."

Just as Andraste was getting engaged with the machine, bringing even the smallest comfort in this situation, Scarlet's fingers clicked again and the picture dissolved.

The sterile white glow of fluorescent lights gave definition to a paneled ceiling and beige walls. The same hands from before, roughened from the factory days, held a pen, filling out information on an application. At the top, the words "PRELIMINARY DOCUMENTATION- U.K. ARMED FORCES" were in block letters. At the bottom, the busy hands filled boxes, answered "yes" or "no," and put down signatures.

A few dotted lines for "parents" appeared. Paul and Vanessa Dillon, both deceased.

"A soldier with nothing to lose can be a powerful thing," Scarlet said with a hint of lamentation.

It started to come back to Andraste. Her mother died when she was a toddler, and the mere notion of her father hurt. She remembered his love, but not his face. Tears ran down Andraste's face without restraint.

The vista faded again, and Scarlet left the colors suspended for a few moments before continuing. "You remember that mantra of yours? 'Don't run away again'?"

The last fragment of awareness that Andraste had went into shock when she heard Scarlet say that. She jerked her head up at the sound.

"Now, let me offer you an explanation for that." The images began to coalesce again as she held her fingers together for another snap.

"How are you-"

"Even in your own head, you can't hide." Scarlet snapped her fingers.

The mist settled into a scene of the Outlands, with the giant trees and thick foliage. It was all familiar, but Andraste waited with bated breath to see the context of it all. Columns of sunlight came out through the canopy, highlighting a route forward as the scene moved along.

Next to coalesce was the tip of an assault rifle's barrel, flash hider swaying in rhythm to the person's footsteps. A pair of familiar hands were wrapped in forest-camouflage gloves, arms covered in the same-patterned sleeves of a jacket at least one size too big. The longer Andraste looked, the more acutely she felt the icy sting of a shocking realization.

"Your first deployment," Scarlet said in a whisper.

For a time, the memory walked along with a group of other soldiers, the rest of them all shooting her second glances, finding issue with the young-faced person following them. Even as she kept her hands in proper position for handling the weapon, they shook and fidgeted.

This continued for a time longer than Andraste could tolerate. The ineffable feeling of dreadful anticipation was overbearing, and the memory of her seemed to feel the same way. Andraste scanned the scene for any sign of danger, any warning sign, while the lost memory of her did the same. Something horrible was going to happen, and they both wished it would hurry and happen.

Torrents of lead and gunfire answered her plea. The soldiers who weren't killed in the ambush dashed behind trees and other bits of cover, while the sounds of returning fire eclipsed orders from the unit leader. Her memory only hid against the back of the tree, not moving and clasping her rifle hard against her chest.

"What are you doing?" Andraste wondered, seeing this again. *"Turn around, fight,"* as if she could influence the memory.

"Dillon!" The commander barked at her from behind a rock outcrop, bullets blasting shards of stone and dust away. "Stay with us! Return fire!"

As she got closer to her squadmate landing shots on the enemy, a bullet ripped through the area and burst the man's head. As he fell, blood and brain matter filling the air, more shots splintered the tree bark in pursuit of Claire. Her arms trembled with electric instability.

"Dillon! Return fire!"

She couldn't hold the gun steady, and she couldn't see straight. Everything was a blur of reds, greens, and grays.

"God dammit, Dillon!"

Andraste realized what was coming next. From the thunderstorm of panic that the soldier felt, she knew what would happen, but she was hoping, with more fervent desperation than ever before, that she was wrong.

"No," she said, in a staggered whisper. "No!"

The soldier disobeyed. Turning away from the commander, she tossed her rifle aside and started sprinting into the greenery and fire of the wilds. Adrenaline carried her far and fast, and the commander's voice was almost lost before his voice joined a chorus of other dying soldiers. Her vision was only clear enough for her to dodge the trees and obvious traps laid out by the Army.

Andraste grabbed her temples, mind ravaged by horror and disbelief. The soldier, her old self, kept running. She wanted to scream until her voice was destroyed, to beat her hands on the ground until they drew blood and exposed the bone, but there was nothing. Her tears were dry, and her body had gone stiff. She could only watch the soldier running, running, and running in a paralyzed stupor.

Andraste tried to fight against the lambast. "No," she said, weak.

"You left your entire squad behind." The scene stopped, and faded into blackness again.

"No," Andraste said, heaving the words out. She was out of tears, and her breaths made her sick. "It can't-"

"It can be." Scarlet grabbed Andraste by the shoulder. "And it is." Scarlet gently pushed her forward, and Andraste slumped on the ground, lacking the energy to pick herself up.

The entire area cracked like glass with another one of Scarlet's deafening finger snaps. The neurons were gone, the glows were gone, and the familiar scene of the Outlands returned.

Andraste was lost in her trauma, mind torn asunder by shock. She couldn't move or think, she only stared ahead with stymied reactions to the world around her.

"Now," Scarlet said as she stood up, "you're coming with us."

Scarlet gestured to the background, and a group of Martyr's Army soldiers emerged, some of whom were nodding, impressed. "Get her on the helicopter. We've got some ground to cover." She saluted the soldiers, who returned the gesture.

Heavy cuffs were latched onto her hands and ankles, and chains were wrapped around her body. Andraste put up no resistance, neither fighting against the soldiers nor raging against her resignation. She was seeing, hearing, and feeling everything as always, but nothing provoked a reaction. Like a stone in a river, she was still as everything around her remained in motion.

Similar to the Holacksi's smoker, she was in a cognitive purgatory, but a sense of dread lay thick over the coldness. While getting loaded onto the helicopter, she was thrown around like a ragdoll, oblivious to the bumps and bruises. Occasionally she would feel a tear down her face, but she was otherwise still. She didn't even know what the soldiers were saying, despite the jeering tones in their voices.

32   Former Czech Territory
19:15   June 8th, 2335

Judicia had been in near-catatonia ever since she spoke with Bashford. While she was never one for small talk or company, Yousef felt a palpable sense of isolation in Judicia's renewed absence.

There was no torture or abuse to speak of while the Martyr's Army held them hostage, but there was nonetheless an atmosphere of malevolence in the fallout shelter. Their cells were almost comfortable on their own merit, with reasonable climate control, decent bedding, but it was this moderate comfort that made the sense of dread even heavier.

The soldiers always wore full face masks with the Martyr's Army sigil on them, never without their guns. While they mostly left Yousef and Judicia alone, there was no shaking the fact that they appeared to be watching their every move.

When a doctor came to bandage his ear after a soldier blew most of it off, he expected the worst. This doctor, also armed and covered in sigils, was quick, professional, and even polite. The sting on the side of his head was long gone and buried beneath clean bandages, but he still kept his guard up.

Kept perpetually on-edge, Yousef couldn't shake the feeling that he saw the interrogations as worse than they really were. Sometimes, they brought them into individual rooms with a druid wearing a sensory deprivation helmet, not saying a word, sometimes for hours. Yousef could constantly tell when these soldiers and bizarre figures were around, stealing second glances at his mind and digging into his subconscious.

He could only sit on his bed, gritting his teeth and clawing at the sheets. He had gone through every behavioral technique he knew for the sake of centering himself, but at the end of the day, he was still petrified.

What worried him most was that no one had called him out about the alarm on the plane. The AUTO alert, as he activated at Andraste's behest, would have drawn a ton of attention to the Martyr's Army and their operations, but they didn't seem concerned about it.

His door swung open, as if answering his questions. A soldier was standing in the doorway, rifle at her side.

"Makkareb," she said, the word sounding awkward from her. "The General needs you." Yousef recognized her accent.

"What does he need me for?" He asked her in Arabic.

She paused for a moment. She tilted her head at him, her gestures hard to read.

Yousef stiffened, biting his lip. He got up from his chair and put his hands behind his head in submission.

She took off her helmet. She looked at him with a conflicted look on her face, one that he stopped to take in. Her complexion was like his.

"Wow," she said, in similar Arabic. "I thought I had gotten better at hiding my accent."

"You-" He began, lowering his hands, "You're from Egypt?"

She struggled to look him in the eyes. "Yes. And I know you are, too."

Yousef forgot his place for a moment. "So, what are you doing here?" He asked in accusation.

She was still.

"Aaron Sennec destroyed Cairo! And now you're working with his- his fanatics?"

The soldier turned to him, a firm look on her face. "I owed nothing to Egypt. And before you even consider going there, I owe nothing to Great Britain."

Yousef lowered his accusatory stance.

"But I owe *everything* to Aaron Sennec." With a quick flourish, she reached into a pocket on her vest and drew out a photo of Aaron Sennec standing next to a young girl, presumably her. "Don't act like you know me just because you know where I'm from." She put the helmet back on and slid the picture back into its place. "Now follow me."

Yousef complied as she cuffed his hands, offering no further protest. Still, he held a silent indignity over this woman's eager renunciation of Egypt.

As they walked down the halls of the compound, whichever one they were being held in now, Yousef found himself thinking of home in Cairo. They lived right near a market, and there was always the smell of sizzling and frying food coming through their windows. They had a loft, which was perfect for entertaining, and Yousef always treasured happy memories of him, his sister, and their friends playing in the rec room while the adults all chatted in the lounge.

This building, while no fallout shelter, still had enormous halls and vaulted ceilings. But, instead of the industrial flatness of the shelter, there were signs of dilapidated grandeur and beauty in the halls of this place. He had never been to many of these places before, but Yousef could tell right away: they were in a cathedral.

He looked around, and saw civilians and soldiers alike packed together into makeshift communities, the pews ripped from the ground and used as structuring. Children crying, sick and elderly people laid out on their backs, and large groups of people surrounding small pots of food. This also reminded him of home. There were always poor people and beggars in Cairo, overflowing from the shelters. He sighed, reflecting that his experience in Egypt wasn't everyone else's experience.

Come the military coup, his family was able to get to England quickly. It wasn't until later that Yousef saw the horror in that news footage. People were thrown off docks, shot on tarmacs, and separated from family members at gates. It wasn't until Quadriyyah and Rowe, the Chancellor of Foreign Affairs at the time, secured more travel options for refugees that the crisis finally started to slow down. Yousef wondered how many people like this were in Egypt, and how many survivors from the Cairo disaster were in this cathedral.

Towards the front of the cathedral, there was a group of people bent over in prayer. All different ethnicities and ages, whispering different languages beneath their breath. The stained glass ahead of them was cracked and missing pieces, but no less gorgeous for it. But as Yousef got closer, it was clear what they were all looking towards. Ancient-looking, but nonetheless respectfully maintained, was a brilliant silver statue, of a man with a halo standing astride a silver casket, held aloft by angels. Pieces of the statue were missing and bent, but for such a pristine piece to be so well-kept after so long was incredible. Yousef, though not resonant with its Christian overtones, was still moved by it.

"Saint John Nepomucene," declared a voice behind them. Yousef and the soldier both turned to see General Bashford, wearing full military gear. His face was streaked with mud, sweat, and blood, much of it from cuts on his face. "He was an old martyr from the 15th century. Stories about him are conflicting, but no one can deny that he died an unjust death." Bashford's words seemed pointed at Yousef.

The soldier turned and gave him the salute over her heart, a gesture he returned.

"Thank you, Fatima." He spoke in perfect Arabic. "I'll take it from here." He handed a large, bulging satchel to her. "This is what the foraging team and I dug up. Hopefully it's enough."

"Thank you, sir." She took the bag and started walking away.

He held the same expression as he looked over him, as if expecting the latter to say something. He kept staring at Yousef while he pulled out some gauze and started dabbing at the gashes on his face.

"I see you and Fatima had a little chat," he began, putting away the gauze. "She's a fascinating woman, and a wonderful soldier. I'm glad you two had the opportunity to talk."

Yousef bit his lip and took a deep breath. "She said you wanted to see me?"

He nodded. "And you replied by calling her a traitor to her country?"

Yousef stood in shock. He didn't know what to do: if he should ask Bashford how he knew, apologize, or return to the original subject.

"You don't have to apologize, Dr. Makkareb," Bashford cut in. "The situation in Egypt was difficult for everyone. I understand that you feel conflicted."

Yousef was silent.

"But please, understand something." He turned away from Yousef. "Look at these people." He gestured towards the civilian camps strewn throughout the cathedral. "These are the people in our charge. United in our allegiance to the Fomorians. The true martyrs." He turned back to Yousef, looking at the people bent over in prayer. "Everyone works so that everyone may thrive, including me. That satchel I gave to Fatima? That was full of roots and herbs for medicine. I had to fight off four wolves for that." Bashford turned back to Yousef. "And I would do it again."

Yousef paused, almost dizzy from turning from one view to the next.

"And then, you call Fatima a traitor for placing her loyalties here." He narrowed his gaze. "I thought you had more vision than that."

His confusion boiled over into rage. "Fuck you!"

Yousef's outcry echoed into the rafters of the cathedral, crashing against the vaulted ceilings and settling back onto the oppressive silence left in its wake. The bystanders were all staring, and the prayers at the tomb had stopped.

Feeling barren and anguished, worsened by all the staring faces, Yousef's anger sloughed away. He looked back at Bashford as if he would do something.

Bashford didn't move or change expression. He held his gaze.

Minding his tone, Yousef began again. "I don't understand, Bashford." He spoke in soft honesty. "You talk of peace, acceptance, and safety like they're all foreign to me. Everything that you described? That's what we want in Great Britain!"

"Of course." Bashford closed the distance between them. "Of course you would say that. Of *course* you would say that your country is the beacon of virtue and prosperity it so fervently claims to be."

Yousef was too frightened to move as Bashford stared him down. In the man's eyes, there was a glint of cold, silver light, as if reflected off a wolf's eyes in the night.

"I see that Rowe and his campaign has gotten to you, as well. Like a rat in a cage, you're conditioned to act a certain way. Rowe espouses his vision of a perfect world, but his vision for Great Britain's future is just a fairy tale."

"Why did you want to see me?" Yousef cut in, trying to restore some clarity to the situation.

Bashford backed down, no less imposing for his relaxed composure. "I need your assistance with something." He walked ahead and gestured for Yousef to follow him.

Yousef followed, still feeling the eyes of the cathedral's inhabitants boring into him. They walked past the tomb, and Yousef winced when he heard someone praying in Arabic.

Bashford led him through a series of doors and stairwells, beginning with the antiquated old building before descending into steel steps and doors. There was nothing to see in the long corridors, and the hushed clamor of the church was far behind them. Every footstep seemed deafening as Bashford sustained his silence.

After a long, circuitous path through the bunker, Bashford stopped and opened a door, leading into an office. After a pause, Bashford gestured for Yousef to go in first.

"I know what your biggest question is going to be, and you'll be satisfied to hear what I have to say." Bashford pulled a chair out in front of the desk, and Yousef instinctively sat down. "Andraste is still alive."

"She is?" Yousef forgot his place and shot out of his chair.

Bashford turned to him with a raised brow and a smirk. Yousef sat down again.

Bashford nodded and chuckled. "It's your concern for her that I find so interesting, Dr. Makkareb." He sat down on his side of the desk. "Despite your persisting terror of Andraste, you continue to offer her genuine support. Why is this the case, exactly?"

Yousef was perplexed. "Is it so strange for a doctor to be supportive of his patient?"

"I find it strange because, though you struggle to understand peace and goodwill towards your human peers, you are able to muster compassion and understanding towards a being of literal alien countenance." He folded his arms and leaned towards Yousef. "You don't understand it when the Martyr's Army helps and shelters people in need, but at the behest of Andraste, a creature made in a laboratory with materials from another world, you activate high-security clearance alarms. Are you really the kind, understanding person I think you are, or are you another cog in the elaborate machine of Great Britain's rabid nationalism?"

"I don't understand you," Yousef rebutted. "Why the hate? You're British!"

Bashford looked down at his desk and sighed. "More's the pity." He looked up and stared down Yousef again. "We're getting sidetracked. I wanted to speak with you because we need your help with Andraste."

Yousef sprang back to attention. "How are you so certain she's alive?"

Bashford straightened his posture. "Because we have her, Dr. Makkareb."

Yousef went pale.

"Why?" He finally asked. "Why do you care? You raise an army dedicated to destroying my home. Now I'm here in your private bunker, and you want me to open up to you?"

"You're a special case, Doctor," Bashford replied.

"I'm a means to an end." Yousef gripped the armrests on his chair as he spoke. "You want Andraste, and you need me to get close to her. Once you've done what you want with her, you're through with me."

Bashford was silent.

"Don't pretend that you care about me. I'll take your open contempt over your empty sentiments."

"I don't speak emptily, doctor." Bashford's fist clenched. "And you know that. You've seen what I've done to Judicia."

Yousef's bitter countenance faded. "Where is-"

"She's working with us on something very important. But, going back to faith in your comrades, I want to ask you something:" he leaned forward and looked at Yousef in the eyes. "Doctor, how would you feel about Andraste if you knew she was a war criminal?"

Yousef squinted at this. "Excuse me?"

"In addition," Bashford said, nodding, "Has Judicia told you anything about the Iconoclast Program?"

"The," Yousef blinked, looking for pieces to put together. "The Iconoclast what?"

33 London, England
15:43   June 9th, 2335

They had gathered in a large group outside his office while the police looked on in wary fascination. Rowe sat at his desk staring at the protestors outside Gower Street, where the most vocal orators had gathered.

Just last night, he had signed an executive order to shut down England's borders- no one could come or go. He had been mulling on it since the Battle of the Shard, and urged parliament into it after the plane was hijacked.

The moment the policy change became known, an organized protest of the closed borders arose online, and the turnout had exceeded everyone's expectations. This protest was in the news, not for its intensity but for its originality.

It was occurring in small pockets all throughout England, with an especially dense concentration in London. Groups of Imams, priests, and Rabbis were gathered, all with their most prominent effects on display.

Prepared and implemented with uncanny readiness, the air in London was filled with songs that spanned at least three major faiths and numerous languages. Passing from one group to the next, Rowe could glean bits and pieces from each shift, all along the lines of "all are welcome" and

"London waits for you." The message was clearest in English.

The chorus seemed pointed at Rowe. Dozens of voices were defying his executive order and the ruling of Parliament overall, dressed in a deliberately kitschy display of cultural diversity to accuse Rowe of basing his decision on xenophobia. Yet, it carried weight. Rowe was moved by the song and images, for he had long wanted to see more of this exact thing. What Rowe resented was being the antagonist in this situation.

In the crowds, he saw plenty of people he recognized. Attorneys, members of the Houses of Commons and Lords, Secretaries of State, and the sight that made him groan and bury his face in his hands: members of the police and homeland security offices. He finally had to turn away when Commander Abaddi, wearing the same uniform he used to fight in the Shard, seemed to glare at him.

The shutters were closed, and he went to his computer, flooded with online correspondence voicing disgust and threats to resign or break deals. Local members of Parliament and executive officials from other countries spared no detail in their disdain. The pit in his stomach was churning, spinning his innards into knots. Rowe didn't want any of this to be the case, but he was making a stance against the Army, and he couldn't stand down now.

His optimism for people to understand his position faded even more when the living contrarian herself, Labibah Quadriyyah, was at his door. Taking a breath and centering himself, he let her in.

She had a look of silent anger, a furrowed brow and a half-lidded gaze. Like a parent disappointed in their child, her presence made Rowe feel both ashamed and indignant. He had to take another breath before continuing.

"Can I help you, Chancellor?" He spoke in a suppressed groan.

"You don't look well, Rowe. Is the demonstration bothering you?" Her tone was less sympathetic than it was reprimanding, and he resented being chided like this.

"Can I help you, Chancellor Quadriyyah?" He spoke through gritted teeth.

"Don't get huffy, Rowe. This doesn't look good for any of us. It's about more than just you." She tilted her head and folded her arms. "If I wasn't so busy, I'd be out there myself."

He put his hands on the table and stood up, his patience at an end. "Can I help you or not, Chancellor Quadriyyah? Or are you only here to remind me of my crimes against humanity?"

"I have heard from another government official who wants to get in touch with you."

"If it's the PM of Australia again, tell him the conversation is over." He spoke with immediacy and dismissal in his voice.

She put a hand on his desk. "It's from the Martyr's Army, Rowe."

Rowe turned back to her.

"George Bashford wants to plan a discussion with you." She looked at him dead-on as she propped herself up on his desk.

Rowe went pale, his arms growing weak at the shuddering elbows. He looked at Chancellor Quadriyyah with wide eyes and a streak of sweat on his brow. She dropped her aggressive countenance and joined him in a look of similar disbelief.

"Since when is he considered a 'government official?'" Rowe began, exasperated.

"His words, not mine." She replied, shrugging. "We received an e-mail from an encrypted address, with photos of the doctors he's held hostage- and a confirmation that Andraste is going to be in their custody."

"How do you know it's authentic? And-and how did another message from the Outlands get through?"

Quadriyyah pulled out her tablet and held it up to Rowe. "The message, we're still working on. As for authenticity, he also sent a video."

A still image of Bashford seated at a table came to life when she pressed "play." He sat up straight, and seemed to look directly at Rowe.

"Mister Rowe, I believe the time is appropriate for us to talk about our respective situations. Andraste's existence, well-known to us at this point, is a sign that you are truly desperate. This sentiment is backed up by your decision to close Great Britain's borders."

Rowe shuddered at Bashford's cutting words. He had never met the man in person, but Bashford spoke with such assuredness and clarity it shook him.

"We both have people sent into the fray, fighting to make our respective goals into reality. You have people you're worried about, as do I. In the interest of keeping as many people alive as we can, let's not dance around the issue any longer. I propose we have a conference, over a live video, and negotiate the terms of your surrender. I have people you want to see returned to your country."

The camera then panned over to another side of the table, where Judicia and Makkareb were tied up and gagged in the chairs.

"And, most importantly, Andraste. I know all about the importance you place on her survival. She has been giving us a rather difficult time, but she has also been brought under control."

At this, Bashford pressed a button on the keypad before him and brought up another video, showing Melissa Scarlet with Andraste tied to a chair. Andraste was slumped over, quietly groaning as Scarlet looked joyfully at the camera, waving. This made him physically ill.

"She is fascinating, Rowe. However, we have reason to believe that she can do some incredible things out here in the Outlands, so I don't want to send her back to Great Britain yet. This is another point we can discuss in our future dealings. I would say it is in your best interest to agree to my terms and hold this video summit, but I cannot influence your decision. By the time you receive this, it will be approximately 1600 hours, and I would like to know your response by 2100 hours. By then, Andraste should be in our custody. Respond to indicate your interest, then we will work out how to connect our video services to one another. I will speak to you alone. I await your answer."

the video stopped. Quadriyyah looked at it solemnly before turning her gaze to Rowe. He was pale and shuddering as he breathed. She sighed as she continued to talk to him.

"This came in just before I came over to see you. What are your thoughts?" Her expression drooped as she spoke, sharing a palpable sense of defeat with Rowe.

"I'm going to tell him, 'yes.'" Rowe stood up from his chair. "Andraste is the key to our future, and I'm not going to let him do any more harm."

"Why are you so certain? Do you really think he's going to be true to his word?" Quadriyyah wanted to be angry, but the situation was too dire. "The lieutenant of the man who sacked Cairo?"

Hearing this, Rowe hung his head. He took a deep sigh and leaned against the wall. "The story of Aaron Sennec is going to be one of his focal points, I'm sure. Yet, something isn't right. After all these attempts on Andraste's life, he suddenly thinks that they need her for something?" He scratched his beard. "Things can't be this simple."

"Definitely not. But, we can't afford to do anything rash. Mr. Rowe, I implore you, be mindful of what you do next. People are depending on you."

Rowe looked outside at the protesters, his expression souring. "Are they?" He went back to his desk. "Write back to Bashford, link me to the conversation, and tell him we've agreed. I'll talk to Laurie and Donahue, hopefully we can track the source of their transmission."

Quadriyyah pressed her lips together, kneading her brow. "Please don't do anything rash, Nathan." With that, she turned to leave.

Rowe didn't acknowledge her parting remarks, and wrote up messages to Laurie and Donahue, who were brought up to speed on the situation. Their response was sent out immediately, and they could only wait as the response from the Martyr's Army came back.

Rowe had no choice but to listen to the people chanting outside as he waited. He tried to ignore them as best he could, but their grim choir stung at him.

"Great Britain hates me," he thought, burying his face in one of his hands. *"I'm doing all of this for them. We've been on the cusp of having normal lives for so long now; I just need one more push."* He sighed, leaning back in his chair and gripping the knot of his tie. *"They'll come around. Once Andraste is safe and the Army is destroyed, the world will be perfect.*

34 Former Czech Territory
19:25   June 9th, 2335

Yousef was beside himself for quite some time. He didn't believe for a second that Andraste was a deserter. Claire Dillon, the last survivor of that unit, had ran from the fight, according to Bashford. He didn't see that in Andraste, but the more he thought on it, the more sense it made.

"No," he kept telling himself, *"Andraste wouldn't do that."* He had spoken with her in doctor-patient confidentiality, and was certain that she was not the type to lie or manipulate, but he had no reason to believe that Bashford was lying, either. All the things he knew about her with such immaculate detail gave credence to his sincerity and knowledge about the situation. Like it or not, Bashford knew what he was talking about. He didn't want to fathom all the things he didn't know.

What kept him steady was that Yousef pledged himself to her well-being. Whether or not, he reminded everyone of what Andraste was at her core: a patient who needed help.

"Doctor Makkareb?" A voice finally spoke up, banging on his cell door and breaking him out of his trance. "The general wants to see you."

"Coming!" He stood up and ran a washcloth over his forehead. He sighed, resigning himself to ruminate on it later. He opened the door, and an armed soldier was waiting for him.

"Turn around, put your hands behind your back." Yousef obeyed and felt the handcuffs around his wrists. He was pulled out into the hallway, where another soldier stood with a smaller woman. Yousef recognized her right away.

"Judicia!" He exclaimed, forgetting his restraints and trying to charge towards her. The soldier reached out and yanked him back into line. "Judicia, what have they been doing to you? Speak to me!"

Judicia didn't respond. She moved with a slow, tilting gait, as if drugged.

"Keep going, Doctor. You'll have a chance to talk later." The soldier prodded him along.

Yousef sighed, plodding down the hallway. His thoughts continued to drift along, unrestrained, going through the same cycles of doubt and fear time and time again. He didn't know where he would begin while talking with Judicia, seeing her so stricken like this. Worse yet, Bashford probably wanted them for something insidious, so he had another conversation to dread.

He couldn't put his finger on it, but there was a bizarre energy hanging in the air of this bunker beneath the cathedral. Not just hearing, but feeling a pulse through the hallways, Yousef had an indelible sense that something else was there with him and the soldiers; alive, feeling, watching. The sense intensified as they marched down the familiar hallway towards Bashford's office. A soldier opened the door and the feeling rushed over Yousef like a gale of hot wind.

Standing in the middle of an elaborate setup of cameras and wires, flanked on all sides by the Martyr's Army flag and commemorative photos of Aaron Sennec, was George Bashford. His furrowed brow and intense eyes hung over a growing smile as he saw the doctors.

While Bashford was always an intimidating man, something about him today was especially frightening. He had a look of animosity and bizarre intelligence behind his gaze that bore inhuman intensity.

He spoke and gestured to the tables surrounded by the cameras. "Bring them in, please. Have them sit down."

Bashford had a wide stance and spread his arms in a way that most would find inviting, but Yousef found terrifying. He looked around at all the cameras and equipment, then back at Judicia, who was barely conscious. They both took their seats without issue, handcuffs locked to the table.

Yousef looked at Judicia, then back at Bashford, doing deep, therapeutic breaths for himself.

"How have you been, Doctor? As I'm sure you've gathered, we have some very big plans for today, and we need you and Judicia's help for them."

His breath was caught in his throat as Bashford spoke to him. He stole another glance at Judicia, who was still.

Bashford noticed Yousef looking at her. "Yes, you two haven't spoken in some time, have you? Well, we're not in a rush." He looked more neutral, but that sudden drop in hostility was even more unsettling to Yousef.

"Judicia!" Yousef turned towards her, going as far as his restraints would allow. "Judicia, what's happening?"

Seated right next to him, she got an earful. She slowly lifted her head, and Yousef saw the dark streaks down her face where blood once spilled from her eyes. Some had coagulated on her eyelids, and the whites of her eyes were streaked with veins.

Yousef stifled a gasp. "J-Judicia?"

Judicia didn't look at him. She looked straight ahead, then sighed. "Bleeding," she muttered under her breath. "Bleeding. It's all bleeding." Her tone was monotone and airy, spoken like she was asleep.

Yousef saw Bashford smiling as she said this. He became more fervent. "Judicia, speak to me! Please!"

She shut her eyes and turned away as Yousef cried out. "I'm right next to you, Yousef. Stop yelling." Judicia slowly turned to him, her face bearing its usual sourness. "I know the situation is confusing right now, but you need to bear with us."

"Who is 'us?' You and Bashford? Just tell me what happened to you! Please!" Yousef pushed himself towards Judicia with such doggedness that he knocked over his chair. The guards, mindful of their guns, only got him back into place.

"I do refer to that, Yousef. Bashford opened my eyes to things that I was once blind to."

Bashford nodded as she said this, folding his arms and grinning.

"The world is going to die, Yousef. Blood is pouring from the heart of the outlands like a river." Then she scoffed lightly, trying to laugh despite her exhaustion. "The heart can change everything, Yousef."

"But," Yousef began, looking between the two of them with desperation, sweat beading on his face, "wh-what are you talking about? The heart of the outlands? Bleeding? I-I don't understand!" He started breathing hard, and a few tears ran down his face.

"You will in time, Doctor. Once Andraste is here with us, everything will fall into place." Basford put a hand on Yousef's shoulder, intending it as a gesture of comfort, but Yousef jerked away from the man's touch.

"What do you want?" Yousef cried out with a desperate shrill. "You have us captured, you've done *something* to Judicia, and you want to get Andraste here on camera? Where is all of this going?"

"This is all going towards the endgame, doctor. Soon we'll have Nathan Rowe on the other end of the line, and we can finally put an end to this whole conflict." He walked back over to the arrangements of cameras.

"Andraste will never work with you!" Yousef continued to berate Bashford, finding strength in his defiance. It was the only way he could stop his hands from shaking in fear.

"She has to, Yousef." Judicia responded, speaking it with a matter-of-fact flatness. "This affects her more than anyone else."

Yousef stared at her, the chains on his handcuffs rattling against the table. Her head was hung in resignation, while Bashford continued overseeing the management of the cameras. Trying to breathe and steady his nerves, he could only clench his fists and gnaw on his lip amidst the situation.

"Where is she?" He said. "All this talk of Andraste, and we have no idea where she is!"

Bashford looked away from the cameras and towards Yousef when he said this. He sighed, folding his arms. "You will see her soon." He kneaded his brow before he continued speaking. "In the meantime, you two will see Rowe on these screens. They have agreed to a video summit with us, discussing terms of surrender."

"Surrender?" Yousef cried out, his voice cracking. "Why would he surrender? What do you have on him?"

"It's for the best," Judicia said again. "Rowe and the others have no idea what's happening out here, or what will happen if they don't act soon."

"J-Judicia, what are you-"

"It's as I said, doctor." Bashford spoke up, quieting them both. "Things will be made clear with time. Judicia has seen things that you have not. The Outlands are suffering, and if the conflict between us and England does not change, then the situation will grow vastly worse." He put a hand on Yousef's quivering fists, bringing them to a stop. "And, yes, Andraste is completely necessary to fixing this situation. She carries an essential part of the Outlands with her, and we have no hope of making reparations without her."

Yousef was silent. Bashford's advance was unexpected, but he held his hands steady without hurting him. There was a strange sincerity to the way he tried to comfort Yousef, which was even more confusing.

"You don't have to understand it yet, doctor." Bashford stood back, looking towards the cameras and screens. "All you have to do is comply. Everything will fall into place."

Yousef sighed, clenching his fists. He hung his head and took his therapeutic breaths. *"Andraste,"* he thought, *"Where are you?"*

35 Former Czech Territory
20:10   June 9th, 2335

The sun was down below the tree line as the helicopter drifted ever onwards towards Prague. Twilight's last few colors were caught on the Vlatava river, leading into the expanse of the city. This was the most urban area that Andraste had seen in a long time, with a handful of pre-invasion skyscrapers and plenty of preserved buildings from an even older time. Kept in the same helicopter as Scarlet, Andraste had no energy for anything but sitting in silence. Scarlet obliged, never speaking or even moving except to coordinate the convoy's landing at the base.

Andraste felt that if she were any more heavy and still, she would turn to stone. Still in a daze after Scarlet brought so many revelations on her, processing the world around her was all she could do.

After a while, Scarlet said something about re-entry into the hangar, and the convoy came to a stop. Beneath them, fractured, weed-ridden cobblestone near the church split down the middle, clean lines marking where the gateways opened. The helicopter began to descend as the false ground opened into a modest air base, where other vehicles became visible as lights around the landing pad came on.

Soldiers came to pull Andraste out of the helicopter, and she numbly obliged. If it wasn't the heart of enemy territory, Andraste would have been impressed at the extent of the machinery surrounding them. They had been hiding under Prague all this time, assembling fleets of planes, helicopters, and everything needed to lay waste to cities that threatened them. A massive helicopter outfitted with almost every weapon imaginable had been decorated thusly; on its side, the names of cities were written in red and then crossed out in white. There was Cairo, Copenhagen, Istanbul, and Madrid all above London, which was left uncrossed. Above all these names was the title, "SAVED."

As she stared, they pulled a bag down over her head and yanked her back into line. Her numb legs and feet made it hard to keep track of her steps. They walked her for what felt like ages, until the bag was pulled off and it was her and Scarlet left standing in front of a sealed door. The general disengaged the locks, keeping a tight grip on Andraste, before leading her inside.

In the room, there was a simple office. Andraste had seen many like it around Central Base, but this was different. At the desk, separated from the rest of the room by the Plexiglas, sat a man. Tall, white-haired, and broad-shouldered, his apparent age did nothing to dull the sharp look in his eye nor the regality of his posture.

"Andraste," he said, standing up. He wore a black military jacket with a Martyr's Army patch on the shoulder, and beneath it, sewn in white letters, the name 'Bashford.' He looked at Andraste in the eyes and nodded. "At last. Excellent work, General Scarlet."

Scarlet let Andraste go and saluted Bashford. "I'll let you take it from here, Bashford. I need to go." Without waiting for his response, Scarlet left through the same door.

Nex to Bashford, handcuffed to desks, were Judicia and Yousef. Judicia's head was down and she sat motionless, but Yousef nearly leapt out of his chair.

"Andraste!" Yousef leaned as close to her as the restraints would allow.

Seeing him sent a current through her, and she felt energized again. "Oh my God," she felt some tears in her eyes. "Dr. Yousef! Are you all right?"

"Yes, I'm fine! But what about you?"

"Better, seeing that you're okay! N-now, how are we going to get out of here!"

"Don't worry about us! I just," he sputtered, trying to smile, but a mix of pain and confusion wracked his expression. "I just can't believe you're alive! But why? You should get to an outpost!"

"I'm not leaving you behind!" Andraste called back at him, her voice harsh as the life returned to her. "It's not fair, what the Army is doing to you! It's me these bastards want!"

"And now you're here," Bashford said, bringing the conversation under his control. "After the debacle with the plane, you must be furious. But there are greater things at work here, and if anyone is to survive, I beg for your cooperation." Bashford glanced over at the doctors.

"Bashford," she allowed the anger to pass, letting her arms hang at her sides. "What do you want, and what makes you think I'll help you?"

Bashford nodded. "First, I want you to understand the risks that plague the Outlands. I know the Martyr's Army espouses much about the end of the world and the heart of the Outlands, but offers little explanation." He stepped back. "It is not something that can be explained. It must be felt."

They stood, looking at one another in silence. Electricity seemed to fill the air from the way they locked eyes. Unlike Scarlet, whose mind was fiercely shielded and inhuman, Bashford had all the emotions and thoughts of a normal man. Yet, his feelings were clear and unclouded, matching everything he said. His mental discipline was unshaking.

"Look into my mind, Andraste," Bashford finally said.

Andraste stared. "I beg your pardon?"

"You heard me. If you want to understand, you must feel what we feel." Bashford folded his arms. "I will offer no resistance, and I have no intention of harming you. Look inside and see."

Andraste narrowed her gaze at him. She could tell from his emotions that he was not lying, but the way he spoke about it so calmly made her suspicious. All the more because she didn't see any alternative.

"Andraste." Bashford commanded her attention. "You know what to do."

Clenching her fist, Andraste ruefully obliged. Both her and Bashford shut their eyes.

Opening her eyes to a blue glow, she stood in the familiar neuronal field. She looked for something familiar, but saw nothing. A sound came from opposite her, like a heavy breath. There stood a shadow, a black outline of a person that obscured the light of the neurons.

"Bashford?"

At this, the figure's eyes opened with dark red circles in its pupils. From there, a lattice of long, circuitous red lines traced over its body and outlined it as the neurons outlined Andraste. They were crisscrossing over one another, branching off at narrow points, and gently pulsing with a dark force. As if in a gruesome parallel to the neuronal field, this creature began to sow a horizon of blood vessels, as the patterns on its feet flowered in the ground beneath it. It was the same color of red she had seen in the Outlands before. The sense of dread made manifest.

Andraste backed away, the creature burning hot with a tangible malevolence. When the red veins mingled with the blue neurons, the entire plane seemed disrupted, radiating with a disorienting force. She fell to her knees, her head pounding and her heart beating out of her chest. The blood veins began to climb onto her legs, and the feelings were redoubled.

"Get away from me!" Andraste tried to swing at it with the blade, but the creature dodged. It caught her arm, less with a hand than with a fraying bundle of loose arteries, and it began to spread onto her. It leaned closer, a hollow cry emanating through the space.

She had a sense of this feeling from elsewhere, like the murderous intent she saw in Listev, but this was much fiercer. It was less a specific emotion and more a manifested concept, so unmistakable and heavy in its existence that it carried a smothering existential weight. She looked up at it and saw blood running from its eyes.

Hot viscera that steamed as it fell and sizzled when it splattered against the ground. This creature was feeling what she was feeling, and it wept over it. A sensation so beyond logic yet so unmistakably real, Andraste and this being were beset by a ruthless black void, a sense of death that was so imminent and pervasive it brought them to their knees.

Andraste fought to pull herself out of this hellish vista, and arose back in the room with tears in her eyes, and rivers of blood falling down Bashford's face. He was on his knees.

"B-Bashford," Andraste stammered, "is that what you wanted to show me?"

"Yes," he grunted. "The Outlands can sense it, and so can anyone attuned to it, like me. An all-consuming death awaits, and it dwells in spiraling agony."

"I've been seeing it this whole time," Andraste was astonished at herself. "Are- are you crying blood?"

"I have no tears anymore," Bashford said, his head still hanging. "I only bleed. Just as the Outlands do." He finally got to his feet, dragging a handkerchief over his face.

"All right, I understand. Something bad is happening out here." Andraste got up, keeping her eyes on Bashford. "But what does this have to do with me?"

"You'll understand." Bashford walked back to his desk. "Primarily, I wanted you to understand our plight before we have another important conversation." He turned to the setup of cameras and screens, then looked at his watch. "We'll have Rowe on the line soon enough."

Andraste was stunned. "What?"

36 Former Czech Territory
21:00   June 9th, 2335

Everyone stared at the screen in unsteady anticipation. Even Bashford was tugging at the sleeves of his jacket after a few minutes.

"They are ready, sir!" A technician called from beyond Bashford's office.

"Turn on the video feed." He stood up as he said this, walking towards the glass wall.

At this, the screen came to life, and in the meeting room, there sat Rowe. As he saw the situation, Rowe's eyes grew massive and he nearly leapt out of his chair.

"Andraste!" He saw her through the screen, eyes fixed on her. "My God, you're alive!"

"Mr. Rowe!" She got closer to the glass, almost forgetting the boundary it posed. "Sir, I-" A few tears began to form at the corners of her eyes. "I-I'm so glad to see you again!"

"Same, Andraste!" Rowe looked teary himself. "I can hardly believe-"

"Mr. Rowe." Bashford spoke up, calling attention to himself. "Do not forget, we have terms to discuss."

Rowe's joyful expression faded, and he sat back down in his chair. "Yes, General. I would presume you claim to have Andraste as leverage."

Bashford's expression was unchanged. "Be that as it may, Andraste has gained some more insight into our plight. She understands what sort of threat the Outlands face. And even she would agree that our bickering is causing more harm than good." He turned to her as he said this.

Rowe looked at her, and even through the screen, Andraste thought she could feel the ice run down his spine in fear. The look on his face spoke of a profound uncertainty that bore through the soul. Looking at Bashford, she felt fear run through her, as well.

"Andraste, what is he talking about?" Rowe finally asked.

It took a moment for her to think of her response. She could not deny what Bashford had shown her. She closed her eyes and took a therapeutic breath. Breathe in, count to five, breathe out, count to five.

"Mr. Rowe," she began, voice shaking, "General Bashford has shown me what is happening. He- He is telling the truth."

As Rowe winced in shock, Andraste felt the knot in her stomach growing tighter.

"I'm sorry, sir! I wish I could explain it better! B- But there is something seriously wrong out here!"

"There is other testimony, as well." Bashford pressed a button, and on the screen was footage of the doctors chained to a table. "Judicia, you are aware of the strangeness out here, are you not?"

"I am," Judicia said. Everyone on screen and in the room turned to her. Yousef was mortified into silence. "These pathetic little human wars of ours are blinding us to everything else. Everyone will die if we don't work together."

"Don't tell me THAT is what you're proposing, Bashford!" Rowe slammed his hands on his desk, flat palms echoing throughout the space. "You want us to surrender on behalf of cooperation? What sick joke is this?" No one could recall the last time Rowe sounded so irate.

"I am not joking, Rowe." Bashford turned back to the screen. "Make no mistake, my efforts have been genuine. A perfect world has no government corruption like yours in it. But I am willing to hold off until we can reach a definitive agreement."

"Or what? You'll kill Andraste? You need her, for whatever damned reason!" Rowe was out of his chair and yelling at the screen, growing red in the face. "And the only thing standing in the way of a perfect world is the Martyr's Army! Murderers and human filth, all of you!"

Andraste was deeply unsettled by Rowe's tone. His fury was almost unnatural.

"Let us not ignore the matter at hand, Rowe. We are facing a disaster, and Andraste is in a unique position to help us avert this disaster." Bashford was unfazed by Rowe's demeanor.

The man reeled. "What?"

"You see, Rowe, you have unintentionally created the key to resolving everything. Whatever form it may take, this upcoming disaster is tied to the Fomorians. The entirety of the Outlands' savage nature is tied to the Fomorians. By reviving a Fomorian, even a hybrid," he gestured to Andraste, "the Outlands has responded, powerfully. With her, we can at last work towards resolving this matter."

"I will never work with you!" Andraste roared at him.

He turned to her with a raised eyebrow. "You have felt the catastrophe approaching, haven't you? Andraste, we both know that you aren't the type of person to simply turn a blind eye to it."

She faltered at this, and she could tell Rowe noticed it. His gaze fell onto her, wide eyes and tense jaw marking his disbelief.

"Andraste, you can't be serious. What has this lunatic done to you to make you even consider helping him?" He grabbed his tie with one hand, giving it a yank to the side, as if trying to strangle himself. "You aren't what the Army needs! You are what Great Britain needs!"

"S-Sir?" Andraste looked at him in disbelief.

"Andraste, you are our goddess! You are the one who is going to finally lead us to victory!" Rowe spoke with a manic grin on his face, sweat beading on his brow. "And after the war, you're going to bring us an even brighter future!"

A moment of crushing silence passed in the room as they stared at the man.

"You're referring to the Iconoclast Program, aren't you, Rowe?" Bashford finally spoke.

Rowe went pale, and his arms fell limp at his sides.

"Th-the what?" Andraste finally spoke up.

The doctors stirred in their seats as the bags were pulled off their heads.

"Might as well open up with it, Rowe." Bashford pulled the camera facing him towards the doctors. Yousef went stiff while Judicia's head only lilted back and forth. "Both of them are well-aware of what's happening."

"Shit," Yousef said under his breath.

"Y-you can't believe him!" Rowe pointed fiercely at Bashford. "Andraste, Makkareb, I don't know what he's told you, but it's all-"

"Judicia is the one who told me," Bashford interrupted. His tone was steady, but it still cleaved Rowe's words mid-sentence. "The Iconoclast Program is the next step of the FH Project. Judicia proposed it, and you agreed to it all."

"It's true," Judicia said, worn out.

Andraste's gaze flicked from one person's face to another, bewildered by the varying looks of comprehension, resignation, and the feeling that they all knew something she didn't.

"What is happening?" She asked, voice wracked. "Someone, tell me!"

Gesturing at Andraste, Bashford raised his eyebrows at Rowe. He turned the camera back to himself as he gestured for the doctors to be gagged again.

The prime minister slumped in his chair. He looked eviscerated, without anything else to say to Bashford. He took a deep sigh before speaking.

"It's true, Andraste." He said heavily. "When the FH project finally proved successful, we were planning on putting even more resources into it. We were going to go public with it and allow anyone to become a Fomorian Hybrid like you."

"But- but why?" Andraste pleaded.

"Because," he stopped to allow a pregnant pause. "Because Judicia and I are tired of the same human mistakes over and over again. If we managed to make something more than a human- like you- then we could slowly phase out humanity."

"Wh-what?" Andraste shuddered when she heard this, thinking back on the truths that Scarlet had coaxed out of her earlier.

"I know, I know, but think about it!" Rowe stammered to save some face. "You're a goddess, Andraste! Humanity was going transcend, and we will finally live in a perfect world! No more 'human nature' to make an excuse for stupid things like war and stupidity! I-it would be brilliant!"

Everything that Andraste endured in the hospital came back to her. The weeks of physical therapy, sensing everyone's emotions, and making them all hallucinate with her came back to her as Rowe said how 'brilliant' it would all be. Her mind thought of an entire hospital full of hybrids like her, making the air in the halls a storm of psychic energy. She started to shake her head.

"No," she said airily. "No! That would be- that would be a nightmare!" She tried to take deep breaths, but struggled.

Bashford looked at Andraste, noting her unease, then turned back to Rowe. "We are getting sidetracked. If you agree to a cease fire, then we will stop the violence, and none of us will expose the Iconoclast Program. If you wish, we can wait until Andraste provides her assistance, and then we can go right back to shooting at one another if that's so important to you."

"Never!" Rowe bashed the table with his hands. "Do something, Andraste!"

Andraste recoiled. "Mr. Rowe!"

"You have superhuman strength and mind powers! Break the glass or give someone a seizure, damn it!"

Bashford turned to Andraste. "Don't do anything rash, Andraste." He kept glancing at Scarlet, putting a hand on the glass to assure her.

Rowe grew redder in the face as she stalled. "Andraste, I am giving you an order! Disobeying me is treason!"

"Sir, what's come over you?" Andraste asked, her shock overcoming her fear of the indignation. "'Goddess? Humanity will transcend?' I agreed to serve my country, not to do whatever you're on about! Besides," she said, looking away. "I'm already guilty of treason."

Rowe flushed, his entire expression fading. He slumped into his chair, a heavy sound echoing throughout the space. From his devastated repose, he looked at her, then at Bashford. "I see." He made a gesture to someone off-screen, a flat hand across his throat.

Bashford perked up at this. "Rowe, don't you dare-" He walked to the screen, pointing at the man, before the broadcast went blank.

Andraste started trembling. She tried to breathe, but the tremors made her breaths harsh and uneven. "Wh-What was," She started to stammer, overcome by all the implications of what she had seen and done. "H-how could

I," Nothing coherent came out of her, and the tremors reached her knees. Andraste struggled to stand.

Nathan Rowe, the man she had respected and worked to impress for so long, going off the way he did was mortifying. A thought crossed her mind that numbed her with fear and made her slump against the wall.

"I failed."

She fell into the corner of the glass cage, panic and fear clawing at her from beneath her skin. Her hands clenched her shoulders and she fought to keep her breathing steady, to no avail. The world seemed to drift into a blurry haze as that same phrase stabbed her mind.

"I failed."

"Calm down, Andraste." Bashford walked over to the glass. "Is it presumptuous of me to say that you're coming around to our side?" He opened glass enclosure and into the office, gesturing for Andraste to follow.

"I am not on your side! You expect me to take orders from you after you splatter one of your own generals on a wall?" She barked at him in indignation. "There may be something happening out there, but that doesn't mean I'm defecting from Great Britain!"

"And yet, you admit to treason and disobey a direct order from the Prime Minister? You saw just as I did! Rowe is losing his mind!" Bashford punctuated this by stabbing the table with the machete. "Don't make this difficult."

She looked away from Bashford at his sentiments about Rowe. He had a point, but she refused to give in to him. "If there is anything to be done about the disaster, I want to do it. But I won't be doing it for the Martyr's Army."

Bashford raised an eyebrow. "Who will you be doing it for, then?"

There were too many things going on for her to think clearly. Rowe's outbursts, Bashford's truths, and Scarlet's death all spun a helix of uncertainty in her mind. She began to feel lightheaded.

"I-I," she forced out a response, trying to center her breathing again. That dreaded thought came back and gripped her mind: *"I failed."* No breath could make her steady as her knees weakened. "I'm doing it f-for-"

"For who?" Bashford tilted his head, his eyes boring into her.

Looking at the man again, she remembered some of his words in the discussion with Rowe.

"Everyone." She righted herself, a current of resolve coming to her. "I'm doing this for everyone. Put the factions aside and let the killing stop."

Bashford kept leering at her, poised over his desk looking ready to lunge, but he relaxed and stood upright after a few moments of taking in this response. A slow, steady smile crept across his face as he pried the machete from the desk.

"Good answer," he said.

Rowe was bent over the desk, fists clenched and blood beating against his veins. His teeth were grinding, and his knuckles were white. Sweat dropped from his forehead onto the varnished wood.

After a few minutes, the door flung open and Quadriyyah marched in.

"What happened?" He demanded, expression tense and glowering. "Why did you cut off the communication like that?"

Rowe looked up at her, red in the face and bloodshot in the eyes. "We've lost Andraste. She's with them."

Quadriyyah leaned over and emphasized her words with her hands. "What. Happened?"

"Andraste thinks they're right!" Rowe nearly jumped out of his chair, and Quadriyyah recoiled from him. "She wants to help them with whatever doomsday nonsense they're purporting! She's betrayed us!"

"Sir, you need to calm down." Quadriyyah kept away from Rowe.

"I will not!" Rowe pointed at her. "We've truly lost, Quadriyyah! This is the time to take action, not to 'calm down!'" He brushed past the chancellor and stormed towards the door.

"And where are you going?" She called after Rowe with annoyance in her voice.

"To my office. I must make arrangements." Rowe turned to Quadriyyah, his eyes wider than what seemed possible. "The Martyr's Army brought the war to London with their attack on the Shard, remember?" A twisted facsimile of a grin formed on his face. "It's our turn, Quadriyyah. We're taking the war back to the Outlands."

37 Former Czech Territory
22:50　　　June 9th, 2335

Andraste was kept with the other doctors in a special cell, surrounded by soldiers. They were prepared for anything, but Andraste had nothing to show them. She only stared at the ceiling from her cot, too tired and disoriented to make any affronts. Judicia and Yousef were already told about everything that had happened. Judicia was as solemn as always, while Yousef stewed in disbelief.

They were advised to get some rest, but there was no rest to be found in their little cell. Yousef kept looking at Andraste, his cot between Judicia and the extra layers of fortified glass between him and Andraste's cell. She kept tossing and draping her arm over her face. After a while, she finally turned to him, her eyes opened just a crack. He opened his mouth to speak, but she spoke first.

"I'm sorry, Dr. Yousef." Andraste whimpered. "I'm so, so sorry. For everything."

"Andy, you were put in an impossible position with Bashford. And Rowe, I don't-"

"That's not what I mean." She cut in as she rolled onto her back. "Yes, I wish that had gone differently, but what I'm really sorry for, is, well," tears began to appear, but she shut her eyes and closed them in. "For me. I'm sorry that I'm such a failure."

Yousef sighed, pursing his lips. "Andy," his voice trailed off.

She looked away from him. "Even before the experiment, I was letting people down. And that's all I've been doing ever since." Finally, the tears came. Soft sobs worked their way into her voice. "I ignored all of your advice. I lied, I killed, I ran away, and now I'm going completely against what I was made to do. I haven't just failed you, I've failed everyone." She buried her face in her sheets. "And I'm sorry! I'm so sorry!"

Yousef felt pangs of sadness worthy of tears. His face scrunched and he covered his expression in his hands, trying to remind himself of the empathy he always had for his patients.

"Andy, please. It's so awful to hear you be this terrible to yourself." He seemed to choke on his own sobs.

"It's the truth, and you know it." She started to shudder as more tears came. "I was a liar and a traitor before I even joined, and now I'm going to HELP George fucking Bashford!" She gripped her hair and twisted around even more. "And Rowe is going mad! I-I don't know what to do anymore!"

Yousef shook his head. "What do you want me to say, Andy? I want to help you, but what can I do?"

"You don't have to say anything, doctor." She took a breath and put her hands down, lying flat. "I thought I had found the strength to move on, but I was mistaken. You don't have to say or do anything. I just wanted to apologize for what I've put you all through."

Yousef got up from his bed. "Do you hear yourself, Andy? This isn't you!"

"Then what is?"

"You've always, well-" he took a deep breath himself before going on, thinking of what Yousef would say, "you've always wanted to improve! To move forward and keep moving! You've had rough spots, sure, but you always get back up and land on your feet!"

Andraste shook her head. "I have nowhere to land this time." Her head rolled to the side. "This whole experiment was a mistake. I never should have signed up for anything."

From the rear of the cell, Judicia spoke up. "I'm certainly glad you signed up, Andraste."

Both Yousef and Andraste turned to her as she spoke.

"Judicia?" Yousef questioned.

"Judicia," Andraste echoed emptily. "I-I don't even know what to say to you, Judicia."

"How about 'thank you'?" She got up, slow, and walked over to the glass. The lethargy hadn't left her, but her voice was clear. "The fact that you are here, bemoaning how much of a failure it was, shows how worthwhile the experiment was."

Andraste sat up, with some considerable effort. "What are you talking about?"

" The Iconoclast Program was what got me out of bed in the morning!" A smile broke across her face, and she started to chuckle. "And on the way, I was going to take a screw-up of a person and make them something amazing! And I did." She pointed at Andraste.

Yousef shook his head at her. "You really felt that way the entire time?"

"Yes, I bloody did." Judicia said emphatically. "I'm surprised you never caught on, Yousef. I thought I made you smart all those years ago."

His expression wilted.

"What is wrong with you?" Andraste begged.

"Me?" Judicia scoffed. "What's wrong with *me?* What's wrong with everyone else?" Andraste saw more emotion in Judicia here than anywhere else. "Humanity is a disease! Humans are petty, stupid animals that destroy themselves and everything that matters to them! War after war, idiot politician after idiot politician!"

"Judicia!" Yousef spoke up, quiet but shocked. "Do you hear yourself?"

"I do, Yousef! It's a sentiment that I've been harboring all my life!" She giggled, moving with a dark spring in her step. "Humans are vile and petty and I want them gone! And YOU-" Judicia pointed at Andraste, "are the answer to all of these problems!"

Andraste got off the bed. "Stop it."

This didn't faze Judicia. "Andraste, shut up! Once Rowe wins his little war, I can do the important work!" She looked back up at the ceiling, lost in a sense of mania. "You were just step one, Andraste! In a few years' time, hybrids like you are going to fill the streets! As generations pass, humanity will get phased out, and we won't have to deal with those wastes of skin anymore! Especially with that Fomorian Heart that Bashford keeps talking about!"

Yousef gasped. "What are you saying?"

"Think of all that Fomorian power, Yousef! Just imagine what we could do with all that!" She looked back at Andraste. "You've seen the power that Bashford was talking about! Once you bring that under control, we can take it for ourselves!"

Andraste stood back, appalled at what Judicia was saying. It was all consistent with what Listev and Scarlet had said, but hearing it from Judicia was bone-chilling. Beyond the approval and watchful gaze of Great Britain's upper echelons, Judicia had schemes. Now she was hearing them, and she didn't have a word for this strange combination of disappointment and horror she felt.

"So that's what all this has been for?" Andraste spoke, her voice flat. "You hate people, so you started mixing them with aliens?"

Judicia turned to Andraste, her head cocked. "I guess you could put it that way." She chuckled with an unnatural-looking smile on her face. "An invasion of unstoppable Fomorians didn't wipe out humanity, so I had to get creative! This is all part of my plan for a perfect world!"

"All part of the plan," Andraste echoed, sitting back down on the bed. "A perfect world, again." She looked away from Judicia.

Yousef looked at her, sitting down on the bed opposite her. They shared the fear of this revelation as they exchanged woeful looks.

Judicia looked back at them, her expression sour. "Oh, spare me the pitiful looks! What, are you going to start telling me how horrible a person I am? That I'm insane?" Her voice was rising. "Go ahead! I've heard it all before! It's a small price to pay for progress!"

"This isn't progress, Judicia." Andraste muttered, reminiscing on everything that the others had said. "This is another apocalypse."

Judicia looked at her, pursing her lips and nodding. "Of course, you wouldn't understand." She shrugged. "It's happening with or without you, Andraste."

"Tell me something, Judicia." Andraste gestured for the doctor to sit down on the bed. "You insist that this project was a success, and since I'm alive, I guess you're right. But, if you weren't strapped for participants, what would have been different?"

Judicia sat down, raising a brow. "What do you mean?"

"I know that I was only accepted into the project because no one else was applying. A traumatized soldier comes shambling in, skin and bones. I don't think I was exactly your ideal candidate." Her eyes narrowed. "In your mind, what did the 'perfect' Fomorian Hybrid look like?"

Yousef turned to Judicia, just as curious to hear the answer. Judicia paused at this question, looking back at the ceiling.

"It's true, you weren't ideal. Yousef gave me quite the earful about how bad your health was, and how we needed to postpone so we could get you sorted out."

Andraste gripped the sheets at the mention of Yousef. "Answer me, Judicia!"

She looked straight back at Andraste. "The perfect hybrid wouldn't have been anything like you!" Judicia's glasses nearly slid off from the whiplash. "None of your tears, none of your traumas, and none of your bloody self-righteousness!"

Yousef got up off the bed, stepping away from Judicia. He stared down at her, his teeth clenched and his hands balled into fists.

"Judge me all you want, Yousef, because I've said nothing but the truth." Judicia fixed her glasses and folded her arms. "We made the best with what we had."

Andraste's breath left her, and she looked down at the floor.

"What, are you going to cry about it?" Judicia was starting to sound tired. Her voice was getting hoarse. "Go ahead, Andraste. You cry about everything else! The truth hurts, and no amount of senseless weeping is going to change it."

"Fuck you!" Yousef roared at Judicia.

"Both of you, stop." She spoke quietly, but there was great force behind her words. The entire room seemed darker with the clarity in her voice. Andraste looked up, tears running down the sides of her face. "I'm sorry I didn't meet your expectations, Judicia. But your expectations are sick." A few sobs broke her otherwise-solid voice.

"I've heard it all before. Trying to see how your tears will fix it?" She looked at Andraste with a grimace. "Get over yourself!"

"So many people are terrified of what this experiment will do, Judicia. And others will abuse it!" She slammed her fist against the glass wall. "Are you planning on doing this experiment on yourself?"

"You think I'd abuse the power? We'll deal with people like that! They're the ones who get phased out, obviously!" Judicia stood up from the bed, clutching her temple. "And will you stop crying?"

"You can't judge people like that, Judicia!" Andraste slammed both hands on the glass, and a shockwave seemed to roll through the cells. The guards watched in fascination, as Judicia struggled to stand. "You can never get the results you want! You expect perfection to come from imperfect people!" Her conversation with Quadriyyah in London came back to her. "If you chase perfection, you'll be running your whole life!"

"I already said that this is just the first step!" Judicia had both hands clutching her head. "We'll expand on it from your success!"

"I'm not a success, Judicia. And not because of my mistakes." Andraste spoke with more conviction, but her tears still fell. "This whole experiment was a mistake! It's been a mistake from its inception! You're a fucking monster, Judicia!"

Judicia was groaning, clutching her head as hard as possible. She fell to her knees and rolled onto her side, the migraine unbearable. Yousef was tempted to help her, but he stopped himself.

"Stop it, Andraste!" Judicia said as she curled into a ball. "My head is killing me! Please!" A few tears even fell from Judicia's eyes.

Seeing this, and feeling the cold emanations of Judicia's terror, Andraste relaxed her stance. She did her therapeutic breathing, which Yousef seemed to notice as he approached the glass.

"Hang in there, Andy." He said before going to help Judicia off the ground. She was taking deep breaths herself and shaking, though she tried to swat Yousef away.

The glass doors opened and a guard came in. He shoved Yousef aside as two more came in to get Judicia. He spoke into his communicator: "Securing Dr. Judicia. She's not safe around Andraste."

"Get off me," Judicia said weakly.

Andraste struggled to see this,

"J-Judicia?" Andraste pleaded. The woman was groaning in pain as the guards put her in a wheelchair.

"Fine, Andraste." She said, voice creaking. One of her hands flipped around in dismissal. "I'm not going to change your mind. Have your convictions and leave me out of it."

Andraste's sense of victory turned bittersweet as Judicia was strapped in and wheeled away. Deflated after the outburst, her knees weakened and she slid back onto the bed. Tears kept falling from her eyes.

"Are you all right, Andraste?" Yousef said.

She wiped some of her tears away. "I-I can't stop," she sobbed, trying to steady her uneven voice. "I keep crying."

"It's all right, Andraste." He put a hand on the glass, and a feeling of warmth filled her room.

She kept breathing, and continued to steady herself. Seeing Yousef's hand on the glass, she put her hand on the same spot from her side of the room. "Thank you, Doctor. I-I," she began, trying to find the words, "I want to say that I really appreciate everything you've done for me. Even at my worst, you've helped me so much."

He smiled at her as she said this. "Thank you, Andraste." His grin was wide, stretching over his thin face. "All I ever wanted was to help you."

"But why?" She asked, choking back the tears. "Do you still mean that after learning what I've done before? And for rejecting your help?" Right as she managed to curb her tears, she felt another surge. "If I stuck with your original plan of treating my amnesia, I could have learned I was a traitor long ago."

He pursed his lips and sighed. "You were confused and scared, Andraste. I can't blame you for either of those things." Yousef sighed, putting his chin in his hand. "I understand where you're coming from, I think. Years ago, when I was having my own problems," as he said this, he ran his fingers through his ponytail. "I was eager to just put it behind me and move on. And moving on is important, of course. But if your past is still hurting you, then you need to address it."

She looked to the side and nodded. "I see," she said solemnly.

"Thing is, Andy," he put both hands in his lap as he looked at her, "I'd say that's what you're doing now."

Andraste looked back at him.

"Yes, you- you made a mistake. You did run away. But look at you now." He smiled. "You came back. Your whole 'don't run away again' thing has been helping you, don't you think?"

Andraste didn't say anything, only looked at him incredulously.

"Andraste, it's been more than just me and Judicia helping you. You berate yourself all the time for your problems, and those problems can be difficult to deal with-" he caught himself, realizing that he was going to sound demoralizing. "But look how far you've made it! You still worked to improve yourself, you saved so many lives in England, and you've survived some of the worst that the Outlands can throw at you." He put another hand on the glass, a tear running down his own face. "Don't you see? You've learned. You're not an idiot or a weakling like you keep telling yourself. All that's left is for you to be a little nicer to yourself from now on." He dragged his sleeve over the tear. "You said it yourself: perfection from an imperfect person doesn't work. So you can't be at the top of your game all the time. But that doesn't make you weak! If you *were* perfect, you- you wouldn't be you!"

Listening to this, Andraste's expression went wide-eyed and hard to read. She broke the silence by putting her other hand on the glass. "Dr. Yousef," she whimpered, sounding happy as the tears fell again.

"You've made me proud, Andy. For what it's worth, despite all the utter fucking insanity around us, I know I can keep counting on you."

She chuckled, and this summoned more conflicted emotions. But she knew Yousef was right. This beaming warmth and sincerity all seemed familiar because she had felt it before from Yousef.

More of Yousef's sentiments became clearer as she reminisced on all the people who had backed her. All the other doctors in the project, Quadriyyah when she came to see her, and the smile on some of the Holacksi family's faces. Ivan came to mind, and she felt warm as she recalled his smile and enthusiasm.

"I wonder how he's doing," she thought as more tears came. She didn't try to stop them.

"People don't cry because they're weak, they cry because they know what it's like to be strong," Nathan Rowe had said. Ages ago, it seemed, he was upbeat and wise and willing to help however he could. What was he now?

"Mr. Rowe," she said under her breath.

"What's that?" Yousef asked, keeping his voice steady for her. "Rowe?"

Andraste nodded, sighing out her grief. "What's happening to him? You heard about the broadcast with him. It sounds like he's lost it!"

Yousef bit his lip and looked to the side. "Yeah, it does. I don't know, Andy. People can do ludicrous things when they're under a lot of stress, but this," he paused, shrugging, "I dunno. I'm still processing the whole 'Iconoclast Program' thing."

She kept looking at her hand as it closed into a fist. "That doesn't matter now. I'm not doing this for him, I'm doing this for everyone." She returned Yousef's gaze. "Now, I need to wait and see what Bashford wants me to do."

He leaned back and sighed. "I hope he's good to his word."

"Bashford is a lot of things, Yousef," she said, disbelieving herself, "but he's not a liar. He really believes he wants me to fix something out here."

"Right," Yousef said, incredulous. "Whatever happens, Andy, please be careful."

She nodded. "I will be, Yousef. I'll figure something out." She couldn't help but glance over at Judicia. "I always find a way."

He smiled as she said this, but then stifled a yawn. "I feel like we've been talking for some time now. And it's late, isn't it?" He looked around for a clock, but the walls were barren. "Some rest would really do us good. Especially you." Yousef looked over at the pillow. "If you don't mind, I think this would be a good time to actually get some rest."

"Yeah, it would. Thanks so much for listening." Andraste yawned herself, drawn to the flat surface of the cot. Her head hit the pillow with a soft thud. "Good night."

"Of course. Good night, Andy." Yousef laid back on his own bed, gratefully sighing as he reclined.

Andraste turned on her side, pulling the thin sheets over herself. For the first time in a while, she felt tired. She welcomed sleep, too tired to acknowledge whatever would come in the morning. When those pangs of uncertainty crept up and told her to prepare, she silenced it with a sentiment from earlier: *"I always find a way."*

She felt the uncertainty creep away as she closed her eyes.

38 Former Czech Territory
09:00   June 10th, 2335

"Andraste!"

She sprang to attention when she heard her name, but not because she was being awoken. It was because of the voice.

She opened her eyes to the field of blue neurons, ringed by that malicious red energy. Looking up, Andraste saw a blue light spinning frantically in place, the Spirit in a spin. The axons and dendrites of the body were all tangling and convulsing, flinging chaotic light. Andraste gasped at it, and even Bashford looked at it with wide eyes.

"I see now!" The Spirit cried, its monotone supplanted by a manic thrill. "It all makes sense! It finally makes sense!" A chorus of other voices seemed to join in its outburst, and the orb began to deform and twist around. A moment of frenzied laughter was heard before it sunk into the floor.

"What the hell?" She managed to say, getting to her feet.

From the glowing center in the ground where the spirit had vanished, an arm sprang out and grabbed at the neurons. It began to pull and heaved out the rest of the body, this time of Scarlet. The general's face and limbs were marked with glowing blue light that also shined out of her eyes and mouth.

"Y-You! What the-" Andraste began to stammer as she backed away. "Scarlet? What's happening?"

"It's okay!" Scarlet put a firm hand on the ground as she yanked herself up. Her voice was an amalgam of her own and the Spirit's, tension underscored by her wide smile. "Andraste, we're so close! I was right, Scarlet is full of answers!"

"What is happening?" Andraste emphasized each word. "Am I talking to the spirit or to Scarlet?"

"Both," the amalgam said happily, before it began to laugh with a hundred voices at once. The massive space began to shake with the echoes. "Next up, Andraste, you need to calm the heart with Bashford. And it's too worked up for us to work with now."

Andraste tentatively regarded it. "Well, how do I do that? I don't even know what Bashford wants me to do."

"You'll learn soon enough." She went for a flap in her jacket and unsheathed her infamous knife. It was glowing in the darkness.

Andraste looked at it with wide eyes. "W-what is this?"

"You'll need it to stop the heart. Think of it like a pointy defibrillator." She held the knife by the blade and extended it to Andraste. "Don't let Bashford see it."

Knowing she wouldn't get any more answers, Andraste took the knife. A sense of dread crept up her spine as she held it, and foreign images of this blade used to torture and murder people started to swirl in her head. She seemed to hold Scarlet's entire history of cruelty and violence, and the severity of it made her hand tremble.

"You'll know when you have a chance to use it. Make the right decision."

"What's the decision?" Andraste pleaded her. "Kill Bashford?"

"You need to see it to believe it. If nothing else, I can tell you this:" Scarlet began to fade from the scene. "Don't let Bashford succeed. Once you see what he wants to do, you'll know why that can't happen."

Andraste fell to her knees, holding the knife and looking at its intense glow. She was tired of waiting, and had too many questions to bear.

"What do you want from me?" She looked up at Scarlet, though she had vanished.

Sighing, Andraste closed her eyes for a moment, trying to center herself. A hard knocking came crashing through the calm surroundings. She opened her eyes again and saw she was back in the cell. A soldier was knocking on the door.

"Wake up. The general needs you."

Looking to the side, she saw that Judicia and Yousef weren't in their cell. She also noticed that she was gripping Scarlet's knife in her hand.

"Alright, on my way." Andraste slipped the blade into the waist of her trousers, handle hidden beneath her jacket. They hadn't given her a change of clothes. With her shoes on, she followed the soldier out of the cell.

Up several flights of stairs, the cruelties held in the knife still seemed to weigh on her. She wanted to anticipate whatever was ahead of her, but she didn't want to lose her focus before confronting Bashford. Ever upwards through rough-hewn tunnels of an abandoned bomb shelter and other structures made to suit the needs of the Martyr's Army, Andraste and the soldier were silent.

After an age of walking, the two of them reached a door that opened into a cathedral. An ancient remnant of the invasion, Andraste was awed by the dilapidated but still magnificent St. Vitus cathedral. Bashford was standing in front of the door to the entrance.

"Were you able to rest, Andraste?" He spoke as he turned. "I hope so. You will certainly need it today."

"I was. But I hope I'll finally find out what you expect me to do." Andraste folded her arms.

He pursed his lips and nodded before he pushed the doors open. "Soon," he said.

Bashford told the soldier to remain at the cathedral as he led Andraste outside. Like she had seen coming in, the city had some remnants of what it used to be- a handful of broken buildings and cracked streets with greenery growing out and around them, some left as a testament to decay and others re-appropriated by the Army. Down the street from the cathedral, its presence marked by an old fountain resplendent with flowers and plants, there was the edge of a tremendous forest.

"Into the heart of our so-called 'jungle,' Andraste. That is where we will resolve this situation." He started to walk.

She followed, looking at the general silence that filled the area. "And it will only be you and me?"

"Yes." His words were terse. "As you saw yesterday, I am deeply affected by the power of the Outlands. You, meanwhile, may be more affected by it than anyone." A few soldiers on patrol would turn and look at them as they went. Some saluted Bashford, but they dropped the gesture when they saw Andraste.

"And that other woman?" The knife seemed to become heavier at her side as she said this. A prickling sensation radiated from it. "General Scarlet, was it?"

"General Scarlet?" He sighed and shrugged his shoulders. "General Scarlet is dead."

Andraste nearly stopped moving as she heard this. Calming herself, she knew giving away more information was a mistake, but something was off here. "I'm surprised to hear that."

"Indeed. She was leading a raid on a British camp and was shot dead. Not like her to be so careless." Bashford's tone seemed intentional, speaking with a lilt about Scarlet's carelessness.

Andraste was unsettled by this news, her pace slowing as she thought on it. It was most apparent when she nearly tripped on an obvious crack in the road, and she caught her breath as she regained her balance. "Well, I'm, er, sorry you lost such a valuable compatriot."

Bashford looked to her, raising an eyebrow. "Yes, it's a shame. But she died for a good cause." He gestured towards the edge the forest, where a lightly trodden path stood beneath the trees. Around the city, there were rows of Outland Spice trees. She followed, with some hesitation.

Uneven root structures and offshoots of massive trees lined the path they walked. With each step, Andraste seemed to notice more and more energy moving around her. Through the roots beneath the ground and up into the great tree trunks, there was a transference of something like water through pipes. As certain as her pulse, it carried life, but had no presence. Tension built in her chest as she followed Bashford.

"Your first time here won't be easy," he said, "But it will answer numerous questions." He kept a steady pace, though the path seemed to go on and on. The sense of uncertainty mounted as they went along, and after several minutes, the movement she noticed throughout the world felt more and more powerful. The pressure in her chest radiated into her head as the energy became more tangible. If she focused, she could pick up what seemed like a heartbeat, becoming more and more pronounced as they went along. Another thirty minutes of silence, pulsing, and pressure passed, and Andraste was ready to burst.

"Do you," she spoke on impulse, forgetting her situation. "Do you feel that?" She had to address it. The sensation was too strong. "I swear, there's a-a heartbeat out here."

He nodded, slowly. "Indeed there is. That should give you an idea of where we're going."

Andraste paused when she heard this, though Bashford kept going. The further along they went, the harder each pulse hit. Even Bashford's steps seemed more staggered. He was sweating and clenching his fists as he walked along. The air seemed to distort from each shockwave, and Andraste was hearing as well as feeling each beat. It radiated through the forest like a gust of wind, and the trees shook with unsteady vigor. With the energy surging through the ground, it felt like walking on an artery.

"He wasn't exaggerating," she thought.

Some time later, Bashford led Andraste into a clearing in the forest. Surrounded by bizarre flowers- green stalks and leaves branching out wildly among iridescent petals that changed color with each pulse- there was a deep hole in the ground, vines radiating out of it that looked more like flesh than wood.

"What the hell?" Andraste asked. She had a feeling of what the answer would be, looking to Bashford for an answer. "Is this-"

"The Heart of the Outlands, Andraste." He finished for her. "In the most literal sense." He stood over the hole and the numerous roots coming from it, a drop of sweat running down his face. "Here, our work begins."

39 Former Czech Territory
11:32   June 10th, 2335

Bashford's serious expression vanished at the sound of a ringing phone on his tablet. He grimaced as he looked at the number.

Fearfully, Andraste looked on. He eventually put set it on a tripod so the two of them could adjust to the Outlands' beating heart. The screen lit up, and Rowe sat in his office, brow furrowed.

"Bashford!" He cried before anyone else could say anything. "You're sorely mistaken if you think you've won!" Rowe was bent over his desk, disheveled and gritting his teeth.

"Rowe, what is the meaning of this?" Bashford demanded as he approached the camera. "I can only hope you've given more thought to my offer from yesterday."

"Mr. Rowe!" Andraste spoke up, walking in front of Bashford.

"Quiet, traitor!" Rowe's look cut into Andraste. "I have considered our situation, Bashford. And I'm here to say that you were too quick to think I've been powerless." With a wicked smirk, Rowe pressed a button on his keyboard and brought up another display. "Perhaps you recognize this, Bashford?"

There was an aerial image of a tanker ship on the open water, going towards the southern English coast. It had no flag on it.

Bashford's jaw dropped as he gasped. "Rowe, what are you on about? That's not one of ours!"

"Oh, of course it isn't," he said in mockery. "It's just a refugee carrier, so blatantly ignoring the decree that we've shut down our borders. And there's no telling how many of your agents and brainwashed servants you're trying to messily throw onto our shores." Rowe appeared again in a small window as he said this, with a complex remote in one hand. "I'm going on the offensive, Bashford. I'm only going to tell you this once:" Rowe spoke with menacing emphasis. "You surrender, drop all your weapons, and release all your hostages. Or, so help me, I will bomb this ship to the bottom of the sea."

Bashford and Andraste both reeled in shock at this command. Rowe was twitching and breathing hard, that same warped smile on his face.

"Mr. Rowe, what are you thinking? That's a civilian vessel!" Andraste spoke up, indignity powering her voice. "Those are only-"

She stopped when the camera on the aerial view zoomed in. There were countless people aboard this ship, appropriately squeezed into this place like cargo, but the sight of one passenger made her breath catch in her throat, turning into a mote of frozen terror. There was a small family on the top deck. An elderly woman with glasses, several adults and grandchildren, and a young boy on a man's shoulders who had his arms in the air. On one of his hands was a thick bandage, covering a part of his hand as if he were missing fingers.

"Oh my god," she shuddered, feeling limp. Andraste fell to her knees. "Rowe, I'm begging you not to attack that ship!" Tears ran down her face, contempt and hate conflicting with the memories of the man she used to know. "You're better than this!"

"I already told you that we had everything riding on you, so now we're forced to seek alternatives! This is on you as well, Andraste!" He looked pained as he said this. "You've both made your intentions very clear, and I can only hope I'm also being clear. I will not suffer more traitors here!"

"Whatever harm you bring to that ship, I will unleash upon London tenfold." Bashford spoke gravely. "One wrong move, Rowe, and you will face the greatest extent of the Army's power."

"Stop! Both of you!" Andraste got up, turning to her side so she could face them both. "I will not tolerate the deaths of any civilians, British or otherwise!" She whipped around to Rowe. "Listen to yourself, Mr. Rowe! I had faith that you would make the right decisions, but this is madness! What perfect world are you making where you murder innocent people?"

Rowe wavered when she mentioned 'perfect world.' He was brought back to the words of Quadriyyah, and his hand went slack on the remote. His expression softened only for a second in hesitation.

"You've made a grand display of what you're willing to throw at us, Rowe." Bashford commanded the attention of the area as he walked back to the crater. "Let me show you what the Martyr's Army can do, Rowe! Andraste, I'll need your help with this!"

She turned to look at him, broken away from the screen by his tone. "Help with what?"

Bashford pointed to a spot opposite him across the gap. "Focus your mind, Andraste! Feel the life beneath our feet!"

As he said this, he extended his arm, and a red energy radiated around him like the times Andraste had focused herself. It was a ferocious red instead of her own soothing blue. She did the same, and felt a mental presence. A massive, pulling presence that almost made her stumble into the crater. She fortified herself, however, feeling the presence radiate and flare out with different emotions and thoughts. The heartbeats from the ground became faster and more frenzied, each one tearing through Andraste's body.

"What are you two doing?" Rowe demanded from the distant tablet.

"Stay strong, Andraste!" Bashford called out, his own voice under duress. "We will not awaken it easily!"

'Awaken?' Andraste went weak at the knees when Bashford said this. Whatever it turned out to be, Andraste remembered the furtive knife that Scarlet had given her, and she continued to press on.

The earth began to tremble as she and Bashford focused their energy, feeling the weight of foreign emotions and thoughts going off like bombs in and around her head. Cold fear, burning anger, electric panic, and cascades of other feelings and elements whirling around and colliding off each other. Tears ran from her eyes, and she could see blood running down Bashford's face. She was shaking as she felt this creature respond to her mental intrusion, reminded of the painful tour she had with the press back in London.

There was no humanity in this underground monster. She took her therapeutic breaths- breathe in, count to five, breathe out, count to five- as she focused on its incoherent thoughts and Bashford appeared to be manipulating its body. After a few moments of tense silence shaken by the beating heart, something started to move.

There was a lurch in the entire landscape, such that a sense of whiplash disrupted Andraste's footing. Re-orienting herself, Andraste saw the overlay of neurons that she usually saw in her mind, with long blue offshoots shooting up into the trees, dendrites extending into the branches and leaves. The expanse of neurons spread out until they came to the hole in the center, where they all converged into a giant blue mass, even larger than the Spirit. Each wave of emotion was distinctly radiating from this massive pile of neurons.

"Keep going, Andraste!" Bashford cried out, an odd glimmer in the blood on his face. It soaked into his white beard and dripped from his chin. Laboriously, he turned his head away from the shifting mass in the crater and back at the tablet. "Witness, Rowe! This is stronger than any bomb you could drop!"

With the blue neurons lit up, red cracks appeared in the figure. Much like what Andraste saw in Bashford's vision, blood-red lines began to weave their way through the blue. Bashford was exerting himself even more, blood falling from his eyes, nose, and mouth.

The more Bashford pushed himself, the more blood veins filled the thing beneath them. The blood started to define the outlines of some creature, as the veins outlined a head, a torso, and limbs. While the neurons were focused in the head, the blood veins were focused in the chest. They piled up together to form a sort of heart, heavily pulsing in time with the other beats running throughout the world. With lugubrious movement, a giant humanoid was pulling itself out of the crater. A hodgepodge of muscle fibers and blood, it opened two massive, pupilless eyes and looked up. Andraste staggered when she saw this.

"N-No! It can't be!" Andraste shuddered as she saw her suspicions confirmed.

"What is this nonsense, Bashford?" Rowe stood up and looked in uncertain horror.

"This is the true power of the Outlands, Nathan Rowe!" Bashford turned to the camera and pointed at the monster. "Your experiment in creating a Fomorian Hybrid was the perfect catalyst for reviving the true Fomorians!"

At the word "Fomorian," the creature lifted its head and screeched. Sinew and flecks of blood flapped around its mouth as its cry filled the air with an unbearable physical force. Andraste was deafened as the sound waves knocked her to her knees. The world around her seemed to warp and deform as the shout rippled through the space, and Bashford was struggling to stand as he looked at the tablet with Rowe. The image was distorted and glitching, with Rowe himself looking pained by the experience.

"Want to drop bombs, Rowe? We'll drop a Fomorian on you!" Bashford had a crooked smile as he watched Rowe squirm.

The beast slumped over when it had stopped screaming. Andraste was able to get her bearings, though carrying the weight of this creature's infantile, cacophonous whirlwind of emotions was a struggle all the same.

Bashford wasn't looking at her, and the creature seemed tired. She saw where the Fomorian's heart and brain were vulnerable.

Andraste took a breath and drew the knife.

"Now or never. You can do this."

Breaking out of her stance, Andraste leapt. Her fingers found purchase on the exposed muscle tissue and veins, and she felt the hot, wet pulse of its blood in its ropey fibers. The Fomorian lurched when it felt her climb on, but it was too slow to react. Grabbing the creature by the shoulder, it reared back, and Andraste felt power run through her body before building up in her arm. Releasing the tension, she buried the knife into the Fomorian's back, going for the heart.

Bashford turned to the creature with a start. He heard another shriek, loud and shrill enough to pierce the world. Its eyes blazed with pain and fury as its limbs spasmed, coming to an abrupt stop when the blade of the knife burst from its heart.

"No," he gasped after an agonizing pause. "No!"

Andraste dragged her arm out of the monster's chest, jumping back as it fell. It struck the ground in front of Bashford, head rolling to the side. Blood gushed from the wounds of the beast before its color faded and it was pulled back into the crater. Its features unraveled, resembling old roots again, before slithering away from the Fomorian's crumpled form.

Andraste and Bashford stared, her arm still dripping wet and clutching the knife. Panting, the fury in her eyes was met by the bereavement in his. His face warped into anger before shouting back at her.

"What have you done?" Bashford pointed at the crater.

Andraste didn't respond, only looked back at the tablet. Rowe was shuddering in his chair as he witnessed this, the remote dangling in his hand.

"Is this what it takes, Mr. Rowe?" Andraste said as she gestured to him with the blade. "Do we need to bring back Fomorians to stop you from killing refugees?" She sighed before looking back at his face. "I've made mistakes, Rowe. And I will make amends for them. But there won't be any amending what you're about to do. This will be tantamount to the death of Aaron Sennec."

Rowe, limp in his chair, looked back with wide eyes when he heard the name. Shaking, he looked at the remote he held, as if he didn't know what it was. After a shuddering gasp, he covered his face with his hand and put it down.

"Rowe!" Bashford grabbed the tablet from its tripod. "This isn't over! Until you and your entire country lie dead, we will fight!" The blood on his face ran down and started splattering on the screen of the tablet. "There will only be justice for the Outlands and the world that Aaron Sennec fought to create!

"And you!" Bashford turned and pointed at Andraste, throwing the tablet onto the ground. "How dare you use Sennec's name like that! We've given you a chance, and you're throwing it in our faces!"

"I said it before, and I'll say it again:" Andraste pointed the blade at Bashford, her voice clear and strong. "I will never work with you!" She got into a stance and readied herself for a fight. "The only way the world will end is if you idiots actually bring back the Fomorians!"

"Look who's talking!" Bashford's eyes grew red, an all-consuming dark crimson that obscured his pupils. "Great Britain has been a thorn in our side for too long! I'll stop at nothing to avenge Sennec!"

"More and more about Aaron Sennec," Andraste groaned, shaking her head. "If he thought that the Fomorians would save the world, then he was as big an idiot as the rest of you!"

Bashford hurled himself at Andraste, becoming a blur of red energy and fists. She ducked out of the way, and his knuckles hit the tree behind her, breaking it in half. He was bent over and breathing hard, steam coming off the blood on his face.

"You don't know the first thing about him." His voice was deep and growling with vicious intent.

"Enlighten me, then." She looked back at him, and her knife went for his throat.

The tree creaked, and a thick branch shot out between them to eclipse the knife point. Andraste froze in shock, not just from branch but from the reflexive speed of it. Bashford grinned as he reached over and grabbed her by the shirt.

"Do you really want to do this, Andraste?" He was able to pick her up and lift her off the ground. "You don't have any allies out here. You're surrounded from every angle."

She struggled against him, only enough to get her bearings and look into his eyes. With a sharp inhale, she focused her mind on Bashford's, feeling the warm corona of his anger from the fiery core deep within. She leapt into his mind, overwhelming it with images, memories, and sensations. This blow left a fracture in his resolve that almost echoed with an audible crack, and he recoiled from it. He held his head in his hands as he released her, stepping back.

Andraste pried the blade out from the tree as Bashford staggered back into his position. He looked up at her, and the red blood flows seemed to glow and dig into his skin. She looked over at the tablet where Rowe was still sitting, bewildered.

"Prague, Rowe! We're in Prague! St. Vitus Cathedral!"

"This is your greatest blunder, Andraste!" Bashford roared as he grabbed the tree branch and stump, wrenching them from the ground as another tree branch fastened itself around Andraste's neck. She felt it grow tense as other roots came up and tied her feet in place. With a hearty roar, Bashford struck her with the improvised root hammer, and the impact sent her flying away from the scene.

Back down the path, she tumbled through branches and brush until she nearly breached the entrance back to Prague. With the same mental energy, she looked into the neurons and dendrites of the life around her. In a desperate effort, she tried to insinuate her own will into the surrounding nature the same way she had spurred other people into moving. To her amazement, she could make these branches fly out and catch her before she struck the ground. From the distance, she heard Bashford again, and the forest shuddered from his cry.

"Andraste!" His voice shook the earth. Down the path, Andraste could feel him sprinting towards her, propelling himself further with the trees.

40   London, England
12:05   June 10th, 2335

Rowe was left hanging, the tablet crushed by the trees being thrown around. He saw Bashford take after Andraste, only guessing at what kinds of atrocities would follow. On the notion of atrocities, he looked at the remote on his desk and felt sick. He drew up the blinds on a window, seeing the protestors. The "Nutty Nathan" image of him had gone viral, and he saw one alongside his own reflection in the glass. Oversized forehead, tiny little eyes, a big mouth full of jagged teeth. He was wounded, not for the criticism or unflattering depictions, but at how he had spent the past few hours justifying them.

There was a beating at his door. He had his door locked and barricaded, but with a sigh, he disengaged the security and allowed it to open. Rowe didn't brace himself for the flood of people as much as he accepted the potential of getting trampled under their shoes.

"Rowe!" Cried a handful of familiar voices as security officers crashed through the door and apprehended the Prime Minister. He put up no resistance. Other members of the Cabinet walked in, looks of judgment and irritation spread equally among them.

"What's going on out there?" Quadriyyah demanded, before looking down and snatching up the remote. She leaned in close and glowered at the man. "Rowe, what have you done?"

"I haven't dropped any bombs, Laurie." Rowe shook his head, knowing his penitence wouldn't mean much to them. "I was trying to put more pressure on the Army by targeting a refugee ship."

"You can't be serious," Quadriyyah spoke up in a temper. "Do you have any idea what you could have done?"

"I do, Chancellor. I do." He nodded at her, feeling limp in the hold of these guards. "I'm not in a position to talk about plans, but you need to know what's going on out there."

Irritated silence became horrified attentiveness as Rowe told them about the situation with Bashford and Andraste. How she had talked him out of the attack, the resurrection of the Fomorian, and how she and Bashford were fighting to the death even as they spoke. The video data confirmed this, and the atmosphere changed from one of justified persecution to one of intense planning.

"Prague? How have we failed to notice until now?" Laurie asked aloud, as if pieces were starting to come together in his mind.

"What's our next move?" Rowe asked, compliant with the security guard keeping him in place.

"Well, Rowe, you managed to get eyes on a ship." Quadriyyah spoke up. "If we can get eyes on Prague, figure out what's happening out there."

"That can be arranged," Laurie responded. "Those images were taken by a drone. I'll get a crew to look onto Prague and get us some information."

"And then what?" Rowe demanded. "We can't keep throwing bombs out there!"

"No," Laurie followed, "But we can keep pressure on them. Get a tactical strike on that Fomorian heart, maybe."

"Then what are we standing around for?" Quadriyyah cried emphatically. "We have lives to save and an Army to suppress! Back to Central Base!"

They all filed out, pulling Rowe behind them onto the secret train car. Rowe didn't object, and had a small sense of pride for his peers showing better judgment than him. He knew his political career was over, but he felt assured that the rest of the Cabinet could handle these situations.

At the base, every manner of military personnel and government official was present, fervently moving around the space as they coordinated with their high-ranking peers.

"Get us a visual on Andraste and Bashford!" Quadriyyah stepped forward.

In a burst of red fury, Bashford leapt out of the forest and lunged at Andraste. As she leapt back, his fist struck the ground and left a crater. Her footing was uneven, but she was still able to keep him off her as he followed up with other blows. Bashford, roaring in exertion the entire time, threw boulders, destroyed buildings, and even sent up dense waves of sharp roots to impale her from beneath the ground.

Andraste kept her distance as best she could, creating illusions in his mind to sidetrack or distract him as she got in a few furtive blows. He was hyper-vigilant about the knife, interrupting her strike each time the blade tried to go for his flesh. Even her hardest punch to his temple only dazed him for a moment.

There were handfuls of soldiers and other druids coming out from the scarce buildings to support Bashford, but they could only distract. Though the spirit was absent, Andraste still felt its power bolstering her, and she turned every gun that was on her towards Bashford. As if anticipating it, Bashford either dodged or created barriers of roots and stone to defend himself. After a few minutes, controlling each individual soldier became too tiresome, and Andraste could only overload their minds, killing them or knocking them unconscious.

"This can't go on," she thought.

Bashford could take every blow, few as they were, and never grew tired from exertion or pain. His face still burned red as the blood on his face smoldered and crusted over. He started to anticipate the next blow to his mind or illusion that she would create. As Andraste looked through his eyes to predict his next blow, Bashford feinted the moment Andraste put up her guard and slugged her from the other side. All his hits were enough to send her flying. This was becoming a battle of attrition, and Andraste knew he had the fortitude that she lacked. Her only advantage was the blade.

After a near miss when he almost kicked a radio tower on top of her, Andraste lost her footing and fell onto her back, fighting to catch her breath again. She looked up and saw Bashford standing over her.

"You're beginning to see it, aren't you?" His tone had calmed down, though his voice was ragged. "This fighting is pointless."

A sense of indignity spurred Andraste. She made a clumsy lunge at him with the knife, which he easily deflected. Never taking his eyes off her, he grabbed her forearm and threw her back on the ground.

"This stupid British patriotism will get you killed. Would you consider working with us if it meant surviving?"

Andraste coughed before getting her breath. "I-I don't understand your hatred of Great Britain," she gasped, knowing she was in no position to get back up and keep swinging. "You used to be a soldier!"

"And I don't understand your unflinching devotion." He spat with a bitter sting in his words. "Your country claims to be an augur of progress and tolerance, but really, nothing has changed about it in centuries." He bent over and looked at her. "I used to work in Outland Reclamation, Andraste. I would go out into the wilderness to fight the original worshippers of the Fomorians. And we would take their lands for ourselves. How is that progressive?" He became more alive with vitriol. "Stealing land and killing dissenters? What makes us any different from our colonist ancestors?" With this, he reached down and grabbed Andraste by the throat. "Hundreds of years, countless technological advances, and an alien invasion later, we're right back where we started. Especially with *you* running around." He picked Andraste up and pinned her to the wall as she struggled against him. "You are the apex of conquest, Andraste. Created to further another agenda at all costs, and to replace humanity with a more 'ideal' variation. Not that this is any surprise to you."

Andraste fought to keep herself breathing as Bashford talked her down.

"So what do you suggest?" Andraste struggled to say. "Do you want me to make another Fomorian for you? Avert this so-called doomsday you keep going on about?"

"The Fomorian heart is the key to the great death, yes. And by bringing it under our control, we can avert the destruction." With a deft swipe, he took the knife from her and let her fall to the ground. "There was always a source of immense power out here, and once you appeared in the Outlands, that power started to lash out at us." He folds his arms and looks at her. "If we can't control it, then we all die." Bashford's eyes were narrowed. "Now that you've seen it, can you refute the power that dwells out here?"

Getting her breath back, Andraste stood up and looked at him, massaging her throat. "No, I can't." She sighed, aggravated. "But do you really think you can control that thing?"

"We have to. For everyone's sake. Once we do, we can fix the entire planet." He spoke with clear conviction. "I'm using everything that Aaron Sennec taught me to keep the land from claiming us. Could you find it in yourself to use what you've learned and save the world?" Bashford's tone carried a mocking weight, as if it were unimaginable that she would say 'no.' "And, furthermore, I haven't forgotten about Judicia and Makkareb." His eyes grew intense again. "If you continue to be difficult, then I will kill them."

She felt her breath catch in her throat, sticking to the insides of her lungs and making breathing impossible. She meant every word when she swore she would never work with the Martyr's Army, but she was racking her brain for an alternative.

The weight of the decision paralyzed her, and she thought she would choke. No other life was worth her own pride, and even though the doctors weren't far, she never felt more alone. Bashford's presence alone cemented it, and considering the scope of Prague, she could feel the pressure on all sides. At this point, the spirit of the Outlands usually came out to get her back on her feet, but she had no idea where it was. As this phrase entered her mind, all the situation's gravity condensed and fell onto her chest: *"No one is coming to save you."*

Bashford looked at her expectantly, as if observing her meltdown. As Andraste labored over the decision, she looked up. A shadow hung in the sky, just as the sun reached its zenith. She heard distant rotor blades: a drone. Bashford broke his gaze to look and stood back in shock.

"Andy!" A voice called from it. She immediately recognized it.

"Chancellor Quadriyyah?" She called back, relieved but perplexed.

"Prague it is, then!" As she said this, there was a powerful hum in the distance before two fighter jets screamed overhead, faster than an eyeblink. The shockwave was enough to knock Andraste and Bashford off-balance.

"George Bashford!" Quadriyyah cried from the drone. "Surrender yourself and all of your weapons now, and you and the army shall be granted clemency." Bashford was too incensed to reply at first. With the pause, Adam Laurie came on. "And, before you start pointing fingers, all of this has been done legally. I have consented to this direct strike on your base."

More and more jets swept overhead. Andraste felt the despair melt away as a tear collected in her eye.

Bashford, however, grew redder and bloodier at this. "Imbeciles!" He barked at the drone. "You're only angering the Outlands with this display! I can feel the blood boiling!" As he said this, he stomped on the ground and a surge of crackling red energy went towards the woods, causing a line of trees to shoot towards the sky. Several jets were caught, their explosions echoing throughout the space.

As Andraste lamented the loss of life, she noticed an energy pulsing throughout the space, just as Bashford described: a frenetic sensation likened to boiling. She felt a hollow echo as the jets struck the trees. Listening closer, she noticed the distinction of the voice.

"The Spirit!" She looked back at the forest, realizing it came from the Fomorian heart back between the trees. Along the same neuronal pathways that she manipulated to control the trees, Andraste focused a message to the Spirit: "Can you hear me?"

"A-Andra-aste," it repeated, voice threshed through fear and pain.

The spirit was interrupted when gunfire echoed from above. Geysers of dirt and grass erupted in front of Bashford, who noticed as much as Andraste that the land was crying out in pain.

"Bashford, the next shot won't be a warning." Quadriyyah continued to speak through the drone. "Surrender."

With this lapse in his concentration, Andraste roused the disturbed vigor of the Outlands into herself. She felt the sensation climb through her feet and up into her mind, as if a cloud of sheer lightning had formed in her head. Struggling to even see Bashford with her shuddering sight, she honed on his mental state and let the lightning latch onto him.

Bashford turned to her just as she launched her attack, and he immediately staggered, clasping his head. He fell onto his knee and clutched his temples to keep his skull from splitting open. With Bashford incapacitated, she took off running to the forest again.

"Andraste!" He roared, struggling to his feet. "Get back here!"

She heard Quadriyyah protest as well, and she would have listened to them, but here, hesitation was death. The Spirit was calling out to her. She ran past gunfire and soldiers screaming orders at each other with the occasional jet roaring by, her focus honed on the entrance to the forest.

Bashford followed, shifting his focus from the tree line to the road ahead. He made a wall of roots burst from the ground, forcing Andraste to stop. She turned to him, keeping herself at ease with deep breaths. She was afraid, but kept her goals in mind.

"What do you even plan to do, Andraste?" He demanded. "Do you *ever* have a plan?" As he spoke, the stone surrounding Andraste shuddered and shifted. "Your dumb luck won't last forever!"

Without breaking eye contact, she could tell there was a disturbance around her. "I have nothing to say to you."

She finished saying this and leapt into the air, dodging the clumps of stone and wood splinters that Bashford tried to crush her with. Andraste found her footing and took off again, anticipating Bashford's other attacks. With the jets keeping them occupied, she was able to sidetrack several Martyr's Army soldiers trying to shoot at her, focusing them onto Bashford. She even landed some hits, but Bashford pressed on despite the injuries.

Having considerable traction over Bashford, Andraste accelerated herself back to the Fomorian Heart with the help of the trees as Bashford had done earlier. She paused, however, when she saw the remains of a crashed plane. Most of the body was in one piece, with one of the wings blown off by an engine failure.

Bashford was gaining ground, albeit with a slower speed from his injuries. Making a snap decision, Andraste ducked behind the plane and disengaged some of the latches that kept the missiles in place. As she emerged, she saw Bashford clambering towards her with even more furious vigor. He threw his arm forward and gathered roots and stones in the air around him, prepared to throw them at her.

"Enough." She stated, as matter-of-factly as she could manage. Like a javelin, she threw one of the plane's unspent missiles at Bashford just as his natural barrage coalesced. The last thing she saw was an uncharacteristic look of rage and utter disbelief on his face.

She turned away, feeling the heat and shockwave of the explosion roll over her. Staggering, she took off running again before she could see what happened to Bashford. Through the ringing in her ears, she catapulted herself along the trees back to the Fomorian Heart.

The crater was in sight, and the presence she felt inside it was beating loud and hard, fracturing the ground around it. Consistent with the pained cries of the spirit, this so-called heart appeared to be having a bout of cardiac arrest. When Andraste touched the ground, she struggled to stay up amidst the tremors.

"Spirit!" She called out to it, desperate for some response. "I'm here!"

"Andraste!" The voice called back to her, loud and distinct. "At last, you're back!"

"What the hell is happening?" Andraste clung to the ground, the tremors relentless. "What's happening to you?"

"I'm fine now that you are here!" As it said this, blue dendrites rose out of the ground like tendrils. "Everything makes sense now! I have so much to tell you!" The tendrils started to drift towards her.

"What are you talking about?" Andraste backed away, but found herself caught by other dendrites that crept up along the ground. They were pulling her into the crater. "Stop it! What are you-"

"You need to see, Andraste. You need to be here to understand it all." The dendrites began to pull.

"No, wait!" She yanked back, breaking a few tendrils off her arms. "It's a war zone out here! We're not safe!"

"Our mutual friend wouldn't dare harm this spot."

Behind her, she heard a heavy footfall. She turned to see Bashford, propping himself up on a tree trunk. His right arm hung mangled and bloody, with deep, bleeding wounds in both of his legs. Breathing laboriously, he glowered at her, face covered in blood and burns. What little was left of him was near-unrecognizable, but Andraste could see that same vitriol and hate in his eyes.

Andraste saw this and felt a different kind of pull. Not just from the heart, but from within. The Fomorian presence beneath the ground was drawing her towards it, and she felt no urge to fight it. She would be escaping Bashford, learning from the spirit, and even more. There was no argument that Bashford would refuse to harm this place. Following the pull and the logic, Andraste kept looking at Bashford before jumping into the hole.

"No!" He cried, stumbling forward before losing his balance and falling on his knees.

The Spirit pulled Andraste from the violent and hectic world above into a dark, quiet one, where neurons surrounded her in a dense expanse. Despite a sense of separation from her body, Andraste found relief in a deep breath.

"Spirit?" She looked out into the cosmos that swirled around her. "Spirit, I've done as you asked! Please, help me understand!" The silence seemed to surround her in response.

Blue pulses traveled along the dendrites, shooting stars in this biological galaxy. They culminated at a point just ahead of her, forming the familiar sphere she was accustomed to seeing. The Spirit manifested with slow, thoughtful movements, more and more resembling a cerebral cortex. Once formed, it moved closer, revealing its sheer size. She felt like a minnow being approached by a whale.

"Oh, at last." The Spirit spoke, its voice occupying all the empty space in the realm. "I feared you would never make it here."

"What is 'here'?" She looked around. "You know what, let's start with what happened in the cell. You were crying out about how 'it all made sense' or something. And what did you do to Scarlet?"

"Well, I told you before that I am just one piece of the Outlands' mind, correct? Well, when you were speaking to Bashford, I finally realized where all the other pieces were, and how to bring them together!" The monotone was gone, and the Spirit spoke with excitement. "Bashford embodies aspects of the Fomorian body, and Scarlet had pieces of the mind! Making that connection with her was astoundingly easy, and she had all these answers!

"That red aura that everyone thinks is the harbinger of the apocalypse is the Fomorian nervous system! It's lashing out at nothing, trying to find its body again!" It laughed when it said this, which mortified her. "Finally, the mind and body of the Outlands are back together!"

"O-okay," Andraste agreed, comprehending but wary. "What does this have to do with the heart? When Bashford and I resurrected the Fomorian-"

"That was no Fomorian!" It barked back, glowing brighter. "A ghost, at best! I was still pulling the pieces of the mind together when that happened! There was no soul in that thing, only blood and sinew!" The Spirit's impassioned voice rose along with the blinding light in the void. "Now, everything is ready. You can finally fulfill your purpose, Andraste!"

This deeply unsettled her. "What purpose?"

"Bringing back the Fomorians!" It cried, radiating its delight.

Andraste's spine went numb.

"The body and mind are coalescing, but they can only do so much on their own. What it needs now is a vessel." The mind floated closer to her. "That's where you fit in, Andraste."

A shred of a moment passed in silence before Andraste responded. "No," she said on impulse. "No, no! You can't be serious!"

"I am serious." The Spirit replied, unoffended. "This is no small thing to ask of you. I understand that. But you need to understand something: your world has been priming for this moment for centuries!"

"Priming?" Andraste heard this and recalled their conversation in the Holacksi's smoker. The way the world was changing seemed to fit the designs of the Fomorians. "The terraforming."

"Exactly!" It cried in delight. "When we came to this world all those years ago, we thought it was perfect. It just needed a few changes."

"What?" Andraste called out to it in shock. "You remember the invasion?"

The Spirit continued despite her protesting. "Fix up the environment, control the population a bit, and this planet would be an excellent addition to the collection!" It began to laugh more, lost in its own glee.

"You're mad!" Andraste shouted at it, wondering where her tears were falling. "Humanity will never yield to you!"

"You would be surprised," the Spirit said, its voice diverging into several different tones. An extension of the neurons came together into a humanoid shape, facing her. Its features developed into those of Scarlet, blooming into full color. It continued speaking in her voice.

"The fragments of the Fomorian mind have taken on numerous forms, Andraste," she narrowed her eyes. "If Scarlet never existed, then the Martyr's Army certainly would have killed you before you could have reached this place."

"You were scheming everything," Andraste said, shaking with fear.

"Oh, even before Scarlet." The figure said, turning to another extension of dendrites creating a human shape. It was a bizarre sight, seeing Scarlet smiling, though Andraste was more concerned with this new person appearing.

A male figure, with a tall forehead, strong chin, and wide smile manifested. Andraste had a suspicion of who he was before his features manifested, and the astonishment hit her hard when she saw the bright eyes and clear skin of Aaron Sennec.

"You can't be serious!"

"I am, Andraste. A substantial piece of the Fomorian mind dwelled within Sennec." He folded his arms, smiling at her. "Explains a lot, doesn't it? How he knew so much about the Outlands and how to help people survive?" He chuckled and sighed. "Even better, his death inspired Great Britain to create you."

Andraste was speechless. These figures were making too much sense. A cold grip of horror crushed her heart, and the sense of helplessness surrounded her like the void she drifted through.

"And now," said three voices in unison- The Spirit, Aaron Sennec, and Scarlet- all smiling as they looked at Andraste, "our vessel is here." They extended their hands. "Don't despair, Andraste. You won't find a greater purpose than this."

At last, she found her voice again. "Everything you did for me," she started, her words trembling, "was for this? Just to get me here?" There was a tangible sense of pain in her tone. There was no hiding her sense of betrayal from the Spirit. As little as she knew about it, The Spirit was the closest thing she had to a connection to the Fomorians. This was not just a betrayal from a friend, but one of the few to understand her.

"Not at first, but that's the reason now. I won't lie to you, Andraste." The trio had died down as the single voice of the Spirit began talking to her. "I understand your feelings, but you must understand, this is your destiny. Don't you see? A perfect world lies within our grasp."

Anger broke through the pain and fueled her next outburst. "Are you joking? Why is everyone so obsessed with making a 'perfect world?' Is that another sign of your meddling?" She forgot the severity of her situation as the memories of Bashford, Jucidicia, and Rowe's arguments came back for her. "It's all anyone talks about!"

"Actually, no. People have taken an intense interest in that on their own." The Spirit was honest, to Andraste's confusion. "That is what makes humanity so fascinating to observe. We see it in you, as well: that constant drive to improve. With our assistance, that improvement will finally be possible."

"Stop! Please!" Andraste clutched the sides of her head, though the sounds of the voices still came through. "What, is all of this just an experiment to you? Nobody asked you to appear and start meddling in things!"

"The same can be said of you." All three voices said this in unison, with Sennec and Scarlet both glowering at her. "And yet, you continued all the same. So who are you to question us? This 'experiment,' as you call it, shall be more than worthwhile for humanity. You've seen them in action. No one knows what to do or how to achieve anything!" Their hands and dozens of other tendrils reached out at Andraste was it said this. "We are not asking you to become the vessel, Andraste. Your destiny is upon you, like it or not."

Petrified, Andraste did not have the wherewithal to struggle when the first few tendrils wrapped around her. She did, however, jump back when Scarlet reached out to her. The gloved hand was going for her throat, and the fingers wrapped around her neck in silent determination. Although Andraste could still breathe, there was no pressure on her throat, but on her entire nervous system. As if her spine itself was being grabbed, she felt the pulse of the tendrils and Fomorian heart rush through her.

"Very good," the voices said. "We don't want this to be painful for you. We've been through so much together, Andraste. You don't think we've forgotten that, do you?" They spoke dolefully, exaggerated but nonetheless sincere. The change from "I" to "we" was most jarring for Andraste. The Spirit was no longer someone she knew.

Relaxing herself as best she could, Andraste met Scarlet's gaze. "No, I wasn't thinking that." Her voice still shook, despite her efforts. "B-but what exactly are you going to do to me?"

She knew it would be pointless to try and lie to this creature, but she wanted nothing to do with it. For a moment, she considered that this was truly the end. This was the culmination of her experiences. Blood, bullets, fire, death and suffering, all unaccountable in the months of her existence. An extra hole in her resolve was dug when she realized. The sum of her frenzied existence had only amounted to a few months.

"Don't be frightened." The Spirit said quietly as more of its tendrils wound their way through and around her. "You will be the host for all of this Fomorian power." It surrounded her in a glowing blue net before drawing her in. "As we said, you will be the vessel. A cohesive body for us to dwell within. As for your mind and personality, they will join the rest of us. You will remain, Andraste, but not as you used to."

"I-I see." Hearing this, Andraste's own grief could not match the fear of becoming the vessel. There was no point in fighting back, and that sense of helplessness almost carried some solace.

"You always find a way," She thought. *"None of this is your fault. You can fix all of this if you try."* It was her own mind speaking to her, but in a tone she barely recognized. She found some resolve from this voice.

Andraste went through her usual drill of relaxing- breathe in, count to five, breathe out, count to five- and spoke to The Spirit again. "All right. Let's do this."

"Excellent! Let's not waste any time!" With a yank, Andraste was pulled into The Spirit's mass before the world went dark again.

Bashford was crumpled over before the crater, dragging his wounded, bleeding body closer to the Fomorian Heart. In the background, there was the din of gunfire and cries of death while more planes flew overhead. As he bled, little was left in him but hate and anger. It was the only thing that kept him crawling forward, even with the occasional blackout from the blood loss.

"Damn it," He sputtered, coughing up heat-fused lumps of blood. "Damn it all!"

Whenever he felt his resolve fail, he imagined Andraste falling into the crater. He felt a shift in the energy of the Outlands while she was in there. Whatever was happening, he was prepared to rip Andraste out of the earth and tear her to pieces. After hauling his destroyed remains across the ground, Bashford had reached the edge of the crater.

As he reached inside, grasping for some semblance of her arm, he was taken aback as something clutched his wrist.

41 Former Czech Territory
13:35   June 10th, 2335

"Bashford," a chorus of voices said, with Andraste's voice in the lead. A monstrous hand rose out and lifted him off the ground, covered in exoskeleton much like Andraste herself. "It's over."

Hanging in the air, beating his fist against each massive finger to free his arm, Bashford looked in a stupor as the rest of the being emerged. A massive, ethereal humanoid lifted itself out of the crater, supporting itself on a free hand. It was too hazy to have clear features, but its outline was roughly feminine with hair made of gray light. The face looked to him, opening into two enormous eyes full of swirling blue cosmos. There was more exoskeleton on its face, split down the middle by a canoe-sized metal mask.

"Andraste!" Bashford cried out in anguish. He stopped fighting and stared, his eyes wide in fear and anger discernible even across his charred face. "What is this?"

"The Fomorians have returned, Bashford." The chorus responded, Andraste's own voice notably absent.

A smile cracked through Bashford's damaged skin. His beleaguered huffs for breath turned into pained laughter. His arm trembling, he reached out to the creature.

"Aaron Sennec would be so proud," he said as a trickle of bloody tears ran down his face. "Harmony will come at last to the world!"

"No!" He heard Andraste cry. The creature twitched, its head lurching to the right. "I will not allow this!"

Looking into the Fomorian's head, Bashford could see a silhouette of Andraste pushing against something. His joy smoldered and started to burn as hate. "Don't you dare interrupt this, Andraste!"

Inside the facsimile of the head, Andraste was sharing her body with countless other forces. She was the conduit for their energy, but she knew they would not relinquish full control and fought for the executive functions of the beast.

"Stop fighting us, Andraste! This is the best thing that could ever happen to your world!" The Spirit insisted, trying to dissolve her into its cluster of lost souls. "Don't you want what's best for it?"

Andraste, rebelling with every ounce of her being, fought through jagged static in her head as otherworldly ghosts assailed her in waves. She only saw Bashford through cloudy glimpses as the Spirit tried to wrest control.

"You don't know what's best!" Andraste argued back, clinging to her views as refuge from the Spirit's onslaught. "You act like you know everything, but you're clueless!" She struck a blow that kept it away for a moment before it came rushing at her again.

"And *you* are some expert, we assume?" It spoke in the voice of Scarlet, bringing a ghostly knife towards her.

"You're not human anymore! You're the newest incarnation of the Fomorians!"

Andraste ducked from the knife and caught the imitation of Scarlet by the throat. "I am not a Fomorian! But I'm not a human, either." With a yank, she pulled the arm off the body. "I'm neither."

As the phalanx of screeching bodies recoiled and reformed itself, it dissipated into darkness and surrounded her. "'Neither?' Then you are nothing! A human and Fomorian hybrid, yet lesser than either!" Each aspect of the Spirit hurled itself at her, trying to bombard her all at once with its alien might.

"You still don't understand at all!" Andraste did not resist. She allowed the energy to pass through her, acknowledging the pain, but not fighting against it. "You have walked among humanity for centuries, but you haven't learned a thing from them."

"And you've learned nothing of the Fomorians! Exemplars of power and perfection! You are worse than any human that we have dealt with!" After a moment of collecting itself, seeing Andraste fail to flinch from the attack, it dove at her with even greater speed. "We've learned that they're fools who never give up, even when they're beaten!"

"Oh, really?" Andraste mused, seeing the cascade of spiritual energy bearing down on her. She tensed her arm and waited for its approach. "Maybe you've learned something, after all!" Andraste's arm shot out and hit the Spirit's attack, swatting it to the side. The sheer force of Andraste's blow was enough to scatter the assembled mass.

The echo of the strike silenced the world for a moment, allowing Andraste to seize control of the body. She was grateful for the silence, allowing her to take a deep breath and collect herself. It seemed as if the Spirit had been truly silenced by her rebuttal.

With the Fomorian body easing as she did, she dropped Bashford and gauged her senses. Her awareness spread out from the ground and went out into the horizon. She thought this magnitude and breadth of perception would overwhelm her mind, but she felt the movements of the Outlands as naturally as she would feel the breeze or the rain on her skin. It was a pleasant experience on its own merits, allowing her tension to diffuse throughout the land.

Bashford looked up at the Fomorian, surprised he was even alive. The creature seemed stunned, its posture slack and its eyes closed. As he tried to regain the feeling in his arm, it came to, eyes opening to show the bright blue irises and oblong pupils of Andraste.

"What have you done?" Bashford demanded, voice hoarse. "This is all wrong! The Fomorian Martyrs were going to save us all!"

"And I will," Andraste said, her voice echoing. "But not the way you want me to." She glared down at Bashford. The fully-realized Fomorian still carried Andraste's distinct tone and the look in her eyes.

"You fool!" The voice in her head cried. She realized it was the Spirit, calling out to her as a distant echo. "You can't handle this kind of power!"

"Watch me." Andraste said out loud, to both Bashford and the Spirit.

Expanding the scope of her perception, Andraste felt herself spread out for hundreds of kilometers, her nerve endings devouring almost the entirety of the European mainland. Taking a breath, she focused on these extensions and drew them back in, as if releasing the tension on a stretched muscle. Slowly, it all began to retract. The masses of dendrites and other neurons spread throughout the land started to pull towards her. Even in the great trees surrounding her, Andraste saw and felt them shudder and withdraw, shrinking back down to a natural size.

"What are you doing?" The Spirit cried. "You're destroying hundreds of years of work!"

"Exactly." Andraste said, resolute.

As these strands of far-flung Fomorian physicality were drawn back into Andraste's body, they bundled together and gave her more form. Andraste's Fomorian body was soon becoming taller and more solid, eventually surpassing the tree line. Lifting the rest of her body out of the ground, she appeared as a massive ghost of herself.

Surveillance photos caught the sight of the giant, spectral Andraste and sent the footage to cities and governments all around the world. It was visible on the internet before anyone from the British Cabinet could comment on it.

"Ladies and Gentlemen, this sight has been corroborated by countless sources all over the internet!" Kennedy Schmidt shouted in disbelief as the footage went on. "Andraste, the mysterious experimental soldier unveiled by the British government only a few weeks ago, has appeared as a giant over a spot in the Outlands! Other sources say that, as her form is developing, the inhospitable and overgrown environment of the Outlands has started to recede!" Another image came up of a building-sized tree imploding on itself while a bear, reminiscent of an armored tank, rolled onto its side as its exoskeleton peeled away. A satellite captured a wave of natural regression that began at the edges of the continent and all centered on a point around Prague. Andraste was a massive specter in the sky, her features becoming more and more defined.

Looks of disbelief, horror, and confusion abounded in Central Base. Andraste wasn't doing anything yet, mostly getting her bearings on the situation as the Outlands' wilderness was brought under control.

"Is there any way we can contact her?" Quadriyyah asked, voice airy with concern. "The drone is still out there!"

"And what would we say?" Laurie interjected. "We don't know what's happening, or if there's anything left of her!"

"That is Andraste out there, make no mistake," Rowe affirmed them with a solemn voice. "And if the rest of the footage is to be believed, she's saving us."

Bashford was contorted in pain on the ground. He felt the energy leave him, seeing translucent red strands pulling away from his body as the Fomorian reclaimed itself. His injuries were mounting, and the onus of his own mortality took hold again. He was doubled over, finally realizing the severity of his wounds. The pain was compounded by the sight of Andraste hovering over him.

She was resplendent, giving off light and a tangible sense of energy. That energy resonated with the light of the sun, and she was surrounded in a blue alien aurora of her own making.

"No," Bashford sputtered as blood filled his lungs. The last thing he saw was Andraste's new form as he painfully expired.

"This isn't over," The Spirit told her, taking hold in a powerful section of her mind. It was only the presence of the Sprit that kept her still, as she battled with it in her mind to maintain control. "You've seen the other countries of this planet! Other Fomorian remains have taken root!"

"I will see to them soon enough," Andraste told it. "I hear them. I hear the people. The fear, the anger, the confusion," she trailed off, wistful. "People are seeing me, and they have no idea what to think."

"You have only delayed us," it went on, indignant. "Soon, your planet will be ours! I'll no longer suffer these wretched humans!"

She finally looked to it. "To suffer is to be human," she said, calm. Her vitriol had faded, and she spoke with direct but soft conviction. "To make mistakes, to be imperfect, is to be human. You say you're fascinated by them, but in your pursuit to create a perfect world for them, you overlook everything that defines humanity."

"What are you talking about?" The Spirit demanded after some silence.

"I'm talking about your flawed understanding of humans," she replied, anger building in her voice. "Everyone has been talking about perfect worlds, but they don't realize that a perfect world will never exist. Not as long as humanity exists." The anger faded, and she took a short breath. "And that's fine."

"What are you trying to say? That you don't want a perfect world?" The Spirit tried to fight back, but Andraste had gathered so much fortitude that it couldn't touch her. She made no effort to deflect its attack, which bounced off her without visible damage.

"A perfect world is an inhuman one," she replied, calm. "There would be no beauty in it." As she said this, in the theater of her mind, a collection of metal gears and tools came together and manifested into a small wind-up toy. "Where is the joy of creation when there's no effort? Without contrast, how can you appreciate anything?" She turned to the Spirit with a flame in her eyes. "I have been in a lot of pain, Spirit. But when it abates, everything looks so beautiful by comparison."

Finally, the giant Andraste came to, looking out at the world around her. The curvature of the earth was in sight, and far, far down below her, sat her old backpack. A tendril brought it back up and pulled out a beloved old keepsake: the wind-up toy she showed Quadriyyah. In her massive hand, she held it tight, feeling warmth inside her.

"Your shepherding has no place here. But there is a place for those who strive to make a difference." She told the Spirit, a tear running down her cheek. She thought of Quadriyyah, of Yousef, of Misha, and all the other people who had shown her kindness. In her booming physical voice, she addressed the entire world. "Don't make a perfect world. Make a better world. Never stop striving to help the world around you and make that difference! Despite all the odds against me, I've never given up!"

"You're absurd!" The Spirit cried, its resolve shriveling and allowing Andraste greater control.

Towards the border of Russia, Andraste felt the impulse of a similar form. Another Fomorian hotbed, as the Spirit claimed, was festering in Asia. Her massive, ghostly figure turned in that direction and vanished.

"What's happening now?" Laurie cried out as the world watched the Fomorian Hybrid disappear.

"Chancellor!" A technician called out, manning a computer, as he pulled up footage from a Chinese website, where Andraste was doing the same thing. She had found a cluster of Fomorian nerves and energy, removing its influence from the mainland. In the center of China, she uprooted a Fomorian heart and returned the country to its natural state. Across the Arabian Peninsula and into Africa, she did the same, repeating the process until she had a bouquet of disinterred Fomorian minds. She hovered over South America looking at the glowing bundle in her hands. Her size breached the stratosphere, and the only ones who couldn't see her were on the other side of the planet.

Soon, world leaders were reaching out to Central Base, begging Rowe to explain why his experimental super-soldier was standing over them. Worldwide, records of the untamed wilderness being violently drawn back were proliferating. The so-called druids were losing their powers, and the more creative were posting online about "our new religion" and other shocking, awe-filled revelations. No one from the British Cabinet could respond, only stare in awe as their creation loomed over the planet.

"She's not just a hybrid anymore," Rowe said with tears in his eyes. "She has become a god."

Andraste was no stranger to any of these sentiments. All these different Fomorian minds were rebelling against her as she usurped their power, and the cacophony no longer troubled her. She heard everyone, all their cries of terror and confusion. Without seeing them, she knew the looks in their eyes. Her magnitude was unrivalled, and anything that could cause these events possessed unconscionable power. She wanted to call out to them, to say "thank you," or maybe even "you're welcome," but she knew that a small taste of her power would be devastating when used improperly.

There was no oxygen where she was, and the radiation of the sun brushed her skin, but she was intact. If surviving exposure to the vacuum of space was this easy, she shuddered to imagine what else was possible for her. Looking at one of her hands, she imagined a simple gear system to calm herself. The gears and machine parts manifested physically, emerging out of light from one of her luminescent hands. Her own power shocked her, and realized that this kind of power couldn't exist in this world.

More than anything, she had the roots of the Fomorians in her hands. Their connection to the world had been destroyed, and they were twitching around in vain attempts to lash back onto something and bend it to their control. Objects of terror and worship to people, much like what Andraste was now. She did not linger on these thoughts for long, for she knew she had to destroy the Fomorians. If not, they would take root elsewhere and try again, one way or another. There could be no room for error with them, or her. The only thing worse than silent controllers of the Earth was a giant one, hovering over people and staring from space. It all needed to end.

She looked up and saw the vehicle for that ending. The sun was overhead, ever untouched by the unthinkable motions of humans.

Andraste felt a tear, collecting at the corner of her eye but refusing to fall. The gravity of the planet was too weak for her. Shutting her eyes, she focused her power on one final project.

With the uninhibited power of her mind, she was able to bring even more of her will into being. She had control over the matter and flesh of the Fomorians, which floated out of her hand. She reflected on all her self-taught lessons on engineering and physics as she twisted the matter into something that could hurl itself into the sun. Her ghost faded from overhead, collapsing into a mass of erupting blue and black energy.

"Andraste, stop this," The Spirit pleaded, its voice weak but distinct. "If not for our sake, then yours! If you think you're above it all, fine! But I know what you're trying to do, and this won't fix anything for you!"

She didn't respond. She focused, the gears and machines that she always imagined for comfort came together into physical reality. Her imagination was given form as she molded gears, motors, and metal from the energy. Even with her intense focus, she kept the sun in sight.

"Please listen!" The Spirit kept on, a wail in its tone. "I looked after you for so long out there! I am begging you, don't throw your life away!"

"I have no choice." She lamented, standing in a ship made of a solid aurora. As a mass of both light and matter, it had sufficient strength to hurtle itself towards its goal.

With a sigh, the energy went off, and it blasted forward. "It's not about me. It's about everyone."

From the ground, a massive aurora traced across the sky, its tail billowing out before it narrowed into a single point in the distant sky, going straight for the sun.

"What is she doing?" Rowe cried out, voice trembling. "She can't be!"

"Andraste, no!" Quadriyyah sobbed. "Don't end it like this!"

Rowe only stared as the others broke down into devastated cries. He watched his creation soar inexorably towards the sun. As it closed in, the lights she cast burned in other, fiercer colors, torn apart by the heat and radiance.

"Andraste," Rowe thought, feeling a great weight on his chest. *"Why is this your solution? You have so much to offer, and not just for the FH Project."* With every breath, he felt the size of his guilt and regret build. *"I've made so many mistakes. I don't expect you to forgive me for any of them."* Finally, he felt some tears and bowed his head. *"What would you say to me, if you could hear me right now?"*

Andraste did hear, her vision going white from the intensity of the sun. The harsh rays of light and radiation were tearing apart her creation and incinerating the rest of the Fomorians. She closed her eyes as she felt the impact approaching. In her last spasm of conscious thought, she reached back out to Rowe.

She told him, *"I'm sorry."*

The bulk of her energy met the surface of the sun, and the Fomorians were annihilated. A black spot was left behind for a few moments, illuminating a brilliant, fluorescent corona that Andraste's machine had created. Blue, black, white, the essence of her, all flowering around the sun as the energy vanished from existence. Visible to the naked eye, cameras and spectators from all over the world had a shared sense of finality. As if the sentiment was tangible, it stuck in everyone's throat until more and more people at last said it.

    Rowe was the first one in Central Base to say it. "It's over." He spoke in a slow, staggered way. "It's finally over."

42 London, England
13:35   September 12th, 2335

Rowe was quickly taken to prison following the unofficial defeat of the Martyr's Army. After Bashford's death, a cease-fire was called that allowed the extraction of Judicia and Yousef, but all was touched with acute bitterness behind the walls of a prison cell.

That autumn, Rowe was ordered to appear before Parliament alongside Judicia to answer for the Iconoclast Program. The British government hoped to put the pieces of the case together before taking the charges to court.

Rowe waited in the wings, head slumped forward. Months of quiet repentance in prison had left him numb to the world, but this hearing inspired something like fervor inside him again. He welcomed whatever closure he could find about the whole affair.

Judicia had a similar air to her, but there was a more distinct note of standoffish defiance embedded in her silence. Rowe heard the stories of her travails in the Martyr's Army prison camp, even though she seemed to be returning to her bitter old self.

"What do you plan to tell them, exactly?" Rowe asked as the silence bore down on them.

"What can I tell them that they haven't already heard? This whole situation is a farce." She scoffed. "We're wasting time. Andraste is dead, and my research is over." She spoke tersely, looking into a corner. "I'm done. Put it in as much writing as you want, nothing is going to change."

Her tone gave him a rise, and Rowe gave her a sad but hard look. "Did Andraste mean nothing to you?"

Judicia kept staring at the corner, only acknowledging his jab with a bitter scowl.

A guard swung the door open, silencing their argument. He gestured for both to come out as he guided Rowe and another guard led Judicia.

A protected courtroom was filled with secretaries of state and the rest of the cabinet. Quadriyyah, stood out from the crowd with her expression of mixed pity and animosity towards them both.

"To order," Quadriyyah began, standing up. "We are present to discuss the illicit nature of the Iconoclast Program, as well as the fate of Andraste. Judicia, Rowe, are you prepared to speak about it?"

"Yes, Prime Minister," Rowe muttered. Hearing that name sucked the resolve out of him.

"Yes," Judicia growled.

Yousef was waiting to be called as a witness in the small gallery, glaring daggers at Judicia. He found some catharsis in directing his hatred at her, but no amount of hate would undo what had been done.

"I tried to do everything I could for Andraste," he thought at Judicia. *"And look what it's come to."*

For Rowe, all was a muddled blur as statements were made among the secretaries. He could only focus on the weight of the situation and how it settled painfully onto his shoulders. Eyes full of strain, he wanted to close them for just a moment, but his face had gone rigid with shame. He only wondered what Andraste would say if she could see them discussing her now.

"Mr. Rowe!"

As if in response to his thoughts, he heard her voice. Rowe shot up in his chair, looking around the room in a frenzy.

"Mr. Rowe!" Laurie shouted at him. "What are you doing?"

"It's all right, Mr. Laurie." Her voice was heard again, this time by everyone. *"I'm sorry to interrupt the hearing."*

In the middle of the room, the three-colored aurora they had seen around the sun that day appeared. Condensing into a single structure of white light, it took the shape of a human before fading into color again. Standing before Parliament was Andraste.

A collective, harsh gasp rose from all sides as she manifested. To her, the shock, disbelief, and confusion were palpable in the air. Immediately, she bowed her head to Quadriyyah in respect.

"Andraste!" Yousef cried, shooting up in his chair from the gallery.

"Yousef!" She turned to him with relief in her voice, but quickly corrected herself. "Mrs. Quad- I mean, Prime Minister- and Members of the British Cabinet," Andraste began, speaking to the room with noticeable conviction. "I deeply apologize for interrupting this meeting. However, I cannot allow judgment to be passed on these individuals without saying my part." Raising her head, her face scrunched as she forced out the next few words. "I am not innocent in this. I believe the implications of my crimes will have a significant bearing on future decisions."

"What are you talking about, Andraste?" Quadriyyah begged. "How are you even alive?"

"Truthfully, I'm still figuring that out myself, Prime Minister. But please, my story is more pressing."

Andraste told them everything. She was a deserter who abandoned her unit, watched her fellow soldiers die, and omitted all this information in her application to the FH Project.

"I may have repressed these memories, but that does not make me innocent. I am guilty of desertion, betraying both crown and country." Shutting her eyes tight, a few tears were visible at the edges. "Please, do not speak of me as a martyr or a victim. I must be held accountable for my crimes."

No one spoke. The members of the Cabinet exchanged some glances, but the silence prevailed. Andraste, tense with shame, decried the silence.

"Please! I know this may be hard to hear, but I won't just pretend nothing is wrong!"

"Andraste, look at you!" Judicia spoke with wide eyes and, of all things, a smile on her face. "You survived a trip into the sun!" Rasping through her lips came a bizarre sort of laugh. "You are the epitome of what my experiment tried to create! No one can hold you accountable for anything!"

Andraste looked at her, face lined with agony. "Judicia, you can't-"

"You're alive," Rowe said in a shaky voice. "Andraste, you- you truly are a goddess now." He shook his head in disbelief. "My god, we all thought you were dead!"

"I know, and I'm sorry about that. But, Mr. Rowe," she gestured to him pleadingly, "your reaction is why I had to look dead! I can't have people worshipping me as a new goddess!"

"How about the replacement for humanity we all need?" Judicia chimed in, head cocked. "You finally amounted to something."

The gallery erupted in angry outcries and derision towards Judicia.

"Order! Order!" Quadriyyah stood, her voice silencing the others. "Andraste, I am frankly uncertain of how to respond. However you managed to survive, the first thing you do is come here and confess to a past crime?"

"People are dead because of me, Prime Minister. I heard what people were thinking when I was uprooting the Fomorians- that I was some sort of goddess. As we've seen with the Martyr's Army," she looked ruefully at Rowe, "and with Mr. Rowe, that sort of idolatry is a very dangerous thing." She hung her head. "I need to be held accountable. I will submit myself to whatever punishment is deemed appropriate for desertion."

"Andraste," Quadriyyah lamented, searching for words.

"She saved the world!" Cried Yousef.

"But desertion is a capital offence!" Cried another secretary.

"She flew into the sun and survived? How on earth are we supposed to detain her?"

The secretary who voiced that concern unintentionally silenced the room. Everyone shared glances with one another as the conversation shifted from the merits of punishment to the possibility of it.

Andraste looked around in disbelief. "Please, you have my full compliance! It's not right to hail me as a hero when I'm not!"

"Andraste, why can't you leave well enough alone?" Judicia spoke with an irritated drawl. "Enjoy your new freedom and appreciate your story! You went from a broken woman to a goddess- be amazed!"

"Judicia, enough!" Andraste rushed her, staring Judicia down. "We're all so tired of your preaching, woman!"

"Andraste!" Rowe cowed at the sight, feeling unworthy just to speak to her. "Please. This isn't going to help your case."

With a deep breath, Andraste centered herself. She looked around at the Cabinet, seeing the looks of fear and awe on their faces. Andraste sighed and turned to them again. "This is what I'm talking about. All of you are too scared to dispute me! No one person can have that kind of power. No one should have the singular power to decide how things should be." She shot a hard look at Judicia as she said that last part.

"I am not disputing that claim, Andraste." Quadriyyah spoke again, sympathetic. "And you have all our respect for owning up to what you've done before. But look at what you've done for us since. You put your life on the line again and again for everyone. You're a hero."

Tears edged at Andraste's eyes. "I appreciate your kind words, but I can't accept this. I can't emphasize enough that my countrymen were killed because of what I did. My past may be behind me, but it's something I must reconcile."

Quadriyyah sighed. "That's valid. And we recognize the severity of what you've done."

Noticing her pause, Andraste filled the gap in conversation. "But, let me guess: you aren't sure how to prosecute me?" She looked around the room. "I can feel it. All of you are terrified of me. As usual."

Quadriyyah looked to the others, who were truthfully all looking in fear. Then a flicker of inspiration came to her. "No, Andraste. I have a better idea:" she stood up from her chair and addressed the room. "You will be ordered to continue serving your country."

Loud murmurs filled the room. Yousef and the people around him all started chittering.

"Excuse me?" Andraste asked.

"You are an exceptional individual, Andraste, and your mere biology can teach us so much. Think of all the nonviolent ways you can continue to help heal the world." Quadriyyah gesticulated as she spoke.

"Heal the world," Andraste said under her breath, warming to the idea.

"Yeah!" Yousef spoke up. "Just- just think of your amnesia, Andraste! You could open up an entirely new understanding of the brain and how memories work!" He stood up, trembling. "A-and the way you see the world and process thoughts! You could teach us all so much!"

"Yousef," Andraste said with happy tears.

Quadriyyah nodded. "Excellent. And do not think this is an extension of the Iconoclast Program, which has been fully terminated. You will be working under federal jurisdiction, Andraste, until you have paid your debt to the country."

She nodded, allowing her tears to fall. "I understand. I will accept these terms."

"Any objections?" Quadriyyah addressed the room.

No one answered but with applause. Even Laurie stood and clapped his hands.

Seeing all of these people cheering, Andraste wept happily. Laughter wove into her sobs.

"Andraste," Rowe sputtered, trying to get out of his chair. The guards caught him and kept him in his place. "I-I don't know if it means anything at this point," he said as he trembled, "but I'm sorry. I'm so, so sorry. For everything." His head slumped and fell forward. "You didn't deserve any of this."

Andraste wiped some tears away before looking at him. His feelings were cold and clawing, true misery within him.

"I can tell you mean that, Mr. Rowe. And I appreciate it." She approached him gently. "But it's never too late to apologize."

Quadriyyah smiled gently as she heard this.

"You've fully lost it," Judicia muttered. "All that power, wasted."

Andraste tried to summon some kindness for Judicia. None came. "I'm sorry, did someone ask you?"

"What would you be without my help, you ungrateful bitch?" Judicia fired back. "You're still that same pathetic, broken thing that wandered into-"

"Enough!" Andraste silenced the room with a stomp of her foot. A shockwave rolled through the room as blue energy flared around her eyes again. "I never needed you to fix me, Judicia. No one needs *your* approval to live their lives."

Judicia was silenced by her, holding the side of her head in anticipation of another migraine. She was slumped over in her chair, reeling from Andraste's sheer presence. The rest of the room stared before applauding again.

The rest of the trial continued with Andraste waiting in the wings. Both Judicia and Rowe were sentenced for crimes against humanity and taken away. Judicia never looked back at Andraste, while Rowe met her gaze with a sad smile. She nodded at him as the former prime minister was pulled away.

The trial was adjourned, and the cabinet came to congratulate Andraste themselves, but ahead of them was Yousef. He dashed at her, and they met in a tight hug, laughing and crying.

"Fucking hell, Andraste! I was so worried about you!"

"I'm sorry, Yousef," she said with a sigh. "I'm here now, though. Does that help?"

"Damn right, it does." He pulled his hair aside, which came undone in his hurry. "You've got a lot of work to do, you know."

"Yes, I'm aware." Andraste said as she held up her palm. A little blue light appeared in her hand, and it took the form of her wind-up toy, becoming tangible in her hand. "I'm looking forward to it, though."

"Glad to hear," Yousef said in awe. "Real quick, though: what was it like going to space?" He asked excitedly.

"Huh?"

"Andy, please. I want you to brag. Must've been fucking amazing!" Yousef's smile was wide.

She chuckled and held the toy close. "Yeah. It was pretty fucking amazing."

"Glad you two are handling things well," Quadriyyah said as she approached. "Also that you're looking forward to the work, Andraste."

"How *are* we going to enforce it, though?" Yousef mused aloud. "She can turn into light and fly into space." He glanced at her. "I bet you could go anywhere in the world after absorbing all that power."

"We'll give her a few holidays," Quadriyyah said with a shrug. "You can stretch your legs a bit, Andraste."

"Don't worry, Yousef." Andraste said. "I'm done running."

Epilogue

"Are you sure he's ready to come outside?"

"Oh, I'm sure." He said, making sure everything was ready to be served. "He's been great with the kids, hasn't he? But if he doesn't leave the house soon, neither will they." The biscuits were all in place, and the tea smelled delicious.

It was a bit of distance from the house to the gazebo, but anyone would make the hike on an evening like this. The bugs were sparse, the sunset was glowing, and the air was warm and fragrant with all the blooms.

"I'm not sure about this, Ivan," she voiced as she looked back at the house. "The man is so old, and he's still unstable."

"Some air will be good for him," Ivan said as he washed his hands. After twenty-five years of missing two fingers, he was an expert on maneuvering around them. "Besides, Jamie, Mr. Rowe will be delighted to see our guest."

"If you say so," Jamie shrugged as she walked back to the house.

She and Ivan inherited this land years ago and decided to put part of it to use as an assisted-living facility. She had no idea how a former Prime Minister arrived at their door, half-dead and continuously spouting nonsense about how "it was all his fault," but he was starting to warm up to them after a few months. She lamented that only Ivan Holacksi would use this "family approach" to therapy, but her husband had surprised her before. Jamie walked into the sunroom and saw the two kids listening to Rowe with rapt attention.

"Misha? Adam? Time for tea!" She called, breaking their concentration. "Mr. Rowe can finish his story once we're all out there, okay?"

After some resigned sighs, the two youngsters ran out as Jamie took the handles on the old man's wheelchair.

"I was just getting to the good part," Rowe complained. Hair as white as cotton, skin hanging limp over his skeleton, and paralyzed from the waist down after a botched suicide, Nathan Rowe bore little resemblance to his old pictures.

"You can get *back* to the good part." Jamie retorted as she wheeled him to the door. With a press of a button, it slid back open and let down a ramp. "Ivan says he has a special guest for you to see."

"I told him, it was just something I ate that day. I'm fine." Rowe spoke more calmly as he felt the warm night air roll over him.

"I promise, it's not the proctologist." Jamie continued, undaunted but unsure about Rowe's petulance.

At the table, everyone had a seat with a teacup and saucer. Some little hands reached for the cakes, but Ivan held them back.

"Not until we have everyone, okay?"

"Who else is coming, daddy?" Misha asked him, doe eyed.

"Any minute now, you'll see." He poured cups for everyone, including the one empty seat next to Mr. Rowe.

"Don't taunt me like this, Holacksi." Rowe said, too calmed by the elements to sound truly indignant. "I don't deserve your kindness."

"No?" Ivan responded, taking a chair himself. "Well, I know someone who would disagree." He looked up and saw a blue flash of light in the sky. "Ah, perfect timing!"

The blue light landed in the yard just a few meters from the gazebo, capturing the attention of everyone present. Rowe saw the figure emerge and felt his breath catch in his throat.

"Here she is! How are you?" Ivan ran up to hug her, which the figure reciprocated.

"I'm doing great, Ivan. Just started my holiday," Andraste said, looking back out over the table. "Misha? Adam? Hello! Oh, you two have gotten so big!" As she said this, she produced two wind-up toys, one for each of them.

Smiles and laughter faded into the background for Rowe. He was frozen, fixed on the life he thought he had ruined over twenty-five years ago. Here she was, not a day older, and none the worse for wear. When she turned to look at him, he nearly fell out of his chair.

"Mr. Rowe," Andraste whispered, calmly walking over to him. She got on a knee and embraced the old man. "I'm so glad to see you!"

"H-how?" He stammered, tears forming in his tired, dry eyes.

Andraste herself cried, though he felt the joy radiating off her. "We have a lot to discuss."

www.ingramcontent.com/pod-product-compliance
Lightning Source LLC
LaVergne TN
LVHW021510151224
799175LV00010B/791